"A fantastic read... A *Da Vinci Code*–e... take on vamp... sex..." —Virna DePaul, author of *Chosen by Blood*

"Bulgarian vampires and nonstop sex (not with the Bulgarian vampires), PLUS an illuminated lost manuscript, in a twisty tale of family mystery, murder, and corporate greed." —Diana Gabaldon, *New York Times* bestselling author of the Outlander series

"A singe-your-fingers page-turner. Don't miss this one." —Shirley Hailstock, author of *Some Like Them Rich*

ACQUAINTED
WITH THE NIGHT

ACQUAINTED

WITH THE

NIGHT

PIPER MAITLAND

BERKLEY BOOKS, NEW YORK

THE BERKLEY PUBLISHING GROUP
Published by the Penguin Group
Penguin Group (USA) Inc.
375 Hudson Street, New York, New York 10014, USA
Penguin Group (Canada), 90 Eglinton Avenue East, Suite 700, Toronto, Ontario M4P 2Y3, Canada
(a division of Pearson Penguin Canada Inc.)
Penguin Books Ltd., 80 Strand, London WC2R 0RL, England
Penguin Group Ireland, 25 St. Stephen's Green, Dublin 2, Ireland (a division of Penguin Books Ltd.)
Penguin Group (Australia), 250 Camberwell Road, Camberwell, Victoria 3124, Australia
(a division of Pearson Australia Group Pty. Ltd.)
Penguin Books India Pvt. Ltd., 11 Community Centre, Panchsheel Park, New Delhi—110 017, India
Penguin Group (NZ), 67 Apollo Drive, Rosedale, Auckland 0632, New Zealand
(a division of Pearson New Zealand Ltd.)
Penguin Books (South Africa) (Pty.) Ltd., 24 Sturdee Avenue, Rosebank, Johannesburg 2196,
South Africa

Penguin Books Ltd., Registered Offices: 80 Strand, London WC2R 0RL, England

This is a work of fiction. Names, characters, places, and incidents either are the product of the author's
imagination or are used fictitiously, and any resemblance to actual persons, living or dead, business
establishments, events, or locales is entirely coincidental. The publisher does not have any control
over and does not assume any responsibility for author or third-party websites or their content.

ACQUAINTED WITH THE NIGHT

A Berkley Book / published by arrangement with the author

PRINTING HISTORY
Berkley premium edition / December 2011

Copyright © 2011 by Michael Lee West.
Cover art by S. Miroque.
Cover design by Rita Frangie.
Interior text design by Kristin del Rosario.

ISBN: 978-0-425-24363-3

BERKLEY®
Berkley Books are published by The Berkley Publishing Group,
a division of Penguin Group (USA) Inc.,
375 Hudson Street, New York, New York 10014.
BERKLEY® is a registered trademark of Penguin Group (USA) Inc.
The "B" design is a trademark of Penguin Group (USA) Inc.

PRINTED IN THE UNITED STATES OF AMERICA

10 9 8 7 6 5 4 3 2 1

PROLOGUE

PERPERIKON ARCHAEOLOGICAL COMPLEX
EASTERN RHODOPE MOUNTAINS, BULGARIA

Nigel Clifford dragged his trowel through the frozen rubble, coaxing potsherds to the surface. The freezing November wind scraped over the excavation site, tugging at his fedora and chilling his hands. Nigel put on gloves and kept digging. He'd just celebrated his seventy-second birthday, and he was better suited to armchair archaeology than fieldwork, but he loved dirt: its texture, the loamy smell, the way it packed under his nails, and the sour, acidic flavor it left in his mouth. The soil yielded more than history; it was the repository of man's secrets.

He worked until sunset, tagging the pottery bits. As he gathered his tools, darkness seeped out of the ground, twisted through gnarled branches, and plunged the mountain into leaden dusk. A ticklish sensation crept up his neck and he cut his gaze to the ledge above him. A figure melted into the shadows. Pebbles hit the path and skittered into the ravine.

Nigel's heart stuttered. Someone was watching, he was sure of it. Despite the glacial evening air, perspiration slid down his neck. He squinted at the ruins. A whirring noise echoed as bats swarmed out of the cave and skimmed over the excavation pit. Nigel tipped back his fedora and watched them scatter into the bruised sky. He'd never seen large colonies in the Rhodopes, especially in November—why so many? And what had disturbed them?

His chest tightened and pain stitched down his left arm. Damned ruddy angina. He pulled off his gloves, pushed a nitroglycerin tablet under his tongue, and hummed "God Save the Queen." He'd come to Perperikon to clear his mind with clay idols and bronze arrows, but after a fortnight of digging, he'd found nothing but potsherds. A pity he couldn't stay in Bulgaria, but a distressing personal matter awaited him in England.

After the spasm passed, he lifted his backpack, climbed out of the pit, and hurried toward the path. He didn't notice the men until they stepped onto the flat boulders above him and stared down with toothy smiles. In the fading light, the duo resembled an Eastern European version of the Blues Brothers—sunglasses, skinny black ties, sport coats. Years ago, Nigel's niece had loved that old film, but the chaps on the rocks weren't cinema actors. They emanated a stygian stink, of earth and beetles and rot.

Steady, old boy. The professor tipped his fedora and strode past the boulder, praying this would be the end of it. The men stood motionless until Nigel passed directly beneath their position, and then they moved swiftly. Too swiftly to see. He started to run, but a black haze blurred past him. Dust spiraled into the air as the men thudded onto the path.

Like the bats. A twinge shot to Nigel's elbow and he grimaced.

"I'm looking for a British archaeologist," the taller man said, each word drilled with a Balkan accent. The wind shifted, carrying the echo of a howling dog. The barbed notes sharpened, and a second animal moaned in the distance.

"How may I help you?" Nigel's breath stamped the air. His right knee shook violently, and the tip of his boot dented the rubble. *Not to worry, old boy. Not yet.* Though it could get sticky if these chaps were thieves.

The man glided forward, his coat rustling. "Where are you hiding your niece?"

Oh, no. Please, no. Nigel's vision narrowed to an obsidian dot. "Sorry, I don't have a niece."

"Yes, you do. Caroline Clifford stole ten pages from *Historia Immortalis.*"

The man knew her name, knew about the book. What were the odds? Nigel's jaw tightened and he nipped his tongue. If you didn't wish to grow old, if you preferred a short but interesting life, get yourself mixed up with *Historia Immortalis.* Each cursed page attracted death— ironic for a tome that celebrated immortality. Twenty years ago, Caro's parents had died because of it, and she'd barely escaped.

The tall fellow waved two long fingers. "Teo, check his backpack."

"*Da.*" Teo wrenched Nigel's bag from his shoulders. Everything spilled onto the path. Pens, documents, tools, medicine bottles, his tattered copy of Herodotus.

Blood oozed into Nigel's mouth. He swallowed, tasting the iron. Two decades of plotting and planning had just gone tits up, and this was how it would end? He gazed past the men, down the winding path. Could he make it down the mountain? He had to try. His need to protect Caro was stronger than life. Stronger than the threat of his own death.

Teo smashed Nigel's mobile phone against a rock, then lifted a medicine bottle. "Georgi, what is Warfarin? We can sell it, yes?"

"Take it." Georgi waved his bony hand.

Teo kicked aside a British passport, reached for a tattered leather wallet, and pulled out a photograph. Nigel swallowed again as he gazed up at Caro's much-younger face. She was his heart, this clever slip of a girl. He remembered the day that picture had been taken and how she'd struggled to tame her wiry blond hair into a strict, shining knot.

"No niece?" Teo laughed and held up another snapshot. It had been taken a few months prior in London. Caro had grown into a beauty, all legs and cheekbones, with her mother's gray-blue eyes. The corkscrew curls were still incorrigible and tumbled past her shoulders. She was just like that hair, feisty and resilient, but she was no match for these fiends.

Georgi grabbed the picture and licked it. "Nice," he said.

"Go after her," Nigel said, "and you'll get a bite more than you can chew."

Georgi shoved the photograph into his pocket and pulled out a knife. Teo knocked off Nigel's fedora, then threw him to the ground and pulled off his boots.

Nigel felt a violent tug on his ankle, as if a meat hook

had snagged it. White-hot spasms pulsed in his heel, rippled into his calf, and throbbed behind his knee. He arched his back and screamed. Bile spurted through his teeth and splashed onto the rocks. Had they hacked off his leg? His head jerked convulsively as he glanced over his shoulder. Blood jetted from a gash above his heel. Dear God, they'd severed his Achilles tendon.

"He wails like a girl," Teo said, then threw his weight onto the professor's legs. Georgi dragged the knife over Nigel's other tendon. A stinging burst of pain slammed into his groin. His bladder let go and warmth gushed down his thighs.

Damn them to hell. To distract himself from the raw ache, he hummed "God Save the Queen."

"Shut up, old man," Georgi cried.

Nigel's lips wobbled, then he began to sing as loud as he could. "From every latent foe / From the assassins' blow / God save the Queen!" *And God save Caro, too.*

Sour breath hit his face as the men fell on him, one on each side. His voice didn't falter until the men bit his neck. He tried to push them away but his arms wouldn't move. Even his feet went numb. A blessing.

Georgi veered away and spat onto the rocks. "Your blood tastes bitter."

Teo jerked back and began dry-heaving onto the stones.

"You're tasting my medication," Nigel said through gritted teeth. "Nitroglycerin and Warfarin. Soon your capillaries will dilate, and your blood will run like wine."

Teo balled his hands into fists and stepped forward, his incisors glinting in the moonlight. They weren't that big, Nigel noted. Stubby little fangs that matched the man's physique.

"No, let him bleed." Georgi scooped up the fedora and shoved it onto Teo's head, then turned back to Nigel. "Tonight you will die. Tomorrow, I find your niece. And it will be so sweet."

The dogs bayed as the men headed down the rocky path. Nigel dragged himself over the cold, rough stones. Perperikon was an ancient place of fire, prophecy, and blood sacrifice—a fitting end for an old tomb raider. But he couldn't die. Not yet.

I must warn Caro. Something only she will understand. His fingers closed on the penlight; he fit it between his teeth and bit down. The beam sliced over his passport and pens. He grabbed them and searched the book for a blank page. His hand shook as he started to write. She'd need to fit the puzzle pieces together before anyone else did. Before those ghouls found her. He had waited two decades to tell Caro the truth. Now the dogs were closing in, and he only had minutes and a scrap of paper.

CHAPTER 1

COVENT GARDEN
LONDON, ENGLAND

Caro dreamed of blood and teeth. She skidded across the icy field, glancing over her shoulder every few seconds at the wild dogs. They loped through high, prickly grass, their breath rising in the chilled air. A tan bitch snagged the edge of Caro's coat and dragged her to the ground. The other dogs closed in, their low, sleek bodies cutting through the weeds.

For the love of God, stop, no, you mustn't.

Uncle Nigel leaped from the shadows, pounced onto the dog, and hurled it into the weeds. The others scooted away, tails tucked under their bellies, and howled. Then their cries morphed into strident ringing.

She lay still, so still, trying to decide if she was awake or asleep or somewhere in between. This recurring nightmare had begun when she was a small girl, right after her parents had died, but in recent weeks, it had grown more violent. Dream or not, she was afraid for Uncle Nigel. Weeks ago she'd begged him to cancel the Bulgarian dig, but he'd patted her head and called her Dame Doom, his pet name for her.

Her shins ached as if she'd really been bitten. She slid her hands beneath the sheet and felt her legs. No wounds. No blood. But the ringing continued, a sharp, stinging sound that echoed through her bedroom.

It was the phone. Again. She tilted the caller display box. The numbers were X-ed out, same as before. Someone had been calling the flat since midnight. She couldn't say why, but she had always attracted unstable people.

She lifted the receiver. The caller laughed, a deep-throated man's laugh. Over his harsh breathing, she heard the distant clang of Big Ben. The same noise drifted through her open window, five peals.

"Why won't you say something, dammit?" she cried. The mattress creaked as she got out of bed and glanced out the rain-specked window. Bow Street was empty. So was the red phone booth on the corner.

The caller meowed.

"Put a bung in it," Caro yelled. She'd spent her childhood traveling with her uncle to archaeological digs and she knew how to curse in seven languages. She was just getting into a rhythm when the caller hung up with a decisive click.

She rubbed her eyes. If she didn't get any sleep, she'd be a wreck tomorrow. But wasn't it already tomorrow? In a few hours she had to pull herself together and escort forty-two Australians around London landmarks. As a child, she'd imagined numerous careers for herself, but none of them had involved riding around on a double-decker bus spouting historical facts into a microphone. Yet here she was. Only a few weeks ago, on November fifth, to be precise, she'd misplaced twelve Americans at Waterloo Station. Since small children were involved, the police had shut down two city blocks. The media had shown up just as Caro was reunited with the tourists. Unfortunately, her photograph had ended up in the *Observer*, along with an unflattering article.

Her reflection moved across the dark window as she walked to her night table. Her hair looked stiff and angular as an Egyptian headdress. She found a plastic razor in the drawer and began thinning her bangs. The curly, dark blond hairs drifted to her knee. The phone rang again and she lopped off a chunk of hair. A vital chunk. Damned bloody pervert. She'd show him.

She reached down to unplug the jack, then paused. Wait, that wouldn't fix anything. The kitchen phone was next to her roommate's bedroom. Phoebe worked at British *Vogue* and didn't like to miss her beauty sleep. If she awoke, Caro wouldn't hear the end of it, so she took a breath and lifted the receiver, steeling herself for Cat Man's encore performance.

"This is Sir Geoffrey McKitterick from the British embassy," said a tinny male voice. "I'm trying to reach Miss Caroline Clifford. Is she available?"

"Speaking." She glanced at the caller display box. It was indeed the main embassy in London. Thank God she hadn't cussed the man, as she had just been about to do.

"Sorry to ring at this hour," McKitterick continued, "but I had a devil of a time finding you. Sir Nigel stopped by our office before he left for Bulgaria, and he left your number in case of emergency. Unfortunately, he transposed the numbers."

Pain spiked through Caro's chest, as if her ribs had turned into ivory tusks. Something dreadful had happened to Uncle Nigel. A broken ankle or, God forbid, another heart attack.

"I'm afraid I have sad news," McKitterick said.

Caro struggled to draw in air, but those tusks were jagged. *Oh, no. Please, no.*

"Sir Nigel is dead."

A ripping sensation tore through Caro's sternum, as if those tusks had cleaved her in half. She pressed a shaking hand over her heart. "He's what?" she whispered.

"I'm so sorry. He was murdered in Bulgaria two days ago. A robbery gone awry at the Perperikon dig site. The Kardzhali police held the news for days. Typical bureaucrats. But the story has already appeared in French and Italian newspapers."

She sat down hard on the bed, and a slat beneath the mattress rattled against the floor. The man's voice reverberated inside her head. Murdered. As opposed to died. Uncle Nigel had taken her in after the fire. He'd raised her as his own, insisting she wouldn't end up like Pip or Oliver Twist. Now she was twenty-five and found herself orphaned for a second time. The heartbreak of losing her family was happening all over again.

"I'm dreadfully sorry," McKitterick said. "We're quite fond of Sir Nigel. The British Museum wouldn't have those delightful Syrian artifacts without him. We owe him a debt of gratitude."

She swallowed. "What happened?"

"The consulate in Sofia will have more details. I

assumed you'd want to get to your uncle straightaway. I'm sending a driver to your flat. He'll have your tickets and itinerary, of course, but I'd like to go over it quickly." He paused. "Are you still there, Miss Clifford?"

"Barely."

"You've got a seven thirty-five flight out of Heathrow. You'll arrive in Sofia before noon. Someone from the consulate will drive you to the station and make sure you get on the correct train to Kardzhali. You'll be staying at the Hotel Ustra. Is this all right?"

"Yes. I'm sorry. I can't talk. I—" She hung up, then fell face first against the bed and burst into tears. Last spring, she had hurt Uncle Nigel horribly when she'd dropped out of King's College to become a tour guide— an odd career path for a Ph.D. candidate in medieval history, but she'd leaped at the chance to leave her uncle's stone house in Oxford. All her friends were either engaged or married, and some had babies on the way.

Caro had desperately wanted to be on her own for a while, but when Uncle Nigel had learned of her plans, he'd developed chest pains. She'd slipped a nitroglycerin tablet under his tongue and blamed her decision on yet another disastrous romance—which was true, but not exactly surprising, considering she couldn't keep a boyfriend longer than two seconds. After much cajoling, her uncle had arranged for her to move into a Covent Garden flat, saddling her with a roommate who lived on sunflower seeds and indulged in biweekly seaweed wraps at a salon around the corner.

Uncle Nigel had made sure Caro's name wasn't in the phone book or even on the mailbox. Even her friends had trouble finding her. During her weekly visits to her uncle's house, he'd claim that Dinah the cat was pining herself into an early grave over Caro's absence, and then he'd lift the corpulent feline, grunting with the effort, and say, "Nothing but fur and bones."

He can't be dead, she thought, dabbing her eyes on the pillowcase. She slid off the bed and began digging through her closet. The few clothes she owned had been bought at the secondhand store. What was the temperature in southern Bulgaria? Cold. It would be icy and cold. She pulled her plaid duffel bag from the shelf and started packing. She'd just slipped into tattered jeans and a striped purple sweater when her bedroom door opened and Phoebe stuck her head through the crack.

"Sorry to wake you." Caro bit her lip. "I was going to leave a note."

"Why? What's happened?" Phoebe frowned at the duffel bag.

"Uncle Nigel. He—" Caro couldn't say the words. Three impossible words: *He was murdered*. She opened a drawer, pulled out a black sweater, and tossed it into the bag. Finally, she managed a terse, "He passed away."

Phoebe's tiny hand slid around Caro's waist, and the lemony scent of Eau d'Hadrien drifted between them: Phoebe's trademark scent. "I'm so sorry," she said. "Was it his heart?"

Before Caro could answer, the intercom buzzed in the hallway. "That's my ride," Caro said.

"I'll tell him you're on your way." Phoebe hurried out of the room.

Caro stood on her toes and reached for the Byzantine icon that hung over her desk. It had belonged to her parents. She traced delicate art. A saint stood at the cen-

ter, her dark hair streaming down the front of the burgundy robe. She held an ostrich egg in one hand, a
gilt-edged book in the other. A bleeding man lay at her
feet while the night sky stretched over a vineyard, a castle,
and a monk in the distance. Uncle Nigel had attached
rules to this relic. If she traveled outside the U.K., the
icon went with her. "Keep it with you at all times," he'd
said. "No matter how inconvenient. You don't want a
hotel maid to nick it, do you?" Caro hadn't questioned
him. It was as if she were protecting her parents, keeping
them with her. She wrapped the icon in a plastic dry-
cleaning wrapper and slid it into the duffel bag.

"All set?" Phoebe called.

"Just about." Caro shoved a red hat over her hair,
grabbed her mittens, and slung her bag over her shoulder.
Phoebe was waiting beside the front door. She straightened Caro's hat.

"There you go. Much better. If you'd stop spinning for
two minutes and fix yourself up, you'd find a boyfriend."

Caro waved her hand. Her last boyfriend had specialized
in Jack the Ripper tours and couldn't seem to get enough
of her. That is, until he was suddenly distracted by a Soho
waitress. A wise move on his part, really, since everyone
Caro loved ended up dead.

"Call me," Phoebe said.

Caro hurried down the stairs and out the front door.
A black Jaguar waited by the curb, its windshield wipers
ticking back and forth. The door swung open and a portly
driver climbed out. Rain drummed against his umbrella
as he escorted Caro to the car. She had started to duck
into the backseat when she heard her name being called.
The sound was coming from across the street. She turned.

A man with a dark ponytail stepped away from a blue Range Rover and came toward the Jaguar.

"Miss Clifford?" he called again. One good thing about tour guiding: She had perfected the art of barely glancing at a person and compiling a profile. Tall. Broad shoulders. Athletic build. Early thirties. Dimpled cheeks. Cut-glass British accent. His eyes were an unnerving shade of blue. Rain slid down his ponytail, streaming down a chocolate leather jacket.

"Yes, what is it?" Caro asked.

"Don't talk to him, Miss Clifford," the embassy driver cried, shielding her with the umbrella. "He's with the paparazzi."

"I am not," the ponytailed guy said. "I only need a moment with Miss Clifford."

"Off with you or I'll ring the police," the driver said, waving the umbrella. He guided Caro into the backseat, shut the door with a flourish, then climbed into the car. Muttering to himself, he handed Caro her tickets and itinerary. As he steered away from the curb, the Jaguar was nearly broadsided by a white Citroën van.

"Blooming punk!" Her driver hunched over the wheel and eased the car into Bow Street.

Caro glanced out the window. The guy with the ponytail stood in the middle of the road. He was a little too handsome, the type of man who usually ignored her and chased after Phoebe. Caro forced herself to look away and sank down in the seat. Uncle Nigel had just died and she was analyzing a reporter's looks. How sick was that? Her throat tightened and she couldn't catch her breath. She'd never had a panic attack, but this was exactly how she'd imagined one might feel. She burst into huge, racking sobs.

"You poor dear," the driver said, and held out a box of tissues.

"Thanks." She pulled out a sheet and blotted her eyes.

"Take the lot," he said. "I've a feeling you'll be needing them."

The Jaguar turned onto the Strand, sped by the Charing Cross station, and looped through Trafalgar Square. She glanced down at her tickets. Today was November 29. Last week, Uncle Nigel had called from Kardzhali, Bulgaria. "I'll be home on the twenty-eighth. Let's have tea on November twenty-ninth."

"I have to work," she'd said. She felt lucky to have a job after the Waterloo debacle.

"It's rather important or I wouldn't ask," he'd said. "I want you to meet a chap from Switzerland. If it's all right, he'll stop by your flat and bring you to Oxford. Say about two-ish?"

"You're matchmaking," she'd cried, instantly suspicious.

"Don't get your knickers in a twist." He'd chuckled. "It's not a romantic conspiracy."

Right, she'd thought, smiling. He'd thrived on code breaking and conspiracies.

Surely the ponytailed man wasn't the man Uncle Nigel had mentioned. No, not likely. The fellow wouldn't have shown up at five A.M. for a two o'clock date. Besides, he'd spoken with a British accent.

Caro pressed her forehead against the glass and imagined her uncle cutting through Green Park, hurrying to St. James Place. She saw the wind tugging his tweed coat as he dashed into the Athenaeum Club. He was everywhere and nowhere, striding ahead of her, just out of reach.

CHAPTER 2

Moose Tipper parked the white Citroën at the end of Bow Street. He turned off his mobile phone and tossed it into the glove compartment. Then he leaned back in his seat and tapped his fingers on the steering wheel, matching the rhythm to a U2 song that was playing on the radio.

He smiled into the rearview mirror. "Hello, love," he told himself. His teeth were the color of slate shingles. He started picking at them when a man with a ponytail walked past the van and climbed into a blue Range Rover. It had a Heathrow sticker, a hired car.

Moose pushed his face against the window for a better look, but the car blasted down the road and turned the corner. With a great sigh, he pulled away from the curb, did a U-turn, and steered the van into a parking slot in front of a redbrick Edwardian. Light pooled down from a fourth-story bay window. The bird's window. She was still awake, most likely from his phone calls.

He exhaled, his breath barely frosting the glass, and studied the building. No security cameras. No doorman. A bit unusual for a posh neighborhood. He loathed how the rich congregated in ritzy-fitzy buildings, insulating themselves from people like himself. This building was close to the theater district, the flats occupied by toffee noses. He'd like to throw the lot of them into the Thames. After he'd drained their blood, of course.

It was time to kidnap the bird. He shut off the engine, reached for his burglar bag, and uncoiled from the van. He huddled on the porch as the rain battered the canvas awning. Mr. Underwood, the head of security at Wilkerson Pharmaceuticals, had told him to chloroform the bird and take her to the laboratory in Hammersmith. If witnesses were about and he couldn't kidnap the bird, he'd have to collect the DNA samples right there in her flat.

"You want a blood or saliva test?" Moose had asked.

"Neither," Underwood said. "You'll need to perform a bone marrow aspiration."

"That's a bit over the top for a DNA test." Moose frowned.

"Just do it," Underwood snapped. "The girl might be Mr. Wilkerson's daughter."

"Crikey." Moose licked each fingertip, as if sending a Morse code message to himself. Harry Wilkerson was the big boss, the owner and CEO of his family's pharmaceutical company; the man had zero interpersonal skills, yet he'd made billions, mainly by eliminating fiscal waste— and his competition, too, but what the hell. So why did old Harry want a bone marrow aspiration when a simple paternity test would suffice? Before Moose had become one of Wilkerson's operatives, he'd worked briefly in the Hammersmith lab as a phlebotomist, so he knew about hematology and all that rubbish. Then again, what the bloody hell did it matter? As long as Moose received his paycheck and daily transfusions, he shouldn't complain.

"Anything else, guv'nor?" he'd asked Underwood.

"Don't kill her," the little man said. "And don't drink her blood."

"No problem." Moose shrugged. Like he'd want to feed from Wilkerson's offspring. *That would be a poisoned well, wouldn't it, mate?* Underwood gave him a snapshot of the girl, but it had slipped out of Moose's pocket. He remembered she was blond and pretty. Just his type.

Now he studied the brass nameplates beside the massive black door. The plates were lined up in two rows and each one had a corresponding buzzer. He couldn't find one with the bird's name, so he pushed the lot, hoping one or more of the wankers would buzz him in.

They didn't.

Moose jimmied the door with a penknife and swaggered into the lobby. It smelled sweet, with rusty undertones. He pulled disposable booties over his shoes and hurried up the stairs. Each floor had the same dark wooden walls and crystal sconces. He took the steps two at a time. His satchel banged against his right leg, and he pressed his wide palm against it to silence the rattling. The bird would have to live on the top floor, but the rich went for rooftop gardens and sweeping views, didn't they?

Number 4-D stood at the end of a long paneled hall. The black door had a peephole. He moved toward it, pausing beside the sconces to unscrew the hot lightbulbs.

Burned fingertips weren't part of his job description. Many things weren't. He didn't like to burgle; his talents lay elsewhere: kidnappings, tracking, extortion, and assassinations. Danger gave him an adrenaline rush that made him feel alive. Moose thought of himself as a BBBS: a brilliant body bag specialist. Not to brag. It was the truth. Even with a bloody obsessive-compulsive disorder, he was top notch—better than the Zuba brothers.

Outside 4-D, he opened his satchel and pulled on a surgical cap, tucking his wavy red hair inside. Next, he pulled on latex gloves and a paper scrub suit. Wilkerson had a "leave no DNA behind" policy. If you didn't leave it, you weren't there. Moose whistled under his breath as he uncapped a black pen and inked over the peephole. Then he leaned close to the door and meowed. This was his most brilliant talent: He could mimic any voice, but he excelled at cats and crying babies. Rich birds were pushovers for mewling kittens.

Before he had time to put the marker away, the girl opened the door and let out a squeak. Clearly she'd expected to find a cat, not a large man in surgical attire. But oh, she was lovely, a wee, wispy thing with golden hair. She didn't resemble Wilkerson, not in the least. So maybe she wasn't his daughter, after all.

She glared at Moose, tugging on the edges of her pink flannel jim-jams. "I heard a kitty," she said.

He meowed. She started to slam the door, but he lunged into the flat. His satchel banged to the floor as he clamped his hand over her mouth. With his other hand, he steered her down the narrow hall. Her muffled screams annoyed him.

"Shut your cake hole. I won't hurt you," he said.

She screamed louder and flailed upward. Her nails scraped down the surgical gown. She twisted, and the pink jim-jams showed her ribs. He dragged her into the living room. No flatmate. No lover. Just him and her. Maybe he could tie her to the bed and slip her a length. As long as he didn't kill her or drink her blood, he could do as he pleased. He'd brought a condom, just in case.

Her eyes bulged, the lids quivering. She reminded him of his mother-in-law, little and toothy. "You're a cheeky one," he said, and she screamed into his hand. He smelled her terror. Something pattered against the carpet, and he saw a damp stain spread on her pajama bottoms. A stench rose up.

"Blinking hell, darling. You've pissed yourself."

Keeping one hand over her foghorn mouth, he dragged her toward the bedroom. She kicked over a lamp, then knocked the phone off the hook. Her sharp little teeth sank through his gloved hand, into his fleshy palm. He winced. Crikey, he hadn't been bitten in a while. Human bites were germy. You could lose your arm to a human bite. But at least she hadn't drawn blood. She needed a good seeing-to. The chloroform was in the satchel and the satchel was beside the door and he'd left the bloody door wide open.

The moment he released her, she scrambled away. He jerked her back. Her teeth caught his thumb and clamped down. One of her hands flapped up, a wren trying to escape the hawk, and her claws lodged in his hair. He heard a ripping sound, felt a wrenching ache. Stupid little bird. Now he'd have to spend the rest of the night hoovering. He couldn't leave his DNA or he'd be in the clink.

One thing at a time, mate. First, make her stop biting.

He slid his other thumb into the side of her mouth, feeling around her molars for an empty space. This was what he did with fighting dogs. It made them quit biting, although sometimes it broke their jaws.

She grabbed another handful of his hair and yanked it out. A scalding pain ran through his skull, searing vessels and nerves, and pooled behind his eyes. Gritting his teeth, he slammed his elbow against her chin. The bone made a crackling noise, as if he'd dropped a porcelain bowl. Her fingers opened and wiry, red filaments floated between them, each strand bearing a chunk of Moose's scalp.

He spread her body on the floor and felt for a pulse. Nothing. Her pupils were dilating, the irises filling with black. She wasn't breathing, either.

"Stone the crows," he muttered. He'd broken her flipping neck. Now what? Should he call Mr. Underwood? Here it was, the worst-case scenario. He supposed it didn't matter now whether he tasted her.

Moose strode into the hall, gathered his satchel, and slammed the door. He hurried back to the bird and hunkered beside her body. He peeled up the jim-jam top. The movement set her creamy breasts to quivering. He'd seen better. Not that it mattered. Not now. As his gaze moved up to her throat, his mouth watered. He pushed his teeth into her carotid artery. Just a little sip, that's all, a sip. The blood was still warm, but it wasn't pumping.

A while later, he remembered the bone marrow test.

The needle was sharp and hollow, roughly the size of a lead pencil. He fit it onto a syringe, aimed it between the girl's breasts, and pressed down. It was like pushing a screwdriver into soft wood. He pulled back on the plunger, but nothing came out. It was easy to go through the bone, so he retracted the needle a millimeter. The syringe filled with dark, venous blood, swirling like dark burgundy with bits of floating cork. Moose studied the white specks. Marrow. Each piece was no bigger than a grain of kosher salt.

He squirted a little fluid onto his tongue. AB negative, the rarest of the rare, with a hint of copper. He capped the needle and eyed the bird. What a pity to let all this blood go to waste—it wasn't like she needed it, did she? He grabbed a handful of syringes and bent closer to the girl. While he drained her, he couldn't decide if he should sell the blood or add it to his private collection.

Keep it, mate, he told himself. *Keep the lot of it.*

CHAPTER 3

HEATHROW AIRPORT, TERMINAL FIVE
LONDON, ENGLAND

Caro walked past the gated shops in Terminal Five, wasting time until the duty-free boutique opened. She'd forgotten to pack a hairbrush, and if her curls were allowed free rein, they'd weave together of their own accord, hardening into woolly knots, and she'd have little choice but to shave her head.

She walked under paper globes that hung from the ceiling. Way off in the distance, a baby cried and cried.

Tears burned the backs of her eyes as she drifted down the sunlit corridor. The Harrods window display caught her attention. A Portmeirion tea set had been arranged on a spill of green velvet, each cup showing a different British flower. These same dishes were in her uncle's Oxford kitchen, lined up in the Welsh cupboard.

Her eyes filled and she pressed her fingertips against

the glass. When she was five years old, thieves had set fire to her family's home in Crab Orchard, Tennessee. An elderly couple had found her wandering on Millstone Gap Road, and they'd driven her to a hospital. Caro was suffering from smoke inhalation, a third-degree burn on her hand, and singed hair. The next day, a man in a brown fedora showed up at the hospital. He had a barrel chest and red cheeks, and he spoke with a strange accent.

"I'm your uncle Nigel," he said. "Well, technically I'm your third cousin, but let's dispense with the proprieties, shall we?"

He checked her out of the hospital, pausing to steal her medical chart from the nurses' station. The uncle had explained that all traces of her had to vanish. "Or those bad men'll get me?" Caro asked, blinking back tears. She wiped her bandaged hand over her eyes.

"Not on your nelly," Uncle Nigel said.

They drove to New Orleans and somehow he'd obtained a new passport for Caro without producing her birth certificate. The next day they'd flown to England and made their way to a cozy, book-lined house in Oxford, then he'd tucked her into a poster bed in the guest room. Caro had tried to sleep, but a striped cat had leaped onto her chest and begun kneading, its claws tugging the wool blanket.

Tears pricked Caro's eyes as she remembered her old house in Tennessee—a white clapboard with green shutters, deep porches, and a flying pig weathervane. Their driveway had a gate that ran on solar power and no one could pass through without a code—or so they'd thought. She remembered limestone, black dirt, coal mines, copperheads, biscuits, syrup running down the blade of a silver knife. Her mother had painted an Alice in Wonderland mural in the nursery. Clocks, chess pieces, the Caterpillar's mushroom, a croquet game with hedgehogs and flamingos. Now everything was gone; the white house had burned.

The next day, Caro and her uncle took the train to London and went shopping at Harrods. They stepped onto the Egyptian Escalator, and her uncle steadied her when her bandaged hand skidded on the rail. In Toyland, her uncle bought her a Paddington Bear, and then they drifted over to the Georgian Restaurant, where a man in a tuxedo led them past tea carts that overflowed with tiny cakes and lemon tarts, to a table in the center of the room. Their waiter's head reminded Caro of a giant volleyball, white and round, with fine black hairs combed just so. He recommended the high tea, twenty-four pounds per person; a glass of champagne added nine additional pounds.

Caro sucked her bottom lip, trying to understand how one drink could cause a sudden weight gain. Her mother, Vivi, had often served champagne and she hadn't grown or shrunk.

"And what for the lass?" The waiter smiled. "A cup of milk?"

"Champagne," she said, eager to sample these magical English foods and beverages. Hadn't *Alice's Adventures in Wonderland* involved cakes and drinks?

"Er, it's a bit unseemly for a child to drink an alcoholic beverage," the waiter said.

"Oh, all right. Bring her a pot of Moroccan mint tea," Uncle Nigel said.

"Sir?" she asked her uncle. "Why is it called a high tea? Because it's served on a high floor?"

"I like how your mind works." Uncle Nigel's lips

tugged into a smile. "Tea is a fancy meal. American tourists add the *high*, my darling."

While he lectured her about the history of British food, the waiter brought a three-tiered serving tray. The bottom layer was crammed with tiny crustless sandwiches; the smaller, higher plates held scones, crumpets, and tartlets. Not a single one had EAT ME written on it. She sighed and reached for a raisin scone, but her bandage was cumbersome and it knocked the pastry to the table. She lowered her head and her eyes filled.

Uncle Nigel dragged an enormous handkerchief from his pocket. "No tears before bedtime. We'll get on famously, but for your own privacy and security, it might be wise to establish some ground rules. Do you know what those are?"

"You lay a ruler on the ground?" She wiped her eyes. The handkerchief smelled faintly of tobacco, and one edge was monogrammed in black. *C* for *Clifford*.

"You're quite precocious for a tot. Let's just call it a list of 'mustn'ts,' shall we?" he continued. "First, when people ask how you came to live with me, you mustn't answer. I want you to shrug. Like this." He demonstrated. "And roll your eyes. Got it?"

She nodded. Her daddy had played games like this.

"Second, you mustn't tell anyone you are from Tennessee—don't even mention America. Third, you mustn't speak of the fire."

Caro didn't ask why. Something ghastly had happened to Mother and Daddy, but she didn't know the whole story. Her uncle's reluctance to discuss the fire was like a red ribbon pulled tight between them. She wanted to thrum and pick at that ribbon, but he just smiled and poured milk into her tea.

"I don't suppose you can tone down that Southern accent," he said.

"What's an accent?" she asked.

"Never mind, darling. I'll hire a speech therapist. Here's another scone. Do you want clotted cream?"

"What does *clotted* mean in British? Spoiled or just lumpy?" How would she ever remember that tea was another word for supper? And what about that nine-pound glass of champagne? Her uncle had taken quite a few sips, but he didn't seem heavier. Yet. Great Britain was looking more and more like a place where the English language wasn't English and food had whimsical effects.

"Clotted cream is delicious," he said. "Rather like a British version of whipped cream, but thicker." Her uncle had smiled and patted her hand. "Caro, you're a dandy."

All these years later, when she heard the word *tea*, she still thought in dualities. Tea was a beverage *and* a late-afternoon meal. Meatless teas were her favorite. She liked nothing better than eating scones and jam and clotted cream while she watched old movies. Once she'd plowed through an entire jar of Devon cream while Olivier had attacked the Spanish Armada in *Fire over England*.

She blotted her eyes with tissues the embassy driver had given her. The overhead speakers crackled and a crisp voice announced that Flight 1887 was boarding—not her plane. There was still time to look for a hairbrush.

She turned away from the Harrods display and bumped into a man. He wore a brown leather jacket and carried a backpack. It was the man who'd been lurking outside her flat. His eyes were blue, with brown chips in the left iris. He resembled the actor in the Dunhill Cologne commercials, but his dark, expressive eyebrows were just like Humphrey Bogart's. Normally she was skittish around strangers, especially handsome ones who seemed to be following her, but the news about her uncle had left her numb.

"You were on Bow Street," she said. "Did you follow me?"

"I'm sorry if I frightened you," he said, sounding anything but sorry. He stepped sideways, giving off a gust of cologne. Caro was surprised that it wasn't Dunhill, after all, but Acqua di Parma, the same scent Uncle Nigel wore. Used to wear.

"Are you following me?" She narrowed her eyes. "Wait, are you a reporter from the *Observer*? Or a staffer from the *Daily Star*?"

"Yes, I followed you. And no, I'm not a reporter." His lips twitched as if he were repressing a smile. "I'm a biochemist."

"That was my next guess. Biochemists are always skulking outside my flat." Her voice sounded clear and confident, but his quick smile was getting to her. His upper lip was well-defined, forming a wide M. Her hands began to shake, and she tucked them behind her back.

"There's a Starbucks ahead. Do you have time for a sit-down?" He pointed at the corridor, where people with backpacks and tote bags were rushing to their gates. A crooked line was forming outside the ladies' room.

"I shouldn't," Caro said, though she desperately needed a gingerbread latte.

"It's rather urgent or I wouldn't pester you," he said. "I won't take much of your time. When does your flight leave? Mine's leaving at eight forty."

He unzipped his backpack and pulled out a folder that

held his ticket and passport. Behind him, a young woman in a plaid coat struggled to control her three toddlers. A chubby girl in a white bunny coat broke free and ran past Caro, straight for a nearby construction zone.

"Lacie, no," the mother cried, holding on to the other children.

Caro shuddered as she remembered the family she'd briefly misplaced at Waterloo Station. She stepped around the biochemist and ran. Just before little Lacie ducked under the scaffold, Caro caught her. A burgundy tint suffused the tot's pale cheeks as she pummeled Caro.

"Put me down!" Lacie cried.

"Let's go find your mum, shall we?" Caro said.

"Bugger off!" Lacie yelled.

The mother rushed up, dragging the other children. Caro set the squirming child on the ground "Be good," she said, patting Lacie's shoulder.

"Oh, thank you, miss," the mother said, pulling the children off to the side. Lacie scowled at Caro.

The biochemist caught up with her. "If you can give me five minutes, I'd be grateful."

She glanced at her watch. In ten minutes her flight would start boarding. She'd have to buy a hairbrush in Kardzhali. "I don't mean to be rude," she began, "but I've suffered an enormous loss, and I'd just like to be alone."

"Yes, I'm dreadfully sorry about your uncle. That's why I've been dogging you. He invited me to tea. I was supposed to give you a lift to Oxford. Then I learned about his death."

Her throat tightened. He'd known Uncle Nigel? Wait, was this the man from Switzerland? "How did you find out?"

"The Zürich airport. It was all over Sky News. They referred to Sir Nigel as England's most beloved tomb raider."

She put one hand on her hip. "Just who *are* you?"

"Sorry, I should have introduced myself straightaway. I'm Jude Barrett." He extended his hand, but she ignored it. Had he really been invited for tea or was he a clever paparazzo trying to pump her for information?

They stepped around a queue outside Plane Food. Morning light spilled through the tall windows, falling in brilliant stripes along the corridor.

"How did you meet my uncle?" she asked.

"Actually, I didn't. We corresponded. His letters were baffling."

Her pulse sped up. "Do you have them?"

"Yes." Jude paused under a departure monitor and glanced at the schedule. Then he pointed to a desk. "That's my gate. Perhaps I could change my reservation. I've got a dreadful layover, anyway. What's your flight number? If I switched, we'd have three and a half hours to talk."

He walked to a British Airways counter and explained his dilemma to the ticket agent, whose face was shaped like a fist. "I'm terribly sorry," the agent said. "I'm afraid all seats are taken."

Jude turned back to Caro. "Well, I tried. Perhaps we can reconnect at the Sofia airport. It's a big ask, but could you wait there until my plane arrives?"

"Someone from the embassy is meeting me." She felt a pinch of disappointment. She was dying to know what was in those letters. From the overhead speakers, a woman with a clipped voice announced Caro's flight number.

"That's me," she said. "I should go."

"But how shall I find you?"

"I'm staying at the Hotel Ustra in Kardzhali. Let me give you my mobile number."

"I don't have a mobile." He stepped backward, toward his gate. "I'll hire a car and make my way to Kardzhali. Perhaps we can have tea and discuss your uncle."

The loudspeaker kept announcing Caro's flight. She reluctantly turned and ran to her gate. It wasn't until her plane taxied down the runway that she realized she'd forgotten his last name. It started with a *B*, she was sure of it. She was so discombobulated, all she remembered was Jude. If he forgot her hotel, she'd never find him. And those letters would be lost. *If they existed.*

CHAPTER 4

WILKERSON PHARMACEUTICALS
EAST LONDON, ENGLAND

Harry Wilkerson rose from his desk and paced in front of the long windows. His office was on the twenty-fifth floor of Wilkerson Pharmaceuticals, the newest building in the East End of London and home to the biggest pharmaceutical company in Europe. He clasped his hands behind his back and stared down at the River Thames, watching a tourist boat chug through the gray water.

If Caroline Clifford was out there, he would find her. Maybe she was his daughter, and maybe she wasn't. Either way, nothing would change for him.

He turned away from the view, stepped over to his desk, and reached for an old newspaper. It was dated November 5, Guy Fawkes Day, and showed a photograph of a pretty, but apparently ditzy, London tour guide who'd lost an entire family at a tube station. Days ago, when he'd read the article, he'd been captivated by the girl's heart-shaped face and wide-set eyes that slanted upward just the slightest bit. Except for the bushy, shoulder-length hair, which appeared to be dishwater blond, she was the image of his dead wife, Vivienne.

At first, he'd thought the girl *was* Vivienne—had she somehow survived the fire? If Vivienne hadn't perished, she would now be in her forties. He found a magnifying glass and held it over the photograph. This girl was younger. Her skin was plump, glowing, and unwrinkled. Yet the resemblance to Vivi was uncanny. Surely her daughter, Caroline, had died in the inferno. But the remains of only two bodies had been found in the ashes. Wilkerson abhorred loose ends, and his experts had assured him that the bones of a five-year-old child would have been cremated in that blaze. Now, decades later, here was Vivi's dead ringer in the newspaper. He threw down the newspaper, strode to the bar, and poured a glass of scotch.

Twenty-six years ago, on the Ides of March no less, he'd sent Vivienne to Sotheby's to bid on ten pages from *Historia Immortalis*. Vivi had been a manuscript curator, quite the little know-it-all on Psalters and whatnot, and according to her, scholars were divided about the book. Some believed it was an account of early astronomers who'd mapped the evening sky; others claimed it was a history of vampirism. Whatever it was, *Historia Immortalis* had launched a crusade in southern France and had played a role in the Inquisition. A tremendous role. Then it had vanished for nearly eight hundred years, only to resurface at the auction.

He'd told Vivi to bid on a medieval icon, too—a sort of companion piece to the manuscript.

"How much are you willing to spend?" Vivi had stood in front of the gilt mirror, brushing her shoulder-length hair. The straight, shiny locks were precisely the color of Earl Gray tea.

"Whatever it takes," he said. "You've got carte blanche."

That afternoon she'd called to say she'd won both the icon and the pages. She brought them to their Kensington flat and stood off to the side, watching with a curious expression as Wilkerson locked the items in his safe. He slipped into a burgundy robe and uncorked a bottle of Merlot, but Vivi wasn't in the mood to celebrate. She pleaded exhaustion and went straight to bed.

Weeks later, on an unseasonably warm morning in April, Vivi left the flat in a hurry. Later, Wilkerson found a home pregnancy test in the trash bin. He held up the pink stick as if it were a mouse tail and blinked at the plus sign in the display grid.

Damn her. Vivi knew he wasn't ready for a baby. She'd clucked sympathetically when he'd told her about his workaholic father and his barmy, social-climbing mother. His parents had dumped young Harry into a boarding school where older boys had tormented him. He'd endured their tricks and insults. Now they were dead, the whole lot, and Wilkerson had restructured his late father's pharmaceutical company. He'd worked eighteen hours a day, sometimes sleeping in his office. Vivi hadn't complained. Her job as curator sent her around the world. What kind of parents would they make? Terrible ones, that's what. Without fail, they'd used contraceptives. Yet here she was, carrying a snot-nosed imp in her belly. Well, she'd just have to get rid of it.

Wilkerson stayed home from the office that day. He poured a glass of scotch and rehearsed a speech. The pregnancy wasn't negotiable. She'd get an abortion or face the consequences. After four years of marriage, he'd grown tired of her. True, Vivi was both exquisite and educated, but she was a bore, and besides, his mistress was far more titillating in bed.

He waited all day for Vivi to come home. At dusk, he began to worry. Had something happened? Was she injured?

I do love her, after all, he thought.

When first light rose over the steep rooftops in Kensington, he'd changed his mind about fatherhood. What would his child look like? Would it have his hazel eyes or Vivi's strange pewter ones? Would it inherit the Wilkerson square chin?

He began to panic when Vivi didn't show up the next day. A sharp-edged fear, hard as shattered granite, sliced through his chest. He ran to his safe, spun the dial, and opened the steel door. Empty, except for a first edition Evelyn Waugh and Vivi's wedding rings. The bitch had left him. His detectives said she'd run off with a wealthy Frenchman she'd met at the auction, taking her unborn child and the artifacts with her.

For a time, Wilkerson went off the rails. His detectives lost Vivi at the Rome airport. Her passport had cleared Customs, and then she'd vanished. His men turned Italy inside out, but they hadn't found her.

It took him years to track down Vivienne. By then, he'd put vampires on the payroll, and they'd tracked Vivi and her Frenchman to a remote hilltop in eastern Tennessee, where they were raising a small girl.

Wilkerson sent six of his toughest Bulgarians to murder the Frenchman; the men were supposed to retrieve Vivi, the child, and the stolen artifacts. But the vampires had gone into a frenzy when the lovers had fought back. The house went up in flames. Everything had burned. Vivi, the child, the icon, and all ten pages of *Historia Immortalis*.

Now, years later, Vivi's doppelgänger had gotten her picture in the newspaper for being a little fool. Again, Wilkerson had investigated, on the off chance that she *had* made it out of the burning house with the artifacts. His in-house detectives had quickly learned the girl's name: Caroline Clifford.

Wilkerson's men had pressured the tour agency for more information. Not only did the director hold a low opinion of Miss Clifford, he swore he didn't have a London address on file, only an emergency contact at Norham Gardens in Oxford. A rather posh address for a silly guide. Until recently, she'd lived with an archaeologist—supposedly her uncle—but no one knew where she'd gone.

Vivienne had never mentioned relatives, except for some giddy cousins in Wiltshire. Wilkerson put his head detective on the case. Mr. Underwood learned that Sir Nigel Clifford was Vivienne's second cousin. But the cousin was excavating in southern Bulgaria.

Wilkerson had dispatched operatives to Kardzhali with instructions to kidnap the archaeologist and shake him down for information. But they'd shaken too hard.

Mr. Underwood shuffled into the office, carrying a stack of papers. He was a dainty-boned man who wore off-the-rack suits from Marks & Spencer. Before joining Wilkerson Pharmaceuticals, he'd worked at Interpol, where his talents had been underappreciated.

He gaped up at Wilkerson and took a step backward. He breathed so hard, the lenses in his thick glasses fogged.

"I thought you were at lunch, sir," Underwood said in a high-pitched voice. His eyes were completely obscured by the mist.

"What do you need, Mr. Underwood?"

"We should have Miss Clifford soon." Underwood set the papers on Wilkerson's desk, then pulled off his glasses. "I traced her mobile phone number to a Covent Garden flat."

"Brilliant," Wilkerson said. "Get someone on it."

"I already have, sir."

"Who'd you send?"

Underwood polished his glasses with his tie, as if afraid to meet Wilkerson's gaze. "Moose Tipper," he said.

"Not him!" Wilkerson slammed his fist against his desk.

"He was the only available operative, sir."

"And do you know why, Mr. Underwood? Because he's a buffoon." Wilkerson waved an imperious hand. "Ring him this instant. Tell him to back off."

"I believe it's too late, sir."

Wilkerson's jaw tightened. "Find him."

Underwood's hands shook as he pulled out his mobile and punched in numbers. The call went straight to voice mail. Wilkerson sneered when Moose's nasal, Cockney voice boomed from the phone: "Sorry, mate, I can't take your bloody stupid call. Leave a message if you dare, but I won't ring you back."

"Mr. Underwood, I want Moose off this case. Send your men to Covent Garden this instant."

"But that's just it, sir." Underwood's Adam's apple

clicked. "There's no one to send. They're at the Hammersmith facility, getting transfusions. And that's where Moose will bring the girl."

"You'd better hope he does," Wilkerson said. "Or you'll end up as a guinea pig in my lab."

CHAPTER 5

SOFIA, BULGARIA

Caro stepped into the arrival hall at Sofia International Airport and walked past a throng of taxi drivers. A short, stubby man began to follow her, and she flashed a stern glance over her shoulder to discourage him. A tall man loomed in the background. Both of them were wrapped head-to-toe in reflective capes, the type worn to deflect light in the desert. They wore wraparound sunglasses, too.

Their odd attire drew stares from the people around them. A woman in a red puffer jacket crossed herself. Two punks with blue hair called out something in a Slavic language—Croatian, maybe? Caro wasn't sure. She'd almost made it to the Hertz counter when the squatty man hollered, "English girl! Stop!"

She had the impression he was speaking to her. But how did she know she was a Briton? Surely the embassy hadn't sent him. If they had, forget it. She wasn't letting this freak drive her to the train station. She'd take her chances with a taxi. Then cold air whooshed over her, and suddenly the man was in front of her. He snatched her duffel bag and bolted.

Dammit. Son of a bitch. Caro choked down a scream. Rule one for a tour guide: Don't panic. But her icon was inside that bag. As she vaulted down the corridor, her hat flew off, and her hair burst out in every direction. All around her, the airport traffic seemed to blur. She heard shouting and a screech. In a flash, she was behind the man. She grabbed his ears and twisted, hard. He tripped over a suitcase and fell against the tile floor.

"Let go, you bloody lout!" Caro grabbed one end of the bag and yanked hard. The man rolled over and tugged in the opposite direction. He jerked the bag out of her grasp and started to rise. An officer blew a whistle and ran toward the commotion.

"He snatched my bag," Caro explained.

The policeman seized the thief's arm. Caro found her hat and slipped it over her head, tucking the militant curls inside. With as much dignity as she could muster, she unzipped her fanny pack and showed the policeman her passport.

He shoved the thief down the aisle. Caro looked for the man who'd yelled and the tall man who'd also been following her, but they'd vanished. She lifted a shaky hand and wiped her eyes, then she started down the crowded hall. Uncle Nigel had always made traveling seem easy. Negotiating with taxi drivers had been a snap because he'd spoken all of the Romance languages, including some Romanian. As soon as Caro had come to live with him, he'd placed one hand on her elbow and steered her through the world.

Over by the Supertrans window, she saw a man in a brown Harris Tweed jacket with a sign that read *Clifford*. She took a breath, walked over to him, and introduced herself.

"Lovely to meet you," he said in a loud, nasal voice. "I'm Thurston Hughes, from the embassy."

She smiled, then pulled off her gloves. They were black angora, patterned with sequined cats; Uncle Nigel had given them to her last year as a gag gift—*Happy Christmas, Love, Dinah*, he'd written. He'd always given presents from their felines.

"So sorry about your uncle." Mr. Hughes paused. "Was he your only relative?"

"Yes." Her hands shook as she tucked the gloves into her pocket. *Be strong*, she told herself. Uncle Nigel had always said that tears were for the living. The dead needed an Irish wake with lots of whiskey and laughter. God, she'd miss him.

———

"You won't be taking the train, after all," Mr. Hughes said. "We weren't sure if you knew the Cyrillic alphabet. It's frightfully easy to mix up the platforms. So I'm driving you to Kardzhali."

Caro followed him through the glass doors, onto the sidewalk. Taxis and vans were lined up along the curb. Mr. Hughes stopped in front of a black Mercedes with a British Embassy seal on the doors. He helped her into the passenger seat, then scuttled around to the other side of the car. He eased into the leather seat, advising her to buckle her seat belt, and without further ado, started the engine.

"The ambassador was outraged about your uncle's death," he said. "He's pressuring the Interior Ministry." Mr. Hughes pursed his lips as he drove down a narrow concrete incline, steering past a row of taxis into the spitting snow. "I've arranged for you to meet one of their officials, Ilya Velikov. Quite bureaucratic but incorruptible. You're to meet him at your hotel this evening. Around seven-ish. I believe he said the mezzanine bar."

"That will be helpful, thanks."

"Not at all," he said. "You look a bit peaky. There's bottled water in the backseat. And a pillow if you wish to nap. It's two hundred forty kilometers to Kardzhali."

She looked out the window. A girl with blue-tipped hair and a nose ring jogged down the sidewalk. When Caro was her age, in a punk phase and longing to get a butterfly tattoo, Uncle Nigel had taken her on a dig near St. Petersburg. He'd bloodied the nose of a KGB agent who'd sold artifacts to black marketers. Uncle Nigel had been arrested, and the British embassy had made a diplomatic protest. The incident had made her uncle an archaeological rock star. She'd been left alone at the Dostoevsky Hotel for two days. Without adult supervision, Caro had entertained herself by hoarding room service rolls and throwing them off the balcony at BBC reporters.

"I don't want to alarm you," Mr. Hughes said, "but do be careful while you're in Bulgaria. It's not a hotbed of crime, but it's not exactly bucolic, either."

"You aren't kidding. A man in the airport tried to steal my bag. He was rather peculiar—all covered in a foil poncho."

"I saw him—he was with another chap, wasn't he? They were wearing sunglasses. Probably to hide their pupils. I'm sure they were drug addicts."

"I chased him. And I got my bag."

"You were brave." Mr. Hughes chuckled, and then his lips drew into a frown. "But next time, you might not be so lucky. Not all of the dangers are human. Not too long ago, wild dogs killed a British tourist."

Caro thought of her dream and hugged herself.

"Not to scare you," Mr. Hughes said, looking rather alarmed himself. "But it was frightfully grisly. Of course, we have the mundane, mafia-style killings. The European Union is pressuring Prime Minister Stanishev to deal with organized crime. But the country is steeped in it. People have gone missing, too. Of course, vanishings have always occurred in this part of the world."

"But that was when Bulgaria was part of the Eastern Bloc," she said. "People were defecting like mad, weren't they?"

"That accounted for some disappearances. Now, of course, there's no reason for defection. Last month, a town near the Greek border reported dozens of missing people."

"What happened?"

"To the people? No one knows. The Interior Ministry looked into it. Apparently it's not a communicable disease, and it's not the Mafia." He cast a sidelong glance. "But never mind that. Have you been to Sofia before?"

"Ten years ago." She frowned. All this talk of missing people was making her jumpy.

"Bulgaria has joined the European Union since you were here," Mr. Hughes said. "But the roads haven't changed.

They're paved but pocky. And the Bulgarians don't believe in marking the lanes. Sometimes it's slow going. The ruddy drivers don't signal or observe the speed limit. One could reach Kardzhali sooner on a bicycle, I daresay."

She smiled into her hand. Uncle Nigel had disliked the sluggish, rural traffic even more than he hated warp speed on the Autobahn. The summer they'd driven from Sofia to Polovitz, they'd kept stopping for goats and horse-drawn carts.

Caro leaned closer to the window. The capital was just as she remembered, tidy and modern for an eight-thousand-year-old city, with Byzantine architecture juxtaposed against gray, Stalinist-era buildings. But the traffic! Just then, a green car cut across two lanes and plowed into the side of a lorry.

"Welcome to Bulgaria," Mr. Hughes said.

CHAPTER 6

WILKERSON PHARMACEUTICALS
EAST LONDON, ENGLAND

Harry Wilkerson sat on the edge of his desk and watched the flat-screen television on the far wall. A BBC reporter stood in front of a Covent Garden flat, the site of an early-morning murder. The victim was described as a twenty-five-year-old woman. Her name was being withheld pending notification of relatives.

Wilkerson looked away from the television and put one hand over his eyes. He had no doubt who the victim was or who had committed the crime. Moose. That pervert had killed the Clifford girl, and now the police had her body. Wilkerson would never know if she'd been his daughter. He'd never find his icon or those ten priceless pages of *Historia Immortalis*.

This was Underwood's fault. He shouldn't have sent that obsessive-compulsive oaf to Covent Garden. Years ago, when Moose had worked at the Hammersmith laboratory, he'd been banned from participating in bone marrow aspirations or biopsies on patients because he couldn't control his feeding frenzies. What had Underwood been thinking? He should have sent a human technician.

Wilkerson lowered his hand, then traced his finger along the blue veins that forked below his knuckles. Having vampires on the payroll carried risks, so he'd found a way to deal with their hunger and manage them. He'd implemented a company policy requiring all vamps to receive daily transfusions at the Hammersmith facility. This allowed his researchers to perform covert studies, mainly clinical drug trials. It was a risky project, because if the vamps knew the truth, they'd revolt. In minutes they could overpower the scientists and guards.

That was why Wilkerson had ordered SSRIs to be added to the transfusions. It was best to keep the immortals cheerful, but they were discouraged from setting foot in Wilkerson Pharmaceutical's headquarters on Waterloo Road. Some of the bolder ones paid no attention to rules. As a precautionary measure, Wilkerson hired a bodyguard, a Cambodian named Yok-Seng, who could put his foot through a man's chest. No immortals, not even the Zuba brothers, messed with Yok-Seng.

Wilkerson glanced back at the telly. The BBC reporter was still talking about the murder. Wilkerson poured scotch into a crystal glass. If he could live for centuries—never aging, never succumbing to disease—he would accumulate a staggering fortune. He wouldn't let anyone, or anything, threaten his dynasty, and that included loose ends.

The dead girl on Bow Street was more than a loose end. She'd been Wilkerson's last chance to find *Historia*

Immortalis. The book was much more than the history of vampirism: It held secrets to longevity and, interestingly enough, methods of destroying the immortals. If the tome fell into the wrong hands, it would pit science against religion. Men would lash out against vampires, depriving them of rights, but the battle would inevitably disintegrate into a predictable man-against-man conflict. Some humans would oppose the immortals, and some would offer support—or even breed with them.

Initially, the outing of vampirism would cause a social upheaval. The affluent, centuries-old clans would be ostracized. After all, the royals were a bit finicky about bloodlines. However, that would be the least of the vampires' problems. The wealthy and common alike would go into hiding. While they reorganized, they'd be sought by fringe groups and bounty hunters. Enthusiasts might hunt them for sport.

Wilkerson took a sip of scotch, grimacing as the liquid burned his throat. It would be gratifying to watch the predators become prey, but the carnage would be short-lived. Humans were no match for the vampires' longevity and superior physical abilities, not to mention their otherworldly skills such as telepathy and telekinesis. The lot were canny survivalists. For thousands of years, they'd endured in a symbiotic relationship with humankind. They'd restrained themselves. If they got the upper hand, humans would be openly slaughtered, and as the earth was depopulated, widespread panic would erupt. A polarized society is a weak society. Civilization would disintegrate. The immortals would roost in Buckingham Palace, feeding on animal blood, and humans would go the way of the Neanderthal.

But this won't happen, Wilkerson thought. He was developing a biochemical means that would give humans like himself an edge. He took another sip of scotch and walked to the framed black-and-white photographs that lined the far wall. Each picture featured an herb or plant associated with longevity: water droplets sliding down an ephedra leaf, snow on mayapple blossoms, a spiderweb laced over ginkgo biloba. Higher plants were the foundation of many pharmaceuticals, and "green," natural drugs were fashionable. As always, Wilkerson Pharmaceuticals would be on the cutting edge, creating products for aging baby boomers.

He patted his thickening midriff and frowned. He was getting older, and bursitis was settling into his joints. His Romanian biochemists were working on a promising drug. They called it "a facelift in a pill." No surgery, no needles, no allergy testing. The effects were temporary, of course, but once the medication was perfected, women would line up at clinics, demanding prescriptions. Wilkerson would rise to the top of the Fortune 500 list. *Time* would name him "Man of the Year."

The Romanian facility was also toying with stem cells, searching for biochemical ways to control aging—something far more permanent than an antiwrinkle pill. He'd recruited promising researchers from around the globe, and they were near a breakthrough in genome therapy. When that happened, Wilkerson would spend eternity without plucking gray hairs or enduring Botox and collagen injections. Laugh lines, his girlfriend called them. She should know, she had a few. Wilkerson didn't. His face was a tight, unlined mask. He never laughed. Laughter was for bloody fools with nothing better to do.

Wilkerson walked back to his desk and glanced at the television. Perhaps Yok-Seng could handle Moose. If not, Wilkerson would have to bring in the Zuba brothers.

God, he hated to do that. The Zubas were two Russian vampires with impulse control issues. When vampirism collided with any type of neurosis, the results were unpredictable. Savage, you might say.

From the desk, the intercom phone clicked, and his secretary's tinny voice rose up. "Mr. Wilkerson? I have Mr. Underwood on line two."

Wilkerson tossed down the scotch and picked up the receiver. "Yes?"

"Sir? We have a situation." Mr. Underwood's voice sounded quivery and high pitched.

"Go ahead." Wilkerson lifted his glass and held it up to the light. Just a dribble of scotch remained.

"It's the Clifford girl," Mr. Underwood said. "She's alive."

"Are you sure?" Wilkerson sat up straight. A pulse ticked in his neck.

"Quite sure," Underwood said. "Her passport surfaced on the grid. Heathrow's cameras show a young woman fitting her description in Terminal Five. She's flying to Bulgaria."

"Make sure there's a greeting party at the airport." Wilkerson poured another shot of scotch. Well, why not? He had a reason to celebrate. A few moments ago, the wheel of fortune had scraped the bottom, but now it was turning upward. The way it always did, always would.

CHAPTER 7

HOTEL USTRA
KARDZHALI, BULGARIA

Caro was leaning against the steel railing in the mezzanine bar, watching for the ministry representative, when a man in a brown leather jacket strode through the doors and up to the reception desk.

She drew in a ragged breath. It was the ponytailed man from Heathrow—Jude something-or-other. Caro couldn't decide if she should get his attention or spy a bit longer. Why was he really here? He might not be a reporter but he was acting like an archaeological groupie. Better to hang back, right?

She grabbed her duffel bag and stepped into the shadows, watching as Jude rested his elbows on the fake marble counter. He had a square face with a boyish, cleft chin. The collar of his jacket stood up against his neck, a tender, boyish neck. He shifted, and his ponytail fanned across his back. Dense shoulders filled out his jacket, the kind of biceps you'd see on a rugby player.

He looked up at the mezzanine and smiled at her. Dimples. God, she couldn't stand it. He passed under the chandelier, and the lighting washed over his face. His nose was straight except for an endearing bump near the bridge.

Breathe, Caro. Count to twenty. But he was already climbing the steps, his glossy ponytail spilling down his back. He stopped in front of her and extended his hand.

"I was hoping to see you," he said.

She shook his hand. Firm grip. Smooth palm. No calluses. Just how tall was he? She was almost five foot eight, but his chin could easily fit on top of her head. This morning his face had been smooth, but now there was a grainy shadow along his jaw. Through the stubble, she saw a tiny white scar on his chin. His eyes had a sleepy, jet-lagged look, and she felt an urge to sit him down with a cup of tea and a biscuit.

"You look lovely tonight," Jude said. He slipped one hand in his pocket, and his jacket parted, showing a cornflower-blue sweater.

"So," she said. Small talk wasn't her métier. Ask anyone and they'd confirm that she was a cut-to-the-chase sort of girl. Not one of her better qualities. Not by a long shot.

"Do you have time for a sit-down?" He stepped closer, and light from the chandelier passed over his face. He no longer resembled an exhausted boy who needed coddling. He looked like a man who wanted to get laid.

"I'm waiting for a ministry official," she said. "But I really want to see my uncle's letters."

"We could talk later. Over dinner, perhaps?" He smoothed one hand down the front of his sweater, the gesture of a man who was accustomed to wearing a suit and tie. But wasn't he a biochemist? Maybe he was into polo, pageantry, the peerage.

"I don't know how long the meeting will take," she said, but she was thinking, *I'm vulnerable tonight. I don't trust myself with you.*

"Not to worry. I'm in room three fourteen. Ring me, if you get a moment." He unzipped his backpack and pulled out two creamy envelopes.

"Your uncle's letters," he said.

She started to thank him, but her uncle's boxy handwriting caught her attention. The first envelope was addressed to Dr. Jude Barrett in Lucerne, Switzerland.

When she looked up, Jude was halfway down the stairs. She stepped closer to the railing and watched him stride toward the elevators. Caro stuffed the letters into her duffel bag. Just then, the black entry doors swung open, and an entourage stepped into the lobby: A balding, pear-shaped man marched past the front desk, followed by three men in uniforms. The bald man wore an official-looking black coat, but he was gripping a red backpack under one arm. The ministry official, no doubt. As he stopped beneath the chandelier, light bounced off his round eyeglasses. He looked up, spotted her, and walked up the stairs.

"Miss Clifford?" he asked.

"Da. Dobar vecher," she said in halting Bulgarian.

"I speak English." He produced a business card and waited while she tucked it away. "We meet under sad circumstances."

He turned toward the windows, where club chairs and glass tables were grouped into conversation pits. Behind them, snowflakes hit the glass and instantly melted. Caro hadn't realized how tired she was until she sat down and tucked one leg beneath her hips.

"Would you like wine? Have you tasted our Mavrud?" Velikov draped his overcoat on the back of his chair, then sat down. "It is a spicy red."

"I've sampled your national drink. Some type of fruit brandy?"

"Rakia." He smiled and wrinkles fanned out from his eyes. "I think you will prefer Mavrud."

A waiter set napkins on the glass table and took their drink orders. After he left, Velikov set the backpack on the table. "Your uncle's personal items," he said.

Caro leaned forward to examine the bag. It looked new. When had Uncle Nigel bought it? He'd hated shopping alone. Before she'd taken up tour guiding, she'd always helped him select his jackets and trousers. She placed her hand on the zipper and wondered if she had the nerve to open it. Not just yet. She folded her hands and leaned back in the chair.

Velikov tilted his head and swallowed. "Miss Clifford, I have difficult questions."

He paused as the waiter set down their wineglasses. "I did not know if you wanted your uncle's remains cremated or returned to England. If you prefer cremation, it is offered in Sofia. Otherwise, I will arrange a casket and a flight. It will take a week to do paperwork on both."

"No cremation." She reached for her napkin and dabbed at her eyes. "I'm so sorry."

"Please, do not apologize for your grief," Velikov said.

She lifted her glass, hoping the alcohol would help her relax, and took a long swallow. Over the rim she saw a tall, gangly man step into the bar. He had thick black hair and wore a black dinner jacket over a red floral Hawaiian shirt and jeans. Wait, she'd seen him at the airport with the purse snatcher. He sat down in one of the chairs and crossed his bony legs.

Velikov turned sideways in his chair. He glanced at the man and swiveled back to Caro. "Is he bothering you?"

"I saw him today at the Sofia airport. He was with a man who tried to steal my bag."

Velikov's eyes cut to her plaid duffel, but he made no comment.

"Now this creep is in Kardzhali." She leaned forward. "At the Hotel Ustra. Don't you find that a little strange?"

"You think he followed you?" Velikov asked in a conspiratorial tone.

Caro's hands began to shake, and her heart sped up. She nodded. Then she remembered that in Bulgaria a nod means no and a head shake means yes. She shook her head.

Velikov turned around to stare, but the man in the Hawaiian shirt wasn't looking at her. Now the ministry official would think she was a kook. Uncle Nigel had sheltered her to an extreme, and she'd grown into a cautious woman—okay, paranoid. But he'd also taught her to view the world through an archaeologist's eyes, paying attention to details.

"He does not look familiar." Velikov's eyes narrowed, and then he turned back to Caro. "But I know his type, and it is not good."

"I'll say."

"He will not harm you." Velikov patted Caro's hand. "I will make certain of it."

Caro looked past Velikov. The chair was empty. She

looked around for the man. When had he left? He wasn't at the bar, either. "Where did he go?" she asked.

Velikov frowned. "Most odd. I will have my men check the hotel. Also, I will alert the front desk. I will tell them to screen your calls and not to reveal your room number."

"Thanks." She took another sip of wine. "I'm not normally this nervous."

Liar, she thought.

"Your fear is justified." Velikov paused. "Considering the brutal way your uncle was murdered."

Brutal? The word slammed inside her head, and she stiffened. A Bulgarian would not use this word casually. The Ottomans had slaughtered them in the fourteenth century and, even today, a good part of Kardzhali was Muslim.

"Perhaps I have spoken out of turn," Velikov said.

"Someone needs to." She stared into her glass. "They didn't beat him, did they?"

He nodded. *No.*

"What happened?"

"The cause of death was exsanguination," said Velikov. "That means—"

"I know the term. Uncle Nigel took a blood thinner for his heart."

"I hesitate to continue. It is not for the faint of stomach."

"I need to know."

"This was more than a robbery. Your uncle was tortured. Both Achilles tendons were severed. And he was bitten."

"Did you say *bitten*?" She abruptly set her glass on the table, and the wine swayed.

"Yes." Velikov shook his head.

"By an animal?"

He shook his head. *Yes.* "And human."

No. Not possible. She rose abruptly and her knee hit the table. The wineglass tipped over, spilling Mavrud across the glossy surface, red drops pattering to the floor.

CHAPTER 8

WILKERSON PHARMACEUTICALS
EAST LONDON, ENGLAND

Moose Tipper sat at the far end of the mirrored conference table, its surface reflecting lights from nearby buildings. Wilkerson stood in front of the broad glass window, his hands clasped behind his back. The Thames stretched out in front of him, black and twisty.

"How did you bungle it *this* time?" Wilkerson asked.

"It went tits up," Moose said, but he was thinking that Wilkerson was absolutely wet. And, he wasn't immortal.

"What happened?" Wilkerson turned.

"I already told you." Moose extended his hand and pointed to the purple bite marks. "I didn't make a total bollocks of it. I got the samples. Isn't that what you wanted?"

"Have you looked at a newspaper?" Wilkerson leaned forward, his reflection moving along the mirror. "Listened to the news?"

"I don't watch the telly. It's too horrid." Moose brought his hands together, tapping each finger, right to left, left to right. Ten times. Perfect. When he noticed that Wilkerson was staring, Moose made a fist and slammed it against the table. "I got your fucking samples."

Wilkerson flinched.

"Didn't break it." Moose lifted his hand. The imprint of his fist had left a smudge on the mirror. He had heard that Wilkerson was sent down from Cambridge. Disgraced his family.

"You got the tissue samples, all right." Wilkerson paused. "From the wrong woman."

Moose narrowed one eye. "Say what?"

"The woman you murdered wasn't Caroline Clifford. You killed her flatmate. The girl's father was Sir Edmund Dowell."

"Never heard of him." Moose shrugged.

"He's the Lord Speaker in the House of Lords."

"Oh, *that* Dowell," Moose said, trying not to roll his eyes.

"Scotland Yard is crawling all over her flat."

"But you never said the Clifford girl had a roomie. I assumed—"

"I don't pay you to make assumptions. I pay you to complete a task. Wilkerson Pharmaceuticals is a billion-dollar corporation, and the cosmetics division will surpass that. I will not see this corporation destroyed by a blood sipper."

"I don't sip it, mate. I'm brilliant at what I do. You know I am. The situation isn't a total cock-up. I just killed the wrong girl. Tell me where to find the right one, and I'll bring her back." Moose clenched his fists, repressing an urge to straighten the pencils on Wilkerson's desk.

"It's too late," Wilkerson said. "I can't risk another botched assignment."

"I'll use chloroform this time. And I'll get your samples in half a tick."

"Sorry, I can't trust you."

"Sure you can." Moose opened his fists and tapped his fingers. Right to left. Left to right.

"You don't get it, do you?" Wilkerson cried. "This murder is all over the news. I can't afford another mistake. Mistakes lead to scandals. Scandals attract journalists. My company could end up on the BBC."

"So?" Moose's eyebrows went up. "I thought you liked publicity."

"A scandal would wreck my company. Worse, you and I could be locked up at Her Majesty's pleasure."

"Quit borrowing trouble, mate." Moose's fingers moved in a blur, tapping against the mirror. Wilkerson was a chinless wonder with a knack for turning pills and face creams into money. Lots of money.

Wilkerson pressed the intercom button. "Sandra?"

"Yes, Mr. Wilkerson?" answered a woman.

"Have the Zuba brothers arrived?"

"Y-yes, sir," the receptionist said, her voice quavering.

Moose's head jerked up. He knew about those blokes. They weren't *just* assassins; they were sadists. Their victims didn't plead for their lives, they begged for death.

The door opened and two men walked into the room. They had cropped, platinum hair and icy blue eyes. One wore a tweed jacket over a pink T-shirt; the other wore a Burberry sweater and ragged jeans.

They smiled.

Moose jumped out of his chair and backed up against

the window. Stone the bloody crows, those teeth. They'd been filed.

"Take him," Wilkerson said.

The men's reflections moved along the mirrored table. Moose grabbed the chair and shoved it through the window. The glass ruptured, clattering to the floor. He leaped through the jagged opening and plunged three stories. He landed feet first on an overhang. That was lucky for him. But it was also lucky for the Zubas.

He bolted toward the fire escape. His right foot snagged on a metal pipe and he toppled over. He heard a crack and pain exploded in his leg. He pulled up his trouser—no protruding bones—and got to his feet. He limped to the fire escape. By the time he reached the ground, his ankle was throbbing. Above him, the fire escape rattled as the Zubas climbed down.

Moose hobbled off into an alley. In the distance, he saw the Hungerford Bridge. He shambled to the Thames and jumped. The dark water clamped over his head like an iron lid. He couldn't stop, couldn't rest. *Just keep going, mate*. You had to play when you were wounded.

CHAPTER 9

———

HOTEL USTRA
KARDZHALI, BULGARIA

After the meeting, Velikov insisted upon searching Caro's room. His coat rippled as he strode to the window and flattened the curtains, presumably making sure no one was crouched behind them. He opened the closet and swept one hand over the coat hangers. His eyebrows quirked and he turned into the bathroom. Caro jumped when the shower curtain hooks scraped over the metal rod.

He stepped back into the hall. "Make sure you bolt the door tonight."

"Why?" She crossed her arms, trying to decide if she'd brought this on with her silliness over the man in the bar or if the extra security was related to Uncle Nigel's murder.

"I have four grown daughters," Velikov said. "And the world is wicked."

The moment he left, Caro sat on the bed and rang

Jude's room. When he didn't pick up, she felt a pinch of disappointment. She hung up and stretched bonelessly across the bed. Above her, the ceiling squeaked as someone paced back and forth, shouting in Russian.

"Zavali yebalo!" a man yelled.

"Nyet," a female voice cried.

Caro slid off the bed and turned on the television. The satellite weather channel showed a smiling sun over Bulgaria. An exotic, dark-skinned woman delivered the forecast in an elegant British accent. The Balkans could expect rising temperatures and overcast skies, followed by a blast of Arctic air and snow.

Her stomach growled. She found a package of Jammie Dodgers in her bag and stuffed a biscuit into her mouth. Then she picked up Uncle Nigel's letters and returned to the bed. The first envelope bore no address or postmark. Scrawled across the front, in his distinct, boxy handwriting, was *Please Forward to Dr. J. Barrett.*

25 October

Dear Dr. Barrett,

Quite by chance, I stumbled upon your article in the British Scientific Journal; I searched for companion articles but couldn't find one. You'd simply vanished from academia. I might not have found you at all, but your name sounded familiar. I'd known a John Barrett at Eton back in the early 1950s. His given name was John Fleming Dalgliesh Barrett from York. We had quite a bit in common, and not because our fathers were in the House of Lords.

We were incorrigible mischief makers. One time, we

caused a ruckus at St. George's Chapel, and the Windsor guards came rushing down. We narrowly escaped. Another time we made false ID cards, took the train to Piccadilly Circus, and got positively sozzled. There are more tales, of course. What else could you expect from two teenaged softies? However, I'm digressing. I was terribly saddened to hear of Sir John's passing.

Once I made the connection, I traveled to York, to Dalgliesh Castle. Your stepmother, the Lady Patricia, wouldn't say if you were dead or alive. Considering the subject of your article, I decided she was protecting you.

In case you are alive and in hiding, please allow me to introduce myself. I'm a professor of archaeology at Oxford, with a special interest in minority cultures during the antiquities. I apologize in advance for my boldness and for my lack of knowledge about your area of study; however, I was simply gobsmacked by your research. Moreover, I was consumed with unanswered questions.

Whilst it's a rather big ask, I hope you'll contact me.

Sincerely,
Nigel H. Clifford, Ph.D.
Norham Gardens, Oxford
Oxfordshire, U.K. OX2 6QD

Caro smoothed the paper with the flat of her hand. Jude was a Briton, just as she'd suspected, and posh. His father had attended Eton and had known Uncle Nigel. Why had Jude's stepmother refused to say if he was alive or dead?

She mulled over the words, hunting for subtext. *Considering the subject of your article, I decided she was protecting you.* What kind of article required protection?

A controversial one. She lifted the second letter. The envelope was addressed to Dr. J. Fleming in Lucerne, Switzerland.

9 November

Dear Jude,

I was a bit puzzled when I received your letter, as I didn't recognize the name "Fleming." Then I read your explanation regarding the pseudonym. For this reason, I'm extremely honored that you're willing to travel incognito to meet me. I applaud your bravery as I'm sure this wasn't an easy decision. I also agree that we shouldn't speak on the phone.

I have many questions about your article, and only you can answer them. I will be leaving the country for a few weeks—just a routine dig in Bulgaria—but I shall return to Oxford on 28 November. Let's have tea at my house on the afternoon of the 29th.

If you are hiring a car, I'm right off the motorway. I do hate to be presumptuous, but perhaps you could give my niece a lift to Oxford? Caro lives in London, Flat 4, 32½ Bow Street. It's out of your way if you're leaving from Heathrow. I'll be happy to reimburse you (and I'll rest easier knowing Caro is with you). During your visit to Oxford, you are welcome to lodge at my home. There's plenty of room to kick about; however, if you are allergic to cats, be forewarned: one on the premises.

Looking forward to meeting you.

Sincerely,
Nigel Clifford

P.S. I've added Caro's telephone number, along with her photograph—not for matchmaking purposes but clarification: Her flatmate is blond, too, but rather short and hobbit-like. They have been known to pose as each other to chase off undesirable guests. I wouldn't want you to bring the wrong girl to tea.

Hobbit-like? Caro smiled and traced a finger over his signature: the square *N*, curlicue *C*, and upswept *d* at the end of *Clifford*.

Not for matchmaking purposes. What an odd statement; yet it was probably true. Her uncle wouldn't have known if Jude was young, old, married, or warty, much less if he was her type. She'd never told anyone, not even Phoebe, about her secret weakness for tall, big-shouldered men with dimples, blue eyes, and dark hair.

So what had been the purpose of this meeting in Oxford? Jude had written an article, one so inflammatory that he'd gone into hiding, and it had caught her uncle's attention. She rubbed her eyes. If only Phoebe were here. They could sort these letters and decide what to do with Jude.

Caro swept biscuit crumbs off the bed, grabbed the phone, and punched in the numbers to the Bow Street flat. She smiled. By now Phoebe had doubtlessly found the carb stash that Caro kept in the medicine cabinet. The phone rang and rang. Caro glanced at her watch. It was eight P.M. in Kardzhali; London was two hours behind. Phoebe should have been home, pulling her wardrobe together for the next day.

As Caro hung up, she remembered a line from one of the letters. *I have many questions about your article.* Had Uncle Nigel been looking into experimental treatments for heart patients? Maybe the answers were in her uncle's backpack.

She pushed the phone aside, grabbed the pack, and dumped the contents onto the bed: ink pens, pill bottles, tiny flashlight, rabbit's-foot keychain, wallet, and passport. The objects were flecked with red. A tear slid down her cheek, fell off her chin, and hit the flashlight. The dried blood there reconstituted and ran down the metal barrel. She turned on the penlight and aimed the beam over medicine bottles and keys. Ordinary items from an extraordinary life.

Then she saw Uncle Nigel's passport. Blood droplets were scattered across the burgundy cover. She dropped the penlight and reached for the booklet. Dark whorls obliterated the *PEAN* and *UN* in *European Union* along with the *U* in *United Kingdom*.

She swallowed around the knot in her throat and flipped pages, following the bloody trail to page fourteen. Uncle Nigel's boxy handwriting filled the red-and-white grids, forming a tidy column.

14 ENTRIES/ENTRÉES VISAS DEPARTURES/SORTIES	15 ENTRIES/ENTRÉES VISAS DEPARTURES/SORTIES
A Gee Creme Mock Ion N Tore	
Ellen vumv canola Bravo ice Bark boy toe foes Tax by fit	

Caro traced a shaking finger over the ink. When had Uncle Nigel written these phrases? Years ago? Or were they quick notes he'd made at the Perperikon dig site? He'd been a list maker with a fondness for word play, subtext, and puzzles. From the time she'd come to live with him, she'd spent Christmas mornings solving intricate anagrams and simple ciphers, and the clues had led to her presents. When she was older, Uncle Nigel had always included a small coded message in his notes to her.

She read the phrases again but felt even more confused. They looked like anagrams, but her uncle would never throw in a garbled word like *vumv*. He would have taken pains to create three actual phrases, like *Naval Cum Novelle* or *Cave Man Oven Lull*.

So what were these odd scribblings? An inventory of some sort? Her hair swung forward as she leaned closer to study her uncle's handwriting. It was firm and unwavering until the last two phrases. Below them, a comma of blood covered the bottom of the page.

A shiver ran up Caro's backbone. She took a slow, deliberate breath and released it. *A Gee Creme Mock*. He'd written these phrases after the attack. She hoped they weren't complicated ciphers. Despite Uncle Nigel's best efforts, she'd never been able to crack anything involving multiple alphabets. In his haste, he would have left simple anagrams. And *vumv* was the saddest clue of all: He'd written it—to her—while he lay dying.

She carried the passport to the desk, opened a drawer, and grabbed a pen. Then she decoded *A Gee Creme Mock*, transposing the letters on her wrist. When she and Uncle Nigel had played word games, he'd insisted that she write the solutions on her arm or leg because a good cryptographer wouldn't leave a trail for the enemy. "If you lose your paper," he used to say, "then you've lost control of your secrets."

The tip of the pen dented her flesh as she wrote *Rock Meg Meece*. That didn't make sense. She moved a little higher on her arm and wrote *Cockermeg*. But *E*, *E*, and *M* were left over. No, that wouldn't work, either.

The ceiling shook, followed by a thud, and the Russians began to shriek. A door slammed, and her concentration snapped. She leaned over the passport and struggled to find her place, but she couldn't focus. Then she remembered that Uncle Nigel sometimes added a twist, transposing a phrase from each line. She ran her finger under *A Gee Creme Mock* and moved down to the next line, *Ion N Tore*. Her heart sped up when she exchanged *Mock* and *Tore*.

A Gee Creme Tore.

Yes, this felt right. She opened her hand and in tiny letters wrote *Ergometer* on her palm. But what to do with the leftover *C*, *A*, and two *E*s?

From the hallway, she heard a rattling sound. The nighttime housekeeper, no doubt, wanting to pull back the sheets and leave a chocolate. Or maybe the Russians had stumbled downstairs, bringing their argument into the public domain.

Caro fought the urge to look through the peephole and squinted at *A Gee Creme Tore* until her vision blurred. The letters seemed to dodge and push each other as they formed a coherent arrangement. *Meteora, Greece.*

CHAPTER 10

Georgi Ivanov ran across the hotel parking lot, climbed into his brown Dacia, and hunched down in the seat. He'd been so close to the girl. So close he could smell her musk. But that bigwig from the Interior Ministry was guarding her. She'd recognized Georgi, too, and she had alerted the bigwig. Thanks to Teo's misbehavior at the airport, their faces would be familiar to many.

The hotel's doors swung open and three policemen walked out of the lobby. Georgi scooted lower in his seat. His mobile phone buzzed and spun around on the console. He picked it up. "Yes?"

"It is me," Teo said. "I am still in the Sofia jail. But they will release me soon. Can you pick me up?"

"Me, me, me. That is your problem, Teo. You suffer

from me-ness." Georgi saw a flash of movement by the
black doors. They opened again, and the ministry official
stepped onto the sidewalk.

"I followed your instructions, and now I am caught,"
Teo said.

"I will call back."

"Wait, no—"

Georgi threw down the mobile and leaned toward the
windshield. The policemen climbed into a white
Opel Astra. The back tires kicked up snow as they drove
out of the lot. Georgi pulled a wrinkled fax from the
glove compartment. Caroline Clifford's image stared
back at him. His fingernail scraped over the paper as he
traced her pewter eyes, following the slight tilt at the
edges. *Nice.*

He grabbed his mobile and punched in the numbers
for Hotel Ustra. When the clerk answered, Georgi asked
her to ring Clifford's room. The woman rudely demanded
to know who was calling. Georgi slapped his mobile shut.
"*Лайно,*" he said. *Shit.* He had time. He had more time
than they knew.

He lifted his arm and sniffed his floral shirt. The fabric reeked of its previous owner. Time for a new outfit.
Something with a hood or a designer label. He was in the
perfect place to shop. He watched the black doors, hoping
a tall, lean man would emerge. A woman darted out and
rushed down the sidewalk, her bleached blond hair spilling down the front of her white jacket. Very nice. But she
wasn't the Clifford girl.

Georgi licked his lips as the woman moved down the
sidewalk. From the rear, she looked even better, her tight

black pants showing the flexion of her perky buttocks and slender thighs.

He got out of the car and vaulted over the slick pavement, landing on a rock-lined path. He lifted a large, jagged stone and slipped it into his pocket. His long legs cut through the air like scissors as he ran over to the woman.

"Dobar wecher," he said, drawing his lips into a grin. "Do you speak Bulgarian?"

"A little," she replied. "I'm from Moscow."

"You need taxi?" He gestured in the Dacia's direction.

"I need time alone." She flashed him a discourteous look and headed down the sidewalk. Georgi glanced around. No one was out. It was too cold. But not too cold for him. He pulled the rock from his pocket and slammed it against her head. Her knees buckled, but he caught her before she fell. He slipped his hand around her waist, pulling her firmly against his chest. She moaned, and her head lolled against his shoulder.

He stepped off the sidewalk, holding her upright, and started toward the lot. Her long legs stretched behind her and her boots dug two trenches through the snow. When he saw the Dacia, he slipped his free hand into his pocket and clicked the remote trunk release. The lid creaked open, dislodging a chunk of snow to the ground. He swung around to the rear and dumped the girl in the trunk. Her jacket gaped open, and her breasts spilled out of a leopard-print blouse. She stirred a little, flinging a hand over her face.

"Soon," he told her, and slammed the trunk. Her muffled screams rose up as he drove off. On his way out of town, he saw shapes following the car. The wild dogs had caught the scent of blood and death. But they would not feast tonight. He pressed his foot a little harder against the gas pedal, and then he turned up the radio and hummed along with the children's choir as they sang "I Want to Go to Heaven."

CHAPTER 11

Caro sat cross-legged in the wooden chair and flipped pages in Uncle Nigel's passport. She couldn't assume he'd been lucid while he'd written these anagrams. What did *Meteora, Greece* mean? Was he directing her somewhere or warning her to stay away? Why name a specific place? Why hadn't he named his murderer?

She stopped on page sixteen and examined a faint red mark. It was an immigration stamp. She flipped another page. No blood. No more anagrams.

Caro squinted at the second phrase, *Ion N Tore*, and transposed the words into *Ion N Mock*, just as Uncle Nigel had taught her. *Nick Moon? Coin Monk? Monk Icon?*

Definitely the last one. *Monk Icon.* The clifftop monasteries were in Meteora, Greece. The churches were filled with Byzantine relics, including icons. When she was a tiny girl, she'd visited the area with Uncle Nigel, but she couldn't remember anything except red-tiled buildings that sat atop huge boulders. Now, he was sending her back to look for a monk and an icon. He'd known she would bring hers, so this wasn't a wild quest. He'd left directions. She was to travel to Meteora, Greece, locate a monk, and show him her icon. But her uncle hadn't indicated which monastery she should visit, nor had he named the monk.

She pressed her tongue against her upper lip and started to decode the next set of clues, but her doorknob rattled.

"Miss Clifford?" a British voice called. "It's Jude."

"Just a moment." She shoved the passport and pen into the desk drawer. Then she hurried to the bed, scooped up her uncle's belongings, and fitted them into the backpack. On her way to the door, she darted into the bathroom and scrubbed the ink off her arm.

"Coming!" she called and leaned toward the mirror, raking her fingers through her hair. After a day of travel, she resembled a hedgehog.

She strode into the hall, leaned against the door, and squinted through the peephole. Jude gazed straight ahead. He'd discarded his sweater and jacket. His white shirt was unbuttoned at his neck, and she saw the start of curly black hairs on his upper chest. He reached up and smoothed his ponytail. His previous stubble was gone, and she noticed a tiny nick on his chin.

Cute guy, bad timing. She stepped away from the door. Part of her wanted to be alone with the anagrams, but another part wanted to quiz Jude about those letters. Were they the only reason he'd followed her to Bulgaria?

Couldn't the matter have been settled over the telephone? Never mind that he didn't own a mobile.

She removed the chain lock and opened the door. The poignant scent of Acqua di Parma drifted over her.

"Miss Clifford," he said, bowing slightly. "I hope I'm not disturbing you."

"Not at all." She smoothed her hair. He disturbed her in more ways than she wished to count.

He pointed at the elevator. "I was on my way to the mezzanine bar. Would you like to join me?"

"I'm a bit tired." Translation: *You're as baffling as the anagrams. I don't need more puzzles.*

"We'll give it a miss, then."

"But I'd like to talk." *Because you're exceptionally intriguing.*

She opened the door wider. He stepped past her and she caught the scent of his cologne again. Handsome men made her nervous, but Jude also looked as if he could defend himself in a pub brawl.

"Would you like a drink?" she asked. "There's wine in the mini fridge."

"That would be lovely."

"Not much of a choice, I'm afraid." She knelt beside the icebox. Bottles clinked as she pulled out a Chablis. She tipped the bottle over two glasses and handed one to him. "Cheers," he said.

She raised her glass and repeated Uncle Nigel's favorite toast: "Here's mud in your eye."

After she took a sip, she set her glass on the desk and picked up the letters. "Why were you using an alias?"

"I didn't want to be found." He stared down into his wineglass.

"Why not?" She sat on the edge of the chair and tucked her feet around the rungs.

"Long story." He tossed down the wine and grimaced. "Several things happened. Including a broken romance."

A romance. Not surprising. Had it broken from Jude's end or the woman's? And why was he bringing it up? To show that he wasn't a pervert? Or unattached? No little wife waiting for him in Switzerland?

Caro set down the letters. "Uncle Nigel had a heart condition. Did your article concern cardiac issues?"

"No, genetics."

"Why would my uncle be interested in that?" She lifted her glass and drained it.

"I was hoping you could tell me." He nodded at her glass. "I'm empty, too. Shall I open another bottle?"

"Open two, if you don't mind. Not that I'm a sot. The bottles are awfully tiny."

"Indeed they are." He walked to the fridge.

"Do you have any idea why my uncle wanted us to meet?" she asked.

"I assumed you were a biochemist, too," Jude said.

"Nothing of the sort." Her voice sounded too cheerful, and she cringed. Dammit, the wine had fizzed straight to her brain, making her unnaturally chatty. Worse, she couldn't control it. "I was a Ph.D. candidate, but I quit. Now I'm a tour guide."

"A Ph.D." His eyebrows went up a little, as if he hadn't expected her to be a scholar. "What did you study?"

"History. Specifically heretics in the medieval church."

He fell silent as he opened another bottle of Chablis. "Why did you give it up?"

She shrugged, as if she were always going off on tangents. The truth was scarier. She wasn't free-spirited or capricious. She was so vigilant her motto was *semper paratus*, always prepared.

Jude handed her a swaying glass of Chablis, and his shirtsleeve pulled back slightly, revealing a sturdy wrist. He stepped back to the wall, reestablishing the neutral space between them.

"I'm sure you're a fantastic guide," he said. "I can see you wearing pearls and escorting groups through Windsor Castle."

"Quite the opposite." She lifted her free hand and rubbed her forehead, trying to smooth out her thoughts. The Chablis had loosened her up, and in a bad way. She squashed an impulse to tell him about her secret specialty: wicked history, the smuttier the better. Once she got going, she'd never shut up. Lecturing this man about Catherine the Great's sexual preferences would be grossly uncouth, wouldn't it?

He smiled, as if he'd heard her thoughts. "When you aren't leading tourists through the Tate, what do you do?" he asked.

She shrugged. Better not mention her daily walks to the bakery, followed by evenings alone in the flat, eating treacle tarts and watching old movies, most recently Bogie and Bacall in *To Have and Have Not*.

He took a sip of wine, and she tried not to stare at his hands. They would have fascinated a medieval sculptor. She wasn't drawn to perfect men, but now that she'd had a chance to study him, she noticed that his right eye was rounder than the left. The disparity gave depth and expression to his face. So did the brown dots in his left eye, which were scattered like ground nutmeg.

She squirmed in her chair, trying to ignore the slight scratchy sound that his hand made as it slipped into the front pocket of his faded jeans. She imagined him clutching a pen, writing equations and notes on a yellow legal pad, adjusting dials on a microscope. Then she imagined his fingertips on her body.

Focus, Caro. Ask him about Uncle Nigel.

"I read the letters," she said.

"What did you make of them?"

"Not much." They'd told more about him than her uncle's secret plan. Jude had grown up in the north country. The land of plucky orphans. Jane Eyre, Heathcliff, and Mary Lenox. "You're from York?" she asked.

"Ripon. North of Harrogate."

"I've been there. Ripon is a cathedral city, right?"

"Yes." A smile—or was it a frown?—tugged at the edges of his lips. "There's a line in *Jane Eyre* that refers to our old pile of rocks. Everyone thinks it's about the Norton-Conyers house, but it refers to Dalgliesh Castle."

Keeping her eyes on him, Caro reached for her glass. Had the wine made him loquacious or was he boasting? She tried to look suitably impressed. "You lived in a castle?"

"I wasn't there often. My father sent me to boarding school."

"And your family is old and stodgy?"

"Old enough."

"Dalgliesh sounds familiar."

"It's popular with tourists. After my father died, Lady Patricia couldn't afford a new roof. It was a positively astronomical sum. Over a million pounds. Lady Patricia had to prostitute the home-place."

"Lady Patricia is your stepmum?"

"Yes." His voice held no inflection and his face was unreadable.

Caro rubbed her temple. She was on the edge of remembering something about the castle. "Does Dalgliesh have a tree in the dungeon?"

"We don't have a dungeon. But there's a hawthorn tree in the cellar. Lady Patricia turned the area into a gift shop."

"That's where I bought my luggage." She pointed to the plaid duffel bag.

"Here's to small worlds." He lifted his glass.

And huge houses. Caro tried to imagine a much younger Jude playing in the garden maze or running into the moor with friends named Dickon and Colin. They'd play hide-and-seek in the turrets, overturn tea tables, smash priceless Staffordshire figurines, kick balls into the knot gardens, and attack Lady Patricia's roses with clippers.

"The castle had four Scottish terriers," she said, hoping he'd elaborate. When he didn't, she added, "Tourists were lined up, snapping their pictures. They were well behaved—the dogs, not the tourists."

"They're Lady Patricia's," Jude said. "They know the sound of her car, and they form a greeting party at the end of the lane. At least, they used to. I haven't been home in years."

"Because you don't get on with Lady Patricia?"

"I'm quite fond of her."

So, his stepmother wasn't wicked. And he was from a powerful Yorkshire family. Why was he living in Switzerland if everything was so cozy? Caro felt more confused than ever, and she was smashed. The alcohol had dissolved the last vestiges of civility. "Why did you leave Ripon and move to Switzerland?"

"I like to move around."

"That's why you followed me to Bulgaria?"

"I was hoping you could interpret Sir Nigel's letters."

"That's only part of it, isn't it?" She leaned forward. "Why are you here? Morbid curiosity?"

"No, indeed not." His eyebrows angled up. "I was intrigued by the letters."

"Why fly from London to Bulgaria to hand them over? You could've given them to me at the airport. I would have called you."

"I told you before, I don't have a phone."

She swallowed the rest of her wine. "Would you open another bottle?"

He hesitated, but only for a moment, and then he stepped over to the fridge, grabbed a bottle, and peeled back the foil. Once again she found herself looking at his hands. His face was interesting, too, changing from second to second, mainly because of his eyebrows—they seemed to have a language all their own, moving when he talked, and even when he was silent.

An intense sexual desire rippled through her, and she didn't have the decency to blush, much less look away. His blue gaze was both appealing and unsettling, and that smile always flickered at the edges of his mouth. Probably because she couldn't stop staring. She hadn't traveled to Kardzhali to have a fling. She was here for the saddest of reasons: to bring her uncle home. The backs of her eyes burned, and she turned away.

"Are you all right?" Jude asked.

She started to tell him she was fine, just fine, but her lips were stuck to her teeth. She couldn't explain that the house on Norham Gardens filled her with an odd blend of homesickness and despair. Their housekeeper, Mrs. Turner, would urge Caro to empty her uncle's closets, to pack away the Harris Tweed jackets that always smelled of tobacco, whiskey, and chalk dust. She would sort through his desk while the cat, Dinah, stretched on the floor, sunning herself on the oriental rug. Without Uncle Nigel's vigorous presence, the house would be cold and empty.

She blinked, and tears ran down her cheeks. The air stirred as Jude knelt beside her. "It's all right, lass," he said. "It's all right."

Her head tipped forward and landed on his shoulder. She breathed in the aromas of cologne, leather, wine, and soap. There was a sturdiness to him, a fixed strength, reminding her of a house on a damp evening, a light glowing behind diamond-paned windows.

"There, there," he said, almost a whisper. "No tears before bedtime."

What a strange coincidence that Jude would use the same words to soothe her that Uncle Nigel had. She wiped her eyes and leaned back. His eyes were so blue, she wanted to jump into them.

His fingers grazed her chin. "Better?" he asked.

Yes. No.

His hand fell to his side, and he stood. "I should go, shouldn't I?"

"Please don't." She got to her feet and stepped closer. She wanted to touch him, to press her face against his face and feel the weight of his body, the whole length of him pushing her down into a warm place. It felt wrong somehow to be consumed by these feelings in the wake of her uncle's death, and yet it somehow seemed right. She wanted Jude to take her out of all that, to distract her and make her feel something other than the immense pain and loneliness that had surrounded her since that horrible phone call.

She stood on her toes and pressed her lips against his, tasting wine and salt. His tongue pressed against hers, lightly at first, but the delicate dance quickly morphed into something more urgent. Her knees began to shake. She wanted more than a kiss, and she wanted it now. She slid her hands up his chest, brushing over the smooth cotton, feeling the hard curve of his muscles.

Still kissing him, her fingers grazed his collar. As she undid the top button, her hand froze. What was wrong with her? How could she feel pleasure amid so much emotional pain?

No, she couldn't do this. She broke the kiss and stepped backward. "I'm sorry."

His eyebrows came together. "What for?"

She felt dizzy and put a steadying hand on the desk. Better not get into that kiss. Better to tell a plausible lie. "I'm just exhausted," she said. "Can we talk tomorrow?"

"Of course." He walked to the door and opened it, then he turned back. "Are you certain you're all right?"

She almost told him to whistle. It had worked for Bacall and Bogie, but it wouldn't work for her. So she just nodded.

"Well, good-bye, then." Jude stepped into the hall. The door clicked shut behind him, a hard, final sound. Now that he was really gone, she was sorry. There was still time to call him back, wasn't there?

No, of course not. She flopped onto the bed. She'd saved herself a world of embarrassment. Him, too. Especially him. She pushed the pillow over her head. Drunken idiot. But not so drunk that she'd slept with him. That really would've taken the biscuit.

CHAPTER 12

Daylight blazed through the curtain, shining into Caro's eyes. It felt rather pleasant until she tried to sit up, and then pain shot through her head. God, how much had she drunk last night? She wasn't in the habit of kissing strange men—not because she was a prude, but because she was a cynic. The London dating scene was flooded with married men and players. Without exception, she'd been drawn to commitment-phobic chaps. In fact, she'd compiled a list of her failed relationships, which she privately referred to as the Lost Boys.

Her first beau, a thirteen-year-old football player, had shattered her bedroom window with a rock, only to later claim temporary insanity after Uncle Nigel had charged the lad with vandalism. Her big love was a college boy who'd almost gotten into her knickers, but Uncle Nigel's relentless hoovering in the next room had quashed that romantic interlude. That particular boy dropped her for a girl who didn't have a nosy, and noisy, uncle. The love-birds had gotten married and now raised show-quality dachshunds.

The most cringeworthy entry in the list was her engagement to an Oxford banker named Robert Thaxton. Their romance was one of those sad tales that tour guides love to embellish on castle tours, but in her case it was true.

Caro had still been living with her uncle when Robert had proposed. Uncle Nigel had wanted to make a huge fuss, so he'd arranged a lavish party at Danesfield House, near Marlow-on-Thames. Then he'd taken her shopping at Harrods, and she'd picked out a gray-blue silk dress went nicely with her eyes. The night of the party, she fashioned her frizzy hair into a sleek chignon. Uncle Nigel looked smashing in his ancient tuxedo. They stepped into the Oak Room, arm in arm, and greeted their guests.

The night deepened. Robert's parents took their place in the receiving line, but their son still hadn't arrived. Uncle Nigel signaled the waiters to keep passing wine and champagne. While guests exclaimed over Caro's engage-ment ring, she kept glancing over her shoulder, searching the crowd for her fiancé.

"Robert was supposed to be back from London now, wasn't he?" Mr. Thaxton asked his wife. "Shouldn't we ring his mobile?"

Mrs. Thaxton kept punching numbers into her phone, sweat beading on her broad forehead.

Robert's eight-year-old brother, Dennis, zoomed around the Oak Room, his short pants riding up over his chubby knees. A red bow tie pushed against his triple chins. Waiters maneuvered around the boy as they replenished the buffet with smoked trout and salmon and tiny, fragrant bowls of horseradish.

Caro followed the Thaxtons onto the terrace, with Dennis bobbing in their wake. Someone must have told him that Danesfield House had been the RAF headquarters in World War II, because the child spread his arms wide and made zooming noises. "Bombs away!" he yelled.

The summer air felt cool and smelled poignantly of roses. Even though it was only seven P.M., the sky resembled blue enamel. Through the trees, a boat drifted down the Thames. While Caro chatted with Mr. Thaxton, his wife kept ringing Robert.

"What was he doing in London, anyway?" Mr. Thaxton asked, his forehead puckering.

"A meeting," Caro said, wishing she'd gone with Robert. The appointment had ended hours before, but she didn't see the point of adding to Mr. Thaxton's gloom.

Dennis careened over and yelped, "Caro's been stood up!"

"Stop that," Mrs. Thaxton said in a mild voice. She was a portrait painter of the royal dogs, which required infinite patience and an ability to deal with the unexpected.

Dennis stuck out his tongue.

"Please return your tongue to its proper position," Mr. Thaxton said, and put his hand on the boy's head.

Lady Sarah, Robert's cousin, walked up behind Caro. "Young Dennis has been into the brandy," she whispered.

"I'll marry you, Caro," Dennis called.

"She won't marry into this family at all if you don't straighten up," Lady Sarah said.

"Come along, Dennis." Mr. Thaxton grabbed the boy's shoulders and steered him down the steps to the riverbank.

Uncle Nigel put his arm around her. "I'm sure the meeting ran over," he said. "Any moment he'll pop through those doors."

As the evening passed into night, the guests grew tipsy. One of them was a flinty-eyed cashier who worked with Robert. "He won't be joining us tonight," the cashier said, his cheeks flushed with wine. "Do you remember his secretary? The one with enormous breasts? Well, she and Robert have gone missing. Apparently the bank was about to charge him with embezzlement."

Caro ran onto the terrace, flew down the steps, and stopped at the river. She heard footsteps behind her, and she whirled. Her uncle stepped out of the shadows.

"You aren't planning to throw yourself in the Thames, are you?" he asked.

"What's wrong with me?" She wiped her eyes. "Why can't anyone love me?"

"I love you, my darling." Uncle Nigel paused. He seemed on the verge of saying something, but he merely patted her arm. "Don't cry. The right chap will come along."

But he hadn't. Meanwhile, the Lost Boys list had gotten longer and longer. It didn't matter if Caro slept with them or not; the results were always the same. In the beginning the men mailed love letters and dirty haiku. They rang her house at odd hours and loitered in her uncle's front yard until he called the police. After each brief but intense courtship, the suitors always lost interest, only to take up with women they later married.

Of course, not all of the men had left her for other women. Some had died. A six-car pile-up on the M4 had claimed one beau. Another had perished while pruning his roses—flotsam from a jet plane had fallen from the sky, smack onto his head. Still another had entered the priesthood and gone to Monaco, of all places. He'd written her a postcard that featured the casino and signed his name *Chip Monk*.

After that, she decided a change in geography would solve her problems, and she told her uncle that she was moving to London. "It's a wicked city," he'd said. "Nothing but perverts, molesters, fiends."

"If someone grabs me, I'll kick him into tomorrow."

"You can't kick a can to Parks Road and back." His white, shaggy eyebrows went up in alarm. "Don't throw away your education. Wait until you have your doctorate."

She hadn't waited, and nothing had changed.

Traffic noises outside the Hotel Ustra made her sit up straighter. She rubbed her forehead. What the bloody hell had been wrong with her last night? She did not want to add Jude's name to the Lost Boys. She wished she could throw herself into a high-powered career. Perhaps she could take up volcanology. Studying magma held more appeal than sifting through dry, crumbling texts about the Great Inquisition, which had once fascinated her. She could move to Iceland, enroll in graduate school, and plant tremor sensors around active volcanoes. She might even fall in love with a tall, blond Icelander named Jón and they'd live in a farmhouse beneath the Mýrdalsjökull glacier.

Her stomach rumbled. She hadn't eaten anything since last night's Jammie Dodgers. Her mouth watered as she pictured a room service trolley filled with toast and sausage and apricot jam. A large pot of tea and a broiled grapefruit sprinkled with sugar would be perfect for a hangover. She reached for the phone to order room service.

"We are no longer serving breakfast," said a woman in heavily accented English.

"What time is it?" Caro got out of the bed, pulling the phone with her, and glanced out the window. Dirty clouds scudded over the sun. The temperature was rising and water dripped from the eaves as snow melted from the roof.

"Noon," said the woman. "May I recommend our restaurant? The buffet lunch offers the best of Bulgarian cuisine."

Caro thanked her and hung up. The headache pulsed behind her eyes as she got dressed. On her way to the loo, she saw a note lying just under her door. She bent down to get it. The handwriting looked like a printed invitation, each letter tiny and precise.

Dear Caro,

I still have questions about your uncle. And I'd like a chance to know you better. Let's have dinner tonight.

Jude

She had questions, too. Was Jude's penmanship indicative of a controlled and self-contained personality? Or was he just another English chap with proper manners? She scanned the note again, picking his words apart, searching for hidden meaning. The first and last sentences were to the point, but the middle one was open to interpretation. *I'd like a chance to know you better* could also mean *I'd like to get you into bed.*

Her stomach rumbled again and she set the letter aside. She reached for her duffel bag. It was a bit cumbersome to lug around, but she didn't dare leave it in her room. If anything happened to her icon, she would lose the last tangible link to her parents. She opened her bag, tossed in her uncle's letters and passport, and headed to the lobby.

Three Bulgarian policemen stood under the chandelier, talking to a man in a red shirt who spoke Russian. Caro walked around them and veered toward the reception desk. The clerk looked up, her hoop earrings swinging.

"Excuse me," Caro began, "but why are the police here?"

The clerk leaned across the desk. "A hotel guest is missing," she whispered.

Caro glanced over her shoulder at the Russian man and remembered the shouting and door slamming. A lover's quarrel, no doubt, but the police were ruthlessly questioning him.

"You need help, miss?" the clerk asked.

"May I leave a message for the guest in room three fourteen?"

The clerk pushed a pen and notepad across the desk. Caro bent over the paper and wrote, *Dear Jude*. She remembered the pressure of his lips against hers and the smell of Acqua di Parma. Maybe she should have finished that kiss.

She jolted, then glanced down at the notepad. She was still writing, and the *e* in *Jude* had squiggled across the page. She ripped off the sheet and started over. *Jude, I'll be out for most of the afternoon. But I'm looking forward to dinner. Caro*

She handed the note to the clerk and headed toward the Ustra Restaurant. She glanced furtively over her shoulder for the thug in the Hawaiian shirt, but she saw only men in business suits. She walked over to the buffet, grabbed a plate, and spooned up hominy with garlicky walnuts, lamb kabobs, and cucumbers floating in olive oil. Soon there was no room left on her plate. Uncle Nigel used to say the Bulgarians served a multitude of dishes because they were excellent hosts, but they also used the abundant food as symbols for fertility and prosperity.

When she couldn't eat another morsel, she settled her bill and walked back to the lobby. The clerk was bent over the desk, studying a ledger. Caro gazed at the knotty-pine cubbyholes on the wall behind the desk. The slot for her room was empty. So was Jude's.

"When did the gentleman in three fourteen pick up his message?" Caro asked the clerk.

"I cannot remember. Maybe ten minutes ago?" The woman shrugged. "It has been crazy around here. A tourist has never gone missing."

When Caro stepped into her room, hot, sour bile spurted into her mouth. The mattress hung off the bed. Drawers gaped open. The trash bin had been emptied and rubbish lay on the floor. Uncle Nigel's backpack had been turned inside out. What had the burglars been looking for? She didn't wear jewelry or flashy clothes. More to the point, who were the burglars? The purse snatchers, of course. But she couldn't rule out Jude.

She found the phone under the mattress. It was time to call Phoebe. Her roomie might not know what was going on, but of all people, Phoebe had the means to find out through her father, Sir Edmund. Caro punched in the number to the Bow Street flat. A man answered on the second ring. "May I speak to Phoebe?" she asked.

"I'm sorry, I—" The man's voice cracked.

"Sir Edmund?" Caro asked. "Is that you, sir?"

There was a grappling noise, and a woman came on the line. "This is Olivia, Sir Edmund's personal assistant. To whom am I speaking?"

"Caro Clifford. I'm Phoebe's flatmate," she said. In the background, Sir Edmund began to wail.

"We were just discussing you," Olivia said. "Are you in London, or have you gone to see about your uncle?"

"I'm in Bulgaria."

"We were shocked to hear of his murder," Olivia said. "First your uncle, and now Phoebe."

Caro dug her fingers through the telephone cord. *And now Phoebe?* What did this mean? "Sorry, I didn't quite catch that."

"Phoebe was killed in her flat, she was," Olivia said.

Caro sucked in air. "Not possible," she whispered.

"It's beyond shocking, isn't it? You were lucky not to be here or that madman might have gotten you, too. Women aren't safe anywhere in this world. The police are saying that it's random. But is it random to be drained of blood?"

CHAPTER 13

WILKERSON PHARMACEUTICALS
EAST LONDON, ENGLAND

Wilkerson paced in front of the boarded-up windows. He'd demanded a rush order to replace the glass, but the Kent factory couldn't promise a delivery date. Wilkerson missed his view, and the gloom was unbearable. Throughout the day, the overhead fluorescents blazed with a sour green intensity that left him headachy.

The door creaked open, and the secretary led Mr. Underwood into the room.

"What is it now?" Wilkerson asked.

"Sir, a woman has gone missing from Kardzhali."

"Not Caroline Clifford, I hope."

"Not directly, sir." Mr. Underwood licked his lips, leaving behind a glossy sheen. "I'm mainly concerned about a Russian tourist."

"Why is this my problem?"

"Because your operatives might be involved." Mr. Underwood's voice shook while he explained the fiasco at the airport, Teo's arrest, Georgi's solitary pursuit of the Clifford girl, and the missing tourist.

Wilkerson blinked. "And you think Georgi snatched her?"

"I asked him and got nowhere. He's like China—he denies everything. I've arranged for his partner's release."

"That's good—Teo calms him down. But make sure the Bulgarians don't rape and murder Miss Clifford." Wilkerson sat down on his desk and grabbed a pencil. "By the way, Underwood, how is your wife?"

"She's quite well, sir."

Wilkerson wrapped his fingers around the pencil and leaned forward. "You're married to a portly dominatrix who forces you to commute twice daily from Twickenham to London. I hear she has a lavish rose garden. Would you like her to keep it?"

Mr. Underwood nodded. He was breathing so hard, his glasses fogged.

"Then control your men." Wilkerson snapped the pencil in half.

Underwood stumbled out of the office and shut the door behind him. Minutes later, Wilkerson heard shouting. His secretary threatened to call the police, and a strident, Cockney voice told her to shut her cake hole.

Wilkerson's door banged open, and Moose limped into the room wearing a motorcycle helmet and a silvery, reflective jumpsuit. He threw a bulging garbage sack onto the conference table, then propped his leg on a chair. "Like my air cast?" he asked Wilkerson. "I got it when I dove through your window."

He pulled off his helmet. Damp red curls were plastered to his head. His hands and face were covered with zinc oxide, but scratches were visible through the white ointment.

Wilkerson blinked. Some of the crazier vamps came out in daylight, smearing themselves with sunblock and piling on the protective gear. You'd think Londoners would have caught on by now—realized that immortals walked among them—but there were so many punks and weirdos in the city, the vamps slipped under the radar.

The secretary stood in the doorway, clutching a folder. "Sorry, Mr. Wilkerson. I tried to make him wait."

"Where's Yok-Seng?" Wilkerson asked.

The secretary pulled a face. "The loo."

Wilkerson picked up the phone.

"Are you ringing the Zuba brothers?" Moose cried. "Let go of that phone or you'll be making future calls with a stump."

Wilkerson dropped the receiver into the cradle and frowned. He wasn't frightened. Not yet. "I thought I'd seen the last of you," he said.

"It takes more than the Zubas to scare me. They might have caused me to break my blooming leg, but I can still get around. So don't get ideas." Moose winked. "You should be flattered. I came out in daylight just for you."

"I'm late for a meeting." Wilkerson shifted his eyes to the boarded-up window.

"Surely you have time for a sit-down." Moose looked at the secretary, who was still hovering beside the door, her breasts heaving. "Boo!" he yelled, waving his hands.

The woman squeaked and ran out of the office, slamming the door behind her.

"Are you tapping that bird?" Moose asked Wilkerson.

"What?"

"Are you diddling your secretary?"

"My private life is none of your concern."

"Maybe not. But is it Cynthia's concern?" Moose leaned forward. "That's your girlfriend's name, isn't it? Poor Cynthia is clueless. Living by her lonesome self in that big manse in Kensington. Nothing but a snub-nosed dog to keep her company while you do the big nasty with others."

"Get to the point." Wilkerson's eyes narrowed.

"I'm a tracker. I know where you live. Send the Zubas after me, and Cynthia hears about your bloody affairs. I've got mates. They know about you. And *her*." He nodded at the door. "Your crumpet."

"I don't care what you tell Cynthia." Wilkerson folded his hands.

"Maybe I'll do more than talk to her. You care what the other toffee noses think. A dead girlfriend won't get you knighted."

Wilkerson's right eyelid twitched. "Why are you here?"

"To finish the job."

"The assignment has been passed on."

"To who? Don't I rate a second chance? Maybe I'll ask your crumpet."

"Leave her out of it." Wilkerson said.

"I'd love to, mate. But I can't." Moose waved at the boarded-up window. "Don't you want to hear about last night? I stole the air cast at Saint Mary's—it was a fucking madhouse, by the way. Humans are so fragile. Then I went back to the crime scene."

"That was foolish," Wilkerson said. When vampires

had OCD, they wreaked havoc. No matter what the bloody sods began, they felt compelled to finish. Wilkerson frowned. In his social circle, and in the circles just beyond his reach, a murder would be delicious fodder for the gossips. They would descend like magpies on an apricot tree, picking and shredding until nothing remained. The negative buzz could reach the newspapers, and he didn't want anyone scrutinizing his company.

Moose's head disappeared inside the garbage bag. He muttered to himself about toffee noses, then emerged holding a fuchsia leather scrapbook. With a flourish, he flipped back the cover, pulled out a small photograph, and slid it across the table. The snap showed a messy bedroom: an unmade bed, books piled on the floor, a tiny painting of some sort above a desk.

Moose waved at the picture. "This is *her* room, Miss Clifford's. Rather tacky, innit? The snap was taken before I spent time with Miss Dowell—by the way, her blood was red, not blue."

Wilkerson's jaw tightened. "Quit pottering."

Moose pointed to the photograph. "It was taken two weeks ago. The date is stamped in the lower right corner. We'll call it the 'before' picture."

Wilkerson shifted his gaze to the door. Where was Yok-Seng?

Moose reached into the bag again and pulled out an eight-by-ten glossy photo. It looked like something from an official crime scene. Moose arranged the snaps, whistling "Drowsy Maggie."

"Tell me what's different about these photos, mate."

Wilkerson blinked. The eight-by-ten glossy showed a larger version of the girl's messy bedroom. But the wall above the desk was empty. He looked back at the small scrapbook photo. The vibrant painting hung on the wall.

Moose thumped the tiny snap. "The art is missing, mate."

Wilkerson shrugged. "Maybe it broke, or she threw it away. You know how women are. Always fussing with the décor."

"I bet she took it," Moose said.

Wilkerson squinted at the small photograph. The art resembled a plaque, roughly the size of a hardback book, but the top portion was curved. A buzzing filled his ears. His heart vaulted inside his chest, leaping painfully against tissue and bones. This was a Greek Orthodox icon—his icon. He'd thought it was lost forever and yet here it was, hanging on an idiot girl's wall, exposed to environmental insults.

Moose stood, and the air cast squeaked. "Am I fired or not?"

"I haven't decided." Wilkerson looked away. "Come back in a few days and we'll talk."

"No tricks?" Moose's forehead wrinkled. "No Zubas?"

"I thought you weren't afraid."

"I'm not, but I don't want trouble." Moose slung the bag over his shoulder.

The door opened, and Yok-Seng charged into the room. He lunged toward Moose, but Wilkerson pushed between them. "Moose was just leaving."

The Cambodian gave a short nod and stepped against the wall.

"He's a man of few words, isn't he?" Moose laughed.

"Yok-Seng doesn't need a vocabulary." Wilkerson paused. "Mind if I keep these snaps?"

It wasn't really a question, but Moose pursed his lips, as if giving the matter deep thought. Then he shrugged. "Sure, why the hell not?"

After he left, Wilkerson rummaged in his desk drawer for a magnifying glass and held it over the small photograph. A red-robed figure materialized, a woman holding an ostrich egg in one hand, a book with gilt pages in the other. Wilkerson reached across his desk and buzzed his secretary.

"Get Mr. Underwood," he said.

CHAPTER 14

HOTEL USTRA
KARDZHALI, BULGARIA

Caro stepped out of the bathroom, pressing a damp cloth to her face. She'd lost her lunch and didn't think she'd ever eat again. Two murders in two days and both victims had bled to death; yet the deaths had occurred in separate parts of the world. They couldn't be related. Or could they?

The night she'd been informed of her uncle's death, a prankster had kept calling the Bow Street flat. Maybe he'd been outside watching. And waiting. Jude had been on Bow Street that night. He knew her telephone number because her uncle had given it to him. How much time had elapsed between the time he'd approached her on the sidewalk and when he'd shown up at the airport? An hour maybe? Was that long enough to kill Phoebe and dash off to Heathrow?

Yes. No. His clothes would have been disheveled and

bloody, right? But they were clean. She set down the washrag. *Think, Clifford. Concentrate.* The murders had to be related.

Maybe Phoebe's killer had killed the wrong girl.

Adrenaline spiked through Caro's veins. She felt an urgent need to leave the hotel and make her way to the embassy in Sofia. Her hands shook as she scooped up her clothes, her uncle's pens, the rabbit's-foot keychain, and the tiny flashlight. She stuffed everything into her bag and ran to the lobby.

The clerk with the hoop earrings stood behind the desk, but Caro didn't take the time to settle her bill, just hurried outside and looked for a taxi. Clouds swabbed over the hills, blending into the scrubwater sky. Everything was damp and gray, reminding her of London, the winter days and nights forming a drab continuum.

Two men in red jogging suits walked toward her, ones she'd seen in the hotel. They wore wraparound sunglasses that reflected trees and buildings. Chalky, white cream covered their faces. Why were they wearing Kabuki makeup?

The tall man lifted one hand. *"Miss Clee-ford!"*

She'd seen him last night, in the bar. And the stumpy fellow had tried to steal her bag in Sofia. Her heart slammed against her ribs, and her mouth went dry. *Run, run, run.* She sucked in a mouthful of cold air, then sprinted in the opposite direction. She stopped at the first taxi she saw and climbed into the backseat, dragging the duffel bag onto her lap.

"Avtobusna spirka," she cried. "Hurry! *Pobarsai!"*

The cab jolted forward and its headlights swept over the road. She clutched the seat as the driver pulled into traffic.

The other cars had their headlights on, too, and it was only late afternoon. She looked out the taxi's back window, her breath fogging the glass. The men in jogging suits hurried across the parking lot and got into a brown Dacia. On the rear bumper was a sticker: I'LL NOT DIE TODAY.

What's that supposed to mean? Caro thought. She saw a flash of movement near the front of the hotel. Jude ran out of the black doors and skidded on the sidewalk. He stared at her taxi, waving both arms. Caro almost told her driver to stop, but those men in the red suits alarmed her. She watched Jude run into the parking lot and climb into a white car. Then she lost sight of him as her taxi turned the corner. St. George's golden domes flashed by. She couldn't remember where the bus station was located, and she hoped her driver was going in the right direction.

She glanced out the back window again and looked for the Dacia and Jude's car. She didn't see either one, but that didn't mean she'd lost them. Trucks and smaller vehicles jammed the boulevard, their headlights shimmering over the damp pavement.

Caro turned around and pulled a map from her bag. She found the Hotel Ustra and drew a line to the bus terminal on Bulgarian Boulevard. She glanced up just as a red Moskvitch darted out of a side street and plowed into the taxi. The jolt knocked her against the door, and her map went flying. The taxi spun around and skidded onto the sidewalk.

The taxi driver got out and waved his fist in the air. His forehead was bleeding. Behind him, the Moskvitch's horn blared in a flat monotone, and smoke drifted up from its hood. The car's occupant lay motionless over the steering wheel. The taxi driver opened Caro's door. Blood ran down his chin and hit the pavement. He pointed east. *"Avtobusna spirka,"* he said.

He was telling her to make her own way to the bus station. Fine, she could do that. People circled the red Moskvitch and peered through the shattered windshield. She reached into her bag, yanked out a T-shirt, and handed it to her driver.

"To stop the bleeding," she said and slid out of the taxi. Cars stretched out in both directions. No brown Dacia. She didn't see Jude's car, either. She stepped into the crowd and walked toward the intersection. While she waited for the light to change, she decided to call Ilya Velikov. As she groped inside her bag for the phone, a brown Dacia whizzed by. The taillights blinked, and the car angled into a parking slot. The creepy men got out, ignoring startled glances from pedestrians, and turned in Caro's direction. She ran to the end of the block and darted in front of a redheaded woman who yelled something in Bulgarian.

"Sorry," Caro said. Still gripping the phone, she looked over her shoulder to check on the men. The sidewalk was jammed with pedestrians, but she didn't see anyone in sunglasses or red jogging suits. She turned around and bumped into something solid. She looked up into a man's white-washed face. He smiled, and his makeup cracked at the edges. It was the tall, gaunt man, and his sidekick stood beside him.

He slapped the mobile phone from her hand. She started to run, but he grabbed her shoulders and spun her around. She ground her heel against his instep. He cursed, then a thin smile creased his face and he tightened his grip. His companion seized her right elbow. Their cold bodies gave off a foul smell.

"You're hurting me, dammit!" She kicked the tall man's kneecaps. He jammed his hands under her armpits, lifted her off the pavement and bolted down the sidewalk toward the brown Dacia.

"Help!" she yelled in English. She jabbed the man with her elbows, smearing the white makeup into his hairline. People stepped out of the way as the squatty man flashed a badge. The tall Bulgarian carried Caro to the Dacia. As he started to toss her into the car, she reached out blindly and her fingers sank into the runt's bushy hair. He tumbled into the backseat with her, cursing and peeling back her fingers.

She bit his hand. He howled and kicked the back of the seat, denting the leather. A red blur moved past her and something sharp pricked her jaw. "Release Teo or I will make you bleed," the tall man said.

Her fingers relaxed. Teo scooted away, rubbing his scalp. "The bitch is strong," he said.

"And she is not afraid. Yet." The tall man leaned back, and Caro saw the glint of a knife. Her stomach tensed. Oh, God. Oh, God. Was he going to stab her? What about witnesses? Pedestrians flowed past the Dacia in a colorful blur of Christmas sweaters, and not a single person looked her way.

"Do not move or scream," the tall man said. Without waiting for Caro's response, he put away the knife, got out of the car, and climbed into the front seat. She immediately reached for the door handle. But there wasn't one. It had been torn off.

A buzzing started between her ears, as if bees were

flying inside her skull. These men had tried to steal her bag at the Sofia airport and they'd probably burgled her room at the Ustra—but why?

My icon. It was quite old, but she'd assumed its value was sentimental. So why had they kidnapped her *and* the bag? Why hadn't they knocked her to the sidewalk and stolen the icon? Or did they want Uncle Nigel's passport with its odd clues? What if these creeps were mixed up in the Bulgarian mafia and were escorting her to an underworld boss?

Rivulets of perspiration streamed down Caro's face. She cut her gaze to the plaid bag—had she packed anything that could be used as a weapon?

The tall man gunned the engine, and the car jolted into traffic. Teo grabbed Caro's hair. "Hurts, yes?" he said, then let go of her hair and shoved her against the window.

"Asshole." She jerked the duffel into her lap and folded her arms around it.

The driver laughed and glanced over his shoulder. "Permit me to introduce myself. I am Georgi Ivanov. My comrade is Teodor Draganov. But you may call him Teo."

"And I'm the bloody queen of England," she cried, sounding braver than she felt. "Stop the car."

"I cannot do that, Your Majesty." Georgi steered the Dacia down a side street and angled into a parking garage. The first level was crammed with vehicles. Why had the men picked this place? Were they going to change vehicles or drag her into the building? An echo rose up as the tires slapped over the concrete segments and screeched around corners. Only a few cars were on the second tier; the third was empty. She wiped her sweaty face and glanced out the window. No cars, no people, no one to hear her scream.

Georgi parked beside a dirty plaster column. Caro glanced at Teo. He rubbed his scalp, grimacing as wiry hairs broke loose and drifted. She turned back to the window.

Okay, Caro. Get ready. When Georgi opens the door, you only have seconds to leap out and run like hell.

She felt a little shaky and took a deep breath, then she inched toward the window. Georgi got out and opened her door so swiftly that she lost her balance. She veered forward, arms windmilling, and crashed to the pavement. The duffel landed beside her with a terrible, final thud. She expected Georgi to brandish his knife, but he stepped to the front of the Dacia and beat on the hood.

"Stop acting like girl!" he yelled at Teo.

Caro pressed her lips together, feeling a steely determination take hold. She was going to die, but these thugs weren't getting her icon. She'd rather fling it over the ledge. Her hands shook as she tucked the duffel's strap across her shoulder.

Footsteps shuffled closer. Georgi yanked Caro to her feet and towed her around the car, to the open trunk. She bent her knees and pulled hard in the opposite direction, trying to throw him off balance. She heard a scuffling noise behind her, then something crashed against her head. Pain spilled through her skull and the pavement sloshed forward, a solid wave of gray, then the light sputtered and went out.

CHAPTER 15

———

DOWNTOWN KARDZHALI

Caro awoke in a dark, foul-smelling place, and wherever that place was, it was moving. Her nose twitched as she breathed in petrol fumes and an underlying stench of dirt and decay. The back of her head throbbed. Had she fallen into a cave? Where the hell was she? Her hand shot out and hit something hard. Chunks of memory floated up. A door without a handle. An open trunk. Men in jogging suits. They'd knocked her out and stuffed her into the damn trunk.

The brakes squealed, and the car stopped abruptly, slinging her backward. A hard edge poked into her back. She reached around and felt a rectangular object. Her fingernails scratched over the surface. Nylon. Her bag. In the distance, she heard honking horns and sirens. Muffled voices seeped from the deepest part of the trunk. Those bastards were listening to music.

She pushed her hand along the bag, searching for the zipper. She couldn't find it, couldn't get inside. And she needed a weapon. She'd packed her uncle's pens, right? She finally found the tiny metal zipper, slid it open, and reached inside the bag. Her fingers brushed over plastic and a square edge.

Okay, good. Her icon was still there. So the men hadn't looked inside the bag. If they weren't after the icon, then what? Maybe they knew it wasn't going anywhere. She couldn't just sit here while they drove to a secluded spot. She had to find a way out.

She thrust her hand deeper into the bag, and her knuckles grazed what felt like a long, cylindrical object. Her thumb passed over a tiny knob. She pushed it, and a circle of light filled the bag with an eerie red glow. Her uncle's pens lay in the bottom—maybe she could stab Georgi in the eye or pick the lock. Not too long ago, the *Observer* had published an article about women and safety, with a sidebar on how to escape from a trunk. Digging into the backseat was one option, and kicking out the brake lights was another. Newer cars had glow-in-the-dark tags.

Caro didn't see one. Not a good sign. She wasn't sure if she could pick the latch with an ink pen, but she had to try. She grabbed a pen, then swept the light around the trunk. Dirty blue carpet. Brown metal roof. Plastic bag filled with jewelry. A child's stuffed bunny. A brown fedora with a crease in the rim, just like Uncle Nigel's.

She jolted. The light wavered and hit a gray, waxen figure with long, dark hair. A mannequin? But why would a mannequin have blood splattered on her jacket? Caro leaned closer, trying not to breathe in the stench. The woman's throat was slashed, stringy tendons hanging down. She was dead, dead, dead.

Caro choked down a scream and scrambled to the far side of the trunk. The woman's hair was caked with blood. All of her fingernails were torn. She was naked from the waist down, with bite wounds along her thighs, and her heels had been sliced open.

Caro winced. Uncle Nigel's Achilles tendons had been severed. And he'd been bitten. She aimed the light over the jewelry, the bunny, and the fedora. It was definitely Uncle Nigel's. The men in the front seat had killed and tortured her uncle; they'd done more to this woman. And they would do the same to her.

The Dacia moved at a sluggish pace, then stopped abruptly. She stuffed the pens into her jacket, then aimed the beam of light at the latch. She didn't see a lock or any type of safety mechanism. This was an older Romanian car, not a Land Rover. The Dacia probably didn't have an automatic trunk release. If it did, it would be connected to the lock by a cable. She looked for one. Nothing.

She put the penlight into her mouth and scooted to the other side of the trunk. She pressed against the dead woman and began ripping up the carpet. The light moved over a bundle of wires and thick cables. She followed one to the trunk latch and pulled hard.

It didn't budge. She rubbed her palms together and grabbed the cable with both hands, wrenching as hard as she could. The cable bit into her palm. She ignored the pain and tugged again. If she didn't get out, she would end up raped and butchered. She pulled again.

Nothing happened.

Okay, one more time, Clifford. She slid her hands along the cable, moving closer to the latch, and braced her feet against the side of the trunk. Then she yanked as hard as she could, ignoring the sharp, searing pain. Pull, pull, pull.

She heard a click, and the lid creaked open. Light spilled around her, stinging her eyes. She scrambled to her knees. Traffic was at a standstill, except for the far lane, where vehicles moved in a blur. The Dacia inched forward. Had the kidnappers noticed the open trunk?

She shoved the penlight into her bag. Then she slung the strap around her chest, bandolier style, and waited for the Dacia to stop. But it kept going.

She grasped the metal edge of the trunk and rolled out. Her feet hit the pavement and she skidded. The car behind her slammed on its brakes. The Dacia stopped, too.

Caro looked under the car. Teo's black tennis shoes appeared. She pulled the pens out of her pocket, then scuttled into the next lane and crouched between two vans. Her pulse thrummed as Teo walked to the back of the Dacia and slammed the trunk shut. He glanced around, straightening his sunglasses, just another cool dude with a penchant for white makeup and dead broads. Then he headed in Caro's direction.

The back of her neck tingled. If she didn't move, the rat bastard would find her. Gripping a pen in each hand, she hurried into the next lane. A taxi honked and hit the brakes. The driver shook his fist.

"Help me," Caro yelled. "Please help!"

Teo jumped onto the hood of a blue Skoda and vaulted to the next car. He was gaining on her. Cars began honking, and a man stuck his head out his window and yelled. Caro ran to the far lane and waited for a gap in the traffic. A cold hand closed on her shoulder and yanked her around. She looked up into Teo's face.

"You sad bastard, leave me alone!" She stabbed a pen into his hand.

Teo stretched his arms like a swimmer and dove toward her. Caro stepped aside and jabbed the other pen into his neck. He tottered on one leg. She lunged forward and pushed him into the far lane.

A white truck honked, but before Teo got his footing, the vehicle rammed into him and sucked him under its wheels. His sunglasses spun up into the air. There was a crunch and the brakes whined. The rear tires stopped on Teo's lower back. Dark blood jetted up, pulsing onto the asphalt.

People climbed out of their cars and pressed closer. A taxi driver elbowed his way through the crowd, yelling in broken English, "She pushed him!"

Caro shook her head, and then she remembered she was supposed to nod. "He kidnapped me. And there's a dead woman in his trunk. He's driving a brown Dacia."

A man in a black sweater charged forward and took her photograph with his mobile phone. She started to run, but he locked his arm around her neck.

"Let me go. You don't understand," she cried. "He tried to kill me."

The man in the black sweater tightened his grip and shouted, "Police!"

His arm pressed hard against her windpipe. She couldn't breathe. Spots whirled in front of her eyes. She pinched his hand, digging her nails into his flesh, and he jerked her to the side. In the distance, she heard someone call her name. Georgi? No, the accent was wrong.

"Caro?" the voice called again. She recognized the heavy Yorkshire accent.

Then Jude pushed through the crowd and lunged at the man in the sweater. There was a crack, and the man tipped forward in a dead faint. Caro felt a warm hand clamp down on her wrist. Jude pulled her up and led her around the truck, across the boulevard. Then she remembered about Phoebe and shook off his hand. He'd been outside their flat that night. Now he was in downtown Kardzhali. He was everywhere he shouldn't be.

"What's wrong?" Jude's forehead wrinkled.

"Leave me alone!" She ran down the sidewalk. Maybe he was in league with those men in the Dacia. If not, why the hell was he here? She cut around a corner, only to stop abruptly and vomit into the gutter. When she looked up, Jude stood two feet away.

"Why are you always turning up?" she cried. She stepped backward. In the distance she heard sirens.

"Calm down," he said. "I followed your taxi, and—"

"Why? Are you a stalker?"

"I'm trying to keep you alive." He pointed. "My car is around the corner. We need to go."

"I don't need you. I can take care of myself." She balled up her fist and slugged him in the jaw.

"Bugger." Jude staggered backward, rubbing his cheek. Behind him, Georgi rounded the corner and pulled off his sunglasses. Jude turned. The two men glared for a long time, making Caro wonder if they were exchanging signals. A smile cut across Georgi's angular face, creasing the white ointment. As he started toward them, the sun skidded out of a gray cloud and shone down, glancing off the asphalt and filling the alley with sharp light. Georgi dropped to one knee and held up his hand, fingers spread into claws.

Caro took off in the opposite direction. She heard footsteps, and then Jude spun her around. She started to hit him again, but he caught her hand and slung her over his shoulder.

"Put me down!"

"Not on your nelly." Gripping her tightly, he jogged across the street and turned down an alley.

She let out a sharp cry and pummeled the back of his leather coat. "I forbid you to take another step, you ruddy punk."

"I'm not going to harm you, I swear it."

Something in his voice broke through her panic and she quit struggling. He carried her into a parking lot and stopped in front of a white Fiat. In one smooth motion, he slung open the passenger door and shoved her into the seat. Then he leaned over and fastened her safety belt.

She immediately unbuckled it.

"Are you mad?" Perspiration ran down his face, and a bruise was forming on his jaw where she'd clipped him. At the end of the alley, police cars flashed by.

"You and that damned Bulgarian man know each other," she said. She was too frightened to cry. She was in survival mode. She started to climb out of the car, ready to fight, but he pushed her back.

"Hold still." He jerked up the hem of his jeans and pulled down his sock. "See the scars?" He pointed to his heel. "My Achilles tendons were cut. Both of them. Just like your uncle's."

Her vision blurred as she stared at the jagged red lines. The police hadn't released details about Uncle Nigel's murder. "How do *you* know what happened to my uncle?"

"Let's get out of the city," Jude said, firmly buckling her seat belt. "Then I'll explain."

CHAPTER 16

Georgi held up his hand, trying to block the light, ignoring the searing pain. The zinc oxide ointment wasn't working. His flesh reddened and his vision blurred. Even with his sunglasses, if he didn't get into the shade, he would go blind permanently. He heard footsteps, then two shapes ran down the pavement. Georgi sniffed. Was it the girl? He smelled guns and leather, the stink of cheap hair tonic. Firm hands grabbed his arms.

"Who are you?" Georgi whispered.

"Police," a deep voice answered.

"Take me out of the sun!" Georgi said, then realized the police might think he was playing at vampirism, that he was a Goth with sunblock and faux fangs. But he'd had quite a bit of experience in quelling the peasants' paranoia.

"I'm a sick man," he added. "I'm taking medication that makes me allergic to sunlight."

The officers carried him into a café and set him down in a chair. Georgi straightened his sunglasses and looked at the men. They were blurry, ringed with halos. "Hurry, or she will get away."

"Who?" one of the policemen asked.

"A woman murderer," Georgi said. "She killed my partner. It happened minutes ago. Her name is Caroline Clifford. A British national."

"Who did she kill?" an officer asked.

"I told you. My partner was killed on Bulgarian Boulevard." Georgi licked the blisters on the back of his hand.

The policemen did not reply.

"If you won't find her, I will." Georgi rose to his feet and wobbled sideways. "She must pay for her crimes."

An officer caught Georgi's arm and led him back to the chair. "Leave that to us," the man said. "It's too dangerous for civilians."

"I am not a civilian." Georgi pulled out an ID badge. Bloodred spots churned in front of his eyes, and his skin tingled. "You are wasting my time. Find the murderer before she kills again!"

"Please calm down," the officer said.

"Calm? How can I be calm? My partner has been bisected." Georgi paused. Truth and lies came as easily as wound-licking, and they were just as soothing. "This woman has murdered others. She kidnapped a Russian tourist from the Hotel Ustra."

Now that Georgi was out of the sun, his vision began to clear. He smelled blood, fresh blood. He surveyed the café.

Not here, he thought. *Not now*. He tried to remember if Teo had closed the trunk. But the pain had clouded his mind.

The bell above the door dinged as customers walked in and out. He blinked at the window. The sun darkened, as if a giant hand had stuffed it back into the clouds; a moment later, it broke free. He reached into his pocket, wincing as his burned flesh hit the fabric, and he drew out a rumpled fax. The picture showed a smiling girl with too much hair.

"This is her." Georgi licked his lips. "Be careful. She is a dangerous woman."

CHAPTER 17

Caro gripped the seat as Jude drove out of the alley and turned onto the crowded boulevard. Lights from police cars whirled along the street, casting a blue tint on the windows of nearby buildings. In the far lane, pedestrians surrounded the white truck.

"We're going the wrong way!" she cried, and glanced nervously out the window. The man in the black sweater was still there. His gaze passed over the Fiat, and then his head snapped around. Glaring at Caro, he held up his cell phone, as if to take her photograph.

"Get out of here, Jude!" She pointed. "That man is taking a picture of your car."

Jude steered the Fiat onto the sidewalk and drove toward an outdoor café. Pedestrians leaped from their tables and scattered.

"Hold tight." Jude's voice sounded amazingly calm, as if he drove on sidewalks every day. He didn't flinch when a plastic chair went flying over the hood.

Caro shut her eyes when the Fiat plowed into a green chalkboard where the daily specials were written in pink chalk. She opened one eye just as Jude drove off the sidewalk, into the boulevard, and zigzagged across four lanes of traffic. He turned down a narrow street, the tires bouncing over cobblestones. A bearded man leaped out of the way and fell into a garbage bin. The can tipped over and rolled down the alley. A policeman on a motorcycle swerved around the corner and rammed into the can.

At the end of the street, three police cars blocked the exit. Jude drove the Fiat toward the opposite sidewalk. The tires jumped the curb and slammed into wooden boxes. Onions and potatoes went flying and rolled down the sidewalk. A metal light pole rose up, but before Caro could scream, Jude swung the Fiat back into the street and cut down an alley. The sirens faded as he navigated down a series of narrow lanes. He took another right, onto a street lined with row houses. In the distance, floodlights shone on St. John the Precursor.

"It's getting dark," Jude said and turned down another side road.

"But that's good. The police will have a harder time finding us."

"Maybe, maybe not."

"I should call Mr. Velikov." Caro fumbled in her bag. A second later, she remembered that her phone was lying in pieces on the sidewalk.

"No." Jude caught her arm. "Don't call anyone."

Every drop of her blood rushed to her head. She jerked

away and scooted against her window. Flashing a malicious gaze, she said, "Mr. Velikov will understand."

"Don't be naïve."

Caro bit down a sharp retort and glared out the window. He didn't know her well enough to pass judgment. Yes, she was naïve, but her deductive skills were intact. Who'd cut Jude's tendons? Was he a victim or some type of assassin?

"Didn't you see me at the hotel?" Jude's calm voice held a flinty edge. "You ran away."

"But you found me. You always do."

"You're sorry I didn't leave you back there? The burly fellow had you in a headlock."

"That doesn't make you a hero."

"I'm not trying to be one." He turned down a street that was lined with empty warehouses.

"Look, Jude, I don't know what's going on, or how you're mixed up in this. All I know is, those men followed me from my hotel and kidnapped me on Bulgarian Boulevard. They stuffed me into the boot of their car. And there was a dead woman inside. They would have killed me, too."

Jude stiffened. "You were kidnapped?"

"But I got away. The short guy chased me. I jabbed him with an ink pen. It's not my fault he stumbled and got smashed. Well, maybe it is. A little." She lifted her chin. "I'm not sorry. Not one bit."

Jude didn't comment. She frowned and shook his arm. "Didn't you hear me? I'm a manslaughterer."

"He deserved to die." Jude shifted gears, and the car passed a building with shattered windows. A skinny dog trotted over to a trash bin and stood on its hind legs. The rest of the street looked deserted.

"You're not telling me everything," she said. "I saw you looking at that creepy Bulgarian. You know him, don't you?"

Jude squeezed the steering wheel, and his jaw clenched.

"You *do* know him!" She unbuckled her seat belt. "Stop the car. Now!"

Jude angled the car to the curb, then shifted in his seat. His legs looked too long to fit comfortably in the cramped car. He started to touch her hand, but she grabbed the door handle and said, "Don't."

"Caro, listen. I *do* know that man. But it's not what you think."

She cracked open the door. Cold air blew around her shoulders, stirring her hair. "Start talking," she said.

"The men who kidnapped you are assassins." Jude stared down at his legs.

"I can believe that. But how did you figure it out?" *Because he's mixed up with them?* She swallowed.

Jude cut his eyes at her. "They tried to kill me."

A tingling sensation started in Caro's fingertips and crept across her palms, as if thousands of baby spiders had hatched beneath her flesh. She slammed her door and took a breath. "When?"

"Two years ago. The guy who got hit by the lorry? Well, he held me down while the tall Bulgarian cut my tendons. Another man was with them. A big redheaded guy. But I haven't seen him in Kardzhali."

She forced herself to keep breathing, but the prickly feeling got stronger, plunging into her forearms. "Why would your attackers come after me?"

"I'm fairly sure they killed your uncle," he said.

Her legs began to shake. She put her hands on her

knees, trying to hold them still. What would Jude think when she told him about her roommate's violent death? Would he claim Phoebe's murder was part of an international conspiracy or the work of two Bulgarian thieves? Were those men mixed up in the underground antiquities trade? She'd gone on digs with Uncle Nigel many times, and without fail, they'd encountered black marketers. Archaeology was a dirty, lucrative business, and it could be deadly. So, yes, thieves could have killed her uncle. But had those same men attacked Jude *two whole years ago*?

"Sorry," she said. "I don't see how this is connected? You. Me. Uncle Nigel."

"I don't know, either." He glanced away.

He's not telling the truth. She looked at her legs. She'd stopped shaking, but the itchy-crawly feeling had moved into her chest and she couldn't get a deep breath. Pressing one hand against her sternum she said, "Mr. Velikov can help. Let's find a phone."

Jude stared out his window, tracking the skinny dog. "And tell him what?"

"What you told me. That those men killed my uncle."

"We'll talk about Velikov later. Right now, we need to get out of the city and hide the car."

"Don't go to the Hotel Ustra. It's not safe." She watched Jude's face, her heart pounding. Had he burgled her room or was he trying to help? And how had he found her on Bulgarian Boulevard—in all that traffic?

He swerved down a wide street. "I know a safe place."

"Good. Then we'll call the embassy."

He glanced away from the road and gave her a penetrating stare. "I don't trust the authorities, especially in Bulgaria."

"Not even the British consulate?"

He shook his head. "You shouldn't trust them, either.

She rubbed her chest, feeling too tired to argue. At least the spiders had finally gone quiet. Through the windshield, a rosy streak held over the mountains, rising into layers of blue. Concrete buildings blotted out part of the sky, with chimneys and satellite dishes jutting up from the rooftops. The buildings looked empty, even though the upper-level windows glowed with fluorescent lighting.

Jude steered the Fiat into the street and drove south. The buildings ended and weedy fields began. He angled up a steep driveway and parked in front of the Akacia Hotel. Through a gap in the evergreens, Caro saw the Kardzhali Dam.

"This is too close to town," she cried. "Let's drive a little farther. The dam is only fifty kilometers from the Turkish border."

"We won't make it through the checkpoint. Turkish border crossings are tough." He opened his door. "Come on, let's go inside."

They walked to the lobby in silence. While Jude spoke to the clerk, Caro tried to calm down. She glanced into the bar and watched a silver-haired man push a white rag over a marble counter. A television hung down from the ceiling, and canned laughter rang out. Behind the bar was a restaurant with knotty-pine walls and a fireplace.

She expected the desk clerk to demand their passports. She pulled hers out, but the clerk slid a key across the polished counter. Jude lifted it.

Caro wasn't a hundred percent sure that he was trustworthy—he seemed rather paranoid—but she wasn't letting him get away until she had some answers. She followed him to room 344.

He unlocked the door and swung it open. She stepped past him and dumped her bag onto the bed. Through the windows, the lights of downtown Kardzhali were starting to shine.

"All right," she said. "How did you know my uncle was tortured?"

"Can you read French?"

"Yes."

He pulled a wrinkled *Le Monde* from his backpack. "Turn to page four."

Her hands trembled as she flipped the pages.

BRITISH ARCHAEOLOGIST
MURDERED IN BULGARIA

Sir Nigel Clifford, a world-renowned Oxford University professor and archaeologist, was murdered Thursday night at the Perperikon cultural site in southern Bulgaria. The seventy-two-year-old professor was found the following morning by tourists. Police refused to speculate on the motive, but a source claimed it was a robbery gone awry. Although details are sketchy, it appears that the archaeologist was tortured—both Achilles tendons were severed, and he was savagely bitten. The Interior Ministry told the British embassy in Sofia that they will bring the murderers to justice. A spokesperson for the embassy said, "We are deeply shocked and saddened by the murder of Dr. Clifford. . . ."

Caro lowered the paper. Okay, fine. Jude hadn't personally known details of her uncle's murder. He'd learned the gory details from *Le Monde*. But he was still holding back.

He rubbed his forehead. "I've been keeping track of odd murders," he said.

"Isn't that an unusual hobby for a biochemist?"

"Not if your Achilles tendons have been cut." His eyes blazed. "In the last two years, there have been four reported cases of severed tendons. Your uncle's case is the fifth."

Caro rubbed the back of her head and winced. How hard had the Bulgarian hit her? She couldn't feel a lump, but her scalp was tender and she was having trouble focusing. Maybe she had a concussion. Jude was watching, so she said, "I got bashed in the head."

"An ice pack will help." He grabbed the plastic bucket and stepped into the hall.

She sat down on the bed and rummaged in her bag for Mr. Velikov's phone number. No, he might not believe her version of Teo's accident. Better to ring Mr. Hughes. His secretary put Caro through right away.

"Miss Clifford!" he cried. "Everyone is looking for you, my dear. Where are you?"

"I'm—" she broke off when she heard a muffled noise from his end of the phone, as if he'd covered the receiver with his hand, and then she heard him whisper, "It's her."

Her? A spider ran up her backbone, and she shivered. *Stop it, Caro. He didn't mean you.*

"Mr. Hughes, I've called to say good-bye. I'm leaving Kardzhali."

"No, you mustn't go. Firstly, there's been a dreadful incident at the Kardzhali morgue. Your uncle's body is missing."

"You mean, like, misplaced?" Her throat narrowed to a pinpoint, but she managed to suck in a breath.

"Stolen." Mr. Hughes paused. "Miss Clifford, I don't wish to alarm you, but a field agent from MI5 is in the building. He needs a word with you, too."

"Why?" She couldn't breathe. The spiders had burrowed under her skin, weaving taut strands around her ribs. MI5 wanted to speak to her?

"I'm not privy to the details," Mr. Hughes said. "But I'm afraid there's more bad news. A fax from the Kardzhali police just came across my desk. A man was killed on Bulgarian Boulevard. An eyewitness claims that a woman fitting your description pushed the victim into the path of an oncoming lorry. Another witness gave the police your name. Normally the embassy doesn't get involved in criminal investigations, but considering the ambassador knew your uncle . . ."

"Wait—a man gave the police my name? No one in Kardzhali knows my name. Except for . . ."

"Except for whom, my dear?"

"It's a long story."

"I'm sure it is. However, the police also faxed a rather grainy photograph of you. Some chap took it at the crime scene with his mobile phone. Now, I'm sure you can explain—"

"I didn't murder anyone, it was self-defense. See, these two awful men kidnapped me."

There was a thrumming silence. Finally he said, "I *see*."

"I know it sounds far-fetched," she said, "but you had warned me about the dangers in Bulgaria, hadn't you?"

"Yes, but—"

"I was on my way to the bus station when two men grabbed me. I'm pretty sure they're the ones who ransacked my hotel room."

"Er, when did the alleged kidnapping happen?"

"There's nothing alleged about it." She paused, wondering if she should mention the dreadful news about Phoebe. She decided against it and plowed on. "I'm sure you can find lots of witnesses because it happened less than an hour ago on Bulgarian Boulevard. The fiends locked me in the trunk, Mr. Hughes. A dead woman was in there, too."

Mr. Hughes released an explosive sigh. "*Dead*, you say?"

"Quite. But I escaped. One of the men chased me into traffic. He caught up with me. We struggled." *And I stabbed him with a ballpoint pen.* "He somehow lost his balance, and a truck ran over him."

She winced. Even to her own ears, she sounded crazy, like a twenty-five-year-old nincompoop tour guide instead of a methodical, reasonable ex-scholar.

"Yes, very well. Stay where you are, Miss Clifford. A car will be there momentarily."

"But . . ." She hadn't said where she was. Or had she? The whole afternoon was gummed together, hanging in sticky webs. Jude stepped into the room. He set down the bucket and frowned. In three long strides, he crossed to the bed and pulled the receiver from her hand. Then he jerked the cord from the wall. It made a loud crack. "I thought you understood," he cried. "You mustn't ring anyone."

"I was only talking to Mr. Hughes at the embassy."

"Right. Only the embassy. I'm sure the police are on their way. We've got to leave." Jude lifted her bag, hooked the strap over her shoulder, and steered her out of the room.

"I'm not five years old," she snapped. "I can walk."

He released her elbow and stepped back, a pulse leaping under his jaw.

She lifted her hand. "Don't take this the wrong way, but we should go in separate directions. MI5 wants to talk to me. And I want to talk to them. I suppose it's about my uncle. His body is missing."

"Yes, I went to the morgue this morning, and—"

Caro's stomach tightened and her hand fell limply to her side. "You what?"

"Don't get your knickers in a twist. I went for information. When I arrived, the morgue was in an uproar."

"But why did you go to the morgue? Why are you poking into my business?"

"I'll explain later. Because I'm sure your friend at the embassy has alerted the police to pick us up. They'll be here any minute." He touched her arm.

She shrugged him off.

"We're wasting time." He gripped her shoulder and directed her down the stairs. The desk clerk waved as they headed out the door.

Jude looked up at the sky. It was streaked with purple, and stars were starting to shine. "Night's falling. We shouldn't linger."

"We shouldn't be together," she said. "You haven't

done anything wrong. I'm the little criminal. Let *me* go to the embassy, and you can drive away."

"I'm not leaving you." He flung open the passenger door. "Now, hop inside before you stir up any more trouble."

CHAPTER 18

Ilya Velikov steered his car onto Bulgarian Boulevard, his headlights moving over the pedestrians. He didn't normally respond to traffic accidents, but he'd made an exception after he'd heard that apparently witnesses had seen a British national, a woman, push a bystander into the path of a truck.

According to the dispatcher, the British woman had long, fuzzy blond hair and she'd been carrying a red plaid duffel bag. Impossible. He had just spoken to Caroline Clifford. She'd seemed sweet and quite genuine, but very, very young. And the young were often impulsive and unwise.

He climbed out of his car and pushed through the pedestrians, flashing his badge.

"Interior Ministry," he kept repeating. "Step aside, please."

Straight ahead, the ambulance blocked two lanes, with police cars parked on either side. The chilly night air snapped his coat as he walked toward the ambulance. Blue lights wheeled over the crowd, sweeping across trees and dingy buildings that lined the wide street. Abandoned vehicles clogged the lanes, their headlights cutting through the dusk. Some of the drivers stood on their cars to gawk.

The crowd parted, and Velikov saw yellow barricades surrounding a white truck. A mangled corpse was wedged beneath the rear tires. Rescue workers knelt around it, arguing about the best way to extract the body. An officer interrogated a man in a black sweater, taking copious notes.

Velikov stepped around them, toward a dark puddle that led to the truck. The undercarriage and doors were splattered with flesh and bone fragments. The body lay under the rear tires. One eyeball stared out of the crushed skull; the other eye dangled from the socket, resting against the corpse's stubby nose.

"Has the victim been identified?" Velikov asked a smooth-faced officer. The young man was impeccably dressed, his navy shirt tucked into his trousers, and the trouser legs were stuffed into Doc Marten bovver boots, the same kind Velikov himself had worn when he'd been in the militia.

"No, Comrade Inspector," the officer said.

Velikov smiled. He hadn't been called that since Bulgaria was part of the Eastern Bloc. The officer looked too young to have remembered the Communist regime, and Velikov was impressed. He started to say something, but a policewoman with dark red hair held out plastic gloves.

"You will need these, Commander," she said.

The young policeman gestured at the man in the black sweater. "Comrade Inspector, this man witnessed the murder," he said. "He took a picture of the woman. I've already sent it to headquarters."

"Let me see." Velikov tilted his head.

The man in the sweater held up his phone. The picture showed a bushy-haired blonde with startled gray eyes. The policeman cleared his throat. "The woman in the photograph is a British national. Miss Caroline Clifford. The witness claims she pushed the victim into the path of the truck."

"She pushed hard," said the man in the black sweater. "The victim fell into the road. I grabbed the woman. Then a man punched me."

"Can you describe him?" Velikov pushed his hands into the gloves.

"Dark hair. Ponytail. Blue eyes. He and the woman ran toward the bus station."

Velikov pushed back his hat and watched the emergency team jack up the truck.

"Careful!" yelled one of the emergency workers as the crew started to lift the victim. Velikov heard a crack, and watched in horror as the victim's pelvis caved in, folding in half. A black crocodile wallet fell out of the jogging suit's pocket and hit the pavement. One of the workers picked it up, flicking off tissue, and handed it up to the policewoman. She opened it. Inside, it was packed with euros. She searched the side pockets and began removing cards.

"Teo Stamboliev of Sofia," said the woman, holding up an ID card that showed a grim-faced man with prominent ears and thick brown hair. Velikov's eyebrows shot up when he saw a card bearing the official seal of the

Interior Ministry. Teo Stamboliev had been a member of the Special Forces Unit at the IVth Police Station in Sofia, but it had disbanded years ago because of allegations of corruption.

The policewoman whistled as she shuffled the cards—Barclay Platinum, Capital One, Virgin Money, MBNA Platinum.

"May I see those, please?" Velikov held out his hand, and the woman passed them over.

A shiver ran up his neck as he shuffled through the cards. The same name was stamped on each one: SIR NIGEL CLIFFORD.

CHAPTER 19

Balkan folk music etched over the radio while Jude drove along the Vurbista River. Caro's head throbbed, and she couldn't string two thoughts together. How hard had the Bulgarian man hit her? As the dark landscape sped by, she kept seeing the dead woman in the trunk. Then she pictured her uncle's empty mortuary slab, and her stomach lurched.

"Stop the car," she said.

Jude glanced away from the road. "What's wrong?"

"I'm going to be sick."

He swerved, and gravel flew up around the tires. She flung open the door and retched. She felt his cool hand brush against her neck, and then he lifted her hair out of the way.

"Hang in there. We'll be in Momchilgrad soon," he said.

"Is that where we're going?" She wiped her mouth on her sweater. "You can drive now. I'm okay."

She leaned against the window as he angled onto the highway. *Breathe, Caro. Focus on the sound of the tires. Ignore the gooseflesh and spidery shivers. Breathe, breathe, breathe.*

She felt calmer when they drove into downtown Momchilgrad. The town square was empty, except for two men hanging back in the shadows, watching a girl ride a bicycle down the sidewalk. Caro tucked her hair behind her ears and sat up.

"I've been here with my uncle," she said, switching automatically into tour guide mode. "You can feel the Ottoman influence everywhere—the language, cuisine, architecture."

Jude nodded.

"Am I talking too much?" she asked.

"No." He looked surprised. "Why?"

"I tend to talk when I'm nervous."

He patted her shoulder. "Feeling better?"

"Yeah, some." She tried to remember if Momchilgrad had been this sparsely populated when she and Uncle Nigel had passed through. In the distance she saw a tall, modern building. A neon sign blinked HOTEL KONAK.

Jude drove up to the hotel, turned into the lot, and parked at the bottom of the hill. "Can I trust you to sit here while I check in?" he asked.

"Why? You think I'll run back to Kardzhali?"

"I'm not sure what you'll do. But if you stay here, you'll be safe."

"From what?"

"Just keep the doors locked."

"You're scaring me." She reached for her bag. "I'm coming with you."

"You'd better not. The hotel might want your passport."

"The other place didn't."

His eyebrows angled up. "Do you want to take that chance?"

"You'll have to give them your passport. What if the police tracked your license tag?"

"It's stolen."

"I thought you'd rented a car in Sofia."

"The tag's stolen, not the car. Don't look so worried. I'll get rid of both soon enough." He shrugged off his leather jacket. "You're shivering."

After he walked to the hotel, she folded the coat over her legs and tried to remember the scanty information in her uncle's letters. Jude had published one research paper and dropped out of sight. All this time she'd searched for a link between the two men, but now that she'd found one—severed tendons—she was more confused than ever. What was the common denominator between a biochemist and an archaeologist?

A few minutes later, Jude came down the hill, his hands jammed into his pockets. "Sorry I took so long, but it took forever to find a clerk. The hotel was deserted. They must be running a skeleton crew tonight."

They walked up the hill, cut through the lobby, and took the lift to the third floor. Their room was at the end of the hall. Red curtains were drawn tightly across the windows. Caro dropped her duffel bag on the floor, sat on one of the twin beds, and pulled off her sweater. He picked up her hand and frowned at the purple gashes on her palm.

"That's where I pulled the trunk cable," she said, frowning at the marks. The back of her head throbbed, too, and her knees jogged nervously, but she didn't want to complain. She felt damn lucky to be alive.

"You were brave today." He sat down beside her.

"But I can't stop trembling. I guess it's hitting me. Being locked in the trunk. All of these senseless deaths. First Uncle Nigel and now Phoebe."

"Who's Phoebe?"

"My flatmate. She was murdered the day I left London."

Jude's eyes widened. "I'm so sorry, Caro."

"You were outside our flat that morning," she said. "Did you see anything suspicious?"

"No. Except a white Citroën almost plowed into your car."

"What are the odds that my uncle *and* Phoebe would die of blood loss?"

"Sorry?"

"My uncle bled to death. Apparently Phoebe did, too."

He abruptly stood and reached for his jacket. "I'm going out for a bit. When I return, we'll have a sit-down."

"Must we?" she asked, stifling a yawn.

"I'll be back in half a tick." He started out the door. "And don't make any phone calls."

"I'll try to resist." She stretched out on the bed. Calling the embassy was the right thing to do, but it felt wrong. And why was MI5 involved?

She pressed a pillow over her face and wished someone would feed her chocolate. When she was a small girl and felt out of sorts, her mother would pop a Hershey's Kiss into Caro's mouth. She remembered how one time her father had climbed onto a ladder to hang glass wind chimes that he'd bought in town. A breeze had stirred the glass slides, and the tinkling had echoed across the porch. Vivienne had stood at the bottom of the ladder.

"Perfect, Philippe," she'd said. "Absolutely perfect." He climbed down, and she slipped a chocolate into his mouth. He kissed her, and a moment later Vivienne's throat clicked.

"You swallowed my kiss," Philippe said. Behind him, moonlight touched the river that ran through the valley. Caro strained to remember more, but the past curved up into the air, faint as the sound of her mother's chimes.

Jude returned with a mug of hot cocoa and a chocolate-stuffed croissant. "My mum used to say that chocolate would cure anything," he said. "I thought a double dose wouldn't hurt."

He put the mug in Caro's hands and guided it to her lips. "There you go."

Be careful what you wish for, she thought, and took a sip. A warm flush spread through her chest. Then she lowered the mug. "Why did Phoebe and Uncle Nigel have to die?"

"Evil men don't need reasons to take lives." He folded his hands around hers, steadying the mug. "Try not to think about it. Well, at least for a while."

The lamplight hit his sweater, and she stared at the rounded curve of his shoulder. It was nearly the size of a softball. Maybe he could protect her, but she didn't want to be the sort of woman who needed coddling. She set the mug on the table and folded her hands, digging her fingernails into her tender flesh.

He looked down at her clenched fists. "More chocolate?"

"No, I'm fine."

"I need to tell you something. You won't like it. But I'm telling you anyway."

"What?" She stiffened. If he was involved with the black market, she'd just give him her icon and be done with it. She didn't need it. She didn't have many memories of her parents, but she had enough, and she could summon them any time. Right now, she just wanted her old, simple life—escorting tourists through Hampton Court and Stratford-on-Avon. But even that wouldn't be possible until the madman who'd killed Phoebe and Uncle Nigel was caught. Until then, London wasn't safe.

"You're not mixed up in stolen artifacts, are you?" she asked.

"What? No, nothing of the sort." He ran one hand over his hair, smoothing long, stray wisps that had come loose from the band.

"Then what is this awful thing you need to tell me?" She flexed her toes. Maybe he was married. Or in love with a woman with straight hair and a calm life.

"I'm horrid at explanations," he said. "But I'll try to tell this story in order. I tend to be rather technical—and I can't blame it totally on my profession. I'm a science nerd. So if you feel confused, stop me."

"All right." She leaned against the headboard.

"Two years ago, I worked at a small biotech firm in York," he said. "I was harvesting stem cells from mouse embryos. The marrow is a rich site for hematopoietic stem cells. I made the cells grow into anything I wanted—skin, muscles, nervous tissues, livers. I also induced mutations in mouse embryos. Do you understand what mutations are?"

She shook her head.

"Well, they corrupt the genetic code." He looked up at the ceiling and frowned, as if remembering something disturbing.

"The mutated mice grew into adults," he continued, "and they were aggressive. Sensitive to light. Wouldn't eat or drink. It's hard to explain, but those mice became more physically attractive. Even their fur changed— longer, thicker, with the texture of a mink coat. And they were hypersexual.

"After several days without food, the mice appeared to hibernate. I couldn't wake them. At first I thought it was porphyria."

"That's a metabolic disease, right?" Caro said. "King George the Third suffered from it."

"The mice didn't have porphyria," Jude said. "I intro- duced normal mice into cages with the aggressive mice— the ones that hadn't lapsed into comas. The normal mice were highly attracted to the mutated mice. They wanted to breed with them. And that's when the biting started."

"Biting?"

"And blood drinking. The mutated mice bit the nor- mal ones and drank their blood. Within hours, the bitten mice became like the others. I thought it was a virus. So I sedated the mice and performed surgery. I took biopsies from various organs and examined the tissues under the microscope. Nothing seemed out of order, except that the specimens were loaded with stem cells. I removed a mouse's liver. He survived the surgery, which was shock- ing. The next day he was running in his wheel."

"A Prometheus?" She smiled.

"A fitting name." He nodded. "I operated on the mouse

again. This time, I noticed a bud of tissue where the liver had been. Under the microscope these tissues showed primitive stem cells. And they were forming a new liver."

"Can a liver do that?"

"Of course. That's how liver transplants are done. But it takes weeks, not days."

"You've lost me."

"If you remove a salamander's tail, three days later, you'll see budding tissue. And the tail will regenerate. The aggressive mice were the same. In one cage, an aggressive mouse had its foot bitten off. I isolated it. Within hours, I saw a bud. Twelve hours later, the mouse had grown a new foot."

"That's not possible."

"I eventually discovered the gene that made it possible. I called it R-99, the Resurrection Gene. I thought it existed only in these unique stem cells. But I didn't realize that this gene already existed naturally." He paused. "It exists in a subset of humans."

"I don't understand. What kind of subset?"

"A type that craved blood, was hypersexual, was hypersensitive to sunlight, healed at an accelerated rate, and was basically immortal." He exhaled. "Did your uncle ever mention vampirism?"

"Sorry?" Had she misunderstood? Or had the bump to her head affected her hearing?

"Vampires," he said.

Caro stared at him. Was this a joke? Or was he off the rails? Why did she always attract the crazy ones? Not that she'd attracted him, but still.

She slipped off the bed and reached for her sweater.

"I know this sounds implausible, but it's true," he said. "The men who kidnapped you were vampires."

"Well, I'm glad we've sorted that out." She strode to the door. Better to take her chances with MI5 than to stay here.

"Where are you going?" Jude rose from the bed.

"I need air." She flung open the door. Then she turned. "Even if those men were vampires—and they weren't—it was daylight. Vampires can't come out except at night."

"It was overcast. And they wore sunblock."

"Right. The whole world is crawling with vampires who wear zinc oxide. And nobody notices?"

"The world has a lot of weird people."

"And you're one of them!" She ran out of the room, down the stairs, out of the hotel, into the dark. She heard him calling her name, but she kept on running. He was crazy. A madman. Or maybe he really was in the antiquities market and somehow knew about her icon. Or perhaps her uncle had been in possession of a rare artifact and the evildoers thought she knew where it was?

"Caro!"

She stopped running and whirled. She didn't see him, but she knew he was there. The hotel was built of dark slate, and it blended into the dusky sky. Most of the floodlights had burned out, throwing the entrance doors into shadow. She shivered as the chilly air cut through her sweater.

"Caro, wait!"

She raced down the hill, her hair bouncing against her shoulders. Her only hope was to call Mr. Hughes, but her cell phone lay in pieces in downtown Kardzhali, and the embassy's number was stashed in her bag. Dammit, she'd left everything in her room. And she couldn't go back.

She stopped in front of a restaurant and reached for the doorknob. It spun around, but the door didn't budge.

She peeked through the glass. The chairs were neatly turned upside down, balanced on the tables. A telephone hung on the far wall.

Jude called her name again, and she glanced back at the hotel. He stepped out of the darkness. She bolted down the sidewalk and turned into a cobbled alley. A gust of wind blew over the steep concrete walls into the narrow passage and blew loose newspapers to and fro. At the far end of the alley, she saw a stocky man embrace a woman with frizzy burgundy hair. Above them, a neon strip flickered.

Caro inched backward, ashamed to witness their love-making. The man looked up, blood streaming down his chin. He dropped the woman, and her body thudded against the pavement. The man twisted his head, looking at Caro. His nostrils flared, and he said something in Bulgarian. He smiled, flashing dingy teeth.

She sprinted down the alley. Footsteps pounded behind her. An icy hand closed on her arm and jerked her backward. How had he moved this fast? He'd been clear across the alley. She wasn't sticking around to find out. She twisted his thumb, but he pulled loose and slapped her ear. A buzzing noise filled her head. He tilted her chin until her neck bowed.

A chill rippled from his body as he leaned closer. His mouth opened and he pressed his teeth into her throat. She felt a sharp pain and tried to push away, but her arms moved bonelessly. An acid burn spread into her chest and moved through her limbs. The man withdrew his teeth and began licking her neck.

CHAPTER 20

MOMCHILGRAD, BULGARIA

From a long way away, Caro heard someone call her name. She tried to hit the Bulgarian man, but her arms wouldn't move. Had he severed her spinal column? She couldn't feel anything from the neck down.

The Bulgarian man pulled back and grimaced. His lips turned blue and the veins in his neck bulged, and then he began to wheeze, as if he couldn't get air. He gasped, sucking in little sips of air. She tried to squirm away, but he clung to her.

Footsteps clapped in the alley. "Caro?" Jude's voice echoed.

She tried to answer, but her lips were paralyzed. The Bulgarian caught his breath and shuddered, then tilted his head and looked down the alley. Blood ran down his chin and pattered on the cobblestones, and then he turned his burning gaze on her. She tried to squirm away, but her arms still wouldn't move.

The man's respiratory distress seemed to be worsening, but he managed to open his mouth and lunge for her neck again. This time, she looked for fangs. His teeth were long and tapered at the ends, but nothing like the canines on a cinema monster. She wrenched back, and over his shoulder, she saw Jude creep into the alley. He held a long metal spike above his head. He sprang forward, moving soundlessly over the cobblestones, and shoved the rod into the man's back.

The man grunted. Blood jetted from the front of his sweater, spattering drops into Caro's face. The man stared down at his chest. Jude pushed the spike deeper, and the tip popped through the wool.

The man gasped. Blood spilled down the front of his trousers. He released Caro, and she fell straight to the stones. The Bulgarian staggered sideways, then started to fall on top of her, but Jude pushed him to the side.

"Caro, how many times did he bite you?" Jude leaned down and pulled her into his arms.

She tried to answer, but she couldn't push out the words.

"The numbness will pass," he said. Sure enough, it was starting to recede. Her arms tingled and burned, but she welcomed the sensations. After a few moments, she managed to slide her hand around his waist. He started to help her up, but her legs buckled.

"Let me see your throat." Jude examined both sides of her neck, then pulled a wool scarf from his pocket and jammed it against her throat. "Hold the pressure."

"Okay." Good, she'd found her voice. And her limbs were moving more freely. She placed her hand against the scarf. It felt hot, but it wasn't the wool—the heat was coming from the wound. She was burning up. Jude propped her against the wall and stood over the Bulgarian.

"Is he dead?" Caro flattened her palm against the scarf. Jude nodded.

But surely he was mistaken, because a moment later, the Bulgarian started convulsing. His hips bucked on the stones and blood ran out of his mouth. Her blood. She could smell it. Vomit spurted out of her throat. She wiped her mouth, tasting bile and chocolate. Part of her hand still felt numb. What if she never got the feeling back?

What were the odds of getting bitten by a human? She remembered what Mr. Velikov had said about her uncle's wounds—some had come from a person.

"Fucking vampire." Jude yanked out the stake and wiped it on the man's sweater.

The Bulgarian stopped convulsing and lay still. Blood spread out from his body, running along the cobblestones. Caro looked at the stake, then at Jude.

"H-how did you learn to do that?" she whispered.

"I was in the Forces."

"I thought you w-were a biochemist."

"I did a stint in the Royal Marines—it's a family tradition. Look, we'll talk later. Let's go!"

"Wait, check that woman. She might be alive."

Jude stepped over the dead Bulgarian and squatted beside the woman. He pressed his fingertips to her wrist.

"Is she alive?" Caro asked.

"She's not breathing. And her pupils are dilated."

Caro had to see this for herself. She struggled to her feet. A pins-and-needles sensation shot through her limbs as she took small, cautious steps. The neon lights flickered over the woman's neck, turning the flesh gray around the edges.

"Why did he bite her?" she asked Jude.

"He's a vampire—or he was."

"He was a man."

"We'll debate this later." Jude glanced around the alley.

"No, let's talk now."

"We can't stay. Others will come." He grabbed her arm.

"What about the woman?" She tugged in the opposite direction. "Should we call the police?"

"Police?" His eyebrows shot up. "Every policeman in Kardzhali Province is looking for you."

"We can't just leave her."

"She's dead, Caro. She's beyond help."

"There are two dead people in this alley. I can't walk away."

"You still don't get it, do you? They're undead. And it's not safe to hang around. She could turn."

"Turn?"

"Into one of *him*." Jude pointed at the Bulgarian.

"And if she doesn't?"

"Either way, she's dead."

"How do you know?"

"I'm a vampire expert. And I know better than to call the police or wait for the woman to rise up and attack— and she will."

"You're heartless."

"No, just practical. I'm going back to the hotel. If you stay, you'll need this." He held out the stake. A drop of blood slid off the sharp tip and hit the ground.

"I don't want it." She stepped backward, tucking her free hand behind her back. Her fingers still tingled a little.

"Have it your way." He reached for a loose piece of newspaper, wrapped it around the stake, and limped out of the alley.

She followed him into the hotel, past the restaurant, where the empty tables spread out in a dizzy pattern. A thin waiter leaned against the wall, smoking a cigarette and chatting with the sous chef. Caro pulled her hair into a rope and draped it over her neck, trying to hide the bite marks.

"You needn't bother," Jude said. "They're stoned."

The elevator appeared to be stuck on the fifth floor. They went up the stairs to their room. She dabbed the scarf against the wound.

"Do I need disinfectant?" she asked.

"Won't help." He set his backpack on the floor.

She stepped over to the mirror and lowered the scarf. She'd expected to see two jagged holes, but the wounds were much larger. Serrated tooth marks curved into two half moons, one set above the other, with a circle of unblemished flesh between them. He'd bitten into her the way a normal person would bite into an apple. The bleeding had slowed, and a thin scarlet line zigzagged down her neck.

"He just nicked you to get the blood flowing," Jude said. "Be glad he didn't take out a chunk."

He squatted next to his backpack and tossed the metal stake inside. It clinked against something. Caro peered down. The bag was full of stakes.

"How'd you get past customs with those?" she asked.

"I bought them in Kardzhali."

"Don't tell me—Bulgaria is just loaded with vampire hunter boutiques?"

"You've got to know where to shop." He winked.

Because of that wink, she almost relaxed. Then she glanced inside his bag. It was packed with survival gear, too: a multitool, granola bars, water purification tablets, maps, multiple passports, and a waterproof poncho.

Caro lowered the scarf and felt the wounds. They felt dry. The bleeding had stopped. "When I ran off, how did you know to bring a stake?"

"The last time I was in Momchilgrad, it was bustling. Tonight it was empty, except for a few dodgy characters. They had the characteristic pall of a vampire."

"But it's November. Everyone is pale this time of year."

He shrugged. "I carry those stakes for a reason. I don't take chances. I wanted to be prepared."

"For what? In case you ran into a vampire?"

"We did."

"But I didn't see fangs. Vampires have fangs. This man didn't."

"Fangs are part of the mythology. But they do have prominent teeth. If you'd bothered to look at your attacker, you would have noticed. His incisors were larger than normal."

"Bothered to look?" she cried. "Of course I did. Do you realize how crazy this sounds?"

"I didn't believe it, either. Not in the beginning. I wrote a paper about it. I thought it would create a stir— and it did. Right after my article was published, I was attacked by vampires."

He broke off and looked down at his feet. "I was left for dead in my laboratory. They set it on fire. A night watchman pulled me out of the building. One of the vampires tracked me to the hospital, hoping to finish me off. It's a long story. But that's why I went into hiding. You can imagine my surprise when your uncle stumbled across my article two years later."

"Why would he read something like that?"

"I've asked myself the same question. I'm almost certain that he knew about vampires. I don't know *how* he knew. I assumed that he'd found something during an excavation and was curious about the science behind vampirism. However, I wasn't sure how *you* fit into it."

"He'd never believe something this ridiculous!"

"I didn't seek him. He came looking for *me*." He stepped closer. "Let me see your neck."

"I'm okay." She flattened herself against the wall. "It's stopped bleeding."

"Caro, I won't hurt you."

"No, you've just got a bag filled with bloody stakes. And you like to stick them into people. Don't try to deny it. You killed a man."

"So did you." His eyes met hers. "That makes us even."

"I want you to leave. Now." She nodded at the door. "Get your own room. And take your stakes with you."

"I'm not taking orders from you. I'm staying. *You* leave. Here, take a stake. But don't wander around."

"Keep it." She lifted her bag and started toward the door. She hadn't brought much money, but it wasn't the cost of the room that worried her—it was the empty lobby.

"Before you leave, you need to see something." He switched off the light, walked to the window, and pulled back the curtain. Then he pointed at the boulevard.

Caro eased over to the window. Five people walked down the middle of the street, two women and three men.

"So?" she said. "They're taking a stroll."

"It would seem that way, but look again."

She leaned closer to the glass. A brown-haired woman wore a nubby cream suit, the front covered with dark, chocolate-like stains. The other woman wore a flannel nightgown. A tall, rangy man tripped and fell forward onto the pavement; the woman in the nubby suit stepped over him and kept on going.

"What's wrong with them?" Caro frowned. "And don't tell me they're zombies."

"They're not," he said. "They're prey. They've been attacked by vampires. The blood loss has left them disoriented. They'll be finished off tonight. Or maybe tomorrow."

Caro folded her hands. One week ago, her biggest problem had been dealing with her crazy job. Now her uncle was dead, his body was God knew where, and the Kardzhali police thought she'd murdered a man. All that and she was stuck in a town with vampires.

"Isn't there another explanation?" she asked. "Like what you said before—porphyria?"

"It's vampirism."

"I've been bitten once. In the horror movies, it takes three bites. So I've got two more to go and I'll turn into one of *them*?" She'd aimed for a sarcastic tone, but her voice sounded shrill and panicky.

"It's not the number of bites. It's the number of stem cells that pass from the vampire's body into yours. And how your immune system reacts."

She shuddered. Best-case scenario: Something was making people act like vampires, and a crazy man was trying to protect her. Only she'd been bitten.

"It takes a little while to adjust your thinking," he said. "You'll get there. I have faith."

She sighed. "You're sure I won't turn?"

"Positive." He patted her arm.

"I'd like to hear more about these stem cells."

"Remember my mice? Vampires are packed with stem cells, too. Their saliva is a particularly rich source. One bite will contaminate a human's blood with vampiric stem cells, but it won't be enough to cause vampirism."

"You sure?" She touched her neck. "Because I feel horrid."

He pressed his hand against Caro's forehead. "You do feel warm. And you may experience flu-like symptoms for a day or two. Then your immunity will kick in."

Caro stepped closer to the window. "What about those people in the street? Didn't they have immune systems?"

"It takes repeated exposure to vampiric stem cells to weaken a human's immunity and set off a transformation."

"Then they become vampires?"

"Yes. Although the condition can be inherited, too."

"Vampires can have babies?"

"It happened with laboratory mice. At least, some of the time."

"So whatever this is—are you saying it's contagious?"

He nodded. "Through saliva and blood."

"Like hepatitis?"

"Hepatitis isn't contagious through saliva. Though I wouldn't want to kiss an infected person." His brow tightened. "Vampirism isn't a virus. The condition is caused by unique stem cells. They grow at an extraordinary rate. Faster than cancer cells. My research was terminated before I could learn more."

His hand shook a little as he rubbed his forehead. "Do you know anything about microbiology or histology?"

"I know a test tube from a turnip. But that's it."

His lips tugged into a smile. "All right, lass. We'll skip the science."

"But I want to know how vampirism can be inherited."

"When the aggressive, vampiric mice reproduced with normal ones, their offspring had an abundance of stem cells. Not as many as their vampire parents, of course, but well above the norm." He opened his hand and studied his palm. "Interestingly enough, I determined that the vampiric offspring had the genotype for R-99, but their phenotype wasn't expressed."

"Phenotype?"

"It means the nonaggressive offspring had the R-99 gene, but vampiric characteristics weren't expressed. In other words, the phenotype-negatives—let's just call them baby vampire mice—healed a bit quicker than the normal babies and ran faster in their wheels." His smile dimmed a little. "I've confused you."

Caro nodded. "You lost me at *phenotype*."

"Actually, it's simple, I'm just explaining it poorly." He scratched his head. "Let's try again, shall we? What if two blue-eyed people get married, and their firstborn has brown eyes?"

"The wife had a lover?" Caro was teasing, but Jude's eyebrows went up.

"No, no," he said. "It means the brown-eyed child has the genotype for blue eyes, but the blue color isn't expressed. The child's eyes are brown."

"Got it." Caro nodded. She didn't like how he was watching her, so she said, "What happened when the baby vampire mice got into sunlight?"

"Nothing. The phenotype-negatives weren't sensitive

to sunlight and weren't aggressive. They didn't bite. Didn't drink blood. Didn't regenerate. But they retained strength and agility. Their rapid healing was due to the vampiric stem cells."

Caro turned back to the window. People were still walking down the boulevard, and shadowy figures moved behind them. The woman in the nightgown staggered and fell down. On the opposite side of the road, a man with thick black hair walked over and lifted her arm, then he dragged her across the asphalt to a weedy lot.

"I can't watch this." Caro spun around and lunged to the mini fridge. She grabbed two itty bottles of vodka. She downed one and started on the other. The alcohol burned her throat, but it seemed to numb the bite wound. She just wanted to sink down into the cool sheets and sleep, but she still had questions. When Mr. Hughes had picked her up at the airport, he'd mentioned that people were disappearing in southern Bulgaria. He hadn't named the town, but he'd said it was near the Greek border. Had he meant Momchilgrad?

She sat on the bed and took another sip of vodka, repressing a shudder. "Let's just say there *are* vampires. How do I know you aren't one of them?"

"Are you serious? You've seen me in daylight."

"Yes, inside buildings. Today you were outside, but it was overcast."

"I'm not a vampire."

"I wish you were a physician. Because I feel woozy." *No, Clifford, you're drunk. Sozzled.* "Are you positive I won't turn into Lady Dracula?"

"One more time. That man bit you once and not deeply. You didn't get enough vampiric cells into your system. You'll make a complete recovery in a day or two. Quit worrying, lass."

"Why do you keep calling me that?"

"It's a Yorkshire endearment. Be glad I didn't call you *flower* or *my dear nug*. That's what my father called my stepmother."

"Maybe I'll call you Mickey."

"Why?"

She started to say Walt Disney had Mickey Mouse, and you've got vampire rats, but she hiccupped. The jolt cleared her head a little, and she tossed the vodka bottle into the trash.

He pushed away from the window and sat on the other twin bed. "Caro, I don't want to upset you, but we need to discuss your uncle. Other scientists have been murdered because they dabbled in stem cell research. But this is the first I've heard of an archaeologist getting killed. There's got to be a link. Something your uncle found."

Right. And it was hidden in her bag.

"Why was he in Bulgaria?" Jude asked.

"Digging. Perperikon is an archaeologist's dream. Artifacts are everywhere. Tourists pick up shards that probably date to the Bronze Age."

She rubbed her eyes, remembering the time she'd slipped into a packed lecture hall at St. Cross College in Oxford to hear Uncle Nigel discuss Perperikon's wine rituals, blood sacrifices, and sun worshipping. But she couldn't think about that now because zombies were lurking in the street. She stretched out on the bed. "How many people are out there now?"

"Three." He traced his finger along the windowsill. "You still don't believe me."

"I do. But I wish I didn't." She hugged the pillow to her chest. Uncle Nigel had forbidden her to read Bram Stoker or Mary Shelley. Horror movies were strictly forbidden. Thanks to her girlfriends, she'd seen every horror film that came down the pike, but she'd secretly preferred Herodotus and Will Durant. History to the nth. Lots of juicy tidbits on gods and goddesses. Nothing about vampires. Nothing about the daylight-loving Thracians at Perperikon, either. Why had they built a fortress on that Bulgarian hilltop? Had they been keeping something in or out? How many secrets had died with her uncle?

Down in the street, a woman began screaming. Caro scooted off the bed and peered out the window. The woman squirmed away from a man. He pulled her back, slapped her to the ground, then dragged her across the pavement into an alley.

"We really should call the police," Caro whispered.

"I doubt they'd respond." Jude sat on the edge of his bed and pulled off his shoes and socks. Jagged red lines ran across both heels.

"Tell me again why those Bulgarians tried to kill you," she said.

He fell back onto the bed. "It's a dreary story. Haven't you heard enough for one night?"

"No. Tell me."

He gazed up at the ceiling. "Right after my article was published, a burly, redheaded fellow showed up at my lab. Said he was a headhunter for a London pharmaceutical company. But he seemed dodgy. Rough and unpolished. He offered two million dollars if I'd sell my research."

"That's a lot of money."

"I didn't want money. My research wasn't for sale. But

the redheaded man wouldn't leave. He stood beside the mouse cages, watching them spin in their wheels. Then he said, 'I suffer from the same condition as your mice.' Before I could answer, he shot across the room and knocked me into an instrument tray. Everything clattered to the floor—forceps, scalpels, clamps. He started choking me. From the corner of my eye, I saw a scalpel. I grabbed it. Somehow I pushed it into the guy's carotid artery. That's the big artery in—"

"I know what it is."

"The scalpel jutted out of the guy's throat," Jude said. "I assumed he was dead. Black, tarry blood streamed down his shirt. He yanked out the scalpel and threw it to the floor. Then he ran away. I rang the police immediately. I scraped tissue from the scalpel and put it under the microscope. It was full of stem cells. I compared this to samples I'd taken from the aggressive mice."

"They were the same?"

"Eerily similar." He paused. "The next evening, I was working late. The redheaded man returned to the lab with the two Bulgarians. They held me down. Cut my Achilles tendons. They took the mice and set my lab on fire."

He shut his eyes, as if trying to decide how much more to reveal. "The orthopedic surgeons at York District Hospital stitched me back together. My girlfriend was hysterical. She was horrified about the mice. She loathed the time I spent at the lab. I assumed that she was overwrought because she'd just found out that she was pregnant. But she was at the end of her tether because of my work habits. The moment she walked into my hospital room, I knew she wouldn't stick around."

That bitch, Caro thought. She didn't want to pry, but

Jude hadn't mentioned the girlfriend's name and she was curious. All right, more than curious. "What was her name?" she asked.

"Vanessa." He paused. "Lady Vanessa. She owns an antique shop."

Lady. That figured. "Was she beautiful?"

"Yes." He paused. "She wanted to know if I'd walk again. The doctors didn't know. The police were convinced that my attackers would return and finish me off. They posted a guard outside my door. The big redheaded vampire crushed the guard's neck and sneaked into my room. My stepmother was sitting beside my bed. She pulled out a snub-nosed pistol and shot the vampire."

"Did she kill him?"

"No." His voice sounded clear and firm, not asking for pity. "The next day, I was moved to a clinic in Zürich—under an assumed name, of course. I asked Vanessa to come. She wouldn't leave York."

A muscle twitched in his jaw. "It took seven months of physical therapy before I was able to walk again."

"You were courageous." Caro paused. "What happened to the baby?"

"She had an abortion."

"I'm so sorry." Her fists tightened around the blankets. Those horrible men had taken everything—his work, his country, his love. His unborn baby.

"I was a mess, inside and out. Casts on both ankles. Crutches. I drank myself into a stupor. I was a sot. When I was able to walk again, I left Zürich and began a lurid cycle of drifting from town to town. Drinking at night, researching vampirism during the day. I separated myth from fact. I kept track of industry news. Other biochem-

ists were murdered—one in Paris, three in the Nether-
lands. Their Achilles tendons had been severed as well.
When your uncle contacted me, I thought he had information."

She was barely listening. All she could think about was
the child he'd lost. "Do you still love Vanessa?" She put
her hand over her mouth. "Sorry. It just popped out."

"We were too different. It couldn't have worked."

"Have there been others? After her?"

"Some. Nothing lasting." He crossed his arms behind
his head. "My focus was survival, not romance. Most of
the time I was drinking."

Caro nodded. The night they'd met, he'd hit the wine
bottles pretty hard. But so had she.

"Since all this happened I've learned how to survive,"
he said. "It's a hard way to live. When I step into a restaurant or hotel, I'm memorizing faces, watching body
language. I'm always looking over my shoulder. I used to
be trusting. But that part of me is dead."

He tilted his head. "You're the first person I've told. I
hope I haven't burdened you."

"Not one bit."

"It's a tremendous relief to talk about it."

Caro swallowed. This was not the time to pressure
him, but she still had questions. "How did you find me
today?"

"It wasn't easy. I lost your taxi. I parked my car and
walked down Bulgarian Boulevard. I was just about to
give up, then I saw your hair." He raised himself up. "Do
you have a hat?"

"A what?"

"You'll need a hat to cover your hair."

"Why? Am I a wreck?" She tucked her hair behind her ears. She still hadn't bought a brush.

"No, but it's distinct. You'll need to change your appearance."

She leaned over the side of the bed, fumbled inside the duffel bag, and pulled out the knit hat. "I've got this."

"It looks small. Will your hair fit?"

"Of course." She spread the yarn apart with her fingers, then pulled the hat over her head.

"Tomorrow I'll find a chemist and buy hair dye," he said.

"Buy a brush and some garlic while you're at it." She stifled a yawn. Then she undressed under the sheets and pushed her face into the pillow.

CHAPTER 21

During the night, Caro felt him pull a blanket over her shoulders and tuck the edges around her chin. She rolled over and fell into the old dream where she was being chased by the wild dogs. One leaped up, bit her arm, and dragged her into the trunk of the brown Dacia. Inside, the dead woman was waiting, her eyes glowing like Jude's mice, torn fingernails scritching as she crawled forward, her wide-open mouth revealing sharp, bone-white teeth.

Caro woke up clawing the air. Her hands flew to her neck and grazed the edges of the throbbing wound. Spasms whirled through her body, and she almost climaxed.

Jude leaped out of his bed and hurried to her side. In the moonlight, his T-shirt glowed with a white radiance, the fabric stretched over his wide shoulders. He gazed down at her with a helpless expression.

"I'm okay."

"Shall I turn on the light?" he asked. "Or would you like whiskey?"

She shook her head and snuggled into the covers.

"You don't seem fine." His hand brushed against her shoulder. "You're burning up."

And she was. She was on fire—not from illness but from sexual longing. His lips were plump and moist, and she wanted to feel them pressing against her mouth.

If I don't kiss him now, if I let this moment pass, I'll never forgive myself, she thought. She wound her arms tightly around his neck and drew him against her into the warm blankets. His shirt felt cool against her cheek. He smelled of spring rain and freshly ironed linen. Familiar, comforting scents, with a hint of a man's smell, sweat and leather.

She felt the rise and fall of his chest, the pressure of his long legs. A slant of light fell across the bed, shining on his square chin. Dark stubble ran down his neck. She wanted to put her fingertip into the cleft. Instead, she dropped her gaze and took in the whole expanse of him beneath the sheet.

He smiled down at her. She lay very still, looking up into his eyes. The sheets rustled as he raised his hand and traced his finger over her bottom lip. "I enjoyed our kiss last night."

"Me, too."

"May I kiss you again?"

She answered by leaning forward. Her tongue flitted past his lips, searching for his, flicking playfully at first, then more urgently. He made a soft humming noise and pulled her against his chest. He was stiff as alder wood.

She stroked him gently, feeling him rise. His hands slid along her ribs, up to her breasts. He cupped them in his hands, squeezing them together, his rough knuckles grazing her skin. Then he broke the kiss and pulled back.

"Are you sure you want this?" he whispered. In the faint light, she thought she saw his pupils dilate.

"Yes." Her hands fluttered over him like wild birds. A sweet spasm pulsed through her belly as she imagined him inside her.

"This will change everything," he whispered.

"It better."

He lowered his lips to her nipple, and it stiffened. He gently took it between his teeth, and she tipped back her head. He traced his tongue over her breast, over her ribs, to her flat belly. She felt his breath through the lace of her thong. His tongue moved up the length of her body and stopped on her mouth. The kiss set off another wave of earthquakes inside her.

She wanted to see him, taste him. He inhaled sharply when her fingers circled him. Two words pulsed inside her head like a heartbeat: *I want. I want. I want.*

She withdrew her hand and swirled her fingertips lightly over his stomach, then angled down to his hips. His buttocks felt hard, the flesh slightly cool. She traced each cheek, then moved her palms upward, over his shoulders to his neck.

Her neck began to throb, the wounds pulsing, sending long, pleasurable spasms downward. He sucked her lip and dropped his hand between her legs, the weight of his hand pushing against the thin lace.

"Make love to me now," she said.

"Let's take it slowly. This is our first time. I want to remember everything."

She wanted to remember everything, too: his breath stirring her hair, the faint scratch of his chest hair on her breasts, the pressure of his hands on her waist. He tugged at the delicate lace and pulled it down over her hip bones. He kissed her midriff, then his mouth moved to her other hip while his fingers slowly edged down the lace, down her legs, removing the thong completely and laying her bare before him.

Cool air broke over her skin. She shivered. Her breath came in quick pants as his hands caressed her and shudders rippled through her.

No sooner had the climax ended than another swept forward, great swells that left her weak and trembly. He didn't seem to be in a hurry. He continued caressing her until another peak began to rise. His finger flicked over her most tender spot, sending her into another deep wave of blinding-white pleasure. Her breath came in ragged bursts as the orgasm rose to a crescendo and receded, moving further and further away.

More, she thought. *I want more. I want him with every ounce of my being.*

He moved on top of her, nudging her legs apart. He bit his lip and sheathed himself deep within her. He moved with unbearable slowness, until a shivery warmth ran through her like water, pouring from the deepest part of herself into him.

He made an incoherent sound, then cupped her bottom and lifted her hips toward him. She surged forward, meeting each thrust eagerly, her fingers gripping his tight buttocks. He was pumping so hard, beads of perspiration dropped from the loose strands of his hair. She shut her eyes and floated toward a whirlpool, into a shadowy cone where pleasure spun in an unbroken circle. Her arms tightened around his neck, and she felt him move with her into the swirling dark.

CHAPTER 22

ASHTON HOUSE
BUCKINGHAMSHIRE, ENGLAND

Wilkerson stood on the lawn outside Ashton House, listening to his tutor explain the procedure of clay shooting—only this was laser shooting. Not the same thing at all. Wilkerson tapped his boot furiously and waited for the teacher to get on with it so he could have lunch in the Oak Room.

"Pull!" the tutor called.

A beat late, Wilkerson lifted the disabled shotgun and squeezed the trigger. A pop sounded. But nothing happened. Either the infrared beam had missed the clay or it wasn't functioning. Wilkerson had been missing them all morning, and he was ready to throw down the gun and walk away. But he couldn't. He needed proper lessons, because next weekend he was going to a clay shoot in Yorkshire; one of Cynthia's friends from the horsey-foxy set was hosting the event, and he wanted to seem knowledgeable, clued-up about the sport. At least he was dressed for the occasion: a green waistcoat, corduroy trousers, thick ear mufflers, orange safety glasses, and Wellingtons.

"Don't watch the clay," said the tutor, "or it will beat you."

"I wasn't looking," Wilkerson insisted.

"Put your left foot forward a bit. Now, look over to the old skeet house. Find an imaginary pickup point."

"Pickup point?" Wilkerson asked.

"The place where you first see the whole clay," the tutor said, and went on to explain the muzzle hold point, stance, and break point. Wilkerson tugged at his tweed cap. The sun hit the front of the white mansion and glinted on the bay windows. Yok-Seng stood off to the side, talking on his mobile phone in hushed tones.

"Let's try again, shall we?" the tutor said, but Wilkerson turned to stare at the bodyguard.

Yok-Seng held the phone aloft. The high, nasal voice of Mr. Underwood streamed out.

"Underwood is calling," Yok-Seng said. "He says it is urgent."

Wilkerson sighed and heaved the gun into the tutor's hands; he walked over to Yok-Seng and snatched the phone. "I'm in the middle of a shooting lesson. It better be important, Mr. Underwood."

"Miss Clifford has gone missing, sir."

Wilkerson cursed.

"I'm afraid that's not all, sir. She's killed Teo."

"How can one little girl cause so much trouble?" Wilkerson stared toward the Chiltern Hills. "Shall I call in the Zubas? Is that what you want? Because you've left me no choice. How am I supposed to find her now?"

"If I might make a suggestion, sir. Miss Clifford is being sought by the Kardzhali police. A witness claims she killed Teo. He took photographs."

"Get to the point, Mr. Underwood," Wilkerson snapped.

"The point is, sir, she's a murder suspect in Bulgaria. I could make a few phone calls, and she'd be a suspect in the Dowell girl's death."

"That's ludicrous," Wilkerson said. "She's not a suspect."

"Not yet. A contact at the *Observer* has unearthed articles about the murder of Miss Clifford's mother. The reporter plans to write a feature article, revealing how Miss Clifford went to live with a hotshot archaeologist in Oxford. Now he's been murdered. The article will suggest that Miss Clifford went temporarily insane and murdered her flatmate."

"It won't work. She wasn't even there when the girl was killed."

"The time of death is questionable, sir. It wouldn't be a stretch to say that Miss Clifford killed the flatmate and staged it to look like a break-in."

"The Yard will never believe that." Wilkerson stared up into the trees. "Besides, Moose left God knows how much evidence."

"Not to worry, sir. Moose will never be implicated. He's too slippery."

"Caroline doesn't have a criminal record. Perhaps if she had a history of violence. Women don't kill each other unless a man is involved."

"I could find a man, sir."

"And leave another dangling thread?" Wilkerson scowled.

"I'm merely thinking of options," Mr. Underwood said.

"Do you still have contacts at MI5?"

"Yes, sir. I've spoken to them. Their agents are in Sofia."

"All right, go ahead," said Wilkerson. "It better work or I'll know who to blame."

CHAPTER 23

MOMCHILGRAD, BULGARIA

Morning sunshine zigzagged into the room, stinging Caro's eyes. She pulled the sheet over her head, stirring up the salty musk of last night's lovemaking. As she bent her toes, a delicious tingle floated up her legs into the center of her chest. Just thinking about Jude sent jolts of pure pleasure through her body. A powerful current had run between them, a pitch-perfect balance of positive and negative charges, pulling her into a place where thoughts were vanquished. All her life she'd waited for the perfect lover, someone who would take her beyond the moves of ordinary sex and sweep her into a pulse-pounding dance. Had she found him? Or was she projecting her strong feelings?

She shivered and lowered the sheet. What was the point of fantasizing when the object of her lust was just across the room, sleeping in the other twin bed? Her smile dimmed as she sat up and blinked in the harsh light.

Jude's bed was empty. Not a trace of him remained in the hotel room. His keys, leather coat, and backpack were missing. Her pulse sped up, thumping painfully against her ribs. He hadn't seemed the type to run away. Maybe he'd panicked and left her alone in this dying town. If so, she'd have to solve the remaining anagrams and try to interpret them and continue on by herself. In the old days, her uncle had left clues in order, creating a logical pattern for her treasure hunts. Until proven otherwise, she assumed that Meteora was the first stop on her journey.

Her pulse throbbed in her neck, and she gingerly touched the bite marks. Her skin blazed as if she was running a fever, but she couldn't worry about that. She didn't want to be caught in Momchilgrad after dark. She'd wait an hour. If Jude didn't return, she'd leave the hotel, buy a map, and study the terrain between southern Bulgaria and Greece. Then she'd hire a car to take her near the border, hike to the nearest town, and make her way to Meteora.

No matter what happened between her and Jude, she'd have to decode those anagrams. She scooted to the edge of the bed and reached into her duffel bag for Uncle Nigel's passport. The room brightened as a wedge of sunlight blasted through the curtain and washed over her arm. Her skin tingled and reddened. She scooted away from the light, and the prickling faded.

She took a deep breath and opened the passport, but she couldn't stop looking at the window. All around her dust motes rose from the sheets, churning in dizzy patterns within the light. It seemed threatening somehow.

According to lore, sunlight made vampires spontaneously combust—and she'd been bitten. But that was silly, wasn't it? She didn't have the luxury of being silly or afraid. She forced herself to stare at her uncle's handwriting.

14 ENTRIES/ENTRÉES VISAS DEPARTURES/SORTIES	15 ENTRIES/ENTRÉES VISAS DEPARTURES/SORTIES
A Gee Creme Mock Ion N Tore	
Ellen vumv canola Bravo ice Bark boy toe foes Tax by fit	

The door creaked open and Jude stepped into the room, his arms loaded with paper bags. His ponytail swung forward as he set the bags on the desk. She hastily rolled across the bed, stuffed the passport into her bag, and moved out of the dappled light.

"You're awake." He smiled, and his upper lips widened into a plush, kissable M.

"Come back to bed." She bent her toes, and a warm sensation rushed down her thighs.

"Don't tempt me." He gave her a lingering glance and opened the large bag.

"What did you buy?" she asked.

"Hair coloring. I'm not sure you'll approve. The selection was grim." He held up a rectangular box that featured a smiling woman with straight, luxurious hair the exact shade of a double espresso.

He reached for the small bag. "Would you like to go first—or shall I?"

"Go ahead. I need a moment to work up my courage."

"I shan't be long."

After he walked into the bathroom, Caro slid off the bed, grabbed her bloody sweater from last night, and shoved it into the trash. If only it were that easy to discard her lingering anxieties over her kidnapping and its connection to her uncle's murder. Her heart bumped against her chest as she recounted the events of the past few days. Had it really been just days? It felt like weeks, months maybe.

Rousing herself, she started to unzip her duffel bag. Did she have enough time to decipher the rest of the anagrams? Before she could grab the passport, the bathroom door opened and steam curled into the room. Jude walked out, tucking a towel around his waist. A smaller towel was draped over his shoulders. But it was his hair that caught her attention. It was wet, short, and brutally dark, the bangs rumpled over his forehead, which showed a ragged line of black dye.

"You cut your ponytail," she said.

"It's ruddy awful, isn't it?" He blotted his neck with the small towel, dabbing at the inky stains. "I can't rinse for twenty minutes. Let's get started with you."

The muscles in his back rippled as he opened the large paper bag. "Hair color, madam. And curl relaxer. I bought two boxes of each. You've got quite a bit of hair. The scissors are in the bathroom."

"But if I dye my hair, I won't look like my passport photo," she said.

"You'll need a new one. I've already made arrangements. I'd like to leave Momchilgrad before dark. I'd hate to stay another night."

"Anything but that," she said, thinking of those zombie-like people. She lifted a box. "I thought it was dangerous to straighten and color hair on the same day."

"Isn't it more dangerous if the police are chasing a curly-headed blonde?"

While he mixed the bottles, Caro found the scissors and leaned over the trash bin, forcing herself to cut an inch from her hair. When she finished, the blunt ends were still well below her shoulders. She ran her fingers through the curls.

"Cut more, lass," Jude said.

"How much?"

"To your chin."

"That's too short. I won't do it. I'll wear it up, in a bun or a twist."

He grabbed the scissors. Before she could move, he lopped off several inches—on one side. The blunt hair just hit her shoulders.

"Damn you," Caro said. She was ready to let loose with a string of harsher curses, but he'd turned away to finish mixing the relaxer and hair dye. She didn't want to distract him, so she sat on the counter and cut the rest of her hair. She looked in the mirror, tugging the frizzy ends, and sighed.

"I look like Little Orphan Annie," she said.

Jude lifted her wrist and glanced at her watch. "It's nine fifteen, Annie. Do get a move on unless you want to stay in Momchilgrad another night."

After Caro defuzzed and colored her hair, she pulled it back into a sleek ponytail. She stepped out of the bathroom and found Jude gathering their hair clippings into a plastic trash bag. He fished her bloody sweater from the trash can and added it to the bag. She thought he might pitch it over the balcony, but he slipped it into his backpack.

"Why are you keeping our trash?" she asked.

"If MI5 is involved, they'll do hair and fiber analysis. We can't leave our DNA."

"I hadn't thought about that." She touched her neck, her fingers glancing over the wounds. They were pulsing. She was having trouble thinking about anything except Jude and her hyperpassionate response to him. She wasn't sure that *hyperpassionate* was even a word, but it was the only thing that fit.

"You'd better get dressed or we won't make it to Romania before dark."

She swallowed. This was the first she'd heard of a proposed escape route, but it meant traveling north. She needed to head south. "Jude, I can't go to Romania."

"Are you feeling ill?" He cupped her cheek. "You've cooled down a little."

"I'm fine. But *you* might not be after I show you something." She sat down on the bed and patted the space beside her. After he got settled, she reached into her duffel bag and pulled out her uncle's passport.

"The police returned Uncle Nigel's personal effects," she said. "When I looked in his passport, I found notes."

She opened the booklet, smoothing the crease between

pages fourteen and fifteen, and pointed to the first two phrases.

14 ENTRIES/ENTRÉES VISAS DEPARTURES/SORTIES	15 ENTRIES/ENTRÉES VISAS DEPARTURES/SORTIES
A Gee Creme Mock Ion N Tore	

"What are they?" he asked.

"Anagrams. My uncle wrote them before he died."

"Secret messages?"

She handed him the passport and explained how she'd deciphered a few clues.

A sharp line creased his forehead. "Why didn't you tell me?'

"I didn't trust you."

He glanced up. "Now you do?"

"Completely." She showed him the next set of anagrams.

He frowned. "What do they mean?"

"One says *Meteora, Greece.* The other says *Monk Icon.*"

"'Meteora'? Isn't that where those extraordinary monasteries are perched atop boulders?"

She nodded.

"I suppose they'd have a monk or two," he said. "But what's an icon?"

"Religious art. I've got one of those, too." She pulled it from her bag and unwrapped the plastic. The light hit the icon, glinting on the red-robed saint and the objects she held in each outstretched hand: a gilt-edged book and an ostrich egg. Behind the saint was part of a castle and a hilly battleground that was heaped with wounded men.

"It's a painting," Jude said. He touched the jagged mountains that rose behind the saint. "Look how the scenery abruptly ends on both sides of the wood. Like the artist's brush slipped off."

"My uncle always made a huge fuss over this icon. Now he's dead. I know you say those Bulgarian thugs are vampires, but they wanted more than my blood. I'm convinced they wanted this icon."

"Maybe." Fresh lines cut into his forehead. "But why didn't they take it out of your bag when you were unconscious?"

"The bag wasn't going anywhere. And they didn't think I was, either." She ran her finger along the icon and paused at the mitered corner. "I don't know how they found out about it. I might never know."

"In any case, it must be very valuable," Jude said. "Why did you bring it to Bulgaria?"

"It belonged to my parents. I take it everywhere. It was one of Uncle Nigel's rules. No matter where I traveled, the icon went. I can't let anything happen to it."

"Maybe that's why your uncle wrote the anagrams. To warn you. You've got to find the monk. Could his name be an anagram?"

"Let's find out." She set down the icon, grabbed a ballpoint out of her bag, and lifted the passport. "My uncle added a spin—he taught me to switch the last words in phrases. I'm taking them as he's listed them, in sets of two." She raised the pen as if it were a candle lighting the page and pointed at *Ellen vumv*. "Here, I'm swapping *canola* and *ice*. The new anagrams are *Ellen vumv ice* and *Bravo canola*."

14 ENTRIES/ENTRÉES VISAS DEPARTURES/SORTIES	15 ENTRIES/ENTRÉES VISAS DEPARTURES/SORTIES
A Gee Creme Mock Ion N Tore	
Ellen vumv canola Bravo ice Bark boy toe foes Tax by fit	

She scribbled on her thigh, rearranging letters the way her uncle had taught her. The hotel room dropped away as her concentration sharpened. Nothing existed but twenty-six letters in the Latin alphabet, all of them swirling around her. She switched *ice* and *canola*, and the *V* in *vumv* leaped out along with the double *L*s in *Ellen*.

Vellum. Her uncle had encouraged her to learn about illustrated manuscripts. When she was a child, she'd drawn her own version of *The Book of Hours*. The obsession had continued into adulthood, when she'd seriously thought of moving to Dublin to do an independent study on *The Book of Kells*, but Uncle Nigel had scotched that idea.

"I've got it," Jude said, leaning over the passport. "Venice vellum."

"Brilliant," she said, impressed that he'd decoded the words without a pen. She smiled and continued writing on her arm, sorting *Bravo canola* into *Lavoro banca*.

"The clues are starting to make sense," she said. "Uncle Nigel had an account at the Banca Nazionale del Lavoro in Venice."

"But what's vellum?" Jude leaned closer to the passport.

"Early books. They were written on animal hides—goat and calfskin. They were called vellum leaves."

"And you just happened to know this?" he asked.

"I told you I was a scholar. I lurked in temperature-controlled rooms at the Bodelean Library. I'm rather passionate about fourth-century Bibles. But I love Psalters and herbals, too."

"Caro, you're the most interesting woman I've ever known."

Interesting? So he thought she was a book geek? Any second now he'd run out the door. She pushed away the thought and focused on the next phrases. She switched *foes* and *fit*. *Bark boy toe fit* had two *B*s, *O*s, and *T*s; *Tax by foes* had an *X*. She quickly sorted the letters, scribbling on her wrist.

BARK BOY TOE FIT = RABBIT FOOT KEY
TAX BY FOES = SAFETY BOX

"Rabbit foot key?" Jude asked.

Caro reached into her bag and pulled out a furry brown chain. Dangling from the ring were a dozen brass keys in various shapes and sizes.

"I'm catching on," Jude said. "And one of these keys fits a safety box at the Banca Nazionale del Lavoro?"

"It better."

Jude drew his finger over her hand, tracing the ink marks. "You've written all over yourself."

"An old habit. My uncle taught me to never leave a paper trail."

"He sounds like he was the 007 of the archaeology world."

"Go ahead, have a laugh." She grabbed his chin, giving it a playful tug. "Uncle Nigel's grandfather cracked German ciphers in World War I. He was involved with Room Forty."

"The British Cryptology Department?" He looked shocked. "His grandfather was a spy?"

"A paleographer. But he had a knack for decryption. All the Cliffords were born with it."

"I wish I could have met him." Jude licked his finger, then pressed it against her leg and rubbed out the *f* in *foes*. "So, we're off to Meteora to find a monk, or shall we go to Italy?"

"Meteora. Do you see the line my uncle drew between the anagrams? It was his way of dividing the clues. Placing them in order. He meant for me to go to Greece, then Italy."

"It's getting late. If we hope to make it to Greece by nightfall, we should leave now."

"Wait." She cupped her hand against his cheek. "Are you sure you want to get mixed up in my problems? Too many people are looking for me. If you leave now, you'll have a clean getaway. But if you stick with me, the authorities will assume you're involved."

"But I *am* involved. I murdered a vampire last night."

"To save me."

"You might need my help again, lass."

"I'm a tour guide, for heaven's sake. Travel is my specialty. I can bribe someone to drive me to Greece."

"I'm going with you, and that's the end of it."

While she dressed, he unfolded a map of Europe and marked an *X* over Kardzhali. Then he drew a straight line down to Momchilgrad.

"We're here," he said, then dragged his finger lower. "Greece is less than an hour away. But the border check-point is at Blagoevgrad. The Bulgarians are mildly obsessed with stamping passports. They're the worst in Europe. A checkpoint can take hours."

"Isn't there a new road to Komotini?" she asked.

"The Makaza Pass? I don't know if it's open. Last I heard, it was complete on the Bulgarian side. The Greeks were procrastinating."

"We could backpack."

"Unexploded land mines are all over on the Greek side. Either we go through Turkey—and that border crossing is a nightmare—or we go through Blagoevgrad."

Caro sighed. "Isn't there another way?"

"I don't think so. I was in Bulgaria last spring and had a devil of a time getting out. The border guards were scrutinizing the holograms on passports. Mine was fake with a bloody awful hologram."

He picked up their bags and headed for the door. She sat there a moment, thinking how in the space of a breath, lives can intersect and transform. Her uncle had known Sir John Barrett, of Dalgliesh Castle in Yorkshire. His son, Jude, had grown up to write an article that would catch her uncle's fancy. Caro had herded tourists over Dalgliesh's ancestral drawbridge, and she'd bought a duf-fel bag in the gift shop. Now Jude was carrying that bag out of a hotel room where they'd shared the most intense physical experience of their lives—at least, it had felt that way from her end.

She rose from the bed and hurried after him.

CHAPTER 24

KARDZHALI, BULGARIA

Ilya Velikov dialed the British embassy in Sofia and demanded to be put through to Ambassador Williams. While he waited, Velikov spread the bagged credit cards over his desk, adding other pieces of evidence he'd found in the dead man's wallet—traveler's checks made out to Nigel Clifford and part of a wristwatch with *Love, Caro* engraved on the back.

The operator put him on hold. A few moments later, he heard a click. "Ilya, this is Thurston Hughes. May I ring you back? We've got a bit of a kerfuffle with the Clifford girl."

"That is why I am calling," Velikov said. "I was at the accident scene last night. When I checked the victim's wallet, I found Professor Clifford's credit cards and traveler's checks. The victim even had the professor's watch.

I called the credit bureau and charges have been made to these cards—after Professor Clifford's death. I am waiting for copies of the signature."

"You're saying that Miss Clifford was chasing her uncle's murderer?"

"Or he was chasing her," said Velikov. "I have interviewed witnesses who saw the accident and events leading to it. They say that two men grabbed Miss Clifford in downtown Kardzhali—against her will. Another witness claims he was stalled in traffic and the trunk of a brown Dacia opened. A woman matching Miss Clifford's description climbed out. The witness reports that Miss Clifford was chased by a male passenger in the Dacia."

"Well, this puts a spin on things, doesn't it?" Hughes said.

"She needs protection," Velikov said. "I checked the Hotel Ustra. She wasn't there. And she has not checked out. I am worried."

"Her picture is all over the news. We'll find her."

"Miss Clifford may be too frightened to come forward. And I received a fax from your government. They are saying that she is wanted for questioning about a murder in London."

"Yes," said Hughes. "And I'm shocked. She didn't strike me as . . . unbalanced."

"I talked to Miss Clifford. I do not believe she is capable of murder. Self-defense? Yes. But not murder." Velikov paused. "I believe she was taken off the street and put into the trunk of a car—by a man whose wallet was full of her uncle's credit cards. Whoever killed her uncle is trying to kill her."

"Don't jump to conclusions, Ilya."

"Someone wants Miss Clifford dead, and your government is helping them."

"That's preposterous," Hughes said, his voice cold. "However, I will leave a message for Ambassador Williams. I'm sure he'll want to speak with you."

Velikov hung up and dialed the Interior Ministry. "I need access to the file on Teodor Stamboliev. His last known address was in Sofia."

"Just a moment," said a woman with a nasal voice. In the background Velikov heard the rhythmic click of computer keys. "Does he have an alias?" she asked.

"It is possible."

The clicking started up again. After a moment, the woman said, "There are no records on Teodor Stamboliev."

Velikov shut his eyes. He was chasing a ghost.

CHAPTER 25

MOMCHILGRAD, BULGARIA

Jude parked in front of a small building with a stone façade. Black Cyrillic letters were painted across the plate-glass window, but Caro couldn't decipher the words. The noon sun hit the glass at an angle, and the glare hurt her eyes, forcing her to squint at the window. As her vision adjusted, she saw a philodendron plant looping around the edges of the glass; a striped kitten reached up to swat it.

"What is this place?" she asked Jude.

"A photography studio. But Mr. Kudret runs a tidy business on the side."

"Fake passports?"

"He's honorable. Plus, he'll want my recommendations."

Caro opened her door and turned back to Jude. "Wait, how much will this cost? I only have a few hundred euros."

"Don't worry about it. I'm taking care of this." He touched her cheek.

"But I do worry. This will cost a fortune. Do you have enough money?" She hadn't meant to sound blunt, but she needed to know.

"My stepmother wires money to my account in Zürich."

"Will it take long to get a new passport?"

"Mr. Kudret works fast. I met him last year when I was trying to get out of Bulgaria."

"Why were you here?"

"Buying titanium stakes."

"For a man in hiding, you get around."

A bell dinged over their heads as they stepped into the building. A short man in a blue smock scurried down the hall. He smoothed back his dark hair and grinned, revealing an endearing, gap-toothed smile.

"This is Mr. Kudret," Jude said.

Jude said something in Turkish, and the man's face split into a wider grin.

"Come, come," he said, waving them behind a curtain. The kitten leaped out of the window and followed the man down a hall. Mr. Kudret stepped into a square room that was filled with photography equipment.

"Sit here, please." He ushered Caro to a chair and stepped over to a camera that sat atop a sleek metal tripod. The flash blinded her for a moment.

"You have beautiful eyes," he said, peering into her face.

Jude picked up a bus schedule and quizzed Mr. Kudret about border crossings. Caro lifted the kitten and paused beside a dusty bookcase, its shelves overflowing with rumpled leather volumes. She set the kitten on the floor and pulled out a book. In the margins, Mr. Kudret—or someone—had written notes in Ottoman Turkish script. From the tiny studio, she heard voices, and she slid the book into the shelf.

The kitten shot ahead and climbed up Mr. Kudret's trousers onto his apron, its claws pricking the heavy fabric.

"Ah, there you are, *madame*." Mr. Kudret lifted the kitten and set it on his head. "I have a question—which languages do you speak?"

For a moment, Caro thought he was talking to the cat. Then she realized he was waiting for her answer.

"French, Italian, Spanish—all of the Romance languages, actually." She paused. "A little German and Russian."

"Yes, but fluently?"

"French, Italian, and Spanish."

"Impressive." He smiled. "You must have a soaking mind—no, that isn't right. How do you say it? I mean, your brain is like a sponge."

"Thank you," she said, repressing a smile. "But the truth is, I traveled with my uncle. He spoke many languages, even Turkish. He taught me your Latin alphabet. The extra vowels confused me."

"There are eight vowels. Come, I will give you a lesson over lunch." He touched her elbow and led her toward the curtain.

"I noticed some of your books," she said, pausing beside the shelves. "They seemed to be written in Ottoman script. I couldn't read the titles."

Mr. Kudret drew his hands over the tattered volumes. "Are these the ones you saw?"

"I hope I wasn't snooping," Caro said. Her love of

books was not an excuse. Back in Oxford, she was always curled up in the window seat with one of her uncle's volumes.

"Not to worry. These books on the bottom shelf detail the life of Kazıklı Voyvoda." Mr. Kudret pulled out a thick volume and ran his stubby fingers over the worn edges. As he thumbed through the pages, a faint musty odor rose up, and the kitten sneezed.

Mr. Kudret flattened a page and pointed to an old painting of a man with a beaked, pointed nose and long, almond-shaped eyes. "Ah, here he is."

"Was he a chronicler of the Ottoman Empire?" Caro peered down at the book. The man in the painting stared back.

"No, no," Mr. Kudret said. "He was a prince of Wallachia. Perhaps you know him by his Romanian name— Vlad Ţepeş? *Ţepeş* was added after the prince's death."

"Better known as Vlad the Impaler," Jude said, pointing to a drawing that showed Ottoman soldiers impaled on stakes.

Mr. Kudret patted the kitten. He spoke to it in Turkish, and the animal began to purr. "Come, let us eat," he said.

Jude and Caro ate chickpea soup and cucumber salad while Mr. Kudret worked on the passport. The kitten walked cautiously across his desk, then leaped onto his shoulder. Caro lifted a red crystal glass and sipped *rakia*. She hoped she looked calm on the outside because her mind was racing. Thoughts passed through her the way light hits a prism and refracts into colors. Her life had intersected with Jude's at a tragic event. They had been thrust together into a strange adventure and now they'd become physically and emotionally involved. Not that she was complaining, but . . . could anything lasting arise from such a dark beginning? It could, right? Well, maybe not. Unless mutual exile bound them together.

Mr. Kudret pushed away from his desk, and the cat leaped to the ground. He held out Caro's passport. "For you, my dear."

Caro rubbed her fingers over the dark red cover. UNION EUROPÉENNE, RÉPUBLIQUE FRANÇAISE was stamped on the cover.

"Is it satisfactory?" Mr. Kudret asked.

"Perfect."

"It even has biometric RFID technology," he said. "All new French passports must have them. And yours does, as well."

"What's RFID?" she asked.

"Radio frequency identification," Jude said. "The chip has your digital image."

"Remember, you are Noelle D. Gaudet," Mr. Kudret said. "And you were born in Aix en Provence."

"What does the *D* stand for?" she asked.

"Désirée." Mr. Kudret held out two bus tickets. "If the border police make questions to you, answer in French. And memorize the information on your passport. I hope you will never need to recite it. But it is best to be prepared. Keep your other passport in a separate place so you will not mix them up."

Mr. Kudret glanced at his watch. He placed the cat on a red pillow and spoke softly in Turkish. "No matter what happens, do not give them the stink-eye. Smile—but not in provocative way."

Mr. Kudret turned, staring directly at her. "Time to leave," he said.

Caro walked outside, blinking at the empty space where Jude's car had been. She looked around frantically.

"Do not be alarmed," Mr. Kudret said. "The car is being painted. It will be sold in Turkey next week. There will be no trace of it. And the rental company in Sofia can file insurance. Do not feel bad for them."

Jude and Caro climbed into his van. As Mr. Kudret drove to the bus station, the sun followed the car, moving through the skeletal trees. The sidewalks were deserted, except for bits of trash.

"The Makaza Pass just opened," Mr. Kudret was saying. "The border crossing has been in place for several months. You should have easy passage to Greece."

The van sped by the hotel and down a hill where a woman's purple house slipper lay in the street. Caro glanced over at Mr. Kudret. He wore a tweed Bond cap, and it was perched low over his forehead. She glanced back at the house slipper. She didn't know what was going on in Momchilgrad, but she hated to think of anything happening to the old man.

"Mr. Kudret?" she asked. "You'll be careful, won't you?"

"Do not worry." He reached across the seat and patted her hand. "I am not afraid."

CHAPTER 26

GREECE-BULGARIA BORDER
NEAR KOMOTINI, GREECE

The bus to Thessaloniki was packed with teenagers and their chaperones from a province in northern Bulgaria. Their chatter made Caro relax, and she felt playful.

"See any vampires?" she whispered to Jude, then she cringed. Vampires. She'd meant it humorously, but saying the word out loud felt strange and embarrassing, like she was playing at a fantasy game.

Jude smiled. "I don't see marks on their necks."

"Not yet," she said.

"When this mad quest is over, let's go somewhere warm and sunny," he said. "We'll lock ourselves in a hotel room for six weeks."

"Sounds heavenly." She tucked her hand into his pocket just as the bus lurched out of the Momchilgrad station. She still had questions about the odd happenings in Momchilgrad, but they would have to wait. She couldn't risk being overheard, even by kids.

She laid her head on Jude's shoulder. She was dimly aware of humming tires and the teenagers' chatter. She fell asleep, dreaming that she was back at Norham Gardens, sitting in the drawing room. Her uncle and several students were discussing a dig in Wales. Three more students showed up for tea. They'd just returned from the Languedoc region in southern France. Her uncle had been jovial all evening, but his face turned white as the students described the ruined Cathar castles and how one of them had supposedly housed the Holy Grail.

"It's a document," said the student. "Not a cup."

Uncle Nigel had shooed Caro off to bed, but she hadn't been able to sleep. Her mind whirled with the idea of treasure hunts. She crept back into the hall and knelt beside the banister. Snatches of conversation drifted up. Whoever these Cathars were, they'd gotten into a lot of trouble with the French, and a crusade had been organized to kill them. The students were just getting to the juicy part when her uncle stepped into the hall and glared up the staircase. She shrank back. After a moment, she saw him cross the hallway into the drawing room and shut the pocket doors with a bang.

She awoke with her head in Jude's lap. She lay there a moment, trying to call back the dream. The bus slowed, and the gears whined. She sat up, pushing hair out of her eyes.

Jude squeezed her arm. "Checkpoint," he whispered.

The driver got out of his chair and walked crablike down the aisle, collecting passports. He carried them off the bus, into a building. Near the front of the bus, the

Bulgarian teenagers laughed and sat in the aisle. Caro squeezed Jude's knee. He seemed calm, except for a faint ticking in his neck.

"What's wrong?" She scooted closer.

"Checkpoints make me nervous."

"Then talk to me." She rubbed his hand. "Tell me more about your research. You can whisper."

"There's nothing to say." He shifted in the seat. "Except that I worked round the clock. I slept at the lab. But I've already told you that, haven't I?"

"If your research hadn't been interrupted, what would have happened with your mice?"

"Additional research," he said. "I published a paper. My supervisor asked me to assemble a team. Our company had a contract with a Scottish pharmaceutical firm. We were developing an antiaging compound. It had the potential to be a billion-dollar drug."

"Isn't that a bit steep?"

"Viagra and Lipitor are five-billion-dollar drugs. The profits from an antiaging pill would be unlimited." Fresh lines etched across his forehead.

She looked up into his eyes, sensing passion and regret for the career he'd left behind. "You miss your work?"

"A bit."

"Maybe you'll do it again."

"Not bloody likely."

"Well, I hope you do." She glanced out the window. "What's taking the driver so long?"

"It's Bulgaria," Jude said. "They cling to bureaucracy."

The driver finally returned, the passports stacked to his chin. Walking at a slant, he moved down the aisle, distributing the booklets. When he was finished, he settled behind the wheel. The engine sputtered, and the bus rolled forward.

Jude's face relaxed, then he drew her hand to his lips. "I can't wait until we're alone."

"Me, either." Her bite wound prickled, and she shifted uncomfortably in her seat.

A whistle blew, and a border policeman stepped in front of the bus, one hand raised. The gears shifted again, and the bus rumbled to a stop. The side doors creaked open, and the policeman climbed inside. He spoke to the driver in Bulgarian, flashing a stack of computer printouts, then started down the aisle, his dark eyes scrutinizing each passenger.

Toward the middle of the bus, he spoke sharply to a chaperone with frizzy brown hair.

She handed over her passport and averted her gaze.

The policeman looked from the passport to his printouts; he peered at the woman and spoke again. She nodded and stared at the floor.

Caro slumped down, but Jude pulled her up and slid his arm around her shoulder. "Your hands," he whispered. "The ink."

Her breath hitched. Anagrams covered her palms. She tugged her sleeve over her fingers, trying to keep her face impassive, but her pulse thundered in her ears.

"Relax," Jude whispered. He leaned forward and kissed her. From the corner of her eye, Caro saw the policeman pause beside their row and study the printouts. He fanned the pages, and she glimpsed her picture.

Caro broke the kiss and turned to the window. She no longer resembled the girl in the picture. Her old self hadn't had cheekbones, and her face had been dwarfed by her Medusa-like curls. However, her eyes were the same, and she hoped the policeman hadn't noticed.

Go away, damn you.

The printouts rustled, then he walked briskly to the front of the bus and climbed down the steps. The doors creaked shut. Jude's hand closed over her knee. As the bus lurched forward, Caro pressed her forehead against the window and watched Bulgaria blend into the Greek frontier. Her relief changed to sorrow when she thought of Uncle Nigel. Who had taken his body? Was he still dead—or had he become like that man who'd bitten her in Momchilgrad?

No matter what, she could never return to Bulgaria to search for him. The police were looking for her. She'd killed a man, and she wasn't sorry. Not one bit.

Jude peeled back the wrapper from a roll of mints and offered her one. She held it between her fingers. "How long till we arrive in Thessaloniki?"

"After sunset. But don't worry. Greece is safer." He reached into his pocket and handed her a garlic clove. "Don't say that I never gave you a present."

CHAPTER 27

SOFIA, BULGARIA

Two Royal Guards escorted Ilya Velikov through a line of protesters outside the British embassy in Sofia. A man held up a sign that objected to the guards' fur hats. Velikov clutched his briefcase and followed the guards to Thurston Hughes's office. A plump secretary looked up from her desk and waved him through.

Velikov walked into the paneled room. Hughes sat behind a massive walnut desk, surrounded by folders. Behind him, silver-framed photographs lined a shelf, each picture showing a laughing, silver-haired woman with two black Labrador retrievers. Hughes rose and shook Velikov's hand.

"Lovely to see you, Ilya. Please be seated. I haven't had any luck finding Miss Clifford."

"Perhaps this will help." Velikov opened his briefcase

and pulled out photocopied documents. "When Professor Clifford's body was found, he was holding his passport. Apparently he spent his last moments leaving notes for his niece. I made a copy of the pages and returned the passport to the niece."

"This is amazing, Ilya. Why didn't you say something earlier?"

"I was waiting for the cryptologist to decode the notes."

"And did he?"

Velikov slid the documents across Hughes's desk. "They were anagrams. Miss Clifford is headed to either Greece or Italy. But I do not know what is waiting for her in either place."

"Brilliant work, Ilya." Hughes lifted the papers. "Just brilliant."

"Is your MI5 involved?"

"My official answer is: no comment," Hughes said. "But off the record, yes. Field agents are looking for Miss Clifford."

"To protect her? Or is something else afoot?"

"Miss Clifford may have murdered her flatmate."

"I cannot believe that. And I am shocked that you do."

"I didn't say what I believed, did I?" Hughes's face reddened. "I'm simply reporting facts."

"Whose facts?"

"I've said too much already. Naturally the embassy won't be involved in any criminal investigation. I'm here to assist British nationals."

"But she *is* one." Velikov ran his thumb along the edge of his briefcase. "I pray she is still alive. If not, her death will not end this."

"How dare you threaten me." The tips of Hughes's ears turned scarlet. He picked up a sheaf of papers and swiveled in his chair. "You know the way out."

Velikov left the embassy and steered his Astra through the clogged traffic in Sofia. He listened to Bulgarian National Radio as he drove down the empty highway to Kardzhali. At twilight he pulled up to his stone house and went inside.

He hung his jacket and holster over the back of the dining room chair, then walked to the kitchen. Ursula had died two years ago, and their daughters worried about Velikov's nutrition. They often sneaked into his house and left soup bubbling on the stove.

He turned on his television and listened to the news while he rummaged in the kitchen to see what his girls had left. The media offered blandness. The citizens of Kardzhali would not hear about murdered tourists.

Velikov found a roasted chicken on the counter. While he carved thin slices of white meat, he thought of the professor's missing body and pieced together a list of suspects. Not even the Bulgarian Mafia would steal the mutilated body of an elderly gentleman. The black market had no use for postmortem organs.

Either the professor's body had been stolen to lure his niece or he had risen on his own. Of course, he could voice the latter theory to no one. To the Interior Ministry, vampirism was the elephant in the room—bad for tourism. Sometimes the lines were blurred, as with the wild dog attacks near the Black Sea. It was impossible to know if the attacks were animal or vampiric in origin. Everyone from law enforcement to the coroners looked the other way.

The professor's wounds had been suggestive of an attack by immortals. Velikov's thoughts circled back to his original theories. Could the British government be involved? Would they use the professor's missing body as a way to trap the Clifford girl? And if so—why? Thurston Hughes was capable of orchestrating a ruse, though whether for his government or for someone else, Velikov did not know. The second option, vampirism, was equally possible, but there had been no reports of violent attacks in Kardzhali, human or animal. No thefts from blood banks. No reports of a naked Englishman creeping around the city.

Velikov rubbed his temples. Too much puzzlement for one night. And his dinner was waiting. He set the dining room table with Ursula's china and lifted his cutlery. The white tablecloth stirred around his legs. He looked around for the source of the draft. A man with oily black hair and eyes like poppy seeds stood in the arched doorway. The man's face was white and stunk of zinc oxide. He wiped his fingers on a filthy red jogging suit. Other, darker stains marked the fabric.

"Dear Ilya, always sticking your nose where it does not belong," the man said.

"Who are you?" Velikov frowned. "How do you know my name?"

"One question at a time. I'm Georgi Stoyanov Ivanov." He bowed. "I know everything about you, Ilya. You go to bed at nine P.M. and arise at dawn. Your wife died of uterine cancer. Every Saturday you visit her grave and leave a bouquet of lilies—her favorite, yes?"

"You are observant," Velikov said, struggling to control his voice. He inched closer to his jacket.

The tall man bowed. "Only when I am paid to observe."

"Did Hughes send you?"

"In a roundabout way, yes." Georgi smiled. His teeth pricked the edge of his lower lip. "Do not worry. I will not drink your dirty bureaucratic blood."

Velikov dove for his jacket and reached for the holster. Before he could turn off the safety, Georgi was on top of him, wrenching the gun from his hand.

"Wait. Do not shoot," Velikov said. "Let us sit down and talk."

"No talk." Georgi seized Velikov's neck. There was a snap, and the bureaucrat dropped to the floor. A tiny thread of blood curled from his ear.

Georgi touched Velikov's wrist. Warm. A weak pulse. But the heart would not beat much longer. The smell of iron brought Georgi to his knees. His thoughts dripped down the back of his mind.

"Just one taste," he said, then plunged his teeth into Velikov's neck.

CHAPTER 28

THESSALONIKI, GREECE

Jude and Caro walked from the bus station to the Capsis Hotel—a square building in a bad part of the city, but it was only two hundred meters from the railway station.

When they stepped into their room, she leaned her hip against him. "After we get settled, let's poke around the city. We can find authentic Greek food."

He shook his head. "It's not prudent to walk around at night."

"But you said Greece is safer." For the last fifteen minutes, she hadn't thought about her uncle or his missing body. She hadn't thought about the living dead in Momchilgrad, either.

"The hotel is in a dangerous part of the city." Jude slipped his arm around her. "Not so many vampires, but plenty of other unsavory types."

"I was in Thessaloniki a long time ago with Uncle Nigel and we walked everywhere."

"Where have you *not* been?" Jude laughed.

"Quite a few places, actually. Machu Picchu. The Easter Islands. Antarctica. Come to think of it, I haven't been to Miami or Chicago, either."

She headed straight to the bathroom. While the tub filled, she picked through the miniature toiletries on the counter. She tipped blue bath oil into the water. Suds rose to the edge of the porcelain lip. She pushed her hair into a plastic cap and sank down into the steaming water. She bent her leg at the knee and rubbed soap over the ink, scrubbing away the letters: *Ellen vumv ice = Venice vellum*.

Her uncle was speaking from the grave. With all the museums in Venice, she was sure to find old manuscripts—but where to begin?

But the first clue, *Meteora, Greece*, also fit. All sorts of manuscripts, from papyrus to vellum, were housed in the clifftop monasteries. Had it only been this morning when she'd solved the anagrams? It seemed as if they'd spent years in Momchilgrad.

She pressed a washcloth to her neck, and the water dribbled between her breasts. The faint movement of the streaming droplets made her skin tingle. She soaped the cloth and ran it over her breasts. Her nipples hardened into taut peaks. Every nerve in her body vibrated like strummed guitar strings. Her head almost slipped under the water as she climaxed.

She moaned, and her foot skated along the slick porcelain bottom. One more inch, and she'd slip under the surface. She grabbed the edge of the tub, pulled up, and brushed her toes along the drain, feeling for the chain.

She gripped it with her toes and pulled. As water gurgled, she tried to work up the courage to touch her nipple again. What would happen if she touched between her legs? She leaned back in the tub and waited till the water receded; her hand dropped to her stomach and moved lower and lower. Ripples moved in all directions, and her breath caught.

Even before she reached her most sensitive place, the orgasm broke loose. The sensations slammed into her, hard. It was like falling and having the breath knocked out of you, but in a pleasurable way.

Moving cautiously, she climbed out of the tub, careful not to touch herself. This could be embarrassing. What if someone bumped into her in a restaurant, hitting her breasts in the right spot, and set off an accidental orgasm? She couldn't even become a nun; she'd have to be a recluse. She wasn't fit to be around people.

I'm just like Jude's mice. Her hand moved to her neck. Even light pressure on the wounds felt erotic. Before the man had bitten her, sex had been pleasing but underwhelming, leaving her wondering why the world made such a fuss about it. But she'd been bitten by a vampire and was now at the mercy of a hormonal storm.

She wound a thick towel around her body, flinching at the pressure against her nipples. The bathroom was foggy, so she walked into the bedroom and peered into the full-length looking glass. She pulled off the plastic cap, and her hair tumbled down. Her reflection peered back, still flushed and aroused. Her eyes looked different, too, more blue and rimmed with silver.

Her breasts looked rounder, fuller. Not a lot, but she knew her body, and it seemed to be changing. Would starvation change her this dramatically? She'd eaten a small bowl of chickpea soup at Mr. Kudret's, but other than that she couldn't remember the last time she'd eaten. She started to turn away and saw Jude's image in the looking glass.

"You're beautiful," he whispered.

For a moment, she thought she could hear his thoughts, that he wanted children with her eyes. The towel fell into a puddle around her feet. She stepped out, feeling like Venus emerging from her clamshell.

He drew her into the warm covers and his hand skated over her damp breasts, down to her navel, then slid upward again. Every place he touched seemed to vibrate. He kissed one edge of her mouth, then the other. The sweet, teasing kisses became more urgent. His hand cupped the back of her damp head and his fingers caught in her hair.

"I want to make love to you all night," he said, kneading her breasts, his thumbs rubbing against her nipples. The pleasure swirled around and around, pulling her with it. She suppressed a shudder as a tiny spasm uncoiled like a watch spring.

"Did you just . . ." Jude's eyes widened.

Don't tell the truth, Clifford. She started to shake her head, then nodded.

"But I was barely touching you. Has this ever happened before?"

She shook her head. "Maybe it's a rare event. Like Halley's comet."

"Damn, I hope not." He laughed. "Let's give it another go, shall we?"

Keeping his gaze on her, he drew his finger down her throat, between her breasts, to her navel, then paused.

"Keep going," she said, and pushed his head to her breast. He drew her nipple into his mouth and gently sucked. She began to pant when he flicked his tongue over the tip. She laced her fingers through his hair, then arched her back. A shimmery circle moved inside her, then folded back on itself. He fitted himself between her legs and smiled down at her. "This time, I'm the one who can't wait," he whispered.

She reached down and guided him. As he moved inside her, he tipped back his head.

"My God," he whispered. "This is—I've never—"

The heat in his words seared the air, leaving a smoking imprint. As he throbbed inside her, she moved in ways she'd never thought possible, and each shift of her body seemed to ignite something within him. He began thrusting, and the slow flame within her blazed again. All she knew was his breath. His heartbeat. His touch.

His hoarse cry brought her back. He pulled her hips upward, pressing deeper and deeper. The friction set off a series of jagged streaks, each one shooting through her. She fully expected the sheets to smolder and burst into flames.

She lifted her hips again and again. His back tensed and he cried out her name. A tiny explosion began in her center. Something was building, something colossal, a force of nature, old as time itself, and it moved through her veins like magma seeking a vent. She felt it shoot upward, fire and ice, and she rose with it.

Afterward, she lay under the blanket, watching Jude's muscles flex as he pulled on a shirt. When he sat down to lace his shoes, his hair fell forward. She wanted to run her hands through it. She breathed in the faint scent of lovemaking that hung in the air. A potent sexual chemistry had existed between them from the start, but it was building into something unstoppable.

She reluctantly left the warm blankets and rummaged in her bag. She pulled out a long black skirt and a delicate white blouse she'd found years ago at a thrift shop on Portobello Road.

She slid her warm arms through the cool sleeves. The rounded décolletage showed a discreet curve of white breasts, and the sleeves were sheer. Layers of antique lace fell around her wrists. She tugged at the skirt. It wasn't loose; she hadn't lost weight after all.

It's the straight, dark hair, she thought, leaning toward the mirror. Jude walked up behind her, swept her hair aside, and kissed her neck. She cupped her hand to his cheek and leaned against him.

"If we don't leave now, I'll need a cold bath." He laced his fingers through hers and led her out of the room. They took the elevator to the lobby and walked past the crowded hotel restaurant toward Irene's Piano Bar.

"What an odd name for a Greek pub," she said.

Jude didn't seem to be listening. He led her to a corner booth. As she slid across the leather, she saw a tall, bony man step into the bar. Her breath caught.

"That's not him," Jude said.

"I see him everywhere."

A waiter took their drink orders and returned with a bread basket and a little bowl of cucumber yogurt. After he left, Jude reached under the table and caressed her knee. "It's taking all of my willpower not to kiss you," he said.

"Willpower is highly overrated." She leaned forward,

rising from the seat, and pressed her lips against his. They were still kissing when the waiter returned with drinks. Diet Coke for Caro, water for Jude. She pulled back as the waiter set out the flatware and a flickering red candle.

Jude lifted his glass and clinked it against hers. *"Sláinte."*

"To the Queen," she said. After the waiter took their orders and left, Caro leaned across the table. "Are all immortal beings evil?"

"Haven't met a decent one yet," Jude said.

"How can you be sure they're all bad? My uncle was an honorable man. He didn't ask to be bitten. Now his body is missing. If your theories are correct, he might turn into a vampire."

"That's precisely why I went to the morgue. To examine him."

"Well, I guess we'll never know the truth." She took a sip of Diet Coke. "But if Uncle Nigel turns up in a black cape, I won't throw holy water at him."

"He won't be your uncle."

"Yes, he will."

"He'll bite you."

"Nonsense. I'll feed him steak tartare."

"It won't stop his blood thirst."

"We're discussing hypotheticals."

"No, we're not. Your uncle wouldn't be the same. Vampirism affects the brain's chemistry."

"I've been bitten. And I'm not craving blood."

"You'd want it after a dozen bites."

"For the sake of argument, let's say I ran into a vampire on my way to the ladies' room, and he bit me from head to toe. Let's say I got just enough stem cells to turn. What would you do?"

His jaw tightened. "I don't know."

"Would you run off into the night?"

"Yes."

She didn't ask why. She didn't need to. Vampires had taken everything from him. But whether he stayed or went, she had no intention of getting bitten again.

After dinner, they went straight to their room. Caro sat on the edge of the bed and kicked off her flats. Jude opened his backpack and pulled out the plastic bag with the hair and her bloody clothes.

"We need to stash this in a safe place for now," he said.

"No one is looking for my DNA in Greece. Can't housekeeping take it?"

"Let's put it in a locker. We'll rent one at the train station. When the heat's off, I'll come back to Thessaloniki and deal with the bag."

"Are we leaving in the morning?" she asked.

"It's up to you. But it might not hurt if we stayed here a few days, would it? We've had a hectic twenty-four hours. And Meteora isn't going to be a cakewalk. We've got to tramp through monasteries and find a nameless monk."

She unzipped her duffel bag and rummaged for a fresh T-shirt. She didn't have a slip or a teddy, and she was definitely in the mood for silk and lace. But a woman on the run didn't have time to shop for a negligee.

Jude leaned over her shoulder. "What's a man's wallet doing in your bag?"

"It's Uncle Nigel's."

"From the crime scene?"

She nodded.

"Was anything missing?"

"Money and credit cards. And my photograph."

"Check it again. He may have slipped a paper into a crevice. And I'd like to take another look at his passport."

She pulled it out of the bag and handed it to Jude. He turned the pages slowly, pausing over the section of clues. "Caro? Have you seen this?"

He pointed to the back page of the passport, near the bottom. *Sa kal Okyrv* had been written in shaky, minuscule handwriting, with a slash of dried blood beneath it.

"I can't believe I missed that." She studied the words. *"Sa kal Okyrv?"*

"Here's another one, too." Jude tilted the book. In the crease was another bloody smear. *Nrot hath setaf a* was written in the same shaky, diminutive print. "Could these be more clues?"

She squinted. "How did I miss them?"

"Well, they're tucked in the back. Maybe he wrote them as an afterthought." Jude paused. "Was the passport found beside his body, or in his backpack?"

"I don't know. Why?"

"When the Bulgarian police worked the crime scene, they would have noticed a passport beside the body, and they would have examined it."

"But if Mr. Velikov had seen the anagrams, he would've kept the passport."

"Maybe. Maybe not." He glanced at the pages. "I hope these clues don't lead back to Bulgaria. Because we can't go back."

"No." She squinted at the words. What did they mean? *Sa kal Okyrv. Nrot hath setaf a.* They didn't form semilogical phrases, like anagrams. "I can't crack these clues," she said. "I can't think straight."

"You don't have to solve them this second, do you?"

He tugged the passport from her hands, set it on the bed, and drew her into his arms. She pressed her head against his shoulder and shut her eyes. She'd had other lovers, but she'd never yielded herself mentally to a man. Some part of her had refused to budge, always holding back. Overnight, an untouched part of her soul had opened, and she didn't know quite what to make of it.

He pressed his lips against hers, then slid his hands up and down her back. She closed her eyes as the kiss drew her in, powerful as a current. His mouth was an ocean. And she was breathing underwater.

CHAPTER 29

Harry Wilkerson stood in front of the new window and clasped his hands behind his back. London's skyline stretched up and out in front of him. The rising sun glanced off St. Paul's, and the dome sparkled with a preternatural light. He ignored the view and peered at his reflection, smoothing down his gray hair.

One good thing about the daylight—it forced vampires to lurk in the shadows, waiting for dusk. Except for the trainspotter. Moose wasn't frightened of anything and might show up at any moment. But soon, even he would be under Wilkerson's control. The Hammersmith scientists had finally developed an SSRI that quashed obsessive-compulsive urges; it also rewired the amygdala—a teardrop-shaped structure in the brain that records the memory of fear, among other things. The next time

Moose showed up for a feeding, he would receive his first chemically laced transfusion.

The chemists were also testing skin patches: a time-release derivative of Ecstasy that caused brain cells to release large amounts of serotonin. Unfortunately, the dose that soothed immortals was lethal to humans and laboratory mice. Still, it was a breakthrough. When vampires were floating in serotonin, they were easier to control.

Wilkerson looked at the notes his secretary had left on his desk. Everything was in order. Mr. Underwood's contacts in the London police department had presented the photographs to the task force; several members had rejected the idea that one flatmate had murdered the other. The information had been leaked to Sir Edmund Dowell, and he'd called the prime minister. Now, more MI5 field agents had been dispatched to Sofia. The investigation was expanding. It wouldn't be long before the Clifford girl's whereabouts were known—and he'd be one step closer to his stolen artifacts.

From his outer office, he heard his secretary's high-pitched voice. "You don't have an appointment. You can't go in there."

"Watch me," came a deep nasal voice.

Wilkerson turned away from the view. The door swung open, and Moose stepped inside wearing his sun-reflective jumpsuit. The secretary scrambled behind, her backside moving up and down in her tight black dress. Yok-Seng's heavy footsteps shook the hall, and he rushed into the room.

Moose pulled off his helmet. "You'll get a punch up the bracket if you mess with me."

"Calm down, both of you," Wilkerson said.

Moose winked at Yok-Seng. "For a bodyguard, you're always up a gum tree."

Wilkerson pointed to Yok-Seng and the secretary. "Both of you leave," he said. "Now."

"You heard the lad," Moose called.

After they left the room, Wilkerson folded his hands on the glossy table. His nose twitched as Moose's earthy aroma filled the room—blood and iron.

"So nice of you to drop in," Wilkerson said.

"Not at all." Moose plopped down in a chair, the leather creaking, and began cleaning his nails with a paper clip. "A word of advice: Get rid of the chink. He's always off for a whiz."

"Can I get you a cup of tea?" Wilkerson narrowed his eyes. "Crumpets and cream?"

"Got any B positive in the cooler? It's got a sweet but metallic bite." Moose pinched his thumb and forefinger together, as if holding up an imaginary goblet. "And yet, it's mellow and fruity."

"I don't keep blood in this building," Wilkerson said. "It's in Hammersmith."

"Been there already." Moose rolled up his sleeve and pointed to a red dot on his forearm. "But don't lie to me, mate. I happen to know that you keep bags of A negative in your wee fridge. The one that's hidden behind the paneling. Myself, I don't like A negative. It's too tangy, and it foams. But I'll drink it in a pinch."

The phone buzzed. Wilkerson sat down at his desk and pressed the flashing button. "Sir, there's an urgent call from Romania," his secretary said.

Wilkerson started to lift the receiver to say he'd take

the call later, but Moose shot out of his chair, moving in a streak of colors. He loomed in front of Wilkerson and wagged his finger.

"Not so fast, mate. Where's the button for the speakerphone?"

"This call doesn't concern you, Moose."

"Let me be the judge of that. How's your bloodsucking secretary doing?" Moose smiled. "Actually, it's not blood that she's sucking. Is it, mate?"

Moose leaned over the phone and ran a dirty finger down the buttons. Up close, his smell was pungent and sour, reeking of unwashed flesh. Wilkerson gagged and clapped a hand over his nose.

Moose pushed a yellow button on the phone, and the speaker crackled.

"Er, this is Dr. Popovici," the caller said, his voice deep and exotic. "I have the postmortem results on Teo Stamboliev."

"What?" Moose cried. "Teo's dead?"

"Er—to whom am I speaking?" the doctor said.

Moose motioned to Wilkerson with a karate chop.

There was a thrumming silence as Moose and Wilkerson glared at each other. "Yes, Dr. Popovici, do go on," Wilkerson said.

"Shall I go over the postmortem with you, sir?"

"*No,*" Wilkerson snapped.

"As you wish." The doctor sounded confused. "When will the British woman arrive?"

Wilkerson mashed the red button and disconnected the call.

"Why'd you do that?" Moose cried. "And why didn't you tell me about Teo? He was my mate."

Wilkerson smoothed back his hair and didn't comment.

Moose snorted. "What's the purpose of a postmortem?"

"Company policy."

"What a load of cack. That call came from Romania."

"So? Wilkerson Pharmaceuticals has research labs everywhere."

Moose sat down on the conference table and the mirrored surface cracked. "Why did you order a post on a vampire? Are you studying us?"

A muscle worked in Wilkerson's jaw. "Don't be foolish."

"And who's the British woman that Dr. Dracula wants? Could it be the Clifford girl?"

"She's none of your concern."

"Will it be my concern when you send me to Romania to kill Dr. Dracula? The day *will* come, you know. Either he won't cooperate, or he'll threaten to go public."

Wilkerson flinched.

"Oh, keep your hair on. It's the Clifford girl, isn't it? Why are you really after her? What did she do—badmouth your cosmetics line?"

Wilkerson almost said yes. That would have been a mistake, possibly a fatal one, even with Yok-Seng lurking in the hall. "I have a billion-dollar corporation to run. And you have the audacity to question me?"

"You couldn't organize a piss-up in a brewery." Moose grabbed Wilkerson's neck and squeezed. "Tell me what the bloody hell is going on, and if you lie, I swear on the queen's dogs that I will cut off your billion-dollar balls."

Wilkerson flailed, slapping at the vampire's large hands. He felt his body rise from the chair. His limbs felt heavy and he couldn't breathe, couldn't think. He passed wind. Moose slung Wilkerson to the floor.

"More tea, vicar?" Moose fanned the air.

Wilkerson lifted his head, checking his extremities one by one. Nothing seemed broken. He licked his lips and tried to appear calm, but his mind raced in all directions. If he told the truth, Moose would kill him. He sorted through classified information, plucking out sordid secrets, and emerged with one tidbit. It was death or disclosure.

"Caroline Clifford is my daughter," Wilkerson said. "But you mustn't tell."

Moose blinked. Cor blimey, this was old news; but it wouldn't be smart to mention that Mr. Underwood had already blabbed it. Wilkerson was hiding something bigger. Maybe he was experimenting on vampires. Whatever it was, Moose intended to find out, even if he had to be submissive. He pressed two fingers to his lips and twisted them back and forth, as if turning a key.

"My lips is sealed, mate," he said. "I'd offer to take your secret to the grave, but I'm already dead."

CHAPTER 30

THESSALONIKI, GREECE

Caro dreamed of the wild dogs again. Jude was with her, and they were running into the desert, kicking up waves of sand. The sun beat down, roasting their skin. She woke up with a jolt and felt her forehead. She was burning up.

They got dressed and took the lift down to the lobby. Jude bought aspirin at the gift shop, and they stopped in the café for juice and poppy seed muffins. She shook two tablets into her hand.

"Take one more," Jude said.

By the time they left the Capsis Hotel, her ears were ringing, but her fever had lessened. The chilly air felt good, and she pushed up her sleeves. Jude reached for her hand as they turned down Aphrodite Street. She waited outside the rail station while Jude paid for a locker and stowed the evidence bag they'd brought from Momchilgrad. Then they caught a bus to Aristotelous Square. Through the window, she glimpsed Byzantine architecture here and there, though much of the city had burned during the 1917 fire. They stepped down onto a crowded sidewalk where Aristotle's statue overlooked old manses that had housed shops and cafés. The city still held a hint of Ottoman influence, with a nod to the West. At one end of the square, workmen erected a massive public Christmas tree.

"I'd quite forgotten about the holidays," Jude said.

"Me, too." Caro felt the gloom creeping back, and she tried to distract herself by focusing on the far end of the square, where the Aegean glittered. They stopped in front of a crowded outdoor café. Smells of roasting meat wafted from the tables.

"This smells like authentic Greek food," he said. "Shall we pop in?"

Caro had expected folk music, but American music drifted from the ceiling. As Snow Patrol sang "Run," a waitress led them to a table facing the street. They ordered lemon rice soup, mussels pilaf, and hot tea. Jude traced his finger over the back of her hand. "You look worried."

"I'm thinking about those phrases. *Sa kal Okyrv* and the other one."

"The Internet has a plethora of deciphering tools. After lunch, we'll find a cyber café."

Their waitress returned with their food. Caro broke off a golden hunk of garlic bread, then hesitated. "Garlic won't hurt me, will it?"

He blinked. "Why would it?"

"It repels vampires—and I was bitten by one."

"Garlic has mild antibiotic properties. It might alter the taste of blood." He patted her arm. "You'll be fine."

"What about crosses and holy water?"

"The myths seem to be cultural. Would a Muslim fear holy water and a crucifix?"

"No. I suppose not. What about silver bullets?"

"Lead might cause a mild anaphylactic reaction," he said.

"Anaphylactic?"

"A severe allergic reaction—like with bees or seafood. The blood pressure falls, the airway closes. The silver could react with the vampires' chemistry, preventing the wound from healing." He leaned forward. "I've been thinking of ways to explain the science behind vampirism. So you'll understand."

A shy grin flitted across his lips, as if he were giving her a bouquet of wildflowers instead of simplified information about stem cells. She hid her smile by taking a sip of tea.

"Have you heard of the MRSA bacteria?" he asked. "Methicillin-resistant *Staphylococcus aureus*. It's an antibiotic-resistant bug. To create a strain, all you need is a petri dish filled with staphylococcus. Add penicillin. It will kill ninety-nine percent of the staph. Take the surviving one percent and culture them. You have bacteria that are resistant to penicillin." He paused. "Are you following me?"

"So far."

"Actually, the bacterium's resistance is a defense mechanism," he continued. "If you put the penicillin-resistant strain into a petri dish and apply erythromycin, the antibiotic will kill a majority of the bacteria. Culture the survivors, and you have an organism that's resistant to penicillin *and* erythromycin. If you repeat this process ad infinitum, adding various antibiotics, you will eventually have a superior organism. One that's resistant to all anti-biotics. And indestructible."

"You're saying vampirism evolved like MRSA?" She set down her teacup harder than she'd intended and it clapped against the saucer. Several diners glanced in her direction.

"It's evolution. Survival of the fittest. Vampires began in small numbers and multiplied. They're adaptive—strong, hard to kill. And they destroy the competing organism." He pushed his soup bowl away, its contents swaying. "They're still evolving."

"Into what?"

"We'll have to wait and see. If we're still around."

———

They found a cyber café at the other end of Aristotelous Square. Inside, the air reeked of burned coffee and stale pastries. Cigarette smoke pooled beneath the pendant lights, floating over metal tables where people stared at computer monitors.

Jude paid the clerk, and they found a terminal in the corner. Caro pulled up a chair beside him. The keyboard made soft tocking noises as he typed *Sa kal Okyrv*.

"No hits," he said.

"I hope it's not cipher text." Caro leaned toward the screen. "Wait, could it be backward?"

"Let's try." He typed in *Vrykolakas*. Thirty-five thousand hits popped up. "Wiki says it's a Slavic word for 'vampire.' But there's also a death-metal band named Vrykolakas. They're on MySpace."

"Uncle Nigel stumbled onto something," she whispered. "And it got him killed."

"That goes without saying. What about the other phrase? *Nrot htah setaf a?* Could it be reversed?"

She grabbed a pen and scribbled on her hand. *A fates hath torn.*

Jude typed *A fates hath torn.*

"No results," she said. "Let's try an anagram solver."

After three tries, they found the right website. Jude typed in *A fates hath torn.* "Only 55,452 results," he said. "See anything familiar?"

She leaned toward the screen. "A northeast haft? Afar that honest?"

"Tartan hath foes?" Jude asked. "Or was your uncle referring to torn faith?"

"I don't know." A dull ache throbbed behind her eyes, and she rubbed the bridge of her nose. She'd solved the other clues, but now she couldn't focus. Cobwebs filled her brain, and each thought scattered like a dust mote. She'd have to try later, after she'd rested. But if the phrase was a Caesar Shift cipher, she'd never solve it without a cryptographer. Jude pressed his hand against her forehead. "You're still feverish. Let's go back to the hotel."

On the way out of the café, they passed by a newsstand. Caro's photograph was on the front page, her blond hair flying in all directions.

Jude said something, but she couldn't hear. A roaring sound filled her head. Her picture? It didn't look like her, but still. Why would a Greek newspaper care about a traffic accident in Bulgaria? Or was this about her uncle? She leaned closer to the rack. "Damn, it's Cyrillic," she said. "I can't read it."

Jude lifted a paper. "It says, 'British National Sought

for Questioning.' Then it gives your name and says that three people are dead—"

"Three?"

"Sir Nigel Clifford, Phoebe Dowell, and Teo Stamboliev." He scanned to the end of the article. "There's a toll-free number that people can call if they spot you."

She swore under her breath. "They think *I* hurt Phoebe?"

"You're a person of interest. Eyewitnesses claim that you pushed Teodor Stamboliev into the path of a lorry. You're described as dangerous and unstable."

"Great. I'm the fall guy, like in *The Maltese Falcon*." She made a fist. "Dammit, what are they playing at? I'm *sought* for questioning? That's wicked. Newspapers use *sought* when mass murderers are on the lam."

Jude shoved the paper back into the rack and took her arm. "Let's go."

On the way to the bus stop, they debated whether they should catch a train to Kalambaka or spend another night at the Capsis. "How long does it take to reach Kalambaka?" he asked.

"Two and a half hours," she said. "We change trains at Larissa. I wish I remembered more, but I don't. I was a little girl."

"How old?"

"Six." She hesitated, wondering if she should tell the rest of it. Before she could decide, the bus pulled up to the curb and discharged a plume of black smoke. They found seats near the back.

"I hope we find answers in Meteora," she said. "But that whole period is sketchy. I was still shell-shocked. My parents had died a year earlier."

"Were they in an accident?"

"A fire." She exhaled a little harder than she'd intended. She didn't want to talk about her family. Not yet. He lifted her chin, and she studied his eyes, concentrating on those endearing tree-bark flecks in his left iris. She didn't want to think about herself. She wanted to know more about him. Did one of his parents have chestnut eyes? Or a grandmother? Maybe the dominant brown genes had been repressed by generations of blue-eyed Barretts, only to surface in Jude. She didn't know anything about genetics, but those dark bits seemed strong and defiant, representing something more powerful than color.

He stared down at her hands. "You're shaking."

She knitted her fingers together. Her throat ached, as if she'd swallowed pointy rocks. Could she tell him the rest of it? His lab had been burned, too. Was there a connection? No, that was Dame Doom talking, not her. Besides, fire hadn't been involved in Phoebe's murder, or her uncle's. The events seemed random, without a connecting thread.

"My parents didn't die because someone forgot to turn off the coffeepot or because of faulty wiring." She swallowed around the stones, her throat clicking. "They were murdered."

The color washed out of his cheeks. "God, Caro. I'm so sorry. I'm a bloody idiot. I've dredged up horrific memories."

"No, I need to remember my family." She swallowed again. "I've suppressed everything, even the happy moments. My mother was beautiful. Long, dark blond hair and silver-blue eyes. Tiny, delicate ankles, almost like stems on wineglasses."

"Like yours." Jude smiled.

"No, I'm more like my father. He had lots and lots of blond hair. Curly like mine. Well, it was."

Her hands shook harder as she pictured the long gravel driveway and the white house hidden behind the hackberry trees. Jude clasped his hands around hers. The firm pressure had a soothing effect, and her tremors stopped.

"When the fire started, I was upstairs," she said, her voice barely above a whisper. "I heard yelling in the front yard. My father was arguing with six men. He turned back to the house and yelled, 'Vivienne! Run!'"

"Vivienne was your mother?" Jude prompted.

She nodded. "I don't know where she was. Probably reading in the sunroom. She always had a book in her hand. Daddy called and called, but she didn't come. One of the men had a bottle with a rag hanging out. He touched a cigarette lighter to it and flames shot up. He hurled the bottle through the living room window. I ran downstairs, trying not to breathe the smoke."

Caro broke off, struggling to hold back the tears, but they spilled down her cheeks. "I found my mother in the dining room. She was stuffing things into my backpack. She clamped a tiny padlock on the zippers, shoved the pack into my arms, and sent me out the back door. She told me to hide behind the waterfall. There was a cave, and I used to play there. I started to follow her up the stairs, but she steered me out the back door. She promised she would find me. She said, 'No matter what you hear, do not come out till morning.' I took off running. But halfway to the cave, I stopped."

The backs of her eyes burned, and more tears broke loose, splashing against Jude's hands. The stone in her throat felt like a boulder, and it was growing, but she forced herself to continue.

"I knew my mother would be angry, but I ran back to the house. The men dragged my father up the front porch. He was limp. I could see through the living room window. Our sofa blazed. The fire jumped to the curtains."

Her chin wavered, and she broke off. Jude lifted one hand and wiped her cheek. Each tender stroke made her feel calmer. She swallowed around the boulder, then drew in a shuddering breath. "I waited in the bushes for the men to return. When they didn't, I ran into the house. I couldn't see anything except for a red stain on the floor. I thought wine had spilled. The living room had been ransacked. I heard my mother screaming in her bedroom. I tried to open the door, but the knob burned my hand."

She spread her fingers. A tear fell off her chin and hit her palm, skidding over an almond-shaped scar.

"A man came out of Mother's room. I ran outside and cut down the hill to the waterfall. I crawled behind it, into the cave. I'd breathed in a lot of smoke and couldn't quit coughing. Then I saw lights moving behind the falls. They were looking for me. I pressed my hand over my mouth, trying to muffle my cough. The lights moved back and forth, then cut to the woods. I waited till morning. I crawled out of the cave and ran to the house. It was gone. Nothing but smoke and blackened wood. I tried to open the backpack, but I couldn't undo the lock. My burns were smarting, so I ran to the highway. An elderly couple picked me up. I ended up in a Knoxville hospital. Then my uncle showed up and whisked me and the back-pack to England. While I slept, he picked the lock and found the icon."

She unzipped her bag, pulled out the relic, and peeled off the plastic covering.

"It looks ancient. Like something in a museum." Jude's brows tightened. "How did your parents come to own something this valuable?"

"I don't know."

"What if they were murdered for it?"

A chill spiked up her backbone. Her heart thrashed in her chest, like a hooked fish. "But they kept it in an unlocked dining room cabinet. Thieves could have broken in while we slept. They didn't need to murder my parents."

"I didn't mean to frighten you." Jude picked up the icon and traced his finger over the metal brackets. "What are these?"

"I don't know. I've always wondered."

He turned the icon over. The back was unpainted, except for black symbols and a drawing: the handle of a sword plunged downward through a large X. It ended in a diamond with a cross embedded in the center.

"What do these mean?" he asked.

"A blessing of some sort. The symbols were supposed to protect our family. But they didn't."

The bus stopped at the corner of Monastiriou Street. They got off and walked to the hotel. She flopped onto the bed. The boulder in her throat was gone, but she felt shaky. Jude sat down beside her and pulled her into his lap, stroking her hair.

"Jude, I have a bad feeling. Maybe we should forget the clues. We could go to South America or New Zealand. Someplace far, far away."

"But we're so close to Meteora."

"The Bulgarian authorities think I murdered Teo. My

picture is all over Greece. It's too dangerous. We need to leave the continent. What about New Zealand?"

"I'm not afraid," he said.

"I am." She burst into tears.

"Don't cry, lass. I'll spend my last breath protecting you." He pushed a handkerchief into her hands, then he rested his chin on top of her head. She leaned against the rough nap of his sweater, wiping her eyes and breathing in the smell of Acqua di Parma. She would probably lose this man, but she would never return this handkerchief. Not even if he begged.

CHAPTER 31

————

MOMCHILGRAD, BULGARIA

The new moon scraped up the backside of the sky as Georgi drove through Momchilgrad. Streetlights shone down on the empty sidewalk. This town was his favorite hunting preserve, but from the look of the town, someone was poaching.

He saw a sign for Kudret's Photography Studio and turned into the parking lot. The car dipped to one side as Georgi climbed out and brushed lint from his new suit. He'd taken it from Ilya Velikov's closet.

Georgi looked at the studio and spat. *A Turk*. He hated all things Ottoman, but he especially loathed Bulgarian Turks. The air was thick with smells. Petrol fumes. The bite of paprika and cumin. The ripe, pungent smell coming from the Dacia's trunk.

Between these odors, he detected the Clifford girl. It

was faint, not enough to track her, but enough to make his pulse race. He took a breath. The aroma welled up, clean yet sticky, reminiscent of soap and sugar, with musky, chemical undertones.

Georgi walked toward the studio, scanning the parking lot. He ignored the CLOSED sign and rapped hard on the glass. "Mr. Kudret? Are you there?" he asked in Bulgarian. "Open up, please. It is an emergency."

Inside the dark building, a light snapped on, and a yellow rectangle spilled into the hall. A rotund man appeared, wearing slippers and a robe. He fumbled with eyeglasses, pushing them over his stubby nose. Halfway to the door, his eyes rounded and he stopped behind a desk.

"We are closed," Mr. Kudret called.

Georgi shook the doorknob. His nostrils flared as he breathed in the Ottoman stench. It smelled of oppression, pain, death.

"I am not a customer." Georgi held his badge against the glass. "Open the door, old man."

"Come back in the morning," Mr. Kudret said. "When it's daylight."

"You will open *now*." Georgi rattled the door, and a string of brass bells tinkled. "I know the girl was here."

"Who?"

Georgi pulled the wrinkled fax from his pocket and held it up against the glass. "Her."

"Leave or I shall call the real police," Mr. Kudret called.

Georgi kicked the door. Tiny, circular cracks spread across the glass; the panel bowed inward and fell. Inside the store a burglar alarm bleated. Georgi reached through the opening, unlatched the knob, and stepped inside. Oh, yes, he would take his time with this one.

Mr. Kudret pulled out a gun, drew a bead, and fired. A bullet sliced into Georgi's left shoulder. Mr. Kudret took aim and fired two times in quick succession. One bullet hit Georgi's leg, and the other whizzed by his ear.

"You cannot stop me," Georgi cried. He lunged across the room, then doubled over, clutching his shoulder. These weren't normal bullets. He was on fire. Then, a chill spread through his limbs. He ran back to his car. The little Turk hurried after him and fired again. A bullet dinged against the Dacia's fender as Georgi drove off.

He steered the car up a hill and parked in front of the Hotel Konak. Here, the Clifford girl's smell was strong. He hobbled into the lobby, blood dripping down to the carpet, and banged on the desk until he roused a clerk. A pale woman appeared, blinking at his stained suit. Her lips drew into a tight bow, and she slid a plastic key card across the counter.

Georgi grabbed her wrist and pulled her over the desk. Bite marks ran up and down her neck. He searched for a clean patch of skin and sank his teeth into her breast. Her heartbeat bloomed in his mouth, but she didn't struggle. He drank greedily, sucking her flesh between his teeth. She didn't have more than a few pints. Someone had gotten there first.

He dragged her body behind the desk. On his way to the elevator, he ducked into the dining room and grabbed a steak knife. He ran to his room and bolted the door. The wounds throbbed. His flesh would dissolve if he didn't remove the Turkish bullets.

He leaned close to the bathroom mirror and pulled down his lower eyelid. The membranes were pale. He had lost blood, and the woman had not satisfied his thirst. He peeled off his jacket. Using the tip of the steak knife, he picked at the wounds. He dropped a bullet into the sink, and it rolled around the white porcelain.

Silver.

He couldn't reach the bullet in his shoulder. It would have to wait. But he had time, all the time in the world. When Teo had removed bullets, he would distract Georgi with stories of the Turks. Sometimes people asked how long they had been partners. "Since the seventies," Georgi would say, omitting the century.

His mouth felt dry; if he didn't feed again, and soon, he would lose strength. He scrubbed the dried blood off his jacket, then put it on and dashed out of the room. At the end of the hall he heard a *ding*, and a stout blond woman stepped out of the elevator, pushing a stroller. The wheel snagged in the gap, and Georgi hurried over to help. He lifted the stroller and gently set it on the ground. Inside, a plump baby slept, oblivious to the commotion.

"Thank you," the woman said.

"Don't mention it," he said.

CHAPTER 32

KALAMBAKA, GREECE

The train whistle blew as they pulled into Kalambaka, rumbling past the yellow station. Caro stepped onto the platform and tipped back her head, gazing up at the giant stone pillars. The monasteries were up there, perched on the flattened tops, their red tile roofs glinting in the sun.

Jude grabbed her hand, and they wandered down the main street, past an outdoor café. Blue tablecloths stirred in the cool air. Caro stopped in front of a window where a man was building a display with olive oil jars, baskets heaped with brown eggs, and glass domes filled with cheese.

When she glanced up, a policeman rounded the corner. Jude hooked his arm around her neck and steered her into a souvenir shop. They stopped by a shelf that was filled with mugs and jigsaw puzzles. Perspiration broke out on her upper lip while she pretended to study the mugs. The policeman stopped outside the shop and peered through the glass; he waved to a dark-haired clerk.

Caro let out a huge sigh. She followed Jude to the desk, where he bought postcards, hats, sunglasses, and a field guide to Meteora. They stepped outside. Jude slipped a hat on her head, then bent down until he was eye level with her. He pressed his palm against her forehead. "You're not feverish anymore."

She smiled, then reached up to straighten his hat. "Did anyone ever tell you that you have a rugged chin?"

"I can't say they have." He laughed and ran his hand over his jaw.

"And I love this teeny knob." She touched the bridge of his nose.

"The Barretts have straight noses." He grinned. "Rugby gave me the bump."

A chilly breeze snapped the edges of Caro's sweater, and she shivered. Jude slipped his arm around her and they walked past gift shops and bakeries. A tour guide with long black hair charged down the street, holding a tiny Greek flag above her head, steering a group toward a Byzantine church.

"I made reservations at the Pension Arsenis," Jude said. They cut down a path and walked through an olive grove to the hotel. In the distance, the monasteries loomed, casting long shadows over the valley.

The lobby smelled of herbs and pine, and on the opposite wall, flames crackled in a stone fireplace. Just beyond the fireplace was a crowded taverna. Cigarette smoke floated over the tables.

"You are the honeymooners, yes?" the receptionist asked.

Jude nodded.

The clerk winked and held out the key. "Your suite is on the second floor. Number sixteen. Very private."

Their room was a far cry from the honeymoon suite, with twin beds on one wall and a pine armoire on the other. Jude immediately pushed the beds together.

"Much better," he said, then turned on the television and flipped the channel to Sky News. Caro found a complimentary bottle of ouzo on the dresser and dribbled a little into a glass.

She opened the French doors and stepped onto the balcony. The Thessalian Plain swept up into the Pindos Mountains. Dusk was falling and spotlights blazed around the distant pillars. Why had Uncle Nigel directed her to Meteora? Was she supposed to find a monk who could translate a vellum page? Or explain the mysterious icon? How did *A fates hath torn* relate to *Vrykolakas*?

Jude walked up behind her, slipped his hands around her waist, then brushed his lips against her ear. "I dreamed about you last night," he whispered. "You were climbing a snowy mountain."

"That's strange. I dreamed about you, too, but you were in a white robe. Sand was everywhere. And wild dogs."

"See? We're dreaming in white."

Still holding the ouzo, she turned and slid one hand over his chest. In the background, she heard the Sky News anchorman recite global events, and she wished the hotel had a music channel. A moment like this called for old standards, songs by Frank Sinatra or Tony Bennett.

". . . authorities are still looking for a London woman who has been linked to gruesome murders in the U.K. and in Bulgaria. Caroline Clifford, a twenty-five-year-old tour guide, was last seen in Kardzhali, Bulgaria, where she reportedly pushed a man into the path of a delivery truck. She is a suspect in a brutal murder in the U.K. Clifford is considered dangerous. . . ."

Caro twisted her head and saw her picture on the television. Even though she'd known this might happen, it was still a shock. Sky News was beamed into every hotel on the continent. If she didn't find answers in Meteora, and soon, she'd have to go underground. Changing her appearance wouldn't be enough. She'd have to be invisible.

———

Jude ordered room service and they ate in front of the television while Sky News recycled the same stories. "I've been thinking about that Bulgarian man I pushed in front of the truck," she said.

"Vampire, not a man."

"Will his stem cells make him regenerate?"

"Not after a catastrophic accident. That's where the vampire folklore comes in. The peasants used to behead a suspected vampire—no chance of regenerating a head."

"What about a stake to the heart?"

"Again, a catastrophic injury. Two areas of vulnerability are the brain and heart. They can't regenerate quickly enough."

"Tell me more."

He pushed back her hair. "They're not human. They're predators."

She nodded. "Keep going."

"It's their world, and we're just in it. They own the night. Some track humans for sport. Others are paid assassins. Maybe someone hired the Bulgarians to find your icon. We should hide it. Say, I've got an idea. We could stash it in the lining of my jacket."

He lifted his coat and ran his fingers along the seam.

She felt the leather. "Won't the icon be bulky?"

"Let's try."

She found a tiny sewing kit in the dresser and threaded the needle. Jude spread his jacket on the floor and cut along the seam with their hair-trimming scissors. Then he ripped the cover from a glossy magazine, fit it around the icon to protect the paint, and slipped the wood panel inside the lining.

He put on the jacket and stood. The icon's square edges jutted out.

"It won't work." She frowned. "We've ruined your jacket for nothing."

"But your uncle's passport will fit. We wouldn't want those clues to fall into the wrong hands."

She fitted the passport into the jacket's lining. Jude watched her fingers fly over the fabric as she stitched a tiny series of Xs. When she finished, he pulled a flat leather wallet from his backpack. "I need to confess something."

"About vampires?"

"No." He opened the wallet and plucked out a tattered photograph. "I fell in love with your picture before I ever saw you."

"My picture?"

"Your uncle sent it with his second letter. So I'd recognize you."

She stared at the photograph. It *was* her. Her uncle had taken it last summer when the garden was in full bloom. She wore a white dress with green buttons, and tomatoes spilled out of her apron. Her hair floated around her shoulders, blotting out the rose garden.

"Do you want to hear the whole story?" he asked.

She chewed her lip. Of course she wanted to hear, but if he kept going, she'd fall in love and it would definitely end with tears at bedtime—her tears.

He seemed to misinterpret her silence and continued talking. "After I heard about Sir Nigel's death, I went straight to your flat," he said. "It was the middle of the night. I kept looking at your picture. My plan was to ring you at daylight and show you the letters. Then, at dawn, I saw a gorgeous girl in ragged blue jeans run out of the building, her hair flowing around her, and bang, I fell in love."

"That's the most romantic story I've ever heard." She threw her arms around him and pressed her forehead against his.

"But it's not a story," he whispered. "It's the truth."

CHAPTER 33

———

LARISSA, GREECE

Georgi stopped at a petrol station on the outskirts of Larissa. He climbed out of the Dacia and unscrewed the gas cap. Odd scratching noises came from the trunk. He wasn't ready to open it. Not yet. A howl rose up in the dark and shapes moved along the dark road.

Georgi howled back, and the shapes bolted. He filled his tank and went inside to settle the bill. The clerk sat behind the counter, leaning over the *Novinite*'s sports pages. He didn't look up until Georgi's shadow fell over the newspaper.

"Can I help you?" the clerk asked.

Ten minutes later, Georgi stepped over the clerk's legs and emptied the cash register. As he tucked euros into his wallet, he saw the Clifford girl's photograph that Teo had stolen from the old professor. Nice. Georgi climbed into the Dacia and shoved the picture behind the visor. He was the hunter, and she was elusive prey.

The assignment had been to capture the girl and transport her to a laboratory in Romania. He'd been forbidden to harm her. In Georgi's opinion, it was all how you defined *harm*. The Geneva Convention did not apply.

He drove west, one bony hand draped over the steering wheel. On the console, his mobile phone vibrated and a London exchange popped up on the small display. It was Wilkerson.

"You left an eyewitness in Momchilgrad."

"Not for long," Georgi said. "I plan to stop there on my way back to Bulgaria."

"Good. Have you found Miss Clifford?"

"I am tracking her."

"Where the bloody hell are you?"

"Larissa."

"Can you travel faster?"

"I was shot. But do not worry." Georgi paused, smirking. "I will arrive in Kalambaka later tonight."

"You'd better. It's gone bollocks one too many times. This time, you will do exactly what I say. Are you following me?"

"Yes." Georgi bit down on the word.

"I've got a connection in Kalambaka—he's not a vampire, so behave yourself. Stick to animal blood for a while. Call the police department when you arrive. They'll be expecting you. Go with them to the monasteries. And remember—not one mark on the girl."

I will do as I please, Georgi thought, remembering the

Russian woman in his trunk. There was plenty of room for two women. But he would need to tie up Miss Clifford. She had fooled him before. But not again.

———

An hour later he drove into Kalambaka and checked into a hotel. It was a classy place with piano music drifting from the bar. Nice. The only sour note was the clerk, a pale man with scabs running up his arms. He reeked of drugs and death.

Georgi hung around the lobby, waiting for a tourist or barmaid, but the hotel was deserted. He walked to his room and propped Miss Clifford's picture on the bathroom counter so she could watch while he poured mouthwash over his wounds. His shoulder had festered. The Turkish bullet had left him shaky and nauseated, killing his thirst. But not his desire. It burned. Day and night it shimmered with a red flame.

"This time tomorrow," he told the picture, "you will be mine."

———

The hotel maid kept knocking on Georgi's door. He rose from his hideout in the bathtub, dragging the blankets with him, and walked stiff-legged into his room. The maid was still knocking. He'd forgotten to put out the Do Not Disturb sign.

"Go away," he yelled.

A moment later, he heard a rattle. He looked through the peephole. The cleaning bitch had pushed her cart away from his door. Georgi yawned and scratched the back of his head. He opened the door, hooked the Do Not Dis-

TURB sign on the handle, and bolted the door. He didn't have to leave his nest until dusk. Then he would meet the Kalambaka police and find the girl.

He walked to the sliding glass doors, standing away from the light. His room faced the big, phallic-shaped rocks. Nice. He turned on the television and waited for the weather report. It would be overcast and cold. He thought of the Clifford girl, and his pants seemed to shrink, the fabric tightening over his groin, pressing hard into his erection. "Soon, my love," he whispered. "Soon you will be mine."

CHAPTER 34

———

KALAMBAKA, GREECE

The morning sun cut through the lace curtains, dividing the room into light and shadow. Caro shifted in the narrow bed. Jude's arm fell over her hips, and she pressed against him.

Without opening his eyes, he smiled. "Mmmm, you're warm."

She was close enough to feel the pulse in his neck. She traced her finger up to his chin where the dark stubble began. He scooted down in the bed until his lips were even with hers.

"You're all I think about," he said. "When it's safe, I'll take you to Dalgliesh. I want my stepmother to meet you."

A wild flutter moved through Caro's chest. He'd take her to the castle with the hawthorn tree and the dogs waiting beside the drawbridge? He moved on top of her and caressed her face, his fingertips stroking her cheeks.

"My lady," he whispered. "My beautiful lady."

He kissed her tenderly and their tongues came together like dancers joining hands. The sweet softness of his mouth was a counterpoint to the hardness between his legs. She slipped her arms around his neck and moved closer, pressing her breasts against his chest. The chaotic thump of his heart excited her.

He broke the kiss and drew his fingertip over her lips as if painting them. "You're even more beautiful as a brunette," he said. His fingers drew circles on her wrist, and he guided her hand under the sheet. The tight skin swelled at her touch. She circled him and moved up and down, faster and faster.

A low hum vibrated in his throat. His hand fell away and brushed over her thigh. The tip of his thumb found her again and again until pleasure streaked all around her. She heard a tiny gasp and realized she'd cried out.

"I need you inside me," she said.

"And I need to taste you." He moved down, between her legs, and she felt the wet flicker of his tongue. She was on fire. The heat of it came in intense waves, threatening to drag her under. She closed her eyes and plunged into the flames.

He waited until she stopped shaking, and then he moved up, scraping his chin over her belly, and fit himself on top of her. She shivered when he rubbed himself against her. He entered her for a teasing moment, pulled away, then returned.

She could not breathe. All the air had left the room.

She pulled him closer, and he slid inside her. She grasped a handful of linen, shaking her head back and forth, and flew into the inferno.

They didn't get dressed until midmorning. Caro pulled on a black puffer jacket that she'd bought months ago at Phoebe's urging. "It's on the markdown rack, silly," Phoebe had said. "You can't afford *not* to get it."

"You look awfully gloomy," Jude said. He pulled on his coat and smoothed the leather where the passport was hidden.

"I was just thinking about Phoebe. She's dead because of me."

"If you'd been in the flat, you'd be dead, too." He paused. "If we find the right monk, perhaps we shouldn't mention the icon straightaway. Not until he proves that he's trustworthy."

"But my uncle sent me here."

"Caro, it's too dangerous. We don't know why your uncle was murdered."

"A monk isn't going to kill anyone."

"No, but he could report you for stealing an artifact. Do you have papers that prove it's yours?"

She shook her head.

"Let's find the monk," Jude said.

They put on their hats and sunglasses, then they grabbed their bags and left the hotel. Caro followed Jude down a path that curved through the olive groves to the foot of the Great Meteoron. Two goats ran out of a cave, their bells tinkling, and scampered over the rocks.

"How do we find this ruddy monastery?" Jude asked.

"The entrance is just up those steps," Caro said.

They caught up with a group of Italian and Australian tourists and turned up the rough stone steps. More tourists came down, talking on mobile phones and posing in front of the dramatic drop-offs. In front of Caro, the Australian woman read from a Fodor's guide, snapping her fingers at two bored-looking teenagers.

"How did the monks get up here?" asked a teenager with blue bangs.

"Nets and ladders," said a girl with a nose ring.

Jude and Caro followed the Australians into the Great Meteoron. Inside, it was dark and cool. Caro stood at the edge of the group, listening to the guide's commentary about icons and illustrated manuscripts in the old refectory.

One of the monks took over and explained how food had been hauled to the monastery with a winch-and-pulley system. Caro looked through a peephole in the sacristy and saw skulls and bones lined up on shelves.

"The bones of the monks," the guide said, pointing out that the monastery had a second name, Metamorphosis.

The group entered the shadowy church. Jude and Caro stopped to light candles. The guide explained that the building was shaped like a cross. Christ gazed down from a painting in the domed ceiling.

The church smelled damp and dusty, reminding Caro of the caves in the Gilf Kebir, where her uncle had taken her to see the cliff paintings. Jude stopped in front of a fresco that depicted the raising of Lazarus; he moved down to a futuristic painting titled *The Last Judgment and Punishment of the Damned*.

"What's this all about?" Jude asked.

"The saints are being tortured," she said. She started to

say that it reminded her of a Hieronymus Bosch painting, and then she saw the icons. They were set up in a row on movable tracks. She stepped closer and looked up at the Virgin and St. Nicholas. They were different from her icon, although she couldn't have said why. She reached into her bag and started to pull it out, but Jude squeezed her arm.

"Not yet," he said, nodding at a monk, who glided along in the darkness.

"Are you seeing a theme?" she whispered. "Metamorphosis. Change. Transformation."

They stepped out of the church, into the sunny cloister. The brightness no longer hurt her eyes and she stretched her arms. A chilly breeze moved through the stone arches, stirring her hair. A marmalade cat sunned on the ledge, and Caro sat down beside him.

"Your icon isn't like the ones in the church," Jude said. "It seems incomplete. Unfinished. Like the art was too big for the wood."

His leg pressed against hers, and a fluttery sweetness rippled through her. For a moment, she couldn't think, couldn't follow the conversation. He was talking about Venice, but she had to force herself to pay attention.

"We could fly out of Athens," he was saying.

"Hmmm?" she said dreamily.

"Athens," he said, grinning down at her.

"Well, I don't know." She pushed her sunglasses over her head and looked up at the sun. "Even if we made it through security, your titanium stakes won't."

"I can buy more." He frowned. "Maybe we should rent another locker and stash the icon."

"Before we do that, I'd like to photocopy it."

He shook his head. "We can buy a disposable digital camera and take pictures."

"You'd make a great spy."

He stretched his arms over his head. "What's next? Another monastery? Back to the hotel?"

"Let's just sit here awhile." She opened her bag, found her uncle's passport, and thumbed through the pages, grateful that the sunlight had knocked away the cobwebs in her head. *A fates hath torn*—what did it mean?

She found a pen in her bag, pushed up her sweater, and wrote the phrase on her arm. Jude bent over and studied the phrase. "Jot down *Father* and go from there," he suggested. She printed the letters, the tip of the pen denting her flesh, then she held out her arm. "We've got leftovers: a, s, a, t, h, t, o, n,"

"Oaths ant?" Jude shrugged. "Satan hot?"

She blinked at the letters. "Thanatos?"

He rubbed his finger across her arm, smudging the ink. "Wasn't that in *The Iliad*?"

"Yes!" She squeezed his arm. "Night and darkness became lovers. Their child was Thanatos. Better known as Death. The gods hated him because he represented mortality—and his sisters drank blood."

"It makes sense. Darkness. Night. Mortality. Metamorphosis. *Vrykolakas*. Thanatos. Sir Nigel knew about vampires, I'm sure of it."

"Thanatos might not be a real name," she said. "We could be pursuing a metaphor."

Three monks swept along the walkway, toward the church. Two of the men were tall and spidery, with dark beards. A portly monk with thick eyeglasses lagged behind, struggling with an armful of loose papers.

"Sit tight." Jude kissed her forehead. "I'm going to ask them about Father Death."

"Wait, I'm going with you."

"It's too risky."

From the roof, a bell pealed, the blunt clang reverberating through the cloister. A group of tourists came up the ramp and stopped to take photographs, all of them talking in broad, flat Midwestern accents.

"I'll just be a moment." Jude got up and walked across the stones, through the archway, toward the monks. "Father?" he called. "Excuse me, Father?"

All three monks turned. "Yes?" the round monk said in English.

"I'm sorry to interrupt," Jude said, "but I'm looking for a monk named Father Thanatos."

The tall monks cast long glances at Jude. The round one straightened his eyeglasses. "He is at Varlaam," he said. "But the monastery closes early today."

"Yes, of course," Jude said. "Thank you."

The monks rushed down the corridor, robes billowing, and turned the corner.

"That was too easy," Caro said, walking up. Jude didn't answer. His gaze was fixed over her head. She looked up, puzzled.

"Caro, put your sunglasses back on," he said.

"Why?"

"A lady is staring. Don't look. She's over by the archway."

Caro lowered her glasses. Coming straight toward her was a pear-shaped woman with short coppery hair. "Caro Clifford?" she said in a nasal Midwestern voice.

Caro grabbed Jude's hand and led him out of the archway, across the cloister, toward the church.

"Caro Clifford?" the woman called again.

"Keep holding my hand," Jude whispered. "There you go. Now, let's walk into the church. If she stops us, speak French, and speak convincingly. Tell her you don't speak English. I'll take it from there."

The woman cut across the courtyard, her shoes slapping on the stones. A short, balding man trailed behind her. "Caro? It's me, Angela Young from Springfield, Illinois? Remember me?"

"Je ne parle pas anglais," Caro said, lowering her chin.

"But . . ." The woman's eyes wobbled. "You were our guide for the English Heritage tour last month. We had our photo taken with you in Stratford-on-Avon. You had the worst time keeping everybody together, but you were awful sweet to us."

Jude put a protective arm around Caro's shoulder. "I'm sorry," he said with a French accent. "You're mistaken. My wife doesn't speak English."

The woman ignored him. "Caro? Don't you remember me?"

"We are on our honeymoon, if you'll excuse us." Jude smiled.

"Oh." The woman squinted, and wrinkles cut into her cheeks. "Well, she looks just like our guide. The hair is different. But . . . wow, I'm sorry. I feel like an idiot."

"They say everyone has a twin, no?" Jude smiled.

"I guess you're right." The woman frowned. "But, gosh, she's a dead ringer for our guide."

Jude led Caro through the last arch, into the church. They lit another penny candle and stepped around the movable icons.

"Is she gone?" Caro whispered, her voice echoing in

the gloom. She licked her finger and rubbed it over the ink marks.

"No. She followed us."

He tucked Caro's hand into the crook of his arm and gave it a reassuring pat. The American woman wandered across the nave, casting sidelong glances in their direction.

Caro leaned against Jude. "Let's go to Varlaam."

CHAPTER 35

————

VARLAAM MONASTERY
METEORA, GREECE

Caro ran up the one hundred ninety-five steps to Varlaam, hoping the physical exertion would distract her from Sky News and the American tourist, but her pulse was slow and steady, pounding against the bite wounds.

She stopped for a moment, waiting for Jude to catch up. From somewhere above, the monastery's bell clanged. She gripped the iron rail and tilted her head, searching for a bell. She saw nothing but rippled stones and a sharp blue sky.

Jude rounded the curve, then leaned against the wall, struggling to catch his breath. He glanced sideways at Caro. "I'm dying and you're not even sweating."

"I'm running on adrenaline," she said. "We've not much farther to go."

They stopped outside the Chapel of St. Cosmas and

St. Damien. Three tourists straggled out of the rough-hewn doors and turned down the curved steps. Before the doors shut, Caro caught one and slipped inside. Her shoes clapped over the floor as she walked down the aisle, looking for a monk. Jude walked past her. Above him the sun filtered through a stained-glass window, and dazzling colors splashed across his shoulders.

"It's shaped in a circle," he said, and walked over toward the north wall to examine a fresco.

"Jude?" She tugged the edge of his jacket. "What if that American woman calls the police?"

"They don't know we're staying at the Pension Arsenis. But we probably should move, and soon."

"I don't see how she recognized me." Caro raked her fingers through her hair. "Maybe I should've gone platinum blond. Aren't they supposed to have more fun?"

"She didn't recognize your outer appearance." Jude reached for her hand. "It was your voice, your mannerisms."

"Then I'm screwed."

They left the church and turned up another stone staircase. Caro stopped next to a stone arch and watched a dove wheel through the haze. In the distance, the Piniós River twisted through the mountains. The wind blew over her face and she felt weightless, as if she could rise into the blue air.

"Now I understand why *Meteora* means 'levitating,' " she said. The floating sensation continued as she turned up another series of curved steps. A pomegranate tree grew next to a terrace, and one fruit dangled from a limb. A monk with a white beard set a ladder next to the tree. The wind snapped his black robe as he climbed toward the fruit.

"Father?" Caro said.

The monk turned. "I am sorry, but the monastery closed at one," he said. "Please, come back tomorrow at nine A.M."

"We won't be here tomorrow," Caro said.

The monk grasped the pomegranate. The branch dipped low and creaked, and then the fruit snapped free. The monk balanced it on his palm. "The monastery is closed," he said, a bit louder this time. "I am late for prayers."

He straightened his square hat. His eyes were the shape and color of Kalamata olives. Beneath them, deep grooves cut into the wrinkled flesh. He started to say something but seemed to reconsider. He slipped the pomegranate into his pocket, gripped the ladder, and started down.

"We were told that Father Thanatos lives at Varlaam," Jude said.

The monk turned, blinking at Jude. "I have not heard that name in a while," he said.

"Do you know him?" Jude asked.

"Indeed I do," said the monk. "I *am* Father Thanatos. At least, I was. But that was many years ago. It was a nickname. I earned it by presiding over funerals in Kalambaka. My true name is Father Aeneas."

"We've been looking for you," Caro said.

"May I ask why?" The monk lowered his eyebrows.

"I was hoping you could explain," she said, clasping her hands. How much should she tell?

"Pardon?" The monk looked confused.

"I think my uncle wanted me to find you," Caro said.

"Who is your uncle, my child?"

"Nigel Clifford. He was an archaeologist."

"Yes, yes. I know Sir Nigel. He is your uncle?"

She nodded.

"Why didn't you say this?" The monk smiled. "Sir Nigel and I are old friends. He brought you to Meteora once. I'm sorry, your name escapes me."

"Caro Clifford."

"Yes, yes. Now I remember." Father Aeneas clapped his hands. "Where is Sir Nigel? Will he be joining us?"

Caro started to speak, but her throat tightened.

Jude put a steadying hand on her elbow. "Sir Nigel was killed," he said.

The monk crossed himself and whispered something in Greek. "Please, follow me," he said.

He climbed the wooden staircase, surprisingly agile for someone his age. Jude and Caro followed him into a breezeway with an arched, ribbed roof. The monastery spread out like a tiny town, with cobbled walkways, stone arches, storerooms, and the winch tower with nets and ladders.

The monk turned into a cloister and sat on a bench. He dragged a handkerchief from a deep pocket and wiped his face. In a raspy, wavery voice, he sang a few lines from "*O mio babbino caro.*" "It's a lovely aria, but you do not look like a *Caro*," he said. "You look like a princess. A princess named Caroline. However, you were not named for a Puccini opera, were you?" He broke out into song again: "Oh, my dear papa . . ."

He's senile. Caro looked up at Jude.

"When were you and Sir Nigel here?" Father Aeneas asked Caro. "Wasn't it twenty years ago? Or perhaps you were too young to remember."

Caro had been young, but she recalled the trip. It was the year after her parents had died.

"Oh, my dear Caroline, I can see little flashes of that afternoon," Father Aeneas said. "Your uncle carried you up the last forty steps to Varlaam. I gave you Turkish Delight—the sugar revived you. You were merrily turning cartwheels. Sir Nigel thought you would topple over the edge. I did, too. You had ceaseless energy."

He broke off, gesturing at the cloister. It was surrounded on all four sides by the arched, covered walkways. "You played here. It was summer, and you picked cucumbers in my little garden. I still have one."

He pointed to a straggly vine that snaked up a wall, and Caro saw a ghost of herself, a girl with thick dark blond curls, eating candy and picking cucumbers.

Father Aeneas made a humming noise, then he said, "Sir Nigel and I went into my study and looked at an unusual icon. If I am not mistaken, it belonged to you."

Caro's head snapped up and she placed one hand on her bag. Jude touched her shoulder and said, "Show him."

The monk's eyes widened as she pulled out the icon and removed the plastic. The sun glanced off the colors, sending up a blinding flash of gold.

"This is God's guiding hand," Father Aeneas said. "May I hold it, please?"

Caro placed the icon on his lap.

"Look into the figure's eyes." Father Aeneas pointed to the red-robed woman. "They will follow you, yes?"

Caro nodded. This was a detail she'd figured out long ago. "What else can you tell me?"

"About your icon? I am not an iconologist. But Greece is famous for them. Some of our brothers paint them for tourists. So I know a little." He traced his fingers around the icon, his thick nails scratching over the mitered corners. "Every color is meaningful. Figures are also symbolic. I've never seen another one with a female."

"Is she a saint or a martyr?" Caro asked.

"No, she is a metaphor," the monk said.

"Of what?"

"I do not know."

"What are these metal brackets?" Jude asked, pointing to the brass plates.

"Hinges," Father Aeneas said. "This icon is part of a triptych."

"What is that?" Jude squinted.

"Three individual panels of art. When you put them together they create a larger picture." Father Aeneas placed the icon on his knees and framed it with his palms. He folded his hands, hiding the art, then parted them.

"Now you see it, now you don't," he said. "That is the purpose of the hinges. Caroline's icon forms the center of the triptych."

Caro stared at his hands. It seemed like a small detail, yet her uncle had never mentioned it. Had her icon been stolen? Ripped from its hinges by thieves, the panels sold on the black market?

"Where are the other panels?" she asked.

Father Aeneas ignored her and cut his eyes at Jude. "I didn't catch your name, young man."

"I'm Jude. Caro's friend."

"Come, let's move into the church," Father Aeneas said. "It's on the other side of the cloister."

Father Aeneas rose from the bench. Gripping the icon like a steering wheel, he led them across the cloister, into an archway, toward the church. Outside the door, *Agii Pandes*—"All Saints"—was carved into the stone.

Jude opened the door, and they stepped inside. Light streamed from high windows, illuminating swirling dust motes. On the left wall, candlelight flickered over a fresco that showed St. Sisois kneeling over the bones of Alexander the Great. The monk handed the icon to Jude and nodded at the fresco.

"Life passes on a butterfly's wing," he said. "Death floats behind it on a ceaseless wind."

He moved across the nave. "I came here before the Second World War. I stood on the balcony and watched Kalambaka go up in flames. The smoke was so thick I felt sure God would hide Meteora from the Nazis. But they came. The monasteries were picked clean. Varlaam held many treasures. Crucifixes, codices, icons, gold communion cups—all gone. They even took the monastery's bell."

"Was it returned?" Caro remembered the bell she'd heard earlier.

"Never. A replacement was donated." Father Aeneas pointed toward the south nave. "Do you see the three-paneled icon? It is a triptych. A classic example of dualism."

"Did Hieronymus Bosch paint it?" Caro asked.

"Correct." The monk's small yellow teeth flashed as he smiled. "A reproduction, of course. Notice the demons are blue."

"They aren't frightening in the least," Jude said.

"Those imps aren't what they seem," Father Aeneas said. "They represent every possible emotion. Each demon is unique. The clergy were horrified by Bosch's work. They denounced him as an alchemist and linked him to the Cathars."

"Cathars?" Jude asked.

"French heretics," Father Aeneas said. "I'm not sure

of their origins. But they developed quite a following in the eleventh century. They stopped tithing, and Rome threw a fit. Pope Innocent sent crusaders to teach the backsliders a lesson. It got out of hand, and the Cathars were butchered."

"Was that the Albigensian Crusade?" Caro asked.

"Indeed." Father Aeneas smiled. "You're a scholar like your uncle?"

"Not anymore."

"No? A pity." The monk tucked his hands into his sleeves. "The Albigensian Crusade ignited the Grand Inquisition."

French history wasn't Caro's métier, but heretics were. She nodded politely. Jude gazed at the Bosch triptych, leaning closer to study the demons.

Father Aeneas pointed to the south wall. "You will appreciate this fresco. It depicts Jesus in the wilderness. The devil is here, too, causing mischief. More duality. Good and evil, with precious little in between. If you mix white and black paint, you create gray. You will never see this color in an icon."

"So, in the world of medieval art, duality is good and evil?" Jude asked. "Or anything with two sides?"

"Both," Father Aeneas said. "You've heard of yin and yang?"

"Of course." Jude nodded.

"Augustine believed that God created darkness so we'd be sure to notice the light."

"That's a hell of a way to go about it," Jude said, hastily adding, "Sorry, Father."

"I am not offended." The monk looked up at the fresco. "I hear this daily. Tourists are shocked and fascinated by the graphic art. They wonder why pictures of devils and demons appear in a holy place."

"More duality?" Jude asked.

"It means the devil can be found anywhere," Father Aeneas said. "Even in a monastery."

CHAPTER 36

Father Aeneas fed them figs, cheese, and crusty bread with jam. Then he went off to his prayers. He caught up with them at dusk and led them up a spiral staircase, where blue light spilled through the arched windows. At the top of the stairs, Caro saw tall bookshelves.

"Welcome to my library," Father Aeneas said. "Varlaam's manuscripts were removed to Saint Stephen's and Metamorphosis," he said. "Theft is still a problem. Even the holy are tempted. We had to put the books behind bars—literally. But I managed to keep a few."

"It's an impressive collection." Caro ran her finger along a shelf, over books with ragged spines or no spines at all. At the other end of the room was a niche with glass doors. Inside, a book lay open on a pedestal, the gilt pages opened to brightly colored drawings.

"It's a twelfth-century Byzantine Psalter," Father Aeneas said. "It was stolen from Varlaam during the war. Years later, it was found in Berlin. God's goodness brought it back to us."

Jude walked over to the glass. "It looks well preserved."

"It's in a place where light can't destroy it," Father Aeneas said. "Even ultraviolet light is a danger."

"Do you keep it open all the time?"

"I do. Some people bind them. However, this manuscript has survived a long while. It will be here after I am gone. Would you like to touch it?" Father Aeneas slid open the glass partition.

"Er, no." Jude shrank back.

"Go ahead." The monk stepped away from the niche, his robe billowing.

Jude moved forward, and his fingers grazed the page. "It feels like silk."

"It's vellum. The leaves were made from sheepskin. Turn the page—notice the roughness? It was made from the woolly part of the hide."

Jude and Caro exchanged glances.

"Notice how the handwritten text only covers a small percentage of each leaf." Father Aeneas waved one gnarled finger. "See how the large paintings dominate each leaf? Illustrated manuscripts were pictorial tomes for the illiterate—a brilliant way for peasants to understand God's word."

Father Aeneas walked to a long pine table and cleared a stack of papers. He smiled up at Caro. "Let's take a look at your icon, shall we?"

She set it down. The red-robed martyr seemed large, out of proportion to the background—a starry sky, castle, battlefield, and part of what appeared to be a turret. Behind the turret, sharp-edged mountains plunged into a distinctive V.

"Remember, symbolism is in every detail," Father Aeneas said.

"There's a lot of red in my icon," she said. A shadow crossed over the table as Jude leaned over her shoulder.

"It has many meanings. Fury, enchantment, time without end, and literal bloodshed. A red cloak indicates martyrdom. As a background color, it symbolizes eternal life. These are a few interpretations. There are others. For example, the pomegranate is deeply metaphorical."

He pulled the fruit from his pocket. "It is unusual for this tree to produce in December. See the fleshy red skin? It is an old symbol of blood. The cycle of life and death. Immortality and resurrection. I am sure you know the Greek myths attached to this fruit?"

"Persephone, Hades, and the seasons," she said.

"Look closely, my dear." Father Aeneas pressed his thumbnail into the fruit. The gash instantly filled with moisture. "The pomegranate's juice signifies martyrs' blood."

He set the warm fruit on her palm.

"This is fascinating." Caro hesitated, looking at Jude for help. She didn't want to hurt the monk's feelings, but she found it hard to believe that her uncle had sent her to Meteora for a lesson in icon symbolism. "But I still don't know why Uncle Nigel directed me here."

"So I could fill in the missing pieces," Father Aeneas said. "You see, I have an icon that fits your triptych."

Dots spun in front of her eyes, and her pulse whooshed in her ears.

Jude put his hand on her shoulder. "May we see it, Father?" he asked.

"Yes, indeed," the monk said. "I keep it downstairs. Shall we go?"

A siren echoed in the distance. She dropped the pomegranate and ran to the window. Way down in the dusky valley, police cars swept up the narrow road; they forked off into different directions. One car for each monastery.

She turned to Jude and gripped the front of his jacket, her fingers sinking into the leather. "That woman called the police."

"Who?" Father Aeneas asked.

"A long story, Father," Jude said. "Is there any place we can hide?"

"Hide you—why? What have you done?"

"The men who killed Sir Nigel are hunting Caro," Jude said.

Father Aeneas's beard trembled. "The police will not harm her."

"They'll arrest her. And whoever killed her uncle will hear about it and come after her."

"Arrest her? For what?" Father Aeneas stepped backward.

Jude squeezed Caro's hand. "Get your icon and let's go."

"I left my bag in the cloister." Her hands shook when she picked up the icon.

"Wait!" Father Aeneas held up one hand. "I do not know what you have done. But I will help you both. Follow me to the church, if you please."

Jude ran ahead to fetch her bag. By the time he joined them in the church, the sirens were closer; the same two notes bleated over and over. Father Aeneas led them behind the sanctuary and slid his hand over the rough wall. He grasped an edge of the cornerstone and pulled. The wall creaked open and cool, musty air drifted out. Smooth rock steps plunged down, then curved into darkness.

"This is where the brothers hid from Turkish pirates," Father Aeneas said, and pushed a flashlight into Jude's hand.

"Thank you, Father," Caro said. "I'll explain everything later."

"I'm doing this for your uncle. But please hurry," the monk said, his voice rising. "At the bottom of the staircase, turn right. There's a cave. It's low, at the bottom of the wall. Go inside. I will fetch you when it's safe."

Caro braced one hand against the limestone wall and stared down. The stairwell looked bottomless.

"Peace be with you, my children," Father Aeneas said. The heavy door scraped shut, and everything went black. Even the wailing sirens snapped off. Jude clicked on the flashlight and aimed the beam over the stone wall. He took Caro's hand and led her down the steps. They looked like something poured into a mold.

"Careful," he said at the bend. Here, the steps became steep and uneven, and he gripped her arm. A tumble down this staircase would mean broken bones, or worse. She moved cautiously, trying to shake the feeling that she was traveling into Dante's nine circles of hell. She imagined the door above them sliding open, the police swarming down.

Jude rounded a corner, and the steps ended. He aimed the light over the walls. They stood in a T-shaped corridor. "Father Aeneas said to turn right, didn't he?" Jude's voice echoed.

She nodded, straining to hear noises. There was nothing but the distant trickle of water. They moved down the narrow passage and stopped in front of a rocky outcropping.

"Is that the cave?" she asked.

"Looks like it." Jude squatted. The opening was set low into the wall, just as the monk had said, hidden by a broad rocky lip.

"I'll take a look." Jude crawled under the ledge. "This is a cave, all right," he said, his voice echoing.

She pushed her bag under the rock, then crept through the opening. Jude took her hand and they moved deeper into the cave. It was so cold, her breath stamped the air and goose bumps rushed down her arms. How long would they have to stay down here? Hours? Forever? It was possible—the monk could have a stroke or heart attack. She glanced at the stygian crevices, her pulse roaring in her ears.

Jude ran the beam along the walls; stalactites soared above them, jutting from the rock ceiling. The chamber resembled a vampire's lair, with streaking shadows and gloomy chambers. She stepped closer to Jude, and the noise in her ears subsided, only to be replaced by muffled sirens.

"The cave probably opens to the outside," Jude said. "Let's hope the gap is too small for humans."

"Humans?" The word echoed.

"A small animal could slip through. Remember the goats we saw earlier?"

"If there's an opening, can the police see our flashlight?"

"Better not chance it."

She heard a click, and everything went dark. "Do you think that tourist called the police?"

"The police got here too fast. Bureaucracy moves slowly."

If not the woman, then who? Caro shook violently.

"You're freezing," Jude said.

Her hand bumped into his shirt, and she flattened her palm against it, feeling the rhythmic thump of his heart. "I'm scared. Talk to me."

He drew in a breath. "I guess you've figured out that I'm a bit of a science nerd."

"You're not." She moved her hand down his arm, found his hand, and gave it a squeeze.

"It's true. My second year at Cambridge, I developed a crush on a girl in microbiology class. As a token of my affection, I gave her a petri dish that had grown a perfect specimen of *E. coli*. She pitched the dish into the trash bin and accused me of trying to infect her with bacteria."

"That's the best story ever," Caro said.

"I learned one thing." He laughed. "Never give a dish of germs to a woman as a valentine."

CHAPTER 37

Georgi ran over the stone bridge and turned up the winding path. He paused by the circular steps and waited for the Greek officers to catch up. Their flashlight beams swept along the rocks, blending into the torches that shone upward from the ground. In the distance, police cars moved down the road toward Agia Triada, St. Stephen's, and Metamorphosis.

Georgi raised his head and sniffed. The girl's smell was strong. Now that Teo was dead, he needed a companion. He'd dumped the Russian woman at the base of one of the monasteries. She was comatose and would remain that way until blood was infused into her mouth or veins. Not likely. So he'd decided to turn the Clifford girl. She was much nicer. Shapelier. He liked a woman with curves. Wilkerson would not approve. But it would be too late.

Georgi and the girl would disappear. They would reemerge after Wilkerson had turned to dust. Georgi had comrades in London who would be more than willing to help.

A policeman rounded the bend, then stopped running, as if caught in the black bead of Georgi's gaze. The man behind him stumbled. Georgi smelled their fear. He heard the blood moving through their veins.

"No need to panic." Georgi smoothed one hand down his new jacket. He had taken it from a tourist at the Kalambaka hotel.

The policemen hung back, watching him with hooded eyes.

Georgi sighed. He couldn't communicate with these Greek pigs. He waved toward the stairs, indicating that they should go first, but they huddled against the rocks. Georgi shrugged and started up the stairs, restraining himself from streaking ahead. His knife felt hard and heavy in his pocket, knocking against his thin leg.

He reached the top long before the Greeks. From the stairs, he heard their harsh, rapid breathing as they struggled to climb the last few steps. He heard their overburdened hearts pumping.

The girl's smell grew stronger as he curved up to a terrace. A monk stood on a wooden platform beneath a slanted roof, his arms folded at his waist. The policemen staggered up, wiping their faces on their sleeves. The monk said something in Greek. The words flew past Georgi, to the men. The monk turned to Georgi.

"You are looking for someone?" he asked in Bulgarian.

Georgi nodded and started to explain. The monk's face twisted in revulsion. Georgi knew that look. He returned it with a belligerent gaze and held up the wrinkled fax. "Have you seen this woman?"

The monk's eyes flitted over the picture. "She was here today."

Georgi waited for the monk to continue, but the old man looked at the Greeks and rattled off a long sentence. The words hurt Georgi's ears. He wanted to pick up a stone and crush the monk's skull.

The policemen babbled something, and the monk fixed his gaze on Georgi. "You are welcome to search the monastery. But you will not find the woman."

"Did you see where she went?" Georgi continued to hold up the fax. "Her name is Caroline Clifford. She is a British national—and very dangerous. She has killed two people."

"Clifford?" The monk put one finger to his lip. "A British archaeologist by this name was murdered in your country."

"He was." Georgi's eyelids twitched.

"And you were the investigating officer?" asked the monk.

"I work with the Interior Ministry." Georgi stuffed the fax into his pocket and reached for his badge. He had been flashing it all night, and not one member of the Kalambaka police force had questioned it.

Wind stirred the pomegranate tree, then washed over the monk, flattening his beard. He looked like a wizard, Georgi thought.

"Shall I take you on a tour?" the monk asked. "If not, I bid you good night and Godspeed."

The monk spoke to the policemen. They shook their heads and looked at Georgi. The monk headed toward an arched opening, his robe floating around his feet. Above him, the monastery loomed, dark and forbidding.

Liar, Georgi thought. But the night wasn't over. He watched the monk blend into the darkness. Then he picked up a stone. He threw it over the ledge and waited for it to hit the bottom. But it never did.

CHAPTER 38

Caro heard a scrabbling sound in the outer chamber. Then a broad slash of light moved in front of the cave's opening.

"Are you here?" Father Aeneas's voice echoed. "The police are gone. You may come out."

They grabbed their bags and hurried to the opening, where Father Aeneas's sandals were visible beneath the ledge. After Jude and Caro crawled out, the monk raised a lantern.

"This way, children," he said and turned down the corridor. "We have much to discuss. My friend Demos will be here at dawn. He will guide you out of Meteora— and Greece, if God wills it."

They followed the monk up the stairs and waited while he closed the passageway. He strode out of the church, across the cloister, into a large room with stone walls, a domed ceiling, and a cupboard. On the left side of the room, an arched door opened onto a terrace.

"Sit," Father Aeneas said, waving at a table piled with books.

Jude pulled out a chair for Caro, then he sat down beside her, his hand lingering on her shoulder.

"A Bulgarian man just left. He posed as a policeman." Father Aeneas walked to a small altar table and lit a candle. Light blazed up, shining into the faces of St. Jude and the Holy Mother. The monk crossed himself and walked to the cupboard. He reached for a decanter and turned to Caro.

"The man claimed you murdered two people."

Caro shook her head. "It's not true."

"The Kalambaka policemen were frightened of this man." Father Aeneas set the decanter on a tray, then added three cups. "He asked if you were here. I denied it, but I do not think he believed me."

Jude touched Caro's arm. "We can't stay here. What if he comes back? Let's take our chances in Kalambaka."

"I need a better disguise—red hair or a wig."

"The chemist closed at five," Father Aeneas said. He shuffled to the table, the cups rattling, and set down the tray. "But souvenir shops are still open."

Caro glanced at her watch. Six P.M. Damn.

"You can stay at a hostel in Kastraki." Father Aeneas placed a cup in front of Jude. "I'll arrange for Demos to pick you up in the morning."

"No." Jude held up his hand. "I don't mean to be rude. It's best if you and your friend aren't involved."

"As you wish." Father Aeneas lifted a cup. "I assume you and Caro are not traveling under your real names?"

Jude didn't answer.

"I do not recommend flying out of Athens with false credentials."

"We're not going there," Caro said, and Jude squeezed her arm.

Father Aeneas caught the gesture and frowned. "Leaving by bus or train will be difficult. The military police can be unpredictable—and they will have Caro's picture. The Serbian borders are stringent, too. But you might have luck with a ferry."

"Caro and I will think about it," Jude said.

"Do not ponder too long," Father Aeneas said. "You'll need reservations. Demos has connections, but he will need your passport numbers and the names you are traveling under. If you do not trust him, you may borrow his car, or he can drive you."

Caro reached for her bag. Jude's mouth tightened as he rummaged in his backpack and produced a passport. The cover was dark red, just like Caro's.

"Father, thank you," she said, pushing her passport across the table.

"Don't thank me yet." The monk poured brandy into his cup. "The night is not over. And we must discuss a troublesome matter."

What now? Caro thought. The French doors rattled, and an icy draft seeped into the room. The red candles flickered, and spiky shadows flashed on the wall. The monk fixed Caro with a penetrating stare. "I know why Sir Nigel sent you," he said. "All those years ago, when he brought you to Varlaam, he wanted me to examine pages from an illustrated manuscript."

Caro's heart thrummed. *Vellum Venice. Monk Icon. Yes, it's all connected.*

"The title was *Historia Immortalis*," Father Aeneas said. "You've heard of this book?"

Caro shook her head.

"During the Albigensian Crusade, copies were ruthlessly ferreted out and burned." The monk lifted his eyebrows. "With their owners."

"Over a book?" Jude's forehead wrinkled.

"Many believe it is a history of the immortals. But it is so much more."

"Immortals?" Caro's hand flew up to her neck. "You mean *vampires*?"

Father Aeneas lifted his hand. "Before you question my sanity, let me clarify. I believe in things that cannot be explained. It is called faith. For a myth to exist in so many cultures, it must have truth. I *know* the immortals exist. I have seen them. And I have read their book. To them, *Historia Immortalis* is a sacred text. But for us, it has the power to shake Christianity, and humanity itself."

"You're off the rails," Jude said.

"Not about this," Father Aeneas said curtly.

Caro's mouth went dry. "Tell me about this book."

"It was translated during Charlemagne's era. That's why it is called a Carolingian manuscript. You, dear Caroline, were named for it."

"Me?" She clasped her hands to keep them steady.

"I am surprised Sir Nigel did not tell you." Father Aeneas scraped his fingers through his beard. "Your icon dates from this period. When the triptych is complete, it shows the location of the complete *Historia Immortalis*. At one time it had one hundred vellum leaves. But they vanished. Except for ten."

Jude rose to his feet. "Caro's icon is mixed up with a book about vampires?"

A cold finger scraped down her spine. She leaned back in her chair, shaking her head.

"Your parents were murdered for it," Father Aeneas said, his eyes dark and sorrowful.

Lies. Nothing but lies. All the blood drained from her head, and she felt dizzy.

Father Aeneas leaned closer. "Was your mother's name Vivienne?"

Caro just stared.

"Your mother was a manuscript curator for the British Library," Father Aeneas said. "The year before you were born, Sotheby's auctioned ten pages of *Historia Immortalis* along with the center panel to a triptych. Vivienne's husband collected vampire memorabilia. He sent her to bid on the artifacts. Collectors from all over the world came to the auction. The bidding was reckless. Another collector started bidding against Vivienne. A Frenchman named Philippe Grimaldi. He fell in love with your mother before the auction ended. By the way, the winning bid was one point two million pounds—placed by Vivienne. Shortly after the sale, the book and the icon went missing. So did your mother and Monsieur Grimaldi."

"Wait, I'm confused." Caro pinched the bridge of her nose. "You said Vivienne's *husband* sent her to the auction. My father was Philippe Grimaldi. How could he send her to the auction and bid against her?"

"Vivienne was not married to Monsieur Grimaldi. She was married to someone else."

"This is ridiculous." Caro pushed away from the table. "You're saying my married mother picked up a man at an auction and ran off with him?"

Father Aeneas's eyes wobbled. "Monsieur Grimaldi wasn't a man. He was immortal."

CHAPTER 39

Caro bolted from her chair, and it crashed to the floor. Terror exploded in her chest. "My father wasn't a—" She broke off, unable to say the word.

"He was a vampire," Father Aeneas said.

"This is a bloody outrage," Jude cried. "Where's your proof?"

"I have none." The monk lifted his hands, fingers splayed.

"Of course not." Jude balled his hands into fists. "What are you playing at?"

"It was Sir Nigel's destiny to explain *Historia Immortalis* to Caroline. Not mine." Father Aeneas's voice shook. "Now he is gone, and I am the only one who knows the truth."

"How convenient," Jude said. "And cruel."

"Truth and cruelty are bound together." Father Aeneas glanced at Caro. "Before I took my vows, I was a physician in Athens. I learned about the immortals. They freely mate with humans, but it is nearly impossible for them to reproduce. True, mortal women can conceive children by vampires, but the pregnancies usually end in miscarriages. In less than half a percent of cases, a baby is carried full term. These rare offspring are called hybrids—half vampire, half human. And they possess unique traits."

"Traits?" Jude's face hardened. "Biting? Blood drinking? Regeneration?"

"Hybrids do not consume blood," Father Aeneas responded.

Caro couldn't catch her breath. She sat down in Jude's empty chair and squeezed her hands, forcing herself to gulp air. She wasn't a hybrid. The monk was lying or crazy. Why had Uncle Nigel sent her to Meteora? Maybe he hadn't. Maybe the anagrams had been a warning to stay away.

"In the old days, when a vampire bred with a human, the offspring was called a *Dhampir*," Father Aeneas said. "*Hybrid* is a modern term. They have unusual speed and strength, with an ability to heal rapidly. Most possess a hyperawareness of danger. Some can read minds. Others can sense when immortals are near—that is why hybrids often make successful vampire slayers."

"Why should I believe you?" she cried.

"I am something of an expert on the immortals. That is why your uncle sought me out. I traveled the world, searching for *Dhampirs*. In my whole life, I only found a dozen. But I am well aware of their characteristics. Also, Sir Nigel and I have both studied those ten pages of *His-*

toria Immortalis. He would want me to explain your hybridism, Caroline."

"I am *not* a hybrid."

"No? Do you sometimes know what people are thinking?"

"Never."

"When you were small, did you run faster than the other children? Were you immune to viruses that swept through the classroom? If you scraped your knee, did people marvel when your lesions healed at an accelerated pace?" His gaze sharpened as he stared at her throat.

Her hand flew to the bite marks. The wounds had scabbed over, but the flesh beneath felt warm and prickly.

Father Aeneas fingered his belt and the beads clicked softly. "I know what is written in *Historia Immortalis*. It is prohibited for a vampire to love a mortal. Yet they do, of course. Their libido is as powerful as their thirst. They are irresistible to humans. I like to compare them to cone shells. Their brown-and-white patterns are intricate as a mosaic. *Conidae* are toothed. Pick one up, and you shall feel their bite. They impale their prey and fill them with venom. They are hunters. Built for survival."

"What's this leading to—*vagina dentata*?" Caro glared at him from under her eyebrows.

"I do not mean literal teeth." The monk's cheeks reddened. "But you exude some type of pheromone that attracts, then repels. Halflings like yourself cannot form lasting romantic relationships with any human."

Caro swallowed, and her throat made a precise click. She remembered the mural in her nursery—a corridor of locked doors, a key on a table, the Cheshire cat, the Caterpillar, the Dormouse. She felt like Alice, curiouser and curiouser.

The monk released a feeble breath. "It is awkward to speak of it. But I will try. Have men always wanted you? Chased you? Like bees following sweetness. But after they taste you, the sugar turns bitter and the men fly away. No man can satisfy you."

Jude flinched, his eyes rounding.

Caro's throat tightened unbearably, and her lungs contracted. In a choking voice she said, "Jude gives me great pleasure. The most I've ever felt. And he isn't a vampire."

"You've been bitten." Father Aeneas gestured at her throat. "Hormones flooded your bloodstream—estrogen, progesterone, and even testosterone. You've become hypersexual. A doorknob could give you pleasure."

Her pulse throbbed against her temples. She shut her eyes and saw blood red, a color symbolizing menses, a woman coming of age. A tear ran down her cheek, and she brushed it off. How did the monk know about her Lost Boys? Their lust had dampened when they hadn't pleased her in bed. Even when she'd faked it, somehow they'd seen through her and moved on to more accessible women. Jude was the only man who'd left her weak and shaking, begging for more. She'd been easier to arouse lately, but she refused to believe that the bites had heightened her sexual response. She was falling in love with Jude. That was why she'd responded.

Now he pushed his hand through his hair, his face pale and troubled.

"I have upset you." Father Aeneas reached for her hand.

She jerked away, her eyes filling. Something cold and barbed streaked through her heart.

"Try to be strong, Caroline. Because you must hear why your parents died. A vampire who falls in love with a mortal is cast out of his or her clan. Your father violated this tenet. Your mother became pregnant and somehow carried you to term. You are a miracle, Caroline, but a dark one."

Jude splayed his fingers against the table. "You're saying Caro's parents were put to death because they fell in love?"

"No." The monk shook his head. "This miscegenation is a moral offense rather than a mortal one. It is not punishable by death. Monsieur Grimaldi and Vivienne were killed because they stole an icon, along with ten pages to *Historia Immortalis*. Vivienne's husband wanted those artifacts and had her murdered."

Jude pushed away from the table and stood. A vein ticked under his jaw. "Explain how *you* ended up with part of this bloody triptych."

"Many of my patients were vampires. A hybrid child contracted meningitis. Penicillin saved the boy, not I, but the parent was so grateful, he gave me his most prized possession: an icon. He'd stolen it from a German soldier. Presumably, it was part of a triptych. I believed the other panels would find each other."

Jude slammed his fist against the wall. Bits of plaster hit the floor.

Caro scrambled to her feet and grabbed his hand. He pulled it back. "Don't touch me," he said.

A black, sucking silence descended. Her stomach knotted, and bile spurted into her throat. She ran out of the room, her shoes clapping on the floor, the sound echoing in the empty hallway. Behind her, Jude and the monk began to argue. As their voices rose and fell, she hurried down the stairs, into the cloister, and leaned against a rock pillar. She looked down at the twinkling lights of Kalambaka. If only she hadn't come to Varlaam. She rubbed her arms. The friction over her breasts sent a wave of pleasure through her, but she didn't enjoy it. Now it only reminded her of all the painful things the monk had just told her. Her icon was linked to vampires. *Because her father was one.*

She stared up at the black sky, tears gliding down her neck, stinging the bite marks. When she was a small girl, her uncle had taught her to navigate by the stars. He'd lectured her about night-related things: comets, dusk-blooming flowers, and nocturnal animals, skipping over the immortals and their penchant for drinking blood. Yet he'd known about her connection to *Historia Immortalis.* He'd opted for nature lessons instead of Vampire 101, and he'd almost taken her secret to the grave.

A scuffling sound echoed behind her, and she turned. Jude walked out of the shadows, his backpack slung over one shoulder. She started toward him, but he held up one hand.

"If I don't come back, will you do something for me?"

She gaped up at him, her stomach clenching. Not coming back? Not ever?

His gaze flickered over her. "It's a big ask, but please don't mention the anagrams to the monk. Don't show him your uncle's passport."

Caro tilted her head. He was just like her uncle, whose motto was *Trust no one.*

"You distrust Father Aeneas?" she asked.

"You could put his life in danger. A Bulgarian man tracked you to Kalambaka." Jude's eyes hardened as he stared at the winking lights in the valley. "What if he's the vampire who kidnapped you?"

"You're scaring me."

"Promise you won't tell the monk about the anagrams."

She nodded.

"Maybe your kidnapper thinks you're hiding *Historia Immortalis*."

"I'm not."

"You've got the icon that shows where it's hidden. Father Aeneas has another panel." He pressed his lips together. "Please be careful."

"I'm a trouble magnet. You can't leave." Her chin wavered. "I'm falling in love with you."

He started to say something, then shook his head. He lifted a shaking hand and started toward the stairs.

"Wait." She shivered. "I don't have Uncle Nigel's passport. You do."

He shrugged off his jacket and tossed it into her arms. "Keep it."

She started to throw it at him, but he turned down the stone stairs and rounded a corner. He hadn't even said good-bye. As she slipped the coat over her shoulders, the smell of Acqua di Parma and man sweat wafted around her. His footsteps echoed in the steep rock walls as he ran down the steps. She started to call his name, then pressed her hand over her mouth. He wouldn't come back. Besides, if the Bulgarian vampire was lurking, her voice would alert him.

Tears slid around her mouth and pattered against the leather of his coat. She'd been dumped before, but no one had ever hurt her like this. She'd told him she was falling in love with him, but she'd lied. She was already in love. All her life, she'd waited and waited, yearning for a man she'd created in her head. She'd shown Jude her broken pieces and he'd shown her his. Those cracked bits had fitted together just as perfectly as their bodies had. But she'd turned out to be the one thing he despised.

Her neck tingled. Was someone watching her? She ran to the church, paused in the center aisle, and genuflected in front of the altar. With her knee still on the floor, she curled into a tight ball. Jude's coat covered her legs, and his smell rose up from the leather. No way had her father been a vampire. He'd listened to her prayers at bedtime, put Band-Aids on her cuts and scrapes, and whistled her to sleep with an old Beach Boys song—her song— "Caroline, No."

They'd never had visitors. It had been just the three of them. Philippe, Vivienne, and Caro. Behind their house had been a root cellar with cobwebbed passageways and dark green bottles stacked along the walls. Her father's home-made wine. Or so she'd thought. Could it have been blood?

She pictured him standing beside the stove, Vivienne's white apron tied low on his hips, while he tossed onions in a pan. She couldn't remember seeing him eat a meal. He'd only picked at food, but he'd always had a glass of dark red wine at his elbow.

A tremor began in her chest, as if something alive and buzzing had hatched, and memories swarmed out: a warm Tennessee night on the side porch, crickets shrilling from the weeds, a harvest moon skating over the mountains. Her mother had set out dishes: cold lemon chicken, asparagus, a salad sprinkled with wild pansies. From the hills came the high yipping of coyotes. "I'll see to them," her father had said, patting Caro's hand. He pushed back his untouched plate and rose from the table. He kissed

Caro's mother and stepped off the porch, across the yard, into the shadows. After that night, she did not hear the coyotes.

Now she lifted a shaking hand and stared at the white scar on her palm. If she was half vampire, why hadn't she healed? A tear fell off her chin and hit her Mound of Venus. Her hand wobbled so violently, the liquid lost its shape and spilled to her lifeline. She closed her hand.

No man can satisfy you, Father Aeneas had said.

Before Momchilgrad, she'd been a little frigid. Of course, that was like being a little dead, or a little pregnant. After the Momchilgrad vampire had bitten her, she'd begun to change. She'd made love to Jude, using her body in ways that had surprised her. Yet something greater than pleasure had swept through them. *He had felt it, too.*

A draft swept through the church, and the flickering flames of the candles quivered. She shivered again, rubbing her arms. Was she spiking another fever? She pulled Jude's coat around her and rocked back and forth.

Footsteps echoed behind her. She wiped her face and turned. Father Aeneas shuffled down the aisle, his robe billowing. He looked relieved when he saw her.

"Thank goodness," he said. "You are still here."

She jammed her fists into the pockets of Jude's coat and waited for the monk to mention vampires. Instead, he helped her to her feet and led her to a pew. She slid across the cold wood and clasped her hands. He hooked his cane on the back of a pew and sat down heavily. His spotted hand adjusted the folds of his robe.

"You've been weeping," he said.

"Even freaks have feelings."

"You are a caring young woman. Of course you have

feelings. When you have calmed down, I will explain vampirism."

"I'm a half vampire, so just explain half."

He stroked his beard. "It has taken me a lifetime to study the immortals. Many of the myths are exaggerated. But some have a kernel of truth. For instance, it is true that the immortals are hypersensitive to daylight. It is not fatal, but ultraviolet rays affect the retina. The blindness is temporary unless exposure is prolonged. The sun also causes third-degree burns to the skin. The condition has been confused with porphyria, but it is more severe."

"But I've seen them in daytime."

"If the day is overcast, and they are desperate to feed, they can wear sunblock. It gives them some protection, but not for long."

"Do they drink anything besides blood?"

"They can. It's by choice, not for survival. The purists believe that food and water intensify the blood craving, and they abstain."

"Purists? What do you mean?"

"The old, elite vampires are more conservative. I call them purists. They are morally opposed to killing humans or animals. Your father was one."

"What do purists drink?"

"Many are wealthy. They own blood banks and receive transfusions."

"But some immortals are violent, right? Because the one who bit me seemed . . . crazed."

"A fledgling vampire, most likely. They cannot control the desire to feed until they receive an initial loading of blood. A fledgling needs blood the way a swimmer needs air. But this phase quickly passes."

"I think my uncle was killed by vampires. Now his body has gone missing from the morgue." A fresh surge of tears gathered behind her eyes. "Will he become a vampire?"

"I do not know. It takes two vampires—sometimes more—to create an immortal. As you can imagine, there are rules about *that* in *Historia Immortalis.*"

"Jude says that vampirism is caused by stem cells."

"How would he know this?" Father Aeneas tilted his head.

"The short version? He's a biochemist. He studied vampire mice—until real vampires tried to kill him."

Father Aeneas sketched a cross in the air, then released a heavy sigh.

"Uncle Nigel was bitten repeatedly." Caro swiped a finger under her eyes. "Maybe he got enough stem cells, and now he's . . ."

"I've no idea. Modern science is beyond my scope. I practiced medicine before the age of stem cells and organ transplants."

She folded her arms. "I want to know about my mother's husband."

"His name is Harry Wilkerson. He owns a British pharmaceutical company. He's quite wealthy—and ruthless."

"My mother was gentle. She wouldn't have married someone like that."

"I only know what your uncle told me. Vivienne's parents died in a plane crash when she was twenty years old. Apparently, she was vulnerable, and Wilkerson took advantage. Wormed his way into her heart. Your uncle never met him, but he'd heard tales from Vivi's cousins. It was a desperately unhappy marriage."

"Was he a vampire, too?"

"No."

"So my mother went to an auction and fell in love with Monsieur Dracula?"

"Apparently."

"Wouldn't a ruthless man like Wilkerson suspect that his wife was having an affair?"

"Apparently her curating business required travel. He was accustomed to her absences."

"Then what happened? She married Philippe?"

"No. According to your uncle, Vivienne was afraid to petition for a divorce. She knew Wilkerson would track her down. And he did."

Caro stared straight ahead, her vision blurring as she tried to absorb the information. What if Philippe wasn't her father? She wouldn't be a hybrid. And she could find Jude and explain.

"Do you happen to know if my mother was pregnant with me when she ran off with Philippe?"

"Yes—according to your uncle."

"Then who got her in that condition? She played around with Philippe while she was married to Wilkerson. He could be my biological father."

"It's possible." Sweat beaded on Father Aeneas's forehead. "But unlikely. Sir Nigel said you were born nine months after the auction."

Dammit, she couldn't catch a break. Her birthday was December fifteenth, but with all the chaos, she'd forgotten. In just eleven days she'd turn twenty-six, and she'd gotten an early present: Everything she knew about herself was a lie.

"For a monk, you sure know how to cause trouble,"

she said. "You haven't offered proof that Philippe was my father. And you chased off my boyfriend."

Father Aeneas's beard trembled. "There's an old saying: Do not confuse the message with the messenger."

"I'm trying. But I'm stunned." *And in denial.* "You know what? I'm glad Mother found happiness with her vampire." Caro smoothed her hand along Jude's coat, trying to feel the edges of the passport, but the leather was too thick. "Did Uncle Nigel know that Philippe was a vampire?"

"Apparently Vivi left a letter in your knapsack that explained the icon, the manuscript, her romance—and you."

"Wrong. She put an icon in my bag, not a manuscript."

"Your uncle told me too much and told you too little." Father Aeneas grimaced. "The night of the fire, your mother placed an icon and ten vellum pages of *Historia Immortalis* in your knapsack. She'd won them at Sotheby's. Your uncle made discreet inquiries about the artifacts. His research led him to Meteora and to me. I advised him to destroy the vellum—it's cursed. But he had another plan, one that he refused to share with me."

Vellum. Venice. Her ears filled with a high-pitched buzzing. Shouldn't she tell Father Aeneas about her uncle's passport? She started to remove Jude's coat, then she remembered his parting words. She'd promised not to reveal the anagrams.

Father Aeneas watched her a moment. "Are you telling me everything?"

She bit her lip. "I could put you in danger."

"I am not afraid. Your uncle would want me to know."

Breathe, Caro. Just breathe. Jude was gone, and she

would break every promise that she'd made to him. She plunged her hand into a pocket, ready to tear out the lining, then hesitated. Was she scared for the monk or overly attached to the jacket? Maybe it was better if Father Aeneas didn't see the passport. The fewer who knew about it, the better. But she could give him a summary.

"Uncle Nigel left clues. Anagrams. One brought me to you. Another mentioned vellum and Venice."

Father Aeneas tapped his cane against the floor, the sound echoing like gunfire along the high ceiling. "That's where he hid the ten pages! Maybe the third icon is there, too."

"I'm supposed to find a deposit box, too."

He stopped beating the cane. "Do you know where? Do you have the key?"

"Yes." *Maybe.*

"Then I will help you find a way to Venice. If your uncle had lived, he would have eventually told you the truth. Do not blame him. No one knows when death is coming."

"I think he'd planned to tell me when he returned from Bulgaria. He'd even called in Jude to provide scientific evidence."

"Do not look so unhappy." Father Aeneas's blunt fingers gripped his cane. "Your young man will come back."

"No, he won't. He despises vampires."

"In time his prejudice will lessen. He will see the psychological similarities between immortals and humans. Some are virtuous, others are evil. They can be intelligent, stupid, or greedy."

"He believes all vampires are wicked. He'll never come back."

"If he doesn't, it is God's will."

"No, it's Jude's will."

"You look tired." Father Aeneas stood, leaning against the cane. "I will show you to your quarters."

She followed him out of the church, down the covered walkway, and up a wooden staircase to a large common room. One side was a dining area; the other side held an altar and bookshelves, clearly devoted to reading and prayer.

"Tomorrow, I will show you my icon," he said. "But now, I must rest." He stopped in front of a wooden door with a crucifix nailed on the upper panel. "Here is your room. Please, make yourself comfortable. If you are thirsty, there is brandy in the kitchen. It may help you sleep. If God is willing, I shall see you in the morning."

He sketched a cross in the air and turned down the hall. She walked to the kitchen, thinking brandy would settle her nerves. Jude sat at the table. She jolted, clapping one hand over her mouth. He stood, his chair scraping over the stone floor.

"I'm not staying long," he said.

A glimmer of hope rose up and streaked through her chest, a palpable force that thrashed against her throat, wrists, and fingertips. "Why did you come back?" she whispered.

"My money was in the jacket."

His words slammed against her like a fist, crushing the glimmer, the pieces falling to her feet. She took a breath, and a defiant flash of hope uncurled from the rubble. "That's the only reason?"

"Yes."

"Take it and go." Her hands shook as she pulled off his coat and held it out. He didn't reach for it, so she draped it over the back of a chair. "Before you leave, you need to know something. Philippe Grimaldi might not be my father. I'm going to find a lab and have my blood examined."

"You don't need tests. I know what you are." His eyes were overbright, and he spoke in a confident, imperious tone. "I documented hybridism in my laboratory. You're like the mice."

"And you're a rat bastard." Her eyes burned, but she refused to cry.

"I saw you run after that child in Heathrow," he said. "God, you were fast. And warm. You're always warm. If I took your temperature, it would be more than a hundred degrees."

"That doesn't mean anything. You're a scientist. I thought you relied on empirical data."

"I don't need to. I've spent the last two years studying vampires. Watching them. Hunting them." A muscle worked in his jaw. "When humans are bitten, they become anemic—pale and sickly. But after you were attacked, you looked different. Smelled different. Felt different."

She lifted her chin. "What if it's just an allergy to vampire saliva?"

"You're more beautiful than ever. More alluring. And I want you like I want air."

Their eyes met briefly; he looked past her. *Want*? He'd spoken in the present tense.

"I thought you cared," she whispered.

"I've cared for others." He shrugged. "I got over it."

"What if I don't get over you?"

"You will. It's just chemicals." He shrugged. "Phero-mones."

"Either you care or you don't."

"It's not that simple. There's no future for us. What if we got married? Our children would be part monster."

"We don't need children."

"I do. We can't be together."

"Give one reason why—and make it a damn good one."

"Because you're a fucking vampire," he cried, his voice echoing.

"Half," she said, lifting one finger. "Only half."

"What part don't you understand?" His forehead creased. "You're one of *them*. I can't be with you. It ends right here."

"No!" She flung herself against him, locking her arms around his neck. For a second, she thought he might embrace her, but he grabbed her wrists and pulled her away.

"Do not try to seduce me," he said.

"I wasn't."

The corners of his mouth turned down. His eyelids were swollen, his face mottled. He exhaled, filling the space between them with whiskey fumes. Averting his gaze, he sat down at the opposite end of the table and pinched the bridge of his nose. Two veins protruded on the back of his hand. Caro looked down at her own hands, and her throat clenched. Her veins were smaller but carried a violent history.

She sat on the edge of a chair and shut her eyes, trying to still her thoughts. She'd returned Jude's money—why was he still hanging around? She pushed down another surge of hope and forced herself to picture her old garden in Oxford and how the morning light spilled over the flower beds. When she was a child, Uncle Nigel had showed her how to plant tulip bulbs. He hunkered in the grass with a trowel, pushing the bulbs into the soil. Next, they planted lavender, basil, and parsley near the kitchen door. Later, they played tag; she always hid behind the boxwood niche where a statue of Pan stood, green moss spreading up his woolly thighs.

She pictured her uncle's desk, the cubbyholes stuffed with notes and students' papers. Reference books lay open on chairs and tables, any available surface. Dinah, the cat, was drawn to chaos, and she daintily picked her way through the debris.

The cheerful memories circled back to vampirism. Caro tried to remember childhood illnesses, but she'd been a vigorous child. Once, though, she'd fallen sick. It had been a snowy winter morning. She'd awoken with a sore throat, and by noon she'd spiked a fever. Her uncle had spoon-fed her ice chips until her teeth chattered. By dinnertime, the fever had broken, and she was turning cartwheels in the hall.

Why hadn't Uncle Nigel told her about Vivi and the stolen artifacts? His life's work had centered around pulling secrets out of the dirt. Because the truth wouldn't stay buried. The truth was a force of nature.

CHAPTER 40

A faint, scratching sound echoed on the terrace. Caro lifted her head and squinted at the French doors. Through the bubbled glass, she saw an eyelash moon. How long had she slept?

She glanced at her watch: four A.M. Jude hadn't moved from his chair, except he'd gone to sleep, resting his head against the table. He muttered something and stirred, and then his breathing slowed. Father Aeneas was wrong. She couldn't read people's thoughts. She didn't even know if Jude was really sleeping, much less why he'd stayed.

From the terrace, the scratching continued. She turned, and a shadow flitted by the door.

"What's that noise?" Jude mumbled without lifting his head.

"A scrabbling. Could the police still be searching for us?"

"When I was down there, I didn't see anything."

She pushed back her hair and faced the terrace. A tall, gaunt man stood behind the arched door. It was the tall Bulgarian who'd locked her in the Dacia's trunk.

He kicked the door, and it flew open. Cold air whipped through the room, making the candles sputter.

"V-vampire," Caro yelled and scrambled to her feet.

Jude lunged from his seat and charged the man. There was a blur of arms and legs, and then Jude was flying across the room. He slammed into the cupboard and then dropped to the floor. Dishes toppled from the shelves, crashing around his shoulders. He groaned. One hand scraped through broken crockery. Then he stopped moving.

Caro snatched a cup and threw it at the vampire. He swerved, and the cup whizzed past his head and clattered against the wall.

"We meet again," the man said, then bowed. "Or do you not remember me? I am Georgi. And you are the queen of England, yes? You damaged my trunk, Your Majesty. And killed my partner. But all shall be forgiven."

"Stay away!" She threw another cup, but this time Georgi didn't duck; he caught it in one hand.

"You have something that does not belong to you," he said.

"Stay away, you bloody bastard."

"Give me the pages you stole."

"I don't have them."

"No? Then I will come up with another use for you." His eyes flicked over her. He threw the cup over his shoulder and fished a knife from his pocket. The air stirred as he crossed the room and pressed the knife to her throat.

"Do not move or I will cut you." He pushed the blade

into her flesh. She felt a pinch, and then something trickled down her neck.

"I have longed for this." He licked her throat. She
smelled iron and an acrid, musty smell. She felt a sharp
pain below her right ear, and then he sucked her flesh, his
throat clicking. *Oh my God.* He was drinking her blood.
She tried to claw his cheek, but her arm tingled and
wouldn't move. A numbing sensation crept down her jaw,
seeping into her limbs, just as it had in Momchilgrad.

Georgi tipped his head back, her blood streaming
down his chin. His nostrils flared and he began wheezing.
Caro remembered the vampire in Momchilgrad—was this
some sort of odd ritual or vampire physiology?

His rasping worsened.

Run, run, run. But how much of her body was paralyzed? Her arms hung limply at her sides, and a tingling
buzz moved downward, spiraling through her chest
toward her lower body. Could she move her feet? She
scraped her foot over the floor—good, her legs weren't
numb. Gritting her teeth, she rammed her knee into
Georgi's groin. He moaned and doubled over, clapping
both hands over his groin. Burgundy threads trickled
down the corners of his mouth. Her blood.

Adrenaline spiked through her veins, and her dead
limbs flooded with sensation. She lifted a wooden chair
and smashed it over Georgi's head. He dropped to one
knee, still holding his testicles, and howled.

She ran across the room, skating through broken
china, and hunkered next to Jude. He was still unconscious. She pushed two fingers against his neck. His pulse
was strong, but fast. The air stirred around her. A cold
hand circled her neck. She groped on the floor, grabbed

a china shard, and drove it upward. She felt it hit something solid.

Georgi bellowed, and his hand fell away from her neck. He staggered backward, blood streaming from his eye, and bumped into the altar table. The crucifix and candles fell over.

Caro's breath came in hitches. She snatched another shard and brandished it. The vampire held his hands over his eye, blood gushing over his fingers, and sank to the floor. She crawled back to Jude and pulled his head onto her lap. "Please, wake up."

He blinked. As he began to stir, bits of pottery crackled beneath him.

"Open your eyes, darling," she said.

He blinked, and then a tendril of smoke blew over his face. Caro glanced up. Across the hazy room, flames licked across the altar cloth. Beneath the table, a shadow uncoiled.

Caro released a shuddering breath as Georgi rose from the smoke. He pulled the shard out of his eye and tossed the piece over his shoulder. The smoke wafted as he shot across the room and seized Caro, shaking her until her neck bowed. A gluey, flypaper sensation trapped her conscious thoughts. She felt herself rise as he dug his hands under her armpits and dragged her past the blazing table, onto the terrace. Faint pink light glimmered over the mountains.

A blast of wintry air hit her face, and she sucked in a deep breath. Her head instantly cleared. She started to claw out his other eye, but he caught her wrist.

"Now I will take you," Georgi said.

A raw, ripping pain broke through Caro's neck as he pushed his teeth into her flesh. His throat clicked and clicked. The bastard was sucking the wound as if it were a ripe peach. Tears and blood ran down her cheeks and curved under her jaw. If she didn't break free, Jude would die in that burning room.

She tried to lift her knee again to smash Georgi, but the numbing sensation was stronger this time and her foot clunked against the floor. She tried to move her toes, but they were dead, dead, dead.

As he drank her blood, her other senses sharpened. The acrid stench of the burning altar cloth rushed up her nose, mingling with Georgi's sour breath. From inside the room, she heard two heartbeats, crackling flames, and an odd zipping noise.

Georgi must have heard it, too, because he wrenched his teeth out of her neck and glanced toward the burning room. Black fluid pulsed out of his ruined eye and curved down his cheek. She tried to push him away, but the unusual anesthesia had turned her arms into leaden posts.

He released her, and she fell to the terrace floor.

"You can't kill me, old fool," Georgi said.

Old fool? Caro twisted her head. The monk stood in the doorway, aiming a crossbow.

"Caroline, move out of the way," Father Aeneas said, his voice low and controlled. Smoke billowed above his head and scattered into the dark. The feeling was creeping back into her limbs. Gritting her teeth, she flattened her shoulders against the balcony rail.

The arrow whizzed through the air and thudded into Georgi's chest. It made a hollow sound, like thumping a melon. His long fingers curled around the shaft. Blood surged around his fist and streamed down the front of his trousers. A second arrow slammed into his chest, inches from the first. He staggered backward across the terrace and toppled over the rail. Caro's arms tingled as she rose up and peered over the ledge. Georgi rolled down the embankment. Cracking noises echoed as his body plowed through brush and stumpy trees.

"Vrykolakas," Father Aeneas said.

Until now, Caro had not known how to pronounce that word. It sounded sinister yet exotic on the holy man's tongue: vree-KO-la-Kahss. Vampire.

"He is the one who came to Varlaam last night." Father Aeneas shifted the crossbow to his left hand. Arrows jutted up from a deep pocket of his robe, and they clicked violently as he stepped to the ledge. "Where did he land?"

"The bottom." She pointed. Lights from the base of the monastery shone on Georgi's body. He was so far down, he resembled a crushed spider, but her vision was still sharper than normal and she saw the gruesome details. He lay face up, his arms and legs spread at crooked angles. A bone jutted out of his thigh, poking through his trousers, and dark blood pooled around his head.

Caro grimaced. "Please tell me he's dead."

"Not yet." Father Aeneas reached for another arrow.

Georgi's arm moved, and then his fingers dug into the soil. He dragged himself out of the light, toward shadowy rocks.

Father Aeneas lifted the crossbow and aimed. The arrow zipped down, clunked against a rock, and spun off into darkness. The monk loaded another arrow. It thrummed down and lodged in Georgi's chest.

Smoke rolled past Caro, and she struggled to her feet, her legs wobbling. "Fetch Jude. He's unconscious. And the room is on fire."

"Stay here," Father Aeneas said. "Keep your eyes on the *Vrykolakas*."

A ribbon of blood slid down her neck, and she shivered.

Father Aeneas hunkered beside her. "You were bitten?"

She nodded.

He fumbled in his pocket, drew out a white handkerchief, and pressed it to her neck. "Hold firm pressure," he told her. "Was Jude bitten?"

"No. But he's injured. And he's breathing smoke."

Father Aeneas hurried into the room. She glanced down at Georgi. He hadn't moved. Without turning, she tracked the monk's footsteps. His sandals crunched over the broken china. She heard a splash, followed by a hiss. She turned. The monk heaved a bucket of water onto the table. The flames sputtered, and black smoke coiled toward the ceiling.

Father Aeneas's robe waffled around his feet as he strode over to Jude. She leaned over the ledge. Georgi still hadn't moved. She was certain he was dead. She glanced back at Jude. He sat up, rubbing the back of his head. The monk set a first-aid kit on the table and rummaged inside. He saw her staring and pointed.

"Watch the *Vrykolakas*," he said.

She turned away. The sun inched its way up the mountain, spilling light onto the red tile roofs of Kalambaka. She looked down for Georgi, but he was gone. Her pulse thrummed in her ears. She yelled for Father Aeneas, and he ran to the terrace. Jude limped behind him.

"I took my eyes off him a moment," she said.

Daylight seeped across the valley, moving in a sharp line that divided it—bright on one side, dark on the other. Father Aeneas pointed to a boulder. Georgi crawled on his stomach, his long fingers grabbing weeds. His narrow face contorted as he stared back at the broadening strip of light.

Father Aeneas lifted the crossbow and loaded an arrow. The string hummed. The arrow slammed through the vampire's left calf into the ground. A sharp cry held in the air, bouncing off the rocks. Georgi struggled to pull forward, but his leg was pinned. He tugged at the arrow. The line of daylight inched forward, eating up the shadows. He screamed as it passed over his legs and hips, over his shoulders. The scream snapped off as the light hit his face and moved to his outstretched arms. His head slashed back and forth, and he clapped his hands over his eyes.

"He's blind?" Caro whispered.

Father Aeneas crossed himself. His eyes met Jude's. "He must be decapitated. Caroline should not see this."

Jude nodded and swiped at his nose, smearing blood and soot across his cheek. He sat down beside Caro and pulled her head against his chest. A pinprick of hope seeped through her, delicate as light streaming through a honeycomb. Something wet and warm tapped against her hand. She leaned back. Jude's blood dripped in the space between them.

"You're bleeding," she said.

"So are you." He pointed to the bloody handkerchief that she was holding against her neck.

"I tried to stop him. He was too strong."

Jude shut his eyes. She stared, fascinated, as light moved over his legs, shining on the folds of his trousers, outlining the intricate peaks and valleys in the corduroy. His right leg was bent at the knee, and the other was braced against a stone pillar. She wondered what he'd do if she pushed her thigh against his, if his repulsion was outweighed by his desire to obey the monk.

Wait, what the hell was happening to her? They'd almost died, and she was thinking of seducing him? No, she'd been tainted by Georgi's horrid stem cells. She inched away from Jude and forced herself to take slow breaths.

Father Aeneas returned, gripping pails of fresh water. She didn't know what he'd done to the vampire, and he didn't offer an explanation. Jude helped her to her feet, and she glanced over the ledge. A dark stain marked the spot where Georgi had lain earlier, but there was no trace of his body.

She followed Jude into the room. Father Aeneas handed her a damp washcloth. She wiped blood from her hair and neck, taking care not to touch the wounds. The icy water trickled down her throat, cooling her blazing skin.

Jude sat down. His nose was swelling, but the bleeding had stopped. He pulled off his sweater and threw it onto the table; his shirt gaped open, showing a smooth neck with an even pulse beat. Her mind filled with prurient images, and she forced herself to look away.

Father Aeneas found a broom and began sweeping up the crockery. Jude glanced at Caro's neck but didn't comment. She doused a cotton ball with hydrogen peroxide and dabbed the wound. Jude looked at her again, then away.

"Any minute now, I'll be turning," she said. "So you better watch out."

Father Aeneas stopped sweeping. "Someone is coming."

Jude reached for his sweater. "Should we go to the cave?"

A short, portly man in a gray wool suit entered the room. He pulled off his hat and smoothed a stubby hand over his straight white hair. His beard was white and wispy, reminding Caroline of a giant dandelion. His hand dropped to the scarf around his neck. As he fiddled with it, his dark eyes skipped from Jude to Caro.

"Permit me to introduce Philokrates Xenagoras Demos. But his name is so long, we call him Demos." Father Aeneas propped the broom against the wall. "He will drive us to the ferry. Demos, these are the young people I told you about."

"Kalimera." Demos bowed.

Jude stood and sat down abruptly.

"If he can't make it down the steps, we can lower him in the basket," Demos said. "It may attract some attention, but if there is no other way—"

"Don't worry about me." Jude waved his hand. "I'm staying here."

A band tightened around Caro's chest, and her lungs flattened. So this was it? They'd never see each other again? Her eyes filled, and she dug her fingernails into her palms, welcoming the sharp sting. It meant the vampire's numbing venom had passed through her system. She pushed harder, hoping the pain would distract her from a crying jag.

"We should leave right away," Demos said.

"I'll fetch my bag." Father Aeneas walked toward the hall.

Caro struggled to catch her breath. Her throat was so tight, she had to push out the words. "You're going with me, Father?"

The monk turned. "I have prayed for guidance. Caroline, you have stepped into the dangerous world of the night. Sir Nigel would expect me to protect you."

"Thank you, Father."

He stepped back to the table and put his hand on Jude's shoulder. "Stay at Varlaam as long as you wish. Caroline will not be alone. I will guard her with my life."

A pinched look crossed Jude's face. He leaned across the table and touched the back of Caro's hand. "If you want me to come along, just say so."

The band around her chest snapped and she took a grateful breath. Two days ago, she would have answered with a glib "So." But Jude was plainly struggling with his emotions. The firm set of his jaw clashed with the doubtful, hooded look in his eyes. She imagined his thoughts. He wanted to stay, he wanted to go. He loved her, he loved her not.

"Yes." She steepled her hands. "Please come to Venice."

CHAPTER 41

—

Demos angled the black van down a narrow road that led away from Varlaam. Onyx rosary beads dangled from the rearview mirror, clicking against a blue evil-eye charm.

Caro stared out the window. A rabbit streaked across the valley. It stopped and rose on its haunches. Father Aeneas traced a cross in the air, as if blessing the rabbit.

She crossed her arms, and the slight pressure on her breasts set off tremors between her legs. Her breath caught, and she jerked her arms apart. Those last two bites were more potent than the first.

Jude turned. "Your face is flushed."

She looked at the bruises on his face and couldn't breathe. Because of her, he'd almost died. In a raspy voice, she said, "I'm fine."

"I thought you might be hungry," Demos said. He

lifted one hand from the steering wheel and grabbed a small wicker basket. "Nothing fancy, but I think you will like."

Caro peeked inside. Small water bottles. A box of raisins. Honeyed apples wrapped in a white napkin. A small flask of red wine. Her stomach twisted and she looked away.

"Where are we headed?" Jude asked the men.

"Igoumenitsa," Demos said. "I have made reservations on the *Ikarus Palace*. I took the liberty of reserving deck-class cabins. They are cheap this time of year. The ferry leaves at nine A.M."

"Have you arranged to leave your van in Igoumenitsa?" Father Aeneas asked.

"I'm bringing it on the ferry," Demos said.

"But we won't need transportation in Venice," the monk said.

"Just the same, I will park it at the Tronchetto."

"What is the point? We will be taking water taxis. A vehicle is one more thing to worry about."

"Worry?" Demos cried. "This van is no worry. You curse it with your talk of worry."

"Park it in Igoumenitsa."

"This is a mistake." Demos shook his head. "I don't like mistakes."

The conversation drifted into the best strategy to line up on the passenger boardwalk. "I'll go first," Father Aeneas said. "The military police will be respectful of clergy. Jude and Caroline can stand behind me."

"Where will I be?" Demos asked.

"Behind Jude. You and I will shield the young people."

Caro glanced over her shoulder and squinted at the van's broad rear windows. The highway was empty. Then a small blue car veered around the curve. A twinge of paranoia made her chest tighten. She swallowed and shifted her gaze toward the front seat.

"There's a car behind us," she said.

"I am watching," Demos said, then peered into the rearview mirror.

She leaned her forehead against the cool window. A long time ago, she'd traveled down this road with Uncle Nigel, and they'd stopped at a gas station that served baklava, calamari, and goat soup. All these years later, here she was, driving along this same road with a monk and a biochemist. Both of whom had killed vampires on her behalf.

The leather seat creaked as Father Aeneas turned and slipped two white tablets into her hands. "Aspirin. For the fever," he said. "You may feel parched, as well. Make sure you drink water."

"Or I'll turn into a vampire," she said, not bothering to hide the sarcasm, but it seemed to wash right over the monk. His mouth sagged open, and his eyes rounded.

"No, no. Do not worry. I have not heard of a hybrid transforming. You will feel ill after a bite, but the symptoms will diminish in a few days."

"Or sooner," Jude said.

Caro tossed the pills into her mouth and opened the water bottle.

Father Aeneas's gaze shifted to Jude. "Last night, Caroline said you'd studied vampiric mice."

Jude shot her a startled look, then faced the monk. "Yes? What of it?"

Father Aeneas smoothed his beard. "I've heard of vampire sheep in France, but mice? How did you find immortal rodents?"

"I experimented with stem cells and created an immortal strain. It's a long, boring story."

"An impressive one," Father Aeneas said. "What did you learn, young man?"

Jude didn't answer right away, as if he felt reluctant to discuss his work. Finally he said, "The offspring of vampiric and normal mice—the hybrids—had fantastic immunity. However, a hyper-strong immune system can be just as dangerous as a weak one. An example would be the 1918 Spanish Flu pandemic, when young people died. But I digress." He pushed his hands together, as if repressing the scientific footnote, and continued with more enthusiasm. "When hybrid mice were bitten by vampiric ones, it caused a mild allergic response in both the host and the recipient. The human equivalent would be a reaction to a flu shot."

As Caro listened to Jude talk, she imagined him standing at a lectern, his jacket sleeves dusted with chalk, instructing biology students about amino acids. He was a born teacher, just like Uncle Nigel.

"Interesting." Father Aeneas paused. "I never imagined that hybrids possessed an antibody that is not found in the immortals. Is the opposite true?"

Jude darted a look at Caro, then looked back at the monk. "Yes, vampires have unique antibodies, but they appear to have an exaggerated response to the one found in hybrids."

Caro squared her shoulders with great dignity, preparing to argue that she wasn't a half-breed. The men fell silent as the van sped through a tunnel, the tires singing on the pavement, toward the dazzling archway. An unbearable glow hurt Caro's eyes when the van blasted out of the tunnel. The sun was up now, glinting on the snow-covered mountains. She blinked, and a stomach-churning dizziness swept through her. A second before she keeled over, she seized the door handle and wrapped her fingers around the smooth chrome.

I'm not a hybrid, she told herself. *I'm not.*

The road straightened and her head cleared, but she stubbornly gripped the handle, making her wonder if she was clinging to other, bigger things. Love. Normalcy. False hope. Her hand sprang open, and she glared at her fingerprints on the chrome. She couldn't deny the truth another second. Philippe Grimaldi was her father. She had inherited his blond, unruly hair, along with speed, immunity, and a metabolism that burned calories. As she pictured her father, a fierce surge of love spread through her chest. His genes had collided with Vivi's, and Caro refused to be ashamed.

But she was afraid. Was someone following them or had she imagined that car? A band tightened around her chest as she squinted at the rear window. The road was still empty, except for a blue dot. It vanished around a curve and then reappeared.

Father Aeneas tugged at his beard. "A vampire's hidrosis is unique."

Caro tore her gaze away from the car. "What?"

"Hidrosis is the Greek word for perspiration," Father Aeneas told her. "When vampires sweat, they give off a tang. Some smell of ketones—a musky, overripe-melon fragrance. But the *Vrykolakas* who attacked you reeked of menthol."

Caro drew her lips into a bow, remembering the raw dirt-and-blood aroma of the Momchilgrad vampire and Georgi's pungent armpits. "I didn't notice a minty smell," she said.

"Some humans can't detect it," Father Aeneas said. "Yet their brain chemistry is affected—it produces a psychological result. It always makes me calm."

"Is it a pheromone?" Caro leaned forward, eager to learn more.

"Definitely not," Jude said. "Though it mimics one. It's more like a terpenoid—that's a plant hydrocarbon. They're fragrant, with pharmaceutical properties. That explains the ketones and menthol."

Father Aeneas looked confused. "If the chemical isn't a terpenoid or a pheromone, what is it?"

"I didn't have time to properly analyze it," Jude said. "But it's similar to a terpene. I'm sure you've heard of Nepetalactone?"

"Catnip?" Father Aeneas asked.

Jude nodded.

"That would explain the aphrodisiac effect," Father Aeneas said.

"But my tabby was immune to catnip," Caro said. "Uncle Nigel was always setting out little herb-filled toys for Dinah. She ignored them."

Jude touched his bruised nose and winced. "Perhaps she lacked the olfactory receptor. Some felines have it, some don't. It's genetic."

Caro's mouth curved into a smile. "What does bat-nip do to humans?"

Jude's face went slack, as if offended by the comment. "It depends on the concentration," he said. "In large quantities, the molecule causes sedation and numbness, followed by euphoria and hypersensitivity."

"But doesn't vampire saliva have a toxin?" Caro wiggled her fingers, remembering how they had gone numb after she'd been bitten. "Surely I wasn't anesthetized from *breathing* these souped-up ketones."

"I agree with Caroline," Demos said. "If the catnip theory is true, then people would faint whenever they got near a vampire. Sidewalks and train stations would be filled with paralyzed humans."

Jude lowered his eyebrows, flashing his I'm-not-good-at-explanations look. "When the chemical is excreted by a vampire's sweat glands, it evaporates and diffuses into the air and becomes less potent," he said, but his clipped, controlled voice couldn't contain his passion for science. "If humans inhale it, they feel relaxed. But it's fleeting. A high concentration of this molecule is found in a vampire's blood and saliva. That's why Caro was temporarily paralyzed. She was prey. And predators are made for survival. They stalk, pounce, restrain, feed."

"Why don't vampires succumb to their own chemical?" Demos asked. "Why doesn't it paralyze them?"

"Is a spider killed by its own venom?" Jude lifted one eyebrow. "An effective predator isn't harmed by its own methods of predation."

Demos stopped at a roadside café. The blue car sped past them and rounded a curve. Father Aeneas helped her out of the van. "Tea and baklava will revive us," he said.

Minutes later, as they sped through the mountains, Jude went to sleep, but the sugary dessert had a loquacious effect on Caro. She told Father Aeneas and Demos about her kidnapping ordeal and the dead tourist in the Dacia's trunk. "Will she turn into a vampire?" she asked.

"It depends on when she was killed," Father Aeneas said. "And how much physical damage occurred prior to her death."

Demos grunted. "Also, we cannot know if the vampire released her from the trunk and taught her to feed, or if he left her to starve. How many days ago were you kidnapped?"

"I don't know. I've lost track." Caro rubbed her eyes. Since she'd come to Greece, time had elongated, flipping back on itself.

"Five days," Jude said without opening his eyes.

Caro reached for the door handle again. "What if that woman is still in his trunk?" she asked.

Father Aeneas crossed himself. "If the vampire left his vehicle in Kalambaka, the police will find it—and the woman, if she is still there."

"What if they open the trunk and she attacks them?" Caro asked.

"Not after five days." Demos shook his head. "If she does not drink blood, she will appear dead. And they will bury her."

Jude's eyes blinked open, and his mouth tugged into a suspicious frown. "How do *you* know so much?"

"My family was killed by a nest of *Vrykolakas*." Demos lifted one hand away from the steering wheel and loosened his scarf, revealing ragged scars on his neck. "I was left for dead. Father Aeneas nursed me back to health and taught me about the fiends who'd killed my wife and children. So that is how I know."

"I'm so sorry." Caro released the handle, and shifted her gaze to the rear windows. Dozens of cars looped around the hairpin curves. She saw two blue cars, and her heart stuttered.

Demos saw her looking and waved his hand. "Do not worry. These vehicles are different. I did not mean to derail the conversation with my sad story. You were asking about the woman in the trunk. She will be in a catatonic state. After the police determine who she is and track down her relatives, it is likely that she will be buried alive."

"*Alive* isn't the correct word," Jude said.

Father Aeneas sat up a little straighter, his prayer beads clicking, and looked at Jude. "I have not talked to a scientist in many years. I would like to hear more about your research."

"If the victim receives enough stem cells through the bite wounds, or if he drinks a vampire's blood, he will enter the first hibernation phase," Jude said. "The victim will appear to be dead. No vital signs. No brain activity. Yet the blood is teeming with immature stem cells, and they're dividing at an extraordinary rate. When the transformation is complete, the victim will regain consciousness. He'll need an initial loading of blood. And if he doesn't get it, he'll go into a frenzy."

Caro touched her neck, her fingernails grazing the edges of the Band-Aid. The slight pressure sent a peppery heat rushing between her legs. Damn, she'd become a female roué.

"When a myth is found in many cultures, it must have some truth," Father Aeneas said. "Some people may quibble over etymology, but they're missing the point. Vampires have been around for—dare I say it?—an eternity."

He chuckled, and Demos nodded vigorously.

"The Russians have the *Upyr*," Father Aeneas continued, "yet this word is mixed up with heretics. The *Strigoi* are Romanian vampires—actually, they have several categories, but I won't bore you."

"Albanians have the *Shtriga*," Demos added.

"The Japanese have *Kamaitachi*," Father Aeneas said. "The Aztecs had the *Civataleo*. Serbians and Bulgarians have *vampirs*. Incidentally, the Serbians have a name for a child born of a vampire and a human—the *Vampirdžije*, a vampire finder. And, of course, the Bulgarian *vampir* supposedly has a single nostril."

"That myth has been debunked," Caro said, remembering Teo and Georgi's perfectly formed noses. She hoped the Serbian vampire killer was a myth, too.

"Yes, it has." Father Aeneas paused. "But the mystery of Agathonos Monastery hasn't been explained."

"What happened there?" Caro asked. Despite the grim subject, she felt soothed by the academic discussion because it reminded her of Uncle Nigel.

"A monk was exhumed fifteen years after he went to God's glory," Demos said. "His body was undamaged. No bones, no mold, no rot."

"Well, perhaps a little decay," Father Aeneas said. "But I have heard that the air was clean, with a hint of freesia. The monk appeared to be sleeping. Supple flesh. Robust coloring."

"But no breathing," Demos said.

Caro leaned in closer to Father Aeneas. "But what prompted the exhumation?"

"It is a custom in Greece. Perhaps you saw the sacristy at Metamorphosis?" Father Aeneas glanced out his window. "Burial space is limited. However, when the brothers are exhumed, nothing but bones are found. Normally."

Caro leaned back against the seat and watched the sun inch its way up the sky. Her eyes watered, and she put on her sunglasses. She'd had trouble with her vision after Momchilgrad, but this morning, it was worse. Still, the light was a comfort, an ancient symbol of protection. They would be safe from vampires until sunset.

"Of course, there have been other cases of preserved bodies," Father Aeneas said. "The prophet Daniel was found intact."

"Do not forget Pope John the Twenty-third." Demos lifted one finger. "Four decades in a casket, and his body did not decompose."

"I suppose the story of Saint John of the Cross is the most interesting," Father Aeneas said. "His mortal remains were buried, exhumed, reinterred, and exhumed again. During one of these outings, someone wanted a souvenir and hacked off Saint John's finger. It bled. No one bleeds after death."

"He was a vampire?" Caro asked dryly.

Father Aeneas gazed out the window, as if the answer were floating in the sunlight. "I only know that he achieved a kind of everlasting life."

"Did the Church explain his finger?" Jude asked.

Father Aeneas shook his head. "Perhaps it was a metabolic oddity."

Demos's lips spread wide, showing a mouthful of small, crooked teeth. Then he said, "Or maybe he did not like the taste of blood."

CHAPTER 42

———

The clerk in the Igoumenitsa port office issued four first-class tickets without asking for identification. The luck continued as Caro followed the men down the steps, where they joined the line at the passenger boardwalk. A bold red stripe ran down the length of the ferry, with MINOAN LINE printed in black letters.

Even with her sunglasses, the light hurt Caro's eyes. She narrowed them and watched passengers walk along the dock. Four American teenagers passed by, chattering about Venice and the knockoff handbags they hoped to buy. Not too long ago, Caro had led a similarly normal, if dull, existence. She'd shopped at thrift stores, watered her African violets, and escorted tourists through Windsor Castle. But normalcy had been an illusion. Her mother was a thief, and her father was a vampire.

A commotion rose up from the front of the line as the military police interrogated a passenger. Caro's uncle had once said that Greek border officers were notorious for inventing ways to detain travelers. She glanced back at Jude, but he was studying his ticket. Behind him, Demos's bottom lip slid forward as cars and trucks were loaded into a wide compartment.

Caro turned around, and the hairs on her neck tingled, as if someone was watching. She shrugged it off, blaming her reaction on the chilly breeze, but when she reached down to button her coat, it was already fastened. Nerve endings kept firing in the back of her neck, and gooseflesh rippled down her arms. Someone was definitely watching. She whirled around and bumped into Jude.

"Anything wrong?" he asked in French.

She stared up at him, confused, then she remembered they were carrying French passports; Father Aeneas had warned them not to speak English. She looked past Jude and studied the long line that stretched behind them. Teenagers were listening to iPods; an elderly couple argued about their accommodations in Venice; a mother fussed at a towheaded child. Caro didn't know what she was looking for. None of the passengers wore visibly thick sunblock. If the British authorities were here, wouldn't they simply pull her aside for questioning? Or maybe they were waiting.

Waiting for what?

She thrust her hands into her pockets, and Father Aeneas's words ran through her head: *Do you sometimes know what people are thinking?*

Near the front of the line, the police yelled at another passenger. The man bellowed. Two officers grabbed his arms and led him off the dock toward a squatty building. After a moment, the line moved ahead.

Father Aeneas held out his tickets and passport. The policeman's unibrow formed a crooked ledge over his eyes. He said something in Greek and stepped back to let the monk pass.

Now it was Caro's turn. The policeman studied her passport, and she forced herself to smile. "Where in Greece have you been?" he asked in French.

"Meteora," she said, affecting a provincial dialect.

The policeman leaned closer, and his sour breath hit her face. *Ketones?* she thought. No, the man stood in daylight. But he made her nervous. She sneezed, hoping he'd back off.

He didn't.

She sneezed again, more forcefully this time. *"Excusez-moi."*

He shoved her passport and ticket into her hands, then waved her through the line. The policeman's eyes flickered over Jude's bruised face. Father Aeneas shuffled forward, pointing at Caro, Jude, and Demos, indicating they were together. The monk smiled at the policeman and rattled off something in Greek.

The policeman nodded. Demos rolled his eyes and nodded at Caro. Then he glanced at Jude, raised an index finger and drew a triangle, adding a dot at the apex. The policeman's eyes moved up and down, watching Demos's finger move.

A love triangle? Caro felt a blush creep up her neck. She always blushed when she was nervous, but she hoped the policeman didn't notice. The ferry's horn pierced the air, and Caro dropped her passport. Father Aeneas picked it up and slipped it into her hand, giving her arm a reassuring pat.

"The policeman wants to know if Jude was in a fight," he whispered. "I avoided his questions and said you are French students. But now, Demos has contradicted my story. He is weaving a tale that rivals *The Iliad*."

The policeman let Jude pass and thumped Demos's shoulder. Greek words flew back and forth like tiny birds in an olive grove. Both men drew figures and dots in the air.

"Demos thinks he is Homer," Father Aeneas said, rolling his eyes.

Caro smiled and started toward the ramp. A passenger pushed by her, and Caro felt a stinging sensation in her arms. She looked at her hands. The flesh was red, and when she pushed up her sleeves she saw that the redness extended under her sweater, as if she'd spent a day at Brighton, oiled with suntan lotion. Maybe Jude and Father Aeneas were wrong; maybe she *was* turning into a vampire.

CHAPTER 43

IKARUS PALACE
ADRIATIC SEA

The ferry steamed past Corfu, its pristine beaches glitter-ing in the morning sun. Even though Caro's eyes were still sensitive, she lingered on the deck to watch a pod of bottlenose dolphins slice through the clear water.

"The ancients believed dolphins were a good omen." Father Aeneas folded his hands on the railing. "They are also an early symbol of Christianity."

The dolphins led the ferry to the Strait of Otranto, through a chain of tiny, rounded islands that bulged from the water. Caro looked around for Jude, but he'd vanished. The smokestack belched, sending up a black mushroom cloud, and the ferry churned north into the Adriatic Sea.

Demos had reserved four cabins, but they were spread out on different decks. A steward led Caro to a cabin on the upper deck. Music pressed in from hidden speakers, and the Goo Goo Dolls were singing "Without You Here."

Perfect. She sat on one of the twin beds and wondered if Jude's cabin was this tiny. If so, he would be able to spread his arms and touch the walls on either side.

Stop thinking about him, Clifford. Her stomach growled. She pushed off the bed, grabbed her bag, and headed toward the restaurant.

She found Jude standing in line outside a snack bar. Two middle-aged women stood in front of him, trying to get his attention. They wore cheery red Christmas sweaters and tennis shoes.

Caro slipped in front of Jude. He gave her a helpless look and said, *"Parle français."*

"We were just wondering if his girlfriend would show up," said a woman with a fanny pack. She laughed, and thin, red lips moved over her teeth.

"Just our luck," her companion said. Three diamond rings flashed as she smoothed back her silver hair.

The woman with the red lips extended her hand. "I'm Regina Hamilton from Birmingham—that's Alabama, not England." She turned to her friend. "And this is Truvy Jo Adamson. She's from Birmingham, too. Where y'all from?"

"Je ne parle pas anglais," Caro said, hoping to discourage the women. She looked past them, into the crowded restaurant. Three television sets hung on the walls, and each one flashed her picture. It was the photograph with all the hair, but still.

"Viens avec moi," Jude said and pulled her out of the line. They hurried along the deck until they hit a logjam.

Greek teenagers had set up nylon tents, and they were videotaping each other. Caro lowered her head, and her hair fell into her face but didn't quite cover it. She gripped Jude's arm, and he led her to the other end of the boat. They passed by another snack bar, and she looked up at the television sets. Her picture was gone, and the screens showed an Iraqi man who'd been kidnapped and tortured in Athens.

"Someone's bound to recognize you," Jude whispered. "Where's your cabin? I'll get takeaway and bring it to you."

"You know what?" She rubbed her stomach. "I'm not hungry."

He pressed his hand against her forehead. "No wonder. You're burning up."

"I'm queasy. I always get seasick. I need to lie down and I'll be fine."

The ferry bounced over a wave, and she stumbled. Jude caught her, holding her tight for a moment as another ferry swept by on the port side, leaving a foamy white wake.

"I'll see you to your room," he said. "Where is it?"

"Up there." She pointed.

The moment they stepped into her cabin, everything went pear-shaped. She bolted for the tiny lavatory. *Oh, no. Not this. Not now.* She was dimly aware of him holding back her hair while she was sick. After a while she stood up and rinsed her mouth with water. He helped her out of the bathroom, and she dove onto the nearest bed. He turned back into the lavatory.

"The bites aren't making me ill," she said in a defensive tone. "I'm seasick."

"Maybe. But you're burning up." A moment later she

heard the lavatory tap running. The piped-in music was playing "Unwell," but she was too miserable to enjoy the synchronicity.

Jude stepped out of the room with a cold rag and pressed it against her forehead. "There you go," he whispered.

"When I was a child I was unbearably seasick," she said.

"Can I get you anything?"

"My old life."

His hand felt cool against her skin. "Other than that?" he asked.

"It's just my inner ear. I'm *not* turning into a flipping vampire bat."

"Let's hope not."

"Oh no." Her insides spun around. She was going to be sick again. She leaped off the bed and ran to the lavatory.

Jude left the cabin and returned a while later with ice and ginger ale. The ice melted instantly on her tongue. She closed her eyes and fell asleep. When she awoke she lifted her arm. Her watch was gone. Damn, she'd lost it at Varlaam. The cabin had no window, so she couldn't judge the time of day. Not that she cared. Jude was stretched out on the other bunk, one hand over his eyes.

"Is it night?" she asked.

"It is." He sat up, opened an Altoid tin, and waved it under her nose. "Breathe in the fumes. Peppermint is supposed to help nausea. Can you lift your head?"

"No. I'm sick as a parrot." She opened one eye. "Have you seen any vampires?"

"Can't say that I have," he said.

"You've looked, right?"

"Vampires wouldn't board a ferry in daylight."

"Maybe they hid in a minivan or a truck."

"They'd still need a driver."

"I bet that happens all the time. They hypnotize people into being gofers."

"Well, they can't get to you. Not now, anyway. Try to relax."

"I can't. I want to, but I can't. What if those chatty women recognized me?"

"Your mind never stops, does it?" He smiled. "I've never met anyone with an imagination that's so . . . delicately tuned."

"Is that a compliment? Or an insult?"

"An observation. Try to sleep."

"Now I know why my uncle contacted you. To convince me that vampires exist." She yawned. "Wonder why he didn't tell me?"

"To protect you. Or, more likely, he stumbled across new information. Something that posed a threat to you."

She closed her eyes and whispered, "A threat."

CHAPTER 44

————

WILKERSON PHARMACEUTICALS
EAST LONDON, ENGLAND

Moose swaggered into the Wilkerson Pharmaceuticals building, his reflective coat swirling around his knees. He stepped into the cherry-paneled lift and pressed the LL button, just as Wilkerson's cheeky secretary had instructed. She had even given him a fucking ID badge, and it dangled from his neck by a grubby string. He had never been to the lower level—and didn't want to go now—but the tricky secretary had insisted. Moose didn't trust her. Any woman who shagged her boss would double-cross the pope.

The lift opened, and Moose stepped into a corridor. He followed the signs to the Executive Lounge. A guard asked for Moose's badge. He held it up with exaggerated boredom. *Wilkerson Pharmaceutical Corporation, Edwin Tipton, Jr., Security Division.*

The guard buzzed him through the locked metal doors. Moose stepped into a dark room that smelled of illness and putrid flesh. He started to run back through the doors, but they snapped shut.

"You're on time." Wilkerson's disembodied voice floated out of the gloom.

Moose heard a whirring noise, and he crouched down, hands extended, waiting for the Zubas to attack. Lights clicked on, and huge TV screens flashed on the walls. Each screen showed a pastoral view: green rolling hillocks, trees, and a broad wash of sky. Birds flew in and out of the yew trees. Moose couldn't spot them, but he could hear their bloody chirping.

Wilkerson stepped out of the shadows, holding a shotgun. "How do you like my virtual shooting gallery?"

"Clever." Moose licked the fingers on his right hand and started on his left. He glanced around for the goon bodyguard. "Where's the big guy?"

"There." Wilkerson pointed to a dark corner of the room, where Yok-Seng lay on a black leather couch, curled into a ball.

"What's wrong with him?" Moose's nose twitched as Yok-Seng leaned over the edge of the sofa and vomited into a bucket.

"A bellyache." Wilkerson shrugged.

"Shouldn't he be in hospital, mate?"

"We're waiting for the helicopter." Wilkerson swaggered over to a stone wall that must have cost a bloody fortune. He lifted the gun and aimed it at the screen, which showed a squatty house.

"Pull," he said, and a clay duck shot out of the squatty house. Wilkerson squeezed the trigger, and a cracking noise reverberated through speakers. The clay duck shattered. Moose watched the pieces fall into the virtual weeds.

"Can I have a go?" Moose blinked at the squatty house.

"Later," Wilkerson said. "I'm sending you to Italy. I received a tip about my daughter's whereabouts."

"What kind of tip?" Moose was instantly suspicious. He didn't want any involvement with Wilkerson's girl. It was too risky. One more bungle, and he'd be hunted ruthlessly by the Zubas.

Wilkerson ignored him.

"You must have contacts in very high places, mate." Moose laughed, but he was thinking, *Bloody wanker.*

"Actually I do. The British embassy in Bulgaria knows the Clifford girl's every move."

"Why would they care about this bird?"

"I'm paying the ambassador's executive assistant to care. He arranged for someone to shadow Miss Clifford. Not to stop her, but to see where she's going, and why. Apparently, she's headed to Venice with her lover."

"So the darling young buggers are traipsing around Europe. Having a holiday, are they?"

Wilkerson grimaced. "She's got something I want. And I need you to get it."

Moose wrinkled his nose. He hated to think what would happen if he broke the daughter's neck.

"But I'm counting on you, Moose. Remember the photos you showed me the other day? The pictures with the art missing from her wall? It was an icon. She stole it from me. I want it back." Wilkerson lowered the gun and clapped Moose's shoulder. "You won't let me down, will you?"

"No, sir." Moose preened a little, then grinned.

"If you succeed, there'll be a handsome bonus. By the way, the Zuba brothers will accompany you."

Moose's smile faded. "Bollocks to that," he said. "I'm not sharing this assignment with freaks."

Wilkerson raised the gun and yelled, "Pull!" Again, the virtual clay sailed out of the little house and flew into the sky. Wilkerson pulled the trigger, but the clay fell into the trees.

"You don't want the Zubas near your girl." Moose ran his tongue over his lips. "They won't stop till she's in pieces."

"The Zubas are brilliant trackers. They won't harm her."

"Sure they won't. Send me a postcard from Italy, mate." He stepped backward. Wilkerson was loop-de-loop if he expected Moose to take this gig.

"The Zubas will behave."

"And pigs might fly. I'm not afraid for meself. I'm afraid for your bloody daughter."

"Trust me, the Zubas won't be a problem. We've started clinical trials with a new opioid antagonist. It's effective with ICD."

"Pardon?"

"Impulse control disorders. That's what they've got."

"I don't give a monkey. I'm not going."

"We're flying out of Gatwick in two hours. I want you on that plane. Don't disappoint me."

CHAPTER 45

When Caro awoke it was darker outside, and the piped-in music was still grinding out love songs. Train was singing "Getaway." As her eyes adjusted to the dark, she saw a familiar shape on the other bed. "How many hours until we're in Venice?" she asked.

"Nineteen," Jude said. "Feeling better?"

"A little." She rubbed her eyes. "Where are we?"

"Somewhere between Croatia and Albania. The Croatian beaches were lovely. I'm sorry you missed them."

"Me, too." She pushed her hair out of her eyes. "Jude?"

"Mmm-hm?"

"That vampire accused me of stealing pages from a book. He meant *Historia Immortalis*, didn't he?"

"It doesn't matter. He's dead."

"*Historia Immortalis* could be the history of vampirism. If my mother truly stole ten pages from that book, what should I do? Go to the BBC? Hide? Oh, Jude. These pages could shake the world."

"Maybe someone doesn't want it shaken. Maybe they want to suppress this knowledge."

She shut her eyes and drifted. When she opened them again, the music had stopped, and grainy predawn light trickled into the room. She stumbled to the lavatory. The nausea was gone, but her ribs ached from dry-heaving. She splashed water on her face and rinsed her mouth, then collapsed on the cot and rolled into a ball.

Jude's bed creaked. She felt him slide the blanket around her shoulders, and she turned. "I hope Father Aeneas doesn't know you're here," she said. "He'll think we're shagging."

"Caro, the man killed a vampire." He knelt beside her bed. "He left a monastery to join us on a bizarre quest. I hardly think he'd frown on a little shagging."

"But we're not," she said.

"No," he said.

"I miss you." Her breath caught.

"I'm right here."

"I miss being in your arms."

"Don't start, or I'll leave."

"Quit threatening me. I'm having my say." She swallowed. "I thought you were the one. I still do. Jude, look at me. Can't you see that I love you?"

"You don't know what you're saying."

"Yes, I do." She scooted close, molding herself around him. His body immediately tensed.

"Caro, stop."

"We're not doing anything. I'm barely touching you." An ache uncurled in her stomach, and she shivered.

"I don't trust myself," he said.

"I won't bite." She felt the corners of her lips curve into a trembly smile. Even as she began to stroke him, she knew the monk had told the truth. The bite wounds had changed her. She was like those damned cone shells, more attractive to prey. But definitely not toothed.

He started to rise, but she grabbed his hand and pulled him to her. His sweater made a scratchy sound as he slid his arms around her. Their mingled smells wafted between them, and the ache in her chest slipped lower, morphing into a craving.

He jerked away. "We can't," he said.

She raked her teeth over her bottom lip. "But you want me."

"Caro, we've been over this. You're a vampire."

"Half. Only half. Stop being so bloody prejudiced."

"I'm not."

She rolled on her side and pushed her bottom against his thigh. "You're discriminating against me because of a few odd genes."

"A few?"

"I'm proof that all vampires aren't bad."

"You're not the only one who's hurting. I'm grieving over the future I saw for us."

She held her breath. He'd seen a future? They could still have it, provided she didn't push too hard. But it was difficult to control herself because she'd never felt such raw yearning. She turned over, resisting an urge to climb on top of him, and cast about for an unromantic topic. Something that could help her understand his mind-set.

"Tell me about the night you were attacked." She sat up. "Why didn't the vampires bite you?"

A pulse leaped in Jude's neck. "I don't know. Perhaps they meant to. The fire drove them away. Chemicals were exploding."

"I don't blame you for hating vampires. Not one bit. I hate them more."

He didn't answer. She leaned over him and groped on the floor, looking for her shoes.

"What's the matter?" he asked.

"I need air."

"Don't try to stand up too fast. Here, take my arm."

They stepped onto the deck. Below, on every level of the ferry, the aisles were heaped with bodies—people sleeping in chairs and tents, curled up on benches.

"Peaceful, isn't it?" Jude said. "I've always loved watching the sun rise." He looked up at the grainy sky. A cone of light broke over the water. Caro grasped the rail. It was beaded with moisture, and her hand slid along the metal. Jude started to say something, then shook his head.

"What?" She frowned.

"Never mind. We'll talk in Venice." He raised two fingers in a salute.

She could almost read his thoughts, but there were too many, each one thrashing like a minnow in a bucket. She sensed fear, anger, sorrow, regret. Ravenous desire.

"I don't regret a bloody thing," she whispered.

CHAPTER 46

———

VENICE, ITALY

As the ship approached Venice, Caro walked to the starboard deck and leaned against the rail. Afternoon sun blazed through the clouds, brightening a row of terracotta palaces. Why had Uncle Nigel directed her to Venice? What was waiting at the bank? This could be a wasted trip. But she hadn't given up on Jude. He could have left her alone in Meteora, yet he'd stuck by her.

The ferry puttered down the wide canal, looming over tiny water taxis filled with luggage and tourists. She felt a hand on her elbow, and Jude squeezed in beside her, looking handsome in his leather jacket. "Lovely day," he said, turning his face up to the sun. "I ran into Demos and Father Aeneas at the Internet café. They booked rooms at the Hotel San Gallo. It's near the bank."

They took a water taxi to San Marcos Pier no. 15. As

they walked around St. Mark's Square, pigeons flew up at a slant, blotting out the dome. Jude headed toward Rusolo Campo, and she hurried after him. The Hotel San Gallo was just beyond an old well, nestled at the end of the empty courtyard, a white, three-story building with lime-green shutters framing the windows. Just around the bend, she could see the ornate façade of the majestic Banca Nazionale del Lavoro.

Caro pinched Jude's sleeve, digging her nails into the leather, and struggled to keep up with his brisk pace.

He stopped abruptly, his brow furrowed. "Am I walking too fast?"

"You're practically jogging," she said breathlessly, but her gaze sent a different message. *You're running away from me.*

"I won't go far, lass. Not with these bum ankles." His eyes seemed to say, *I'm damaged goods.*

"I still can't keep up. I'll get lost." *No matter what I do, you'll leave. And I'll be alone.*

The truth was, she was an expert at being alone. She'd always had a wide-open space inside her—Dame Doom's black pit—but now, finally, a radiant streak had forked into the gloom. She didn't know much about human nature, didn't know who or what she was; but she knew how love felt, and it flowed around her, buoyant as the notes in a Puccini aria. No, she couldn't return to the dark. Not now. Not ever.

She gripped his jacket a little harder and breathed in his cologne. "Jude?"

He gazed down at her. "The answer is no," he said in a soft voice.

"But I haven't asked a question."

"Yes, you have." He took a breath and held it, as if he were smelling her, too, and then his face relaxed. "If we're alone, we'll make love. And we can't."

"I always avoided men who say 'can't' in a cultured, I-went-to-Eton way. But you make it sound alluring." She flashed a coy smile. "Do word pheromones exist?"

"At one time, I didn't think vampires existed." A wry smile flickered across his lips. "I never thought I'd be standing in Rusolo Campo, trying to hide a hyper-aroused condition."

"You needn't hide anything." She smiled. "The campo is empty."

"You're relentless."

"If you stop pushing, I'll stop pushing." She released his jacket.

"You're always talking in riddles. I haven't moved an inch."

"I'm quite aware of your position." She cupped her hands over his hands, as if she were holding baby birds, their hearts fluttering against her palms. "I don't want to be alone tonight."

"You'll be on your back in two seconds, Clifford." The vein in his neck leaped against his collar.

"That's your favorite position, not mine."

He winked. "I know."

She felt encouraged by that wink. With his hips pressed up against her, a quivery sensation began in her belly and she couldn't think straight. She locked her hands behind him and looked up into his eyes, studying the brown chips caught in the blue. "Let's take this indoors," she whispered. *Yes. Say yes.*

"I can't." There was that word again. It brushed past her ear, feather soft, barely above a whisper.

"And I know why. Because you love me." She cringed. *Big mistake, Clifford.* She knew better than to pin the L-word on a moving target. Jude would probably think she was stoned on bat-nip, filled with insatiable cravings.

"We'll only get hurt," he said.

"I'll handle it."

"Is it that easy for you?" He pulled away from her, his eyes hard. "It's not me you want. You're flooded with hormones. Right now, you'll sleep with anyone. Check back with me in a few days."

"I'll feel the same."

"Right." He didn't look convinced. "Until then, pull yourself together. Look at yourself. You're a wreck." She felt a prickling behind her eyes. Maybe it *was* hormones or plain old tiredness, but she was going to cry. *Dammit. Son of a bitch.* She strode ahead of him, down the stone walkway and opened the hotel's heavy wooden door.

In the lobby, a sleepy-eyed clerk stood behind the desk, twisting her long blond hair around her fingers. She pushed a clipboard across the marble counter and yawned while Jude wrote down the confirmation number.

Savory aromas wafted from the restaurant, lemony fish with rich undertones of sautéed onions and pancetta. The seasickness had vanished, and Caro was starving. She picked up a hotel brochure to see if the restaurant's hours were listed.

The clerk dropped two enormous brass keys onto the counter.

"*Passaporti, per favore,*" the woman said, stifling another yawn.

Jude tossed down his passport, and Caro slapped hers on top of his. He grabbed a key and left hers on the counter. Then he walked toward a dark staircase.

"Shouldn't we wait for our passports?" she called.

"This is Italy," he said over his shoulder. "We'll get them later."

Caro lifted her key. It was heavy, shaped like a giant toothbrush. Then she hurried toward the stairs. She caught up with Jude on the landing. On either side, halls twisted off into dim passageways. According to the brochure, Hotel San Gallo had only twelve rooms, but they were tucked into corners and at the ends of steep staircases. Her room was three doors down from Jude's.

"I'll see you in thirty minutes," he said. "Then we'll talk to Father Aeneas." His tone was businesslike and dismissive. He fit the huge key into the lock and stepped into his room.

"Make it thirty days," she called after him, and then she closed her door a little too hard.

CHAPTER 47

———

The medicated blood was kept in a chilled compartment in Harry Wilkerson's private jet. Instead of having labels, the bags were color coded.

Moose sat in the back of the plane, transfusing himself. During the flight to Venice, he had sampled the lot. The yellow bags had lessened his finger licking and toe tapping, but they withered his dangly parts. The green bags had been reserved for the Zubas, but Moose had stolen one. The blood had given him a rush reminiscent of his psychedelic days at Piccadilly Circus.

Wilkerson's phone kept ringing, presumably with updates about the girl. When the jet landed at Marco Polo Airport, he briefed the vampires. "My contact just informed me that Miss Clifford will be staying at the San

Gallo. She's registered as Noelle Gaudet—but don't go near her. Just hang back and watch."

"I thought you wanted us to kidnap her," Moose cried.

"And risk another cock-up?" Wilkerson shook his head. "Follow Miss Clifford for the next twenty-four hours. She'll start to feel complacent. If I want you to snatch her, I'll ring you. In the meantime, do try to stay out of trouble."

Wilkerson took off for the Hotel Cipriani, leaving Moose and the Zubas to fend for themselves.

"Now I'm in charge of you fucking sods," Moose said. He tossed two yellow bags to the Zubas, then he selected a bag with a green label for himself.

"Wilkerson told us to take the green ones," said the Zuba with the nose ring. The other fiend stood in the background, rubbing sunblock over his hands—each finger bore a tattoo with some type of fucked up Cyrillic.

"He did, did he?" Moose laughed. "Well, Mr. Toffee Nose isn't here. So you'll get the yellow."

Moose opened a cabinet, pulled out the IV equipment, and slogged to the front of the plane. Something cold hit him between the shoulders, and he turned just in time to see a yellow bag hit the floor.

The Zubas rushed past him in a blur, leaping over the seats, into the aisle. They climbed off the jet and loped across the tarmac. What a pair of donkeys. They needed a big telling-off. They weren't trackers, they were murderers. Moose lifted the green bag and hooked himself to the IV.

He followed the Zubas' distinct smells of blood, sex, menthol, and Dunhill cologne to Campo di Santa Margarita. They stood in the shadows outside the church, dabbing on sunblock.

"So, what are you lot up to?" Moose said.

The Zuba with the nose ring pointed to a medieval building. "We tracked the girl. She is outside the tobacco store with her lover."

"You're sure it's them?" Moose studied the couple. The girl had frizzy, dark blond hair, and she was smiling up at a man. His brown ponytail streamed down his back as he leaned over and kissed her.

The Zubas' mouths opened, fangs slightly extended.

Wankers, Moose thought, and then he grimaced. Ever since those transfusions, his bloody temples had throbbed painfully while the rest of his whole body had grown numb. Had he gotten a bad batch of O negative?

The tattooed Zuba pivoted on his heels and ogled a redhead in tight black pants. She hurried around a corner.

"Hey, stop acting lewd. You're on duty," Moose snapped.

The trio put on reflective capes and followed the couple to the canal. Moose frowned when the people stepped into a gondola. A man in a striped shirt pushed a pole into the water and the boat surged forward, merging with a dozen other gondolas, all of them floating toward a bridge.

"Hurry, duckies, or we'll lose them," Moose said. The Zubas ran behind him along the water. They crossed the bridge and cut down a tangled lane. The gondola skated into a narrow waterway lined with saffron and peach houses. The couple leaned together and kissed. The girl looked like the one in Wilkerson's picture. Yet something just wasn't on.

He and the Zubas jogged along the canal, tracking the gondola. It curved back toward Campo di Santa Margarita. The couple got off the boat and wandered to a gelato stand. Moose's head jerked up when he heard their voices. This wasn't right. The lad with the Clifford girl was supposedly a Briton. These people were Americans.

"That's the wrong couple," Moose told the Zubas.

"No, you are wrong," the tattooed Zuba said.

"You're barking insane. It's not them." Moose pulled out his new iPhone and got the number for the San Gallo. When the hotel operator answered, he cleared his throat. "Hello, dearie," he said in a perfect imitation of a woman's voice. "This is Mrs. Gaudet. My daughter is a guest at your hotel."

He made up a cock-and-bull story about how the daughter shouldn't be disturbed, that Mrs. Gaudet was merely double-checking her precious girl's room number.

After he'd gotten the information, he caught up with the Zubas at the gelato stand. They were still watching the wrong freaking couple. The boy led the girl down a narrow cobbled lane, both of them licking their gelati. The girl's cone was the color of blood but smelled fruity. The tattooed Zuba swaggered after them, and the one with the nose ring followed. Moose grabbed the tattooed vampire's jacket. His hands hit a solid hardness.

The Zuba turned, his eyes flat and cold. Empty.

"You're driving your geese to the wrong pond," Moose said. "Let's go."

"No, you go," said the nose-ringed Zuba. "We stay."

"But you've tracked the wrong people," Moose said. "The real ones are out there, riding in bloody gondolas and feeding pigeons. You're wasting time."

"We will catch up with you later," said the tattooed Zuba, showing his teeth. "After we feed."

"Whatever," Moose said. His temples pounded, and

little fishhooks of pain were spreading into his forehead. He waited until the discomfort faded, then he lifted his iPhone and punched in the number for the San Gallo again. Harry Wilkerson would pay for serving nasty blood. And his daughter would pay with her life.

CHAPTER 48

HOTEL SAN GALLO
VENICE, ITALY

Caro paced in front of the shuttered windows, her shadow dashing over the yellow walls, flitting over blue damask draperies. She fretted over the upcoming bank visit. Then her thoughts turned to Jude. If only she hadn't made a fool of herself in the campo. Maybe it was hormones, but she needed to feel his warm breath on her cheek, his mouth on her mouth, his body inside her body. But that wasn't going to happen because he saw her as an invading, conquering presence.

She turned away from the window and leaped onto the nearest queen-sized bed. The mattress took her body with a slap, setting off unbearably pleasant sensations. She breathed in little sips of air and beat her fists against the pillow until the pulsing in her limbs slowed. After a long while, she slid off the bed, walked to the ornate French desk, and forced herself to look in the mirror.

White face. Mussed hair. Eyes ringed with black mascara. She was a dead ringer for a raccoon. Her pupils were still large and light sensitive, but the flu-like symptoms had vanished. Heaving a sigh, she pushed back her dark brown mane. It had grown longer overnight, falling just past her shoulders, courtesy of Georgi. He was dead, yet his molecules were still alive, burrowing into her DNA.

Her mouth felt dry, as if she'd dipped her tongue in alum, and a glossy sheen covered her palms. The internal changes were beyond her control, but she refused to let a vampire influence her hairstyle from the grave. By damn, she'd cut it off. She started toward her bag, then remembered that Jude had the scissors. She stopped abruptly, but her hair kept moving, snaking around her arms. She needed herbal shampoo and a long, soapy shower. But she didn't trust her body chemistry. What if the dye faded? Actually, that would be a blessing. The straightening solution was another matter. If her militant curls returned, she'd resemble her photograph on Sky News. But if she went to the bank without tidying up, the teller might not reveal information about Uncle Nigel's lockbox. Which was worse—a smelly bandit with straight locks or a clean-smelling girl with crooked hair?

When she was halfway to the bathroom, the phone rang. She sprinted back to the desk, hoping it was Jude. *I'm removing the word "can't" from my lexicon,* he'd say. *We can, and will, be together.* Right before she picked up the receiver, she remembered to answer in French. *"Oui?"*

She heard a faint mewing, followed by a click, then the

line hummed. She jolted, and the receiver fell from her hand. Exactly one week ago, when she'd learned that Uncle Nigel had died, someone had called her flat and meowed.

Breathe, breathe, breathe. Don't get paranoid. Murderers don't impersonate kittens. The caller was a Venetian cat lady who'd dialed the wrong room. Caro wanted to dive onto the bed and yank up the covers, but she forced herself to walk to the bathroom.

She'd just dried her hair when she heard three sharp raps on the door, followed by two softer ones. "It's me," Jude called.

"Just a moment!" She fluffed her hair. The color and texture were intact, and it fell in cold slices against her neck, soothing the wounds.

"Coming," she called and put on an outfit that matched her mood—black jeans and a blacker sweater—then grabbed her bag and hurried out the door.

Jude leaped out of the way, his wet hair swinging forward. The dim lighting in the hall cast shadows over his bruised face. "I fetched our passports . . . "

His voice trailed off. "You look ghastly. Has the nausea returned?"

"You have such a gift for sweet-talk."

The corners of his mouth tugged upward. "So I've been told. What's wrong, Clifford?"

"Someone called my room and meowed." She paused, and a miasma of snark washed through her. "I assumed it was you," she added.

"You're joking, aren't you?" One edge of his mouth kicked up into a smile. "Oh, I see. This is payback for my lecture on catnip."

She tugged the edge of her sweater. Did he think

everything was about him? "It was a real call. By a fake kitten. *Thanks* for your concern."

They walked in silence to Father Aeneas's room. The layout and décor were identical to Caro's. Yellow walls, two queen-sized beds, and ornate French furniture. Afternoon sunlight pricked through blue damask curtains, slashing over the floor. Demos ushered them into the room, running a distracted hand through his white hair. The monk sat in front of a desk, sorting through medicine bottles. When he saw Caro, he smiled and rose to his feet.

"Jude told me you were ill." He grabbed her hands.

"Just a little seasick. I'm fine now."

"Excellent. Please, sit." He waved at a gilt chair.

She perched on the edge, and Jude positioned himself behind her, resting his fingers near her shoulders. The monk's dark eyes swept over her, and then he folded his liver-spotted hands and bowed his head. "Before we discuss your true reasons for coming to Venice, let us pray."

True reasons? She didn't have a clear goal, just a handful of clues. Her thoughts dispersed when the monk began to whisper in Greek. She felt dizzy as words swirled in the air, each one curled and shimmering. Caro felt a tug on her left shoulder, then Jude's hand moved to the back of her neck and gently squeezed. She glanced back. He shook his head, his eyes guarded.

She looked away. Why was he so distrustful? Because vampires had severed his tendons or because suspicion was part of his core personality? Trauma molded a person far quicker than kindness; that much she knew. Her parents had been slaughtered, but she'd survived. Doom and doubt were part of her being, but the pessimism had been balanced by Uncle Nigel's unconditional love.

Now, as the Greek prayer eddied around her, she understood why her uncle had withheld the truth. For whatever reason—probably because she'd moved to London, where he couldn't protect her—he'd changed his mind, and recently, according to the dates on his letters. He'd approached Caro's history the way he would prepare for an archaeological dig. First, he'd unearthed the scientific article, and then he'd burrowed deeper, tracking Jude from Yorkshire to Zürich. Her uncle had set up that meeting in Oxford, hoping to assemble the odd pieces of her life like potsherds. Then, because he loved routines and schedules, he'd left for his annual dig at Perperikon. During his final moments, he'd left clues and the Fates had brought them to her.

Caro sat up straight. Why hadn't Uncle Nigel left any hints about Jude? Had he forgotten? Despite her uncle's condition, his quick mind would have allowed him to jot down a scrambled form of *Jude Barrett—biochemist*. Why hadn't he? Because even at the end of his life, her uncle had been cautious and practical. No need to bring Jude into the fray and endanger him. The monk was a man of God, a former physician, and he knew intimate details about Caro's parents. Uncle Nigel had been deliberately obscure with the anagrams to protect her and Father Aeneas—but was the omission of Jude's name a clue?

Father Aeneas's prayer beads clicked softly as he sketched a cross in the air. His narrow face dissolved into wrinkles as he smiled. "Caroline, what do you hope to find in the safe-deposit box? The third icon? Or ten pages from *Historia Immortalis*?"

She was pretty sure she'd find the vellum, so why was she lying to this good man? Because her uncle's death had created a void. Jude's rejection had created another one. Nature abhors vacuums. She squeezed her hands until her fingertips turned pink.

The monk opened his bag and dragged out a small cloth bundle. His gnarled fingers drew back the fabric. The icon was a bit smaller than hers, and curved at the top.

"Caroline, let me see your panel."

She fished it out of her bag and set it on the bed. The monk pushed his icon beside hers, aligning the colors and images. The night sky filled the top portion of both panels, with mountains jutting up like wolf teeth. Father Aeneas's icon showed a stone sarcophagus. Inside was a man, his eyes wide open, and he seemed to be rising. Below him, a fire raged out of control, flames jutting out of an arched window, with a tiny robed figure racing away from the inferno, carrying a sheaf of papers and a large egg.

Caro tried to look away from the flames, but she felt herself pulled toward them. She could hear crackling wood and smell the scorched flesh. She felt a cool hand on her shoulder and looked up into Father Aeneas's eyes.

"My child, are you ill?" he asked.

"I don't know." She pointed to his icon. "This is the fire that killed my parents. And this figure is a child. She's me."

"Impossible," Father Aeneas said. "The triptych was painted in the eighth century."

"But look at my icon." She pointed to the red-robed woman. "She's holding a book and an egg. And her hair is dark like mine."

"It's not you." Jude touched her neck. "A week ago, you were blond."

Father Aeneas nodded. "This triptych depicts the Albigensian Crusade. Many people burned, and *Historia Immortalis* was at the center of it."

"What does the egg mean?" Jude asked.

"It's symbolic of birth and rebirth." Father Aeneas drew his finger along the line where the icons were joined. "Do you see the beehive and peacock feather? More symbols of immortality. Sir Nigel and I put these panels together a long time ago. We spent days examining the art, trying to decipher the metaphors. The night sky is larger on my panel. And look at the stars—Perseus and the Pleiades. This is significant. Of what, I do not know. We desperately need the third icon."

"Maybe it is in the vault?" Demos spread his hands.

"What time does the bank close?" Jude asked.

"If Caroline leaves now, she should make it before siesta," Demos said.

She grabbed her bag and started for the door. "Wait," Jude called. "Where are you going?"

She turned. "The bank."

"What are you planning to use for identification?"

She reeled backward. "Damn."

"What is the problem?" Father Aeneas folded his hands.

"The bank will ask for identification," Jude said.

Father Aeneas stepped away from the bed. "But Caroline has the key."

"She'll need more than that," Jude said.

Father Aeneas frowned. "The bank isn't interested in Sir Nigel's lockbox."

"They might be interested in *her*." Jude stared into Caro's empty chair. "She can't ask them to look up Sir Nigel's box. She doesn't have the number, by the way.

And they're going to ask for it, along with her relationship to Sir Nigel."

"They'll definitely want identification, too," Demos said. "If her name isn't listed on the account, they won't divulge anything. They may call the police."

Caro leaned against the wall, feeling a headache trying to break loose behind her eyes. Uncle Nigel's instructions had led her to Venice. She had to follow them.

Jude crossed the room and squeezed her shoulder. At first, she thought he was trying to comfort her, but the pressure intensified. She looked up.

"What about your uncle's passport?" he asked.

"Yes, what of it?" She blinked.

"It might be useful." He looked at Demos, who was leaning against the wall, picking his teeth with his fingernail.

Jude shrugged off his jacket and picked at the seam. He pulled out Uncle Nigel's passport and handed it to Caro. She glanced at Demos, then her uncle's photo. Father Aeneas joined them and studied the picture, too. He looked at Demos. "Uncanny," he said.

"They're around the same age," Jude said. "Even the white hair is the same."

This won't work, Caro thought.

"He'll need a haircut," Jude said. "And the beard would have to go."

Demos stopped picking his teeth and scowled.

"It could work," Father Aeneas said.

Jude opened his bag and pulled out scissors. "Caro, you should alter your appearance, too. The bank will have video cameras. Did you bring a dress?"

"No. Why?"

He handed her a fistful of euros and sent her to a boutique with instructions to tart up, without veering too far from her passport photo. She walked to the door and hesitated. Was it safe to go out alone? She started to ask Jude to come with her, but he was already steering the loudly complaining Demos into the bathroom.

She hurried out of the hotel and dashed over the bridge, past tattoo artists and men selling fake Louis Vuitton and Fendi handbags. She cut down a narrow alley and turned into a shop. Her headache vanished when she pulled a black dress from the rack. Finally she was doing something normal. The dress wasn't her size or style, but at six euros it was a bargain. She folded the garment over her arm and reached into a sale basket, scooping up a handful of bangle bracelets. On her way to the register, she grabbed a mannequin's black sweater.

Five minutes later she'd changed clothes and was on her way back to the hotel. Her dress swirled around her knees as she stepped into Father Aeneas's room. The monk did a double take. Jude looked at her legs, and his eyes widened. Before he could speak, Demos emerged from the bathroom. His hair was neatly trimmed, and the beard was gone.

Caro thought she might cry. Demos looked eerily like her uncle.

Jude handed her a black expandable bag, the type that tourists favored for trinkets, then began firing off instructions.

"When you walk into the bank, keep your head down. And when you open the box, put the contents in this bag. Don't look at the camera, either."

Jude pulled her aside. "Find a teller who isn't paying attention. Avoid the obsessive ones. Look for a messy desk.

Offer minimal information, and give it in increments. If the officer prohibits you from accompanying Demos to the vault, insist that he suffers from palsy and needs your help. Demos, shake a little." Jude demonstrated. "Caro, if anyone recognizes you, run like bloody hell. You, too, Demos."

"Okay." She dropped her uncle's keychain into the nylon bag.

"Scared?" he asked her.

"Petrified."

"You can do this," he whispered.

Behind him, Demos was pacing. "I do not look like myself," he complained. "I do not resemble my own passport photo. How will I get back into Greece?"

"Your beard will grow," Father Aeneas said.

"In a few weeks, yes."

"Be thankful we didn't shave your head," Father Aeneas said.

Demos's forehead puckered. "You laugh, but I am serious. It is illegal to use a false ID. I am too old for this trouble."

"After it's over, I'll buy you a hat," Caro said, handing him her uncle's passport. He started to thumb through it, but she put her hand on his. "And sunglasses," she added. "I'll buy you sunglasses."

Demos eyed her. "I want my hair."

"Demos, my friend," Father Aeneas said, "you complain more than fifty nuns on a fast."

———

Caro followed Demos along the Grand Canal, the afternoon light streaking on the water. The back of her neck tightened, and she had the feeling again that someone was watching. She spun around. A gondola glided by, its reflection moving in the dark green water. In one end of the gondola, a man with a dark ponytail aimed a video camera at a girl with curly, ash-blond hair. A Burberry scarf was looped around the man's neck.

"What is wrong?" Demos asked.

"I don't know." She pressed a fist against her chest. Never in her life had she experienced a premonition, but she felt a sense of doom around that couple.

Demos followed her gaze. "The girl, she looks like you. Except her hair is frizzy."

Caro blinked. The girl's curls spiraled around her shoulders, and the man had an uncanny resemblance to Jude before he'd cut his hair.

Demos dismissed the couple with a wave. "Come, we must hurry or the bank will close."

She tucked her hand into the crook of Demos's arm and they headed to the Banca Nazionale del Lavoro. They stepped into the marble lobby, and Caro looked around for a distracted employee. A policeman stood beside a teller's cage. His gaze lingered on a skinny brunette in a tight beige dress who sat on the edge of a desk, surrounded by messy folders. She yelled into the phone, lifting her free hand and making a fist. Dozens of gold bracelets rattled. Caro picked out a few Italian phrases—*Dove eravate* and *Perché telefonate*—and decided that a man had stood up the brunette.

The woman slammed her fist against her desk. Several tellers glanced in her direction and smiled at each other. *"Bastardo,"* she cried.

Perfect, Caro thought. She steered Mr. Demos toward the desk and waited. The woman's eyes flashed as she slammed the receiver over and over. She glared at Caro and Demos, clearly irritated by the intrusion.

Caro explained that her uncle needed to examine his safe-deposit box. She wrote her uncle's name on a Post-it note and slid it across the brunette's desk. The woman blinked at the note and rolled her eyes, chattering under her breath in Italian about old paper and water.

Not a good sign, Caro thought.

The woman spread her arms on the desk, the bracelets chinking, and cast a petulant glance at Demos. *"Posso vedere la vostra identificazione?"*

"He's British," Caro said. "He doesn't speak Italian."

The brunette shrugged. "May I please see ID?" she asked in English.

Demos flashed the passport. The woman glanced at the photograph, then looked at Demos. He sealed the deal by winking at her. She slid off her desk and eased into a chair, then turned to a computer terminal. As her fingers clicked over the keys, she frowned. Caro began to panic. What if this was the wrong bank? What if Interpol had flagged the account?

"This way please," the clerk said in Italian. She slid off her desk and walked down a hallway, her high heels clicking. She glanced over her shoulder to make sure they were following, then she turned up a winding staircase. Demos was gasping when they reached the top.

"This is the vault for paintings and documents," the woman said in halting English. "It is small but far away from dampness. And, it is climate-controlled." She passed through the rounded vault door into a room with green marble walls. Fitted into the walls were numbered brass boxes, the smaller ones on top, with larger ones running along the bottom. The woman stepped around a corner and pointed to the top shelf. "Box 514356," she said. "May I see your key?" The woman extended her hand, the long tapered fingers curling.

Caro hesitated. She wasn't at all sure of the procedure. She pulled the rabbit's-foot keychain out of her bag and held it out. The brunette narrowed her eyes at Demos.

"His eyesight is failing," Caro said. "It's difficult for him to distinguish the keys."

The brunette exhaled, and her bangs lifted from her forehead. She picked out a small key with a round top and slid it into the keyhole. The tumblers clicked. Standing on her toes, the woman slapped open the door and yanked out a metal box. She carried it to a table and set it down, bracelets clanging, then tossed down the key. The violent jangling continued when she pointed to a clock above the door.

"The bank will be closing for siesta in one hour," she said.

"We won't take long," Caro said.

As the woman stepped out of the vault, Caro glanced around for a camera. She didn't see one. Demos sat down with an exaggerated groan, as if he'd fallen ill. His hand slipped under the table, his index finger pointing above the vault door. A tiny black camera hung down from the ceiling, blending into marble veins that ran along the wall.

Caro turned away from the door and opened the nylon bag. Demos stood, blocking the camera's view with his rounded shoulders. Caro ran her hands over the box. She didn't see a lock. She raised the lid. Inside was a smaller cardboard box.

"We'll open it later," she whispered and slipped it, and her uncle's keychain, into the bag.

"Walk behind me," Demos said. He walked through the round door. Caro remembered the camera and lowered her head. She followed Demos down the stairs, back to the lobby. The policeman moved away from the teller's cage and strutted down the aisle, his hands clasped behind his back. He squinted at Caro's bag. Demos steered her toward the main entrance. Halfway to the door, their clerk yelled, *"Arresti!"*

Demos stumbled, and Caro reached out to steady him. His eyes rounded in horror. She leaned over and whispered, *"Arresti* means 'stop.' "

She turned, forcing herself to smile. The clerk tottered over to Caro and Demos, her lips curved into a smile.

"Signore, I checked your account. It has well over two million euros." The woman spoke in perfect English now, and directed her comments to Demos. "If you would like to set up an appointment tomorrow, I can explain how your money can earn dividends."

He lifted one eyebrow and sketched a giant capital *L.* It took Caro a moment to realize that he'd drawn the British pound sign; he meant for her to collect the money.

Caro tilted her head to the side. It was tempting to empty the bank's coffers, but it would take days, even weeks, for the bank to complete the paperwork. And they would need a steamer trunk to haul the money. A bigger question loomed: How had her uncle squirreled away two million euros on a professor's salary?

"Il mio zio penserà a questo proposito," Caro said. *My uncle will think about it.*

The brunette handed Caro a business card, bracelets skating over her thin arm. *"Arrivederci."*

"But . . ." Demos sputtered.

"Time for your pill, Uncle," Caro said, and pulled him out the door.

CHAPTER 49

Caro and Demos walked into the hotel room. Jude and Father Aeneas were stretched out on the beds, watching an Italian soap opera on TV, *Un Posto al Sole. A Place in the Sun.*

Jude sat bolt upright. "How did it go?"

"It was a piece of cake," Demos said, tucking her uncle's passport into her bag. "Except when Caro lost two million euros."

"It's not lost," she said and explained about her uncle's mysterious fortune.

"Caroline, you made a wise decision." Father Aeneas frowned at Demos. "You can always collect the money later."

"If there is a later." Demos snorted. "She is wanted by the authorities. She will never get her inheritance under her real name. This was her only chance."

"It was a chance for both of you to get arrested," Father Aeneas said.

Demos's cheeks turned red. "But—"

The monk cut him off. "Do you not see the dangers? Are you mad?"

"I resent that." Demos lifted a finger over his head. "And I do not like the haircut you gave me, either."

While Father Aeneas and Demos argued, Caro unzipped the nylon bag, removed the cardboard box, and set it on the bed. She pulled off the lid and saw ten vellum sheets, each one lavishly illustrated. Magenta knights held shields, each one woven with infinity symbols, and below the knights, a dead stag lay with its neck ripped open. Many pages showed graphic, alluring illustrations of sex and vampirism.

Caro's bracelets clicked as she tilted the box. The dazzling colors seemed to vibrate, washing over the back of her hand. Obsidian, lapis, topaz, amethyst, shot through with gilt. Each page curled at the edges like dried tobacco leaves.

"All this trouble for a book?" Demos snorted.

Father Aeneas's breath stirred his beard. "It is *Historia Immortalis*."

"How long were the pages stored at the bank?" Jude asked.

"It's impossible to know," Father Aeneas said. "The Gospel of Judas deteriorated while it sat in a Long Island lockbox for years."

Lines slashed across Jude's forehead as he bent down to study the page. "Why would Sir Nigel put a valuable book in a city of water? What if the bank had flooded?"

"The lockbox was in a special room," Demos said. "It would take a tsunami for water to reach that vault."

"But it still seems rather careless," Jude said.

"No," Caro said. "My uncle wasn't the capricious type. He hid the pages in Venice for a reason."

"I agree." Father Aeneas nodded. "He knew the vellum would be safe. It is durable. These pages have lasted over a thousand years."

Jude whistled. "That long?"

Father Aeneas pointed to the lavish black script. "You are looking at the literary brainchild of Charlemagne. Notice the upper- and lowercase letters? The words are spaced and do not run together. It is called Carolingian minuscule. Named after—"

"I just can't believe it." Caro lifted the cardboard lid and flipped it over. An envelope swung down, hanging by a strip of yellowed tape. Using the tip of her fingernail, she opened the envelope and pulled out a bill of sale from Sotheby's auction house in London.

Father Aeneas peered over her shoulder. "The provenance," he said.

"What's a provenance?" Jude asked.

"A list of previous owners." Father Aeneas gestured to the paper. "It helps prevent the sale of stolen artifacts."

At the bottom of the page, Caro stared at the signature. *Vivienne Wilkerson.* So it was true. Her mother had been married to that British man.

"I'd hoped Sir Nigel would have left a note about the third icon." Father Aeneas's eyes drooped at the edges.

"It could be anywhere," Demos said. "You could spend the rest of your days looking."

"Maybe the note is stuck between the pages," Jude said.

"Brilliant idea," Caro said, and bent over to examine them. Hypnotic colors ran along the scrolled border, distracting her for a moment. She sifted through the pages. Nothing.

Father Aeneas held up the cardboard box. Light streamed through tiny circles. "Do you see the pinholes in the cardboard?" he asked, his voice rising. "They were put here so the vellum pages could breathe."

"See if the box has a false bottom." Demos handed his pocketknife to the monk.

Father Aeneas ran the blade along the edges of the box, scraping the corners. The upper right section loosened, curling, and the monk peeled back the cardboard. Hidden underneath was a small envelope.

Father Aeneas's hand shook as he handed it to Caro. When she opened it, a yellowed paper slid out. She recognized her uncle's precise handwriting.

Isla Carbonera
Villa Primaverina
Sig Raphael Della Rocca
Vitas Quest Rev I

Jude stepped closer. "More anagrams?"

"They're not encrypted," she said, tracing her finger over the last phrase. " 'Vita' means life. Uncle Nigel is telling me the quest is over and to get on with my life."

"What about 'Rev I'?" Jude asked.

"The Book of Revelation," Father Aeneas said. "The 'I' doubtlessly refers to the introduction and benediction.

'Blessed is he who reads and those who hear the words of this prophecy, and keep those things which are written in it, for the time is near.'"

Caro drew in a ragged gasp. The time was near for *what*? She glanced at Jude. He looked pale and troubled.

Father Aeneas patted her arm. "Now it is clear why Sir Nigel involved me. He knew you would need someone to examine the vellum. To make sure the leaves aren't forgeries."

"Maybe they are all fake," Demos said.

"How could you determine authenticity unless you had a piece of the original?" Caro lifted a page. Something else bothered her too—the order of her uncle's clues. He'd taught her to pay attention to all parts of a puzzle. Venice hadn't been an arbitrary hiding place for the vellum. Every mark in her uncle's passport, every word, held meaning. If he'd been concerned about forgery, he would have listed the anagrams in reverse—first, she would have traveled to Venice and retrieved the pages. Next, she would have found the villa and Raphael Della Rocca. Finally, she would have gone to the monastery.

Father Aeneas turned to Demos. "We must return to Varlaam immediately."

"Why?" Caro said.

The monk looked puzzled. "Because my tools are there. And I know an excellent paleographer in Meteora. We'll need to arrange for carbon dating, of course."

Demos sighed. "I'll check the ferry schedules."

"I can't go back to Meteora." Caro slid her uncle's note into the box. "My uncle intended for me to locate Isla Carbonera. Then, I've got to find Signore Della Rocca."

"But your life could be in danger. You must come with me to Varlaam. I must inspect the pages. If they are not authentic, there is no reason for anyone to chase you."

"I agree with Caro," Jude said. "She needs to find the villa. It doesn't matter if these pages are genuine. Whoever is chasing her won't be privy to your findings. They'll assume these pages are real, and they'll hunt her until it's finished."

"When I find Isla Carbonera, I'll bring everything to Varlaam. Father, you have my word."

"As you wish." Father Aeneas sighed. "I will examine the pages when God wills it."

"I knew we should have brought the van," Demos said.

"Call the front desk, Demos. Perhaps they will know where to find Isla Carbonera." Father Aeneas grimaced and pressed his fist to his chest. "Too much excitement for an old man."

"And too many gyros on the ferry," Demos said.

"I'll be fine." Father Aeneas twirled one finger in the air. "Call the front desk."

"This can wait." Demos pulled up one of the carved chairs. "Sit, sit."

"Eh." Father Aeneas shrugged.

"Should I call a doctor?" Caro asked. The monk seemed suddenly too frail to lift a gyro, much less a crossbow.

"No, no. I do not trust the Italians. Demos is right. I shouldn't have eaten the gyros. I need bicarbonate of soda."

"Which is first?" Demos rubbed his eyebrows, making them stand up. "Call the front desk or get the soda?"

"Soda," Father Aeneas said. "I will be ready to travel in an hour."

"There's no hurry." Caro tucked the box into her duffel bag. She pointed to his icon. "May I borrow it for an hour or so? I want to study the images."

"Yes, of course. Demos, wrap the panel for Caroline."

Demos pulled a pillow from its case and slid the icon inside. He cradled it like an egg and eased it inside her bag.

"Bah." Father Aeneas waved one hand. "I shall wait. Dusk is coming. It is safer to travel in daylight."

Daylight, Caro thought as she followed Jude into the hall. She hurried after him, her bracelets clinking. "Jude, slow down."

He turned. "Sorry. I'm in a bit of a rush."

"I'll say. Are you going to help me find Isla Carbonera?"

"I wish I could." His lips tightened into a thin line. "My train leaves tonight."

Her chest tightened. She'd been dreading this moment, and now it was here. "Were you going to say good-bye?"

He looked away. "I hadn't thought that far. I'm not leaving until nine o'clock."

She pushed back her sleeve to check her watch, but saw a bare patch of skin. "Dammit."

"What's wrong?"

"My watch. I must have lost it at Varlaam." She rubbed her chest. Any second now she'd hyperventilate. "I thought you'd stay awhile longer."

"It wasn't an easy decision."

"Are you going back to Switzerland?"

"No."

"Scotland?"

"I can't put Lady Patricia in danger."

"Then where?" Her chest sawed up and down.

Jude hesitated and his face contorted, as if he'd just stepped on a nail. "It's best if you don't know."

"You promised you'd stay until I was safe."

His face relaxed. "But you are. Father Aeneas and Demos will look after you."

"So this is it? I'll never see you again?" She squeezed the bracelets, digging them into her wrist. Maybe the pain would prevent her from crying.

"I shall always think about you," he said.

Her mouth grew dry. She wanted more than an occasional thought. She loved him, and she wanted him to love her, too.

"We made a good team, didn't we?" he said.

She squeezed the bracelets a bit harder, and the sharp bite of pain seemed to help. She might be devastated, but she was alive. Jude had saved her life, but perhaps he'd fulfilled his role in this adventure. Fate was pushing him toward another quest, just as it was pushing her to the mysterious villa. Her breathing slowed, and her mouth didn't feel quite so dry. "We did," she said in a clear, calm voice.

"Take care of yourself, Caro."

"Can I buy you a farewell drink?" She fully expected him to decline, but she wanted to delay him a few seconds longer. She looked up into his eyes, memorizing the exact placement of the brown specks in his blue irises. *Please say yes.*

His head tipped back a little, and he blinked. "Yes," he said.

She repressed a smile. "Should I drop my bag in my room?"

"We'd better stay away from there," he said, taking her arm. "Come on."

As Jude and Caro walked along the Grand Canal, afternoon light hit the palaces, staining them pink. Water slapped against the gondolas, and the boats drifted, straining against the ropes that lashed them to the pier. The bells in St. Mark's Square began to clang, and they walked to the church. Cafés rimmed the piazza and the smell of baked bread wafted through the air.

"Let's keep walking," Jude said. "Unless you think we'll get lost."

"You know what those silly tourist guides say—getting lost in Venice is part of the adventure."

"You're struggling with that bag," he said. "Let me carry it for a while."

She gladly handed it over, and they wandered to Campo di Santa Margarita, where smells from the morning fish market still lingered. The campo spread out in a T, each section jammed with tourists. A little boy in a red coat kicked a rubber ball across the square. The fading light hit the tops of the buildings, brightening one side of the square, throwing the other into shade.

"It's crowded," Jude said. "What's the occasion?"

"Campo di Santa Margarita is always this way," she said.

They turned into Café Rosso, and Jude led her to a table in the back. A waiter took their drink orders and stepped toward the bar. Caro leaned across the table.

"What if I can't find Villa Primaverina?" she asked.

"You will. I have faith in you."

"Please come with me."

"Caro," he said, giving her a warning glance.

"Aren't you even a little curious about what I'll find at this villa?"

"Of course." He looked past her, out the window.

She grabbed his hands. "Stay one more day. Just one." She knew how she sounded. Desperate. But she had nothing to lose.

He pulled away. "You know what will happen."

"You make it sound terrible, like being with me is as dangerous as smoking crack."

"It is."

The waiter set down their wine and bustled off. She thought about Father Aeneas's theory. Her predatory genes had attracted Jude. She was a human cone shell. And its alluring effect had strengthened after she'd been bitten.

Jude lifted his glass. "I've already explained why I loathe vampires. You need to focus on other issues, like finding Villa Primaverina. Or going back for your two million euros."

"Don't lecture me." Her stomach tensed as she watched him drain the glass and signal the waiter for a refill.

Without looking at her, he said, "What are you going to do with the vellum leaves?"

"Hide them in another lockbox." She rubbed her finger over the rim of her untouched glass. "Then I'll hide."

The waiter stopped beside Jude, set down a full glass of Merlot, and moved to another table. Jude lifted the glass and took a swallow. "Please be careful. Too many people have died because of those pages."

"If you were truly concerned about my welfare, you'd stay."

"I never said I wasn't worried." He drank the rest of his wine.

Caro slid her glass out of his reach. "When you look at me, you see a monster, but I'm just an ordinary girl in a bar."

He gave her a long, contemplative stare, then he said, "You're anything but ordinary."

Darkness gathered between the buildings as Jude walked Caro back to the hotel. The streets were crowded and she fell in step behind him, pinching his jacket. He hurried past Campo Rusolo and stopped in front of a jewelry shop.

"Maybe they sell watches," he said, and opened the door. A bell dinged over his head as he stepped through a vestibule. Caro followed him inside and stopped at a display table. She lifted a silver goblet that was heavily engraved with hunting dogs.

A lady in a beige dress looked up from the counter and smiled at Jude. *"Desidera?"* she asked.

A loaded question, Caro thought. *Desidera* from *desiderare*, a desire for something or someone you did not have.

"Do you sell watches?" Jude asked.

"None that work," the lady said, and gestured to an aged onyx rosary. "I specialize in antique jewelry. Could I interest you in a brooch or hat pin?"

Jude stared at the glittering objects that lay inside the case. His gaze stopped on an enormous red pendant. The stone was oval, rimmed by a gold border, and the intricate bale was tethered to a double strand of polished red beads. The woman removed it from the case, humming to herself as she arranged the pendant on a plush black pillow.

"Is it a gemstone?" Jude asked.

"Nephrite jade," the woman said.

Caro leaned closer for a better look. "Jade is green. These stones are rusty red."

"Green is the traditional color," the woman said. "But it can be red, white, black, yellow, or purple."

"Iron oxide makes it red," Jude remarked casually.

The woman smiled at Caro. "Does your boyfriend always use strong words to describe delicate objects?"

"The Italians have a rather strong word for boyfriend," Caro said. "*Fidanzato* sounds . . . beefy."

A pink flush spread across Jude's cheeks. "I was merely trying to explain."

"Jade has other qualities," the woman said quickly. "It frightens foes and prevents bodily harm and symbolizes strength. That is because jade is very hard—perhaps the hardest of all gemstones."

"It's tough because of tremolite," Jude said. "That's a mineral."

The woman touched the ornate gold loop that joined the beads to the oval stone. "The bale is formed by two serpents. Notice how they form a circle, as if they are swallowing themselves?"

Jude stiffened, and the pinkness washed out of his face. "Yes, well. Perhaps you can show me a necklace that doesn't have negative symbolism."

Temptation. Eve and the apple. Caro lifted an eyebrow. Definitely not his style.

The woman's eyes rounded. "No, no, no. You misunderstand. On jewelry, the snake motif has a respectable meaning. These serpents are guardians. They deflect evil. No thief will steal a pendant that is watched by these sentinels."

"Perhaps I *do* like it." Jude lifted the pendant and turned to Caro. She tried to control her breathing as he fastened the clasp. Except for the cheap bangles she'd bought today, she'd never owned jewelry. He stepped back. The pendant fell just above her breasts.

"Perfetto," the woman said.

"Sì," Caro said.

The woman's eyes went to the Band-Aid on Caro's neck. "He is desperately in love with you," she whispered in Italian.

"Desidero," Caro said. *I wish.*

"What did she say?" Jude lifted his eyebrows.

"That you'll be sorry if you leave me," Caro said.

"Shall I wrap the necklace?" the woman asked.

"I believe the lady will wear it," he said.

Caro looked down at the stone. It quivered on her chest like a beautiful ticking clock, each woeful beat pushing her away from Jude. They left the shop and turned down Calle Valleresso. A girl with blue-tipped hair squeezed through the crowd outside Harry's Bar. She lifted a giant strawberry daiquiri, and the contents sloshed over the edge of the glass. *"Scusa, scusa!"* she cried. She surged around another group and plowed into Caro. The glass flew out of the girl's hand and smashed on the cobblestones.

Italian words flew out of the girl's mouth as she leaped back. Caro glanced at her dress. A red stain covered the front, bits of ice clinging to the ruffled hem.

"Let's get you cleaned up," Jude said, and steered Caro away from the shards, into the bar. They dodged a waiter and hurried down a staircase, into a dim hallway. A carved door stood ajar, spilling a wedge of light onto the terrazzo floor. The hinges squeaked as Jude pushed open the door and led her inside.

"We took a wrong turn," Jude said. "This is the wine cellar."

The walls were lined with corkscrews and dusty wine bottles. A long pine table stood at the far end, piled with napkins. Jude grabbed one and dabbed it against her collarbone. Their eyes met. She studied the brown flecks in his left iris. Oh, how she loved them. She pressed her hand against his cheek, the dark stubble prickling her palm.

"I'm so afraid you'll forget about me," she asked. "Or maybe that's what you want." *Where's your pride, Clifford? Let him leave. You'll pick up the pieces and put yourself back together.*

He shook his head. "Never."

"I can't get through this without you," she said. He looked away.

She lifted his chin. A tear curved down the side of his nose, over his lips. She touched the tear and slipped her finger into her mouth.

"Don't do that," he whispered. "Or I shall go mad."

His broad Yorkshire accent had an intoxicating effect, like tossing down shots of whiskey. She walked to the door and bolted it.

"Unlock it," he said.

"No." She lifted her chin. "Make love to me," she whispered. "One last time."

"Here?"

She crossed the room and looked up at him. "Yes," she whispered. She grabbed his belt and pulled him against her. His warm, wine-scented breath stirred her hair.

"You're seducing me," he said.

She wrapped her arms around him and held tight. At first, he didn't move, and then she felt his hand slide over her back. His mouth found hers, and his tongue began moving in a slow, familiar waltz. He lifted her skirt and drew it over her thigh. The sweet dance picked up speed, and she felt dizzy. Her thoughts scattered like wild birds. All she knew was his touch, his kiss, his smell.

He unzipped his trousers and pushed them down. She stepped between his legs, feeling him against her hip bone. He led her to the oak table and raised her dress one inch at a time, his fingers gliding under the damp fabric, brushing against her bare stomach. His gaze dropped to her legs and moved up.

"Turn around," he said. "And bend over the table."

So that was how it was going to be. He didn't want to look at her face. He was drawing a bold line between sex and love. She leaned over and flattened her hands against the table, feeling the smooth grooves along the wood. She felt him move against the backs of her legs. He pulled up her dress, then grasped one edge of her lace panties and tugged. As he pulled them down, she felt his hot breath on the small of her back. His lips moved up her spine, each kiss searing her skin.

His hands dropped to the swell of her hips. "Spread your legs," he whispered. She braced her feet apart. His body pressed close, and then he was inside her. The wine bottles started rattling in their wooden cradles. She wanted to see his eyes and fall headlong into the color blue; chips of sky, a swirling current in the Aegean, the haze of distant mountains, forget-me-nots scattering in the wind. He stopped, and the wine bottles quit rocking. She felt him move away from her, and she looked over her shoulder. Before she could ask what was wrong, his hand closed over hers, and he spun her around. He lifted her into his arms, her skirt billowing, and set her on the table, nudging her legs apart. He reached into the space between them, found her center, and entered her. She pushed her hands beneath his leather jacket and squeezed his chest, feeling dense muscles beneath his sweater.

"Please come back to me," she whispered.

"I haven't left yet." His lips crushed against hers. His hands flitted over her cheeks, shoulders, hips, breasts. Her hips rose from the table, and she wrapped her arms around his neck. The air around them seemed to ignite. She was running through fire, and there was no turning back. She arched her back and spread her legs wider, taking him deeper and deeper.

He gasped, then whispered in French, "I'm going to come, I'm—"

His thighs trembled violently, and he pulled out of her. Something warm jetted against her thigh. He wasn't going to risk having a quarter-vampire bastard. He pressed his forehead against hers.

"I know you care for me," she whispered.

"What if I do? You heard what Father Aeneas said. I can't satisfy you."

"You just did."

"It's not me." He shook his head. "It's not. What if I'm keeping you from your true love?"

She smoothed back his hair. "You *are* keeping me from him."

He looked down and groaned. He was growing. "Not possible," he said.

A fierce arousal swept through Caro, and it had a scent,

a musky, sugar-coming-to-a-boil smell. Her knees trembled. She grabbed the table, and the pendant skimmed over her damp chest. Clock's ticking, she thought.

"I've got to have you again," Jude said. His pupils dilated as he took her with a ferocity that left them shaking. She collapsed against him, panting. He lifted her hair and blew on her neck.

The doorknob shook, and a man cursed in Italian. Jude and Caro pulled apart, adjusted their clothing, and walked to the door. Jude threw the bolt, and they stepped past a startled waiter. She started up the stairs, then reached back for Jude's hand. Static electricity crackled, and her fingertips buzzed. He pulled away. Had he felt it, too?

He stared at his palm and made no comment. They walked out of the bar and started up Calle Valleresso. At the corner, two men with short platinum hair strode down Salizada San Moisè. A burly redheaded man ran after them.

"Hold on, wankers," the redhead yelled in a Cockney accent. "That's not the way to the San Gallo."

Jude's eyes darkened with recognition. He wheeled around and seized Caro's arms; he pressed his lips to her ear. "Don't move," he whispered.

"Why, what's wrong—"

He silenced her with a kiss and his hands tightened on her arms. She tried to squirm away but he gripped her tighter. The wounds in her neck began to throb. Something was dreadfully wrong. Over his shoulder, she saw the redheaded man cut down Seconda Calle de la Fava, trailed by the skinny guys. They weren't looking at Caro, but she felt pulled in their direction. The holes in her neck thrummed. Vampires.

A girl in a green dress hurried down Seconda Calle de

la Fava. Her high heels clicked as she turned the corner. The blond vampires shot after her.

"Leave it, you grot bags," the redheaded man yelled.

Their footsteps faded to a distant clap as they ran after the woman. Jude's lips were still jammed against Caro's. "They're gone," she said, her voice echoing in his mouth.

He pulled back. "Did you see those men?" he asked.

"Yes, of course. You know them?"

"The big ginger guy came to my lab in York. He held me down while the Bulgarians cut my tendons."

"How did they track you to Venice?"

"They're not after me." He grabbed her hand. "We've got to get to the hotel and warn Father Aeneas."

"They're moving that way." She pulled him in the opposite direction, down to Campo San Moisè, and stopped in front of the Hotel Bauer. Off to the side, gondolas bobbed in a narrow canal.

"Let's hide in the Bauer," she said, pulling him toward the glass doors. The lobby was jammed with people. Jude and Caro stepped around luggage racks and angled to the pay phones. Caro dialed the Hotel San Gallo and tapped her fingers against the marble ledge while the operator connected the call. Jude walked over to a map of Venice that hung on the opposite wall.

"Father? This is Caro—there's a lot of noise. Can you speak up?"

"Where are you?" Father Aeneas cried. "Demos has been looking everywhere."

"We ran into a snag." She explained about the vampires and their connection to Jude.

"Is he certain?" Father Aeneas cried.

"Yes."

"But why are his attackers in Venice?" Father Aeneas asked.

"They're tracking me. You and Demos could be in danger, too."

"I am not worried for myself."

"Just be careful. We spotted the men by Saint Mark's Square. They were headed to Hotel San Gallo."

"You are certain?"

"One of them mentioned it." She wrapped the phone cord around her wrist.

"When are you coming back to the hotel?"

"I'm not. I'll just get a room at the Bauer."

"Should Demos fetch the vellum sheets and icons from your room?"

"They're with me. I'll take good care of them, Father."

"You are so like your uncle. Meticulous and brave. Sir Nigel would be proud."

Caro glanced toward the map. Jude was tracing his finger over Murano, then out to the lagoon. "I'll call tomorrow."

"Go with God," Father Aeneas said.

She hung up and stepped over to the map. "The lobby is jammed. We shouldn't linger."

"I found Isla Carbonera." He touched a tiny dot on the map. "It's in the north lagoon. Between the airport and Murano."

"Seriously?" She leaned forward, and a wild flutter moved up her spine. Sure enough, there was the island. She squeezed Jude's arm. "Let's go."

"Now?"

"Why not?"

"Why not? Because those vampires are lurking. And we don't know if Villa Primaverina is on that island."

"Let's ask the concierge," Caro said.

"Twenty quid says she's never heard of that villa," Jude said.

"You're on."

They walked to the concierge's desk. The woman smiled and ran one hand over her shiny blond hair. Her smile changed into a frown when Caro asked about Villa Primaverina.

"It's on one of the islands," the concierge said with a faint German accent.

"Isla Carbonera?" Caro asked.

The woman gave a short nod.

"What's the best way to get there?" Caro asked.

"You can't." The concierge narrowed her eyes. "It is private. No tourist boats go there."

"Surely you can arrange a water taxi."

"Are you a guest at the Bauer?"

Jude slid a fifty-euro note over the woman's desk. "Does the Signore Raphael Della Rocca live at Villa Primaverina?" he asked.

"He owns the island."

"Who is he?" Caro asked.

"A rich man who hates tourists."

"We need to see him," Jude said.

"You would have better luck at the Vatican."

"It's important."

"I can arrange a private water taxi, but it will be expensive." The concierge tapped an ink pen against her palm. "Make sure the boat stays. You don't want to be stranded."

"Why not?"

"It's a long swim back."

CHAPTER 50

HOTEL DOMUS CAVANIS
VENICE, ITALY

Moose put his fingers into his ears, trying to block the sound of the girl's screams, but the hotel's walls were thin. The Zubas were in the next room, and each time the girl wailed, the men told her to squeal louder.

No one will ring the bloody police, Moose thought. *Not in this stink-hole.*

"Put a bung in it!" He threw a shoe at the wall.

Everything had gone pear-shaped earlier that night after the Zubas had butchered the young couple. Next, they'd stalked a girl in a green dress and dragged her to their room. Moose didn't know what they were doing, but it wasn't love bites or the old rumpy-bumpy. Drinking blood was one thing, dismemberment was another.

He cringed as one of the Zubas yelled something in Russian. The woman shrieked. Moose wished he had an iPod. He'd turn it up full blast, listening to Leona Lewis sing "Bleeding Love"—God, what a set of pipes.

The girl whimpered. There was a pause, and the Zubas laughed.

Moose's mobile phone vibrated, skidding on the table's smooth surface. He snatched it up and grimaced when he recognized Wilkerson's number. *Pip-pip, cheerio, and all that rot*, he thought.

"You're blown," Wilkerson said. "Find the Zubas and meet me at the airport."

"Now? But I thought the Clifford girl was here." Moose glanced at the wall. The pictures were shaking.

"You can't track her now. The police are looking for you and the Zubas. Someone reported a disturbance at the Hotel San Gallo—were you there?"

"Not by myself, mate." Moose exhaled through his teeth. "I told you not to bring the Zubas. They're wreaking havoc. First off, they killed a couple. Said it was the Clifford girl and her fellow. I told them they had the wrong people, but no, the Zubas think they're bright sparks. They butchered the pair. Dumped their body parts into the canal."

"Why didn't you stop them?"

"Two against one?" Moose cried. "Against *them*? I told you I wouldn't be piggy-in-the-middle. And *you* said you'd take care of it, that you'd drug them."

"It was supposed to work. I don't understand." Wilkerson sighed. "Were there any witnesses?"

"There always are." From next door, a screech rose up. Moose rolled his eyes. *Cor blimey.*

"Did you clean it up?" Wilkerson asked.

"Yes, ducky. And it will cost you extra."

"Find the Zubas and bring them to the airport."

"They're engaged at the moment."

"Doing what?"

"They snatched another girl. They're with her now." Moose held out the phone for a moment. "Do you hear the yelling? And that's just the love bites, I'm afraid."

"Ruddy fuck!"

"I'm sure they did that, too, before they—"

"Never mind," Wilkerson snapped. "Get them."

Bugger that. I'm out of here. Moose disconnected the call. Next door, the screaming snapped off. He dug through the desk and found the number for the Venice police.

"Two men have butchered a woman at the Hotel Domus Cavanis. Room forty-five. Hurry."

He left the hotel, cut across St. Mark's Square, and caught a water taxi to the airport. Two police boats sped by, toward Vaporetto No. 1, where he'd just left. *That was quick*, Moose thought, and leaned against the tufted seat.

When he stepped on the Learjet, Wilkerson was sitting in the back, reading *USA Today*. He lowered the paper, and his glasses slid down his long nose. "Where are the Zubas?"

"Apparently someone heard the woman's screams and called the police."

"The police have the Zubas?"

"It's possible, mate."

"I'll tend to them later." Wilkerson folded the newspaper and stood. "I've got to tell the pilot to submit a new flight plan. We're flying to Bulgaria."

"Is that where the Clifford girl has gone?"

"No, she's still in Venice. But your work here is finished."

"Because of the blooming Zubas?"

"Not entirely. I've got to see a man about a dog," said Wilkerson.

"A real dog?" Moose squinted.

"No, Moose." Wilkerson started down the aisle toward the cockpit, then turned his head. "You have absolutely no sense of humor, do you? It's just my way of saying 'Sod off,' but in a kinder, gentler way."

Moose smirked. "Aren't you the lad."

CHAPTER 51

ISLA CARBONERA
LAGUNA VENETA

The water taxi skidded past Isla Murano toward a brightly lit island with a steep, medieval wall. The driver pointed, shouting into the wind, "Villa Primaverina."

The taxi puttered around the wall toward a rectangular landing. Behind it, the villa rose up. It reminded Caro of a floating hotel, a four-story Italianate the color of oyster shells. Grand, curved steps plunged down to the water.

Nearly every window in the villa glowed. *A generator?* Caro wondered. *Underwater cables?* The taxi passed a sign: *Proprieta Privata—Guardi da dei Cani.* Guard dogs? The concierge hadn't been kidding. Signore Della Rocca didn't want guests. The boat chugged around floats and buoys and approached the rock landing. A tall man with a crew cut stepped out of the shadows. He smoothed his hands down the front of a white dinner jacket, then he straightened a red bow tie.

The Signore? Caro mused.

Lights shone down on the man's scalp, the fine hairs jutting up like wires. His long chin was knobby and dented like a potato. As the water taxi coasted to the landing, Caro saw a sailboat, a yacht, and a speedboat. The tall man glared. *"Proprietà privata."* The driver's knees shook as he explained that Caro and Jude were behind the insubordination.

"Vaffanculo!" The tall man lifted one finger and drew a circle in the air.

"What's he saying?" Jude asked.

"The island is private. He told us to leave, but in a rude way. I'm telling him about my uncle." Caro stood up and the boat swayed. *"Ascoltami!"* she called. *"Il mio zio è un amico del Signore Della Rocca."*

"I speak English," the tall man said. "Who is your uncle? And who are you?"

Caro detected a slight German accent mingled with Italian. "Could we speak privately?" she asked. She didn't know if Sky News reached this island, but even if it didn't, she was leery of giving her name.

"No," the tall man said. "State your business or leave."

Jude unzipped his backpack and jotted a note on a napkin. *Sir Nigel Clifford's niece must see Della Rocca about a triptych.* Then he passed it up to the frowning tall man.

Panic twisted through Caro's stomach as she watched the man read the note. After a moment, he opened a mobile phone and pivoted, giving a full view of his mammoth shoulders. His voice dropped to a whisper as he spoke into the phone.

The driver spat in the water. "The police will come now."

The tall man turned. "Signore Della Rocca will see you."

The driver scrambled to his feet and helped Caro out of the boat. Jude hopped out with their bags. Caro saw a flash of green as wild parakeets flitted into the olive trees.

"This way." The tall man strode ahead, his shoes clapping over the stone path.

"Nice chap." Jude frowned. "Large vocabulary, too."

The island wasn't landscaped so much as sculpted. Stone nymphs danced around a fountain. Further out, boxwood hedges formed crosses. Next to the front steps, topiaries were carved into mythological beasts.

Caro followed the tall man to a terrace. Stone gargoyles peered down from an upper balcony. Music drifted from the house, and she recognized the rhythmic beat of "Closer" by Nine Inch Nails. It was about raw, animalistic sex. Phoebe used to play it all the time.

The music lent a jarring note in this sumptuous atmosphere. Caro wondered just how old Della Rocca was.

Jude grabbed her arm. "I don't like this," he whispered.

The tall man strode toward the main entrance, up rough marble steps to a terrace. Caro stared at the man's wide shoulders. She could have set teacups on them with room for scones and clotted cream. He stepped past the life-sized statuary and opened a massive front door.

Caro stepped into a vestibule, and her reflection moved over a black-and-white checkerboard floor. A grand staircase curved up into the gloom. The tall man strode toward an arched hallway. Caro started to follow, then she heard a tinkling noise and looked up. A six-tiered crystal chandelier swayed from a domed ceiling, the prisms trembling in rhythm with the eerie music. Perhaps Signore Della Rocca was a heavy metal musician.

A word floated into her mind: *Hardly*. She looked up to see if Jude had spoken. But his lips were clamped together. Her mind was playing tricks. She stared at the oil paintings that lined the staircase wall, hunting dogs biting into feathered things.

The music changed to a Type O Negative song. As the goth-metal band sang "Haunted," their dark, heavy voices echoed like liturgical chants.

"Odd music selections, wouldn't you say?" Jude whispered.

"Depends on what you call odd," she said. "At least it's not Cradle of Filth."

They caught up with the tall man in the hall. The violent artwork continued, with hunt scenes giving way to Hieronymus Bosch paintings. Caro peeked into a large, formal room with French antiques grouped around a zebra rug. A bombé chest held a collection of crosses. She relaxed. Crosses didn't mesh with vampires or devil worshippers.

The disturbing music got louder when their escort flung open double doors and directed them into a windowless library.

A man with long platinum-blond hair sat in a plush Bergere chair, petting a small black dog with a monkey face. It growled, the dark eyes shifting from Caro to Jude.

"I am Signore Raphael Della Rocca," the blond man said with a faint Italian accent. "Welcome to Villa Primaverina."

Caro had been expecting an older fellow, but Signore

Della Rocca looked to be Jude's age, early thirties, maybe even younger. His dark eyes and brows made a striking contrast against his pale hair. He wore a black shirt and faded jeans with gaping holes.

Caro started to introduce herself, but Della Rocca held up his hand.

"I know who you are," he said. "Sky News claims you're dangerous."

"I can explain," she said, pushing down a fresh surge of panic.

"Please do." Della Rocca gestured at a carved settee. Jude tucked his bag under a table and sat down. Caro continued to stand, clutching her bag. In case she had to run, she'd be ready.

"Beppe thinks you are disturbed by my music." Della Rocca nodded at the tall man. "But I think you are disturbed by me. Whatever the cause, not to worry. I have changed the selections. I trust they will be to your satisfaction."

Beppe? Caro glanced at the man. He stood beside the doors and stared straight ahead, hands clasped behind his back. She wondered when, and how, he'd shared this information with his employer.

Della Rocca sat down. Pearl Jam began to sing "Alive," something their host was clearly not. Della Rocca laughed. "Perhaps you prefer Smashing Pumpkins? Or Sting?"

She narrowed her eyes. Only a moment earlier, she'd hoped he would play something by Sting.

Caro glanced around the library, wishing she could poke through the books. "Your villa is lovely," she said.

"Grazie mille," Della Rocca said. "A house like this

would be unbearable without books. And yes, you may look at them later."

She tilted her head. Had she spoken out loud? She looked at Jude to see if he'd heard, but he was talking to the dog. The animal showed its teeth, then lurched forward and snapped.

"No!" Della Rocca snapped his fingers at the dog. "Bad Arrapato!"

"*Arrapato* means 'horny,' " Caro told Jude, who immediately withdrew his hand. The dog's silver tags jingled, and he showed his teeth again.

You speak Italian? asked Della Rocca.

"Yes," she said.

Jude sat up straight, looking confused. "Yes, what?" he asked.

"Signore Della Rocca asked if I spoke Italian."

"He did?" Jude frowned. "When?"

Raphael stroked the dog. *Perhaps Arrapato distracted the young man*, he said.

Caro distinctly heard Della Rocca's voice, but his lips hadn't moved. Jude hadn't spoken, nor had the sphinxlike Beppe.

"What are you playing at?" she asked Della Rocca.

I am reading your thoughts, Della Rocca said. Again, his lips didn't move.

Caro's knees buckled, and she sat down hard on the settee. Della Rocca sniffed as if he'd detected something pungent. The little dog raised his head and sniffed, too.

This is impossible, she thought. A warm flush spread up her neck.

I've made you blush. He smiled.

Della Rocca was either a mind reader or a skilled ventriloquist.

She pushed a thought in his direction: *It's rude to read people's thoughts. Stop it this instant.*

I will try. But I cannot promise. Della Rocca raised his brows.

Caro narrowed her eyes. Her thoughts weren't any of his damn business.

You are a feisty one.

I told you, stop reading my mind.

Please forgive me, mia cara. *I'm trying to control it, but there is too much power in this room. I feel it coming from you and from him—so much from him. This kind of power makes angels fly too close to mountains. It has been a long time since I have been near the beginning of love. It builds the way great music builds.*

You don't know what you're talking about. Caro glanced away.

But I'm not talking.

She flinched as Della Rocca's words hit her own thoughts and scattered like dust motes. *You're wrong. He doesn't love me. He's going to dump me here with you.*

Would that be so tragic?

Again, his words flitted away. She met his gaze, and a blinding pain throbbed behind her eyes.

The headache and confusion are less if you do not resist. Relax. Let my words move through you like water. Otherwise the pain can worsen.

His gaze lingered on her neck.

What's that supposed to mean? she thought. Had the bites caused her to read minds? She cupped her hand over the scabs. She had a bad feeling about Della Rocca. Yet her uncle had sent her to Villa Primaverina, and she didn't want to leave without answers.

The bites have enhanced what was already inside you. Della Rocca shrugged. The dog began to pant, its pink tongue curling like a witch's shoe.

She'd known Della Rocca three minutes and he was lecturing her about love, mental telepathy, and genetics. The trouble was, they weren't moving their lips and it was disconcerting, like watching a movie with the audio out of sync.

Please, call me Raphael. Della Rocca is too formal.

Jude crossed his legs and placed one arm on the back of the settee. She didn't need to be a mind reader to know that the silence was making him uncomfortable.

Look at his body language. Raphael tilted his head. *He is telling me that you belong to him. He is warning me to back off.*

"He is not," she snapped.

"What?" Jude's eyes widened.

"It's nothing," Caro said hastily.

A flush spread down Jude's cheeks as he glanced from Raphael to Caro. "Could someone explain what's going on?"

"I shall try." Raphael faced Caro. "But before we begin, please accept my condolences. I was saddened to learn about Sir Nigel's death. He was an extraordinary man."

"You knew him?" Caro asked.

"Indirectly."

Raphael glanced at her duffel bag. "You have brought two icons."

Jude flinched. "How do you know?"

"He's reading our thoughts," Caro said.

"Not all of my kind can do this," Raphael said. "I do it poorly. My talents lie elsewhere."

"Your kind," Jude said. It wasn't a question. "You're a vampire?"

"I prefer to be called Raphael. And don't make the mistake of thinking all immortals are alike. Because we're not. I can sense the presence and thoughts of other vampires, but I cannot read *all* human minds. Some are closed. My gift is stronger if I have an emotional investment in a person. I knew you were coming, Caro, and I knew you weren't alone."

"Why should we believe you?" Jude said.

"You look like you need a drink," Raphael said. "What would you like?"

"A single-malt scotch if you have it," Jude said.

"With ice?"

"Please."

Raphael turned to Caro. "And you, signorina?" *Sei molta bella.*

"Nothing, thank you." *Flatterer.*

Beppe vanished into the gloomy corridor, presumably fetching the scotch. Raphael stroked the dog. "It is late. I am sure you're exhausted. Have you eaten? Beppe's wife is an exquisite chef. Perhaps she can prepare you a meal." A moment later, Beppe stepped into the room carrying a tray. Ice cubes tinkled in a glass.

"A vampire has a chef?" Jude asked Raphael, then took a quick swallow of his drink.

"I love to host parties, even if I choose not to eat. But during my mortal life, yes, I enjoyed food. I still love to smell it. Some of my kind cannot abide it. Arrapato is unusual—he still likes bones and scraps. As I said, the immortals are wildly different in talents and tastes."

Jude choked on the whiskey. "The dog is a vampire?"

"He is immortal, yes." Raphael smiled. "I would be honored if you'd stay at the villa tonight. Arrapato and I love guests."

"I'm sure you do," Jude said. "Especially after dark."

"You are an intractable young man," Raphael said.

"And you're a vampire." Jude glared. "You drink blood."

"You drink scotch."

"But when I want a drink, I go to a bar. I don't bite people."

"I don't bite them, either. Not anymore. Not in centuries."

"How do I know you won't attack us?" Jude asked.

"I'll try to restrain myself." Raphael smiled. His teeth were white and radiant. "I have a blood bank on the lower level. No need to worry. I will not harm Caro—or you. Besides, we haven't discussed the icons."

"Let's discuss them now," Jude said.

"It is late," Raphael said. "We shall talk tomorrow after you have rested."

I have answers for you, mia cara. *If you want them.* Raphael stood, cradling the dog, and bowed. "Beppe will escort you to the kitchen. I will see you tomorrow night. Dinner will be served on the south terrace at dusk. Ask Beppe to show you the way."

CHAPTER 52

VILLA PRIMAVERINA
ISLA CARBONERA

Jude and Caro sat at a long walnut table in the kitchen, watching Beppe's wife ladle potato soup into thick red pottery bowls. Across the room, flames crackled in the stone fireplace. Arched windows lined the opposite wall, showing a thread of moonlight on the black water. In the distance, a bright haze rose up from Isla Murano.

"I'm Maria," Beppe's wife said as she set down their bowls. She added wine and a basket filled with garlicky crackers.

"Anything else?" She tucked her wiry, gray-blond hair behind her ears.

"We're fine, thank you," Jude said.

Caro studied the woman's mouth and complexion, trying to decide if she was human or vampire. But Maria's face held a rosy glow; her teeth were small and white.

Jude must have been thinking along the same lines. "How long have you been Raphael's chef?" he asked.

"Nine years. That's how long Beppe and I have been married. We fell in love over a bowl of gnocchi." She dipped a garlic cracker into olive oil, then bit down. A good sign, Caro thought.

Maria passed by a wall calendar that showed a Christmas scene. Was it still the sixth of December? Caro wondered.

"Signore Raphael wanted me to remind you about tomorrow night," Maria said. "Antipasti will be served on the south terrace at sunset."

"Where's the south terrace?" Caro asked.

Maria smiled. "I'll give you a tour when you are finished with your soup."

"We'll need one," Caro said. A better name for this massive house would be Villa Confusionaria.

Maria lit a cigarette. An even better sign, Caro thought.

Jude tapped his spoon against the bowl. "Do you enjoy working for Raphael?"

"Very much. He is a kind man," Maria said. "He has quirks—but don't we all?"

Maria escorted them through the house, pointing out highlights: a mirrored weight room, an indoor lap pool, and a media center with Swarovski crystals embedded in the domed ceiling. They moved into the game room. A chandelier hung from a mirrored ceiling, reflecting a black leather sofa and a card table. Pinball machines lined the far wall. Jude walked to the billiard table and lifted a cube of blue chalk.

"Do either of you play golf?" Maria asked. "There is a virtual course down the hall." Her cell phone rang and she stepped into an alcove.

"It's not safe here," Jude said. "We should call a water taxi."

"I'm not leaving until I see Raphael's icon." Caro folded her arms. "You're not thinking he's dangerous?"

"You tell me. There's roughly twenty pints of blood between us."

"Raphael didn't seem violent."

"Why? Because he's wealthy?" Jude flashed a doubtful look.

"He owns a blood bank. And if that redheaded vampire gets near the island, Raphael will sense it."

"He's like a canary in a coal mine?"

"Well, he knew we were coming."

Maria stepped out of the alcove. "That was Beppe. Will you be staying in the same room or would you like separate accommodations?"

"Separate," Jude said.

Maria moved into the hall.

"Aren't you afraid to sleep alone?" Caro whispered.

"I've got garlic."

"Suit yourself." So his distaste for sharing a bed with a half vampire outweighed his fear of getting bitten by a real one. But then why had he ravished her at Harry's Bar? Correction, she'd attacked him. Totally. She strained to hear his thoughts, but all she felt was a steely resolve. From his end, it was finished between them. She'd better get used to sleeping alone, the sooner the better.

Maria led them upstairs, down a labyrinth of interconnected halls, and opened a paneled door. "This is your room, Caro," she said. "It has lovely views of the lake. Tomorrow you will see."

If I make it through the night, Caro thought, then

immediately squelched the thought. She lingered in the doorway and watched Jude and Maria turn a corner. She wanted to know where he was sleeping—just in case she dreamed of the wild dogs again. She repressed an urge to follow Maria and stepped into her room. It was violently red—toile wallpaper, velvet draperies, a burgundy Persian rug with bold black swirls. A queen-sized canopy bed was swathed in more toile.

She was too tired to undress. She flopped onto the duvet. Raphael's mind reading had taken its toll. She pushed her face into the feather pillow and fell asleep.

CHAPTER 53

Caro dreamed that the wild dogs were chasing her through brambles, toward a burning house. When she awoke, she thought her room was on fire. A reddish-orange hue tinted the air. She scrambled out of bed, ran to the window, and fumbled with the latch, thinking she'd climb onto the balcony and try to shimmy down the vines, but then she saw the sunset. No fire. No danger. Smoke drifted up from Isla Murano, turning amber as it passed through the late afternoon light.

How long had she slept? She ran her hand over her neck. The flesh was smooth. No new bites. Raphael hadn't slithered under the door, or whatever vampires did, to sample her blood. She hoped he'd extended the same courtesy to Jude.

She heard a timid rap on the door. "It's open," she called.

A bell-shaped woman stepped into the room and curtsied, her black gabardine uniform creaking at the seams. "My name is Dorotea. I will attend your personal needs during your stay. Signore Della Rocca sends his greetings and a welcome gift."

"How did you know I was awake?" Caro asked.

"I heard your footsteps, signorina."

"What day is it?" Caro rubbed her eyes.

"Sunday. I have good news. My master has sent gifts." Dorotea moved back. A young, round-faced maid walked in carrying two black Chanel boxes and set them on the bed.

Caro opened the larger box, flipped back the tissue paper, and lifted the straps of a burgundy dress. The fabric made a soft hissing noise as it slid out of the box. She opened the second box. Red shoes were nestled inside, strappy little sandals. They were her size, but the dress was too small.

The round-faced maid dropped into a curtsy and backed out of the room.

"Mi scusi," Caro said. "I can't accept this dress."

Dorotea looked puzzled. "If it is not to your liking, we shall find another."

"Where?" Caro asked. Did Raphael have deep closets crammed with ball gowns in all colors and sizes?

"Milan," said Dorotea. "Beppe's niece works at Chanel. She sent three dresses by helicopter this morning. The Signore personally selected this dress, but it can easily be replaced."

"No, it's—" Too symbolic. Blood, fire, hearts, claret. She lifted the gown. The afternoon glare shone through the silk and turned it maroon. She pondered that word—maroon. Not only was she stuck on this island, she would be wearing a shade Robinson Crusoe might approve of. Was Raphael trying to tell her she was a castaway? Did he think she needed rescuing?

Dorotea clasped her hands, waiting for Caro to continue.

"I can't accept something this valuable. Even if I could, it's way too small."

Dorotea appraised Caro's figure. "It will be perfect."

"For a Chihuahua."

Dorotea giggled. "Let me put it on a hanger. We can't have this pretty frock getting wrinkled. Shall I draw you a bath?"

Caro glanced at double doors that led to a hallway. She glimpsed black marble walls, beveled mirrors, statues set into niches. A toile chaise longue was angled in front of a crackling fireplace. Beyond that, she saw a sunken tub surrounded by mirrors.

"I do not wish to rush you, signorina, but a hairdresser is on the way. She is bringing an assistant for your makeup. We want you to be beautiful tonight."

"For a casual dinner?"

"Nothing is casual at Villa Primaverina." Dorotea smiled.

Forty-five minutes later, Caro sat on the chaise longue, surrounded by beauty specialists. A hairdresser stood behind her with a curling iron, clicking her tongue about *capelli del bastone*—stick-straight hair. *If only you knew,* Caro thought.

A manicurist spread dark red polish on Caro's nails. On her other side, a makeup artist opened an enormous case filled with rouge pots and blush. She lifted an eyeliner pencil, and Caro shrank back. "I don't ever use that," she said.

"Do not worry." The artist smiled. "It will be subtle."

Another lady doused Caro's pulse points with perfume that smelled of jasmine and mandarin.

"Mmmm, delicious," Caro said, inhaling.

"Isn't it?" The lady smiled. "It's Clive Christian Number One. All of the Signore's women wear it."

"I'm *not* his woman," Caro said.

"No? Then I am sad for you, signorina."

"Why?" Caro asked.

The women looked at each other and giggled.

"What's so funny?" Caro said.

"He is like the wind," the perfume lady said. "A woman is like a kite."

"You know from personal experience?" Caro lifted an eyebrow.

"No." The lady smiled. "But I wish."

The women led her to a three-way mirror. Caro spun around, the gown's hem swishing around her ankles. Not only did the dress hug her curves, it had an alluring slit up the side. The neckline plunged discreetly, showing the top curve of each breast, Jude's pendant floating above them, a slash of red against her creamy skin.

She ignored the beaded evening clutch that Dorotea had set on the bed and grabbed her duffel bag. Those pages from *Historia Immortalis* weren't safe in a vampire's guest room. The dress whispered around her shoes as she stepped into the hall. From hidden speakers along the high ceiling, Death Cab for Cutie was singing "I Will Possess Your Heart."

She started down the staircase, tracing her fingertips down the iron banister, trying to ignore the duffel bag as it thumped against her thigh. The stairs ended in an art gallery. Unlike the brutal images she'd seen in the foyer, these paintings were serene. Sheep grazing at sunset; the ocean at dawn; vineyards spilling down a hillside, the vines forming ragged Xs. The paintings were not united by color, but the theme was consistent: daylight.

"So I won't forget," Raphael said.

She turned. He stood beside the staircase, one arm casually resting on the banister. His hair was drawn back into a gleaming ponytail, and it fell down the back of his tuxedo. His eyes went to her duffel bag. She waited for him to speak, but he just stood there.

"Do you miss the light?" she asked Raphael.

"More than I ever dreamed." His finger skimmed along the rail, an oddly sensual gesture. "I miss the red sheen of the lagoon at sunset. The heat of an August morning. The light melted and poured, clean as glass. These things are lost."

She'd always taken sunlight for granted; she couldn't imagine losing it. Her heart drummed. His head tilted, as if he'd heard, and he stepped closer. "Immortality has its advantages. Samuel Johnson said it best. 'He who makes a beast of himself gets rid of the pain of being a man.'"

"Do vampires feel emotional pain?"

"It depends on the vampire." His teeth flashed, white and radiant. "Did you know the sun has a lingering scent? Olive trees and grass. Lemon verbena and evergreens. It smells like you, *mia cara*."

The music changed. As Muse sang "Unintended," he pulled her into his arms and kissed her. A current traveled from her lips to her breasts. His hands molded to her back. She felt the coolness of his palms and fingers, yet her skin was burning. She wanted the kiss to go on and on. Only he wasn't kissing her, he was possessing her.

She had an image of an obelisk, and the vision changed to teeth and male hardness. Italian words flew in her mind like pebbles. Her hands knotted in his shirt. The music dropped away, and her pulse crashed in her ears.

You could love me, mia cara.

Yes, she could. She wanted to follow him into the dark. But she mustn't. She shouldn't. Then she was climaxing, and she knew he knew. She had no will to stop him until his mouth slid down to her neck. What if he bit her? She balled her hands into fists and pushed away from his chest.

"You shouldn't have kissed me," she whispered.

"Please forgive me. I've smudged your lipstick."

You did more than that, she thought, touching the edge of her lips with a trembling hand. "Please don't ever do that again."

"I never make promises I can't keep."

He led her to a gilt mirror and pressed a handkerchief into her hands. She wiped her lips. Raphael snapped his fingers, and Beppe glided out of the dark hallway.

"Fetch the makeup artist, please," Raphael said.

She stared at his reflection. One more myth debunked. Vampires *do* have reflections.

You are in love with him, mia cara.

"What if I am?" She turned around. "And stop listening to my thoughts."

"You should be more careful to whom you give your heart."

"You don't know everything," she said, her voice glacial.

He shrugged. "I know enough."

"Have you read Jude's thoughts?"

"I sense great ambivalence. When he's away from you, he's strong and analytical. But when you are near, his passion takes over. The allure of the forbidden. Science is no match for that. He is drawn to you, *mia cara*, but sees no future."

"Because I'm half vampire?"

"His prejudice is more powerful than his love. And you cannot break through it."

"If I can't be with him, I won't be with anyone."

"You feel that way now. But you *will* change. You may even fall for me. And if you do, I promise one thing: It will be the best sex you've ever had." His eyes met hers. *"Attenderò. Ho tempo."*

I will wait. I have time.

"It will be so good, *mia cara*."

"You may know how to entice women, but what do you know about love?" She crossed her arms defiantly, ignoring her throbbing breasts. Love was meant to be felt, not explained. Just thinking about Jude sent a deep, red flush spiraling inside her chest. She wanted to wake up in his bed every morning. She wanted to meet Lady Patricia and wander around Dalgliesh Castle. She wanted children with blue eyes, a smidgen of brown in each iris. She wanted a house filled with laughter and cheerful voices, each one stamped with a charming Yorkshire accent.

"These are your wants, *mia cara*. Not his."

Footsteps echoed in the hall, then Beppe and the makeup artist stepped around the corner. The woman opened her box, selected a thin brush, and repaired Caro's smudged lipstick.

Raphael extended his arm in a courtly fashion. Caro hesitated, then placed her hand on his sleeve. He led her down the gallery, through the black-and-white living room, past a tall black vase that held dozens of red amaryllises.

"You are worried about the monk?" Raphael asked.

"Yes." She looked up. What else had he picked from her thoughts?

"Worry will change nothing," he said.

"I promised I'd call. And I have his icon."

Raphael pulled an iPhone from his jacket pocket. She willed her thoughts to be quiet as she called the Hotel San Gallo. The operator informed her that Father Aeneas had checked out that morning.

Caro slipped Raphael's phone into his hand. "I suppose he's gone back to Meteora. If only I'd called sooner."

"You are too quick to assume blame, *mia cara*. Do not worry. Monks are resourceful."

They walked in silence to the terrace. A hurricane globe flickered on a long glass table, casting shadows on platters of bruschetta, smoked salmon, cheese, and olives. Caro felt too anxious to eat, so she leaned against the railing and stared at the water. A dark blue flush spread across the sky. Beneath it, the lights of Murano and Venice glimmered.

Beppe glided onto the terrace holding a round tray. He handed her a glass of red wine, then turned to Raphael.

As the vampire lifted his glass, Arrapato stood on his hind legs and twirled.

Beppe smiled at the dog and set a bowl on the ground, the dark liquid swaying. Arrapato ran over to the bowl and started lapping.

The wind picked up, and Caro smelled the tang of blood. She raised her glass and took a sip—yes, it was wine. She slid her free hand down her dress, trying to keep it from flying up.

"It is the Inverna," Raphael said. "The south wind. It will blow until midnight."

"You pay close attention to elements of the night," Caro said, and took another sip of wine.

He lifted one finger and drew it through the air. "The dark cannot be touched. Yet it is all around us."

Arrapato barked, and Caro turned. Jude walked onto the terrace, the wind snapping the edges of his white shirt. He held a red amaryllis.

"For you, lass." He gave her the flower. "A bit more fragrant than my first gift."

Caro smiled. She still had the garlic pod in her bag, and she planned to keep the amaryllis, too. She pressed her nose to the petals and breathed the spicy, scarlet scent. Red, symbolic of love and sacrifice. The color of lips and hearts and blood.

Jude's lips parted, releasing a tiny puff of air. What was he trying to say? *We'll always have Venice?* Caro felt as if she'd strayed into *Casablanca*, dogged by fiends, bad timing, and a hero who was hell-bent on doing the right thing.

"You look beautiful," Jude said, his Yorkshire accent drifting lazily between them.

"More than beautiful," Raphael said. "She is a goddess." The wind rose up, presumably the Inverna, and lifted Caro's hair. Jude moved closer to the terrace railing and squeezed in next to her. She took a deep breath. Both men smelled poignantly of Acqua di Parma.

Raphael signaled Beppe, then led Caro and Jude to the table. They sat down and Beppe placed a large wooden box in front of them.

"I keep my icon in a temperature-controlled room," Raphael said. His coat sleeves moved over his wrist as he lifted the relic. Before the sleeve slipped back, Caro saw part of a tattoo: an elongated, curved black circle.

He set his icon on the table and waited while she set down the amaryllis and eased her panel and Father Aeneas's from the duffel bag. She laid them beside his.

"A perfect fit," he said. "Just like some people, no?" It did indeed fit neatly against hers, forming the right side of the triptych. A starry sky and jagged mountains curved across all three icons, but Raphael's images were even more confusing: a stone fortress with turrets and a drawbridge; crusaders sprawled on the ground, their blood spilling into a vineyard; a woman in the foreground and a baby crawling toward the dead. The vineyard invaded Caro's icon, then stopped abruptly before it reached the female saint and the bleeding man.

Jude leaned forward and his leg pressed against hers. "Is the castle symbolic or a real place?"

"Both," Raphael said.

"Where is it?" Caro asked.

"Southern France," Raphael said. "The Languedoc region."

"It looks like Carcassonne," Caro said.

"The resemblance is striking," Raphael said, his gaze sweeping over his icon. "But this castle is in Limoux."

"Why are the mountains and castle so distinct?" Caro asked. "I thought Orthodox icons were sketchier."

"They are," Raphael said. "I was the theological advisor to this project. But I took a light-handed approach."

"What do you mean, 'this project'?" Jude's brows came together. "Father Aeneas said the triptych was painted in the eighth century."

"It was," Raphael said.

"You were the advisor?" Jude swallowed. "Surely you weren't alive when this triptych was painted."

"I wouldn't say *alive*. But I was there."

The historian rose up in Caro, and she leaned forward, eager to hear more. "What was it like—the eighth century?"

"Cold and dreary," Raphael said. "Venice froze solid. The ninth century was better—a hotbed of gossip and intrigue, thanks to the Vikings. Murders, invasions, romance, power struggles. And the weather was lovely, too."

"How did an Italian vampire end up in France?" Caro put her chin in her hand and smiled.

"Back in my mortal days, I walked from Italy to Santiago de Compostela to pay homage to Saint James. On my way back, I stopped in Tours. I worked in a scriptorium at Marmoutier—that's a monastery outside Tours. This was during the glorious Carolingian age. I was one of the monks who translated *Historia Immortalis* for Charlemagne. Right after I finished, I got 'neck bit,' as they say. One of the Grimaldis turned me."

Caro's hands went involuntarily to her throat. "Grimaldi? That was my father's name."

"Yes, I know. Philippe Grimaldi was my best friend. Incidentally, he didn't bite me. Philippe saved all that for the ladies. It was his cousins, the bawdy d'Aigrevilles, who turned me into a vampire."

Caro grabbed his arm. "You knew my father?"

"I know this must be hard to fathom, but yes." His eyes circled her face. "The Grimaldis were French noblemen. Aristocratic. Richer than the pope—and immortal. They lived in the Languedoc region, between Carcassonne and Limoux. They began having prophetic dreams about the immortal race. I had them, too. So did many other vampires. The Grimaldis wanted the visions documented. So they commissioned this triptych. They had definite ideas about how it should be painted. Plus, they required movable art, the preferred type for heretics on the run."

Caro's grip tightened on Raphael's arm. All those magnificent details about her father were in Raphael's head. That was why Uncle Nigel had sent her to him. To recover what had been lost. Not pages, not an icon, but the truth of her family.

I will tell you everything, mia cara. *One thing at a time.*

She released his arm and nodded.

Jude pressed his mouth into a flat line, and the *M* in his upper lip vanished. After a moment, he said, "Why are these icons different from the ones in Meteora?"

"There are all types of iconography," Raphael said. "Technically, this is a family icon. Etienne Grimaldi—he was your grandfather, Caro—hired a Greek craftsman to paint the triptych. The artist came from the Iviron Monastery on Athos. The poor fellow traveled all that way only to be bombarded with requests by the Grimaldis.

Things like, 'I don't like the eyes on that owl' and 'Add another vineyard.'"

Raphael lifted his eyebrows. "Talk about finicky. Since I was advising the artist, I was supposed to have the last word, but when I told him the martyr was a female, the artist threatened to quit. He insisted that all martyrs were male. I explained that the triptych should illustrate a prophecy and, like it or not, the artist had to comply with the Grimaldis' wishes. He broke his paintbrush in half and spat on the ground."

"Why didn't he paint what the Grimaldis wanted?" Jude asked.

"It's hard to describe the medieval mind-set. They were obsessed with piety and the seven deadlies. In the wrong hands, art could be exploited. Guilds had inviolable guidelines about iconography. They'd beat an artist to a bloody pulp if he painted anything remotely heretical."

"How did the triptych get painted?" Caro asked.

Raphael framed the outer panels between his hands, his short fingernails gleaming in candlelight. "A pile of money was transferred under the table, and the Grimaldis prevailed."

Caro studied the castle on Raphael's icon, looking for geographical clues. "Do you have a map of the Languedoc region?"

"Several." He glanced up. "But you won't find answers in Limoux."

"Father Aeneas said the triptych shows where the rest of *Historia Immortalis* is hidden," she said.

"He told the truth as he knew it. But he was mistaken." Raphael ran his finger along his panel, tracing the vineyard.

"It shows where the book was located at the time the triptych was painted."

"So it's not there now?" Caro pressed her knuckles against her lips. She wanted this quest to end, but it kept twisting.

"No, *mia cara*. It's a long, convoluted story. Do you wish to hear it?"

She nodded.

Raphael kept stroking the triptych, his nails scratching against the wood. "When the crusade heated up, Philippe and I dismantled the manuscript and the triptych. We took the artifacts to a cave near his chateau. We divided the leaves into ten-page bundles, wrapped each one in silk, and placed them in shallow wooden chests. The same for the icons. We shoved these chests in crevices and piled rocks in front of them."

"How did you keep track of the hiding places?" Jude asked.

"Philippe had what is now called a photographic memory. But we lived in violent times. If he'd gotten killed in the crusade, I wouldn't have found the chests. So I marked the hiding places with rock cairns. After Château de Quéribus fell, your father and I returned to the cave to retrieve our treasures. Some of the cairns had been dispersed by thieves. Philippe remembered each hiding spot. We found one icon and all but ten pages to *Historia Immortalis*. I kept the icon and Philippe took the vellum pages."

"What did he do with them?" Caro asked.

"He wouldn't tell me."

"Why not?" Caro shifted closer to Jude. If her father hadn't trusted Raphael, perhaps she shouldn't, either.

"Philippe wasn't being secretive. He was protecting

the book. After the Inquisition, the book had become a collectible. The Church wanted to burn it, but art dealers were having wet dreams. The fewer who knew, the better."

"Why didn't you just read his thoughts?" Jude's eyes narrowed.

"No one could. Not even me. Philippe was strong in his mind. But his philosophy was simple: When the pupil is ready, the teacher will appear." Raphael stared into Caro's eyes. *Although I am not sure who is the teacher—you or me.*

Caro remembered opening the envelope her uncle had stashed with the vellum. Just below Raphael's name, he'd written *Vitas Quest Rev I*. Good lord, her uncle hadn't meant for her to read the Book of Revelation; he hadn't steered her toward a Biblical prophecy. *Vitas Quest Rev I* was an anagram for *At Vivi's request*. Now she understood why her uncle had stashed those pages in Venice and why he'd directed her to Raphael.

Uncle Nigel had honored Vivi's last request.

Raphael sat up straight, and his dark eyes filled. *I have so much more to tell you,* mia cara.

Jude was studying the panels, his eyes moving back and forth. "If the triptych doesn't point the way to the rest of the book, then Caro's uncle sent her on a nonexistent treasure hunt," he said.

"That depends on how you define *treasure*," Raphael said. He looked away, wiped his eyes, then blinked down at the panels. "But you couldn't be more wrong about the triptych. It figures heavily into the immortals' mythology. And, perhaps, into our future. Because it holds a prophecy."

Caro's stomach tightened. She didn't want to hear the

rest of it. *For the time is near.* No, it wasn't. Her quest had ended.

"So the relevance of the triptych isn't the book's location," Jude said, regarding Raphael with an impassive, academic gaze. "It's the illustrations. They depict the prophecy, correct?"

"A prophecy of what?" Caro's voice shook.

Raphael sighed. As his breath grazed her cheek, she caught a faint bouquet of ripe cherries and pomegranates. Ketones. Her stomach eased, and she leaned back in her chair.

"Some things cannot be explained," he said. "They must be viewed—like art in the Louvre or the Vatican. As I said earlier, symbols in this triptych came from the Grimaldis' dreams. A few events occurred, such as the crusade, but most of their dreams have not materialized. Now that Caro and the triptych have come together, I'm not sure what will come to pass."

Jude stiffened, then flashed a glacial stare at Raphael.

Caro stared at him, too, trying to prick through the vampire's thoughts, imploring him to hush, but he kept talking.

"You have the Grimaldis' beauty and intuition. And your uncle trained you well." Raphael broke off, and his forehead creased. "We will talk later. Someone is coming."

He turned toward the water. A distant puttering noise cut through the dark. Then it got louder and louder. *A boat,* Caro thought.

A beam of light hit the fortress wall and swept across the wooden landing.

Caro's throat tightened, and scalding, bitter fluid

spurted into her mouth. She swallowed, forcing down the bile, then squeezed Jude's arm. "Those vampires found us."

"Caro, so many people are after us, it's hard to guess who might be in that boat."

"No vampires." Raphael stood, the wind tugging his ponytail, the blond hairs spreading in the air like cracks in a porcelain vase. "These interlopers are human."

CHAPTER 54

Beppe stepped out of the shadows, his shoes clicking over the terrace, and pulled out his BlackBerry. *"Telefonare la polizia?"*

"Not yet." Two lines creased Raphael's forehead. "Beppe, please greet the party crashers."

"Does this happen often?" Caro asked Raphael.

"Does *what* happen?"

"People sneaking up on you."

A flush spread over Raphael's cheeks, and he strode to the balcony rail. Jude and Caro followed and gazed down into the dark garden. Beppe moved down the steps, aiming his flashlight at the boat. The beam swept into the startled faces of Demos and Father Aeneas.

"We know them," Jude said, turning to Caro. "It's the monk and his friend."

Raphael's iPhone rang. *"Sì?"* he answered, his face tight and unreadable. "No, it's okay," he said. "They're Caro's friends."

The Inverna picked up as Beppe escorted the men up to the terrace. When Father Aeneas saw Caro, his face split into a grin. Before he could speak, Raphael bowed.

"Welcome to Villa Primaverina," he said. Arrapato was less cordial. He barked and showed his teeth.

"Caroline!" Father Aeneas's prayer beads clicked as he rushed over to her.

"I called the hotel earlier," she said. "The operator said you'd left. I assumed you'd returned to Meteora."

Demos put his hands on his hips, his fingers splayed. He wore a baggy green tweed jacket, and a bottle jutted up from a deep pocket.

"We barely escaped." Father Aeneas shuddered. "Vampires stood outside the hotel—in daylight. They wore some sort of gear. But I knew. So did Demos. We pulled back the curtains and watched."

Arrapato sniffed, then growled under his breath. Raphael snapped his fingers, and the dog's ears drooped. He scooted under the table and put his head on his paws, his eyes darting back and forth.

"How long did they hang around?" Jude asked.

"Until noon, when the sun was strong and the evil ones were weak," Demos said. "And their reflective gear was drawing too much attention. They ran off and we came to Murano. We had trouble finding someone who would bring us here."

Raphael turned to Beppe. "Please bring these gentlemen something to drink."

"Wait. I brought a gift for you," Demos said. He

pulled up the tapered bottle. "Grappa. It is aged. We shall all have a taste, yes?"

Raphael moved two fingers, and Beppe left the terrace.

"Would you like to see the third icon?" Caro asked Father Aeneas.

"Yes, yes." His eyebrows lifted, grazing the rim of his hat. "Where is it?"

"Over here." She led him to the table.

Father Aeneas gazed down at the panels. "The triptych is whole," he said, his voice hushed and reverent.

Caro bit her lip. How could she explain that the triptych wouldn't lead them to the remaining pages of *Historia Immortalis*?

Father Aeneas pointed to the castle on Raphael's panel. "I hope this is not Carcassonne. *Historia Immortalis* is not there."

"It never was," Raphael said. "This castle isn't Carcassonne."

"Then where is this domicile?" Father Aeneas's breath stirred his beard.

"The image isn't relevant." Raphael paused, as if waiting for a reaction.

"What are you saying?" Father Aeneas tipped back his hat, and a vein bulged in his temple.

"*Historia Immortalis* was moved from the Languedoc region during the Crusades," Raphael said. "The triptych no longer shows where the manuscript is located."

Father Aeneas grasped an edge of the table. "The pages are lost forever?"

"I wouldn't say *forever*." Raphael steered the monk over to a chair. "They have an uncanny way of popping up."

"Caroline, your ten pages are all the more valuable," Father Aeneas said. "You must keep them safe."

"I've got them right here." She patted her duffel bag.

Raphael cut his eyes to the bag, and then his cheeks flushed again. So, apparently he hadn't pulled everything from her thoughts.

Beppe walked onto the terrace holding a tray with crystal goblets, each one a different color. Demos held out the grappa and Beppe poured the liqueur into each glass.

"I shall do the honors." Demos handed a goblet to Caro. "Red to match your dress," he said, winking.

She thanked him and took a sip. The grappa was too sweet, but she forced herself to swallow.

"Good?" Demos asked.

"Delicious." Caro smiled.

Demos passed the remaining glasses to the men. "You, too," he said, handing a purple glass to Beppe. Then Demos raised a bright green goblet. "To our host!"

"To Raphael," Jude and Caro said.

Maria walked onto the terrace holding a portable phone. She made an apologetic gesture and said, "A call for you, Signore."

"*Grazie*, I will take it in the library," Raphael said. He took another sip of the grappa and set down his glass. "Please excuse me."

He stepped through the door, followed by Beppe and the little dog.

Demos walked over to the dog bowl and squatted beside it. A bark echoed in the house, and a moment later Arrapato trotted back onto the terrace. He growled at Demos, then lowered his muzzle to the bowl and started drinking. Demos scrambled to his feet and edged over to Father Aeneas. "This is a vampire's lair!"

The monk sketched a cross in the air, and his elbow knocked into his grappa. The glass fell and liqueur spilled across the table. Caro moved the triptych, then grabbed a napkin.

"Bah, I am clumsy." Father Aeneas frowned.

Arrapato bared his teeth, snapping at Demos. The little Greek climbed onto one of the chairs. Arrapato barked twice and ran back into the house.

"Caro, you must leave at once. Signore Della Rocca is a vampire," Demos said.

She repressed a smile. "Yes, but he's a nice one."

"Nice?" Demos made an obscene gesture with his hand. "And the dog?"

"Arrapato is more temperamental."

"We cannot stay," Father Aeneas said, his voice rising.

"We're perfectly safe," Jude said. "Raphael and the dog aren't dangerous."

"Dangerous?" Demos cried. "He will drain us! We shall leave while he is gone."

Caro stood, weaving slightly. "Excuse me," she said to no one in particular. "I'll just be a moment."

"But we do not have a moment," Demos said.

"I'm just going to the powder room," she said.

"There's no time," Father Aeneas said. "Demos is right. We should go."

"I'll be quick." She turned into the house. The powder room was across the hall. Music blared from the speakers, Jim Morrison singing "The End."

Caro turned on the tap and splashed water onto her face. She glanced in the mirror. Her reflection showed a grotesque image. Droplets slid down her cheeks, then floated up and out, spinning in the air. She blinked, and her head separated into a triptych; the middle piece slid down the front of her dress.

Keeping her eyes on the mirror, Caro backed up against the wall. A strange calmness descended as her reflection morphed into a skeleton, then changed back into her face. But her teeth hung down, piercing her bottom lip. She was turning into a vampire. The serenity vanished, and a hoarse cry tore out of her throat. She lunged out of the powder room, into the hallway, where Arrapato paced back and forth. His frantic movement stirred up a vortex of colors.

Caro sucked in a breath of magenta. It tasted like Raphael's wine, with a hint of Demos's grappa. She wasn't transforming into a vampire; she'd been drugged.

CHAPTER 55

SOFIA, BULGARIA

During the flight to Bulgaria, Moose sat in the back of Wilkerson's jet and transfused himself with the medicated blood. The seats around the vampire slowly filled with empty bags, each one wrinkled like a grape skin and prominently stamped with a green label.

When the plane touched down in Sofia, he screamed.

"Shut it back there," Wilkerson yelled.

The vampire staggered up the aisle, cursing the Zubas and railing against toffee noses and chinless wonders. Wilkerson got up from his seat and gathered his bags. Behind him, Moose bumped his head on the overhead baggage compartment. "I can't bear this blooming part of the world," he cried, followed by a string of *bloody fucking hell*s and *ducky*s.

It took forever to clear customs. Moose kept mouthing off to the official. "He suffers from Tourette's syndrome," Wilkerson told the officers.

After an interminable drive to the Grand Hotel, Wilkerson shoved Moose out of the taxi and steered him into the lobby. When they finally entered the suite, the vampire lunged into the bathroom. He started to crawl into the tub, but he was too large.

"It's all sixes and sevens," he muttered, and curled up under the sink.

"Don't get cozy," Wilkerson warned. "We have an appointment at the embassy."

"Go by yourself, grot bag."

"What's wrong?"

"You drugged me, ducky," Moose said. "I don't know what you put in the blood, but it's deadly. I got to sleep it off. Go away."

Wilkerson stared down at the sleeping giant. Days ago, before they'd left London, the Hammersmith chemists had added Tofranil to Moose's transfusions; the bags were clearly marked with yellow labels. It was supposed to help with the OCD. But only God knew what the chemists had put in the Zubas' green bags.

Earlier, he'd watched Moose hide in the back of the plane and set up IV equipment. "Don't get the bags mixed up," Wilkerson had called.

"Fat lot you know," Moose had said.

Now, Wilkerson frowned. Was Moose having a drug reaction? The blood chemistry of a vampire was a conundrum. However, if Wilkerson didn't find a way to drug his operatives, he would have to eliminate them from the program.

He rang the head nurse at Hammersmith. The drug

trials at Wilkerson Pharmaceuticals were conducted with strict secrecy, and normally, the nurse wouldn't know which patient received the drug and which received the placebo; but it was different with the vampires.

Even with the difficulties, Wilkerson preferred working with the Zuba brothers. They never spoke, never screwed up. Well, not until the drug-testing fiasco. Hours ago he'd dispatched Mr. Underwood to Venice to arrange for their release, but if their jail cells had windows, the Zubas would be blind and useless.

"Moose is in the fetal position," Wilkerson told the nurse.

"Did he accidentally receive the wrong blood?" she asked. "The green labels were earmarked for the Zubas."

"Let me ask." Wilkerson lowered the phone. "Moose, when you transfused yourself, which color label was on your bag?"

"Like I remember, ducky!"

Wilkerson pressed the phone to his ear. "He said—"

"I heard." The nurse paused. "It's impossible to tell if he got into the wrong blood, but he appears to be suffering from adverse effects. Discontinue the medicated transfusions, give him fresh blood, and let him sleep it off."

"I'm in Bulgaria. What am I supposed to do? Trap small animals and bring them to the hotel?"

"If I may make a suggestion, sir? You're close to the Romanian laboratory. They have a large blood bank. Shall I tell Dr. Popovici you're coming?"

"Can't they bring the blood to me?" Wilkerson sputtered. "Wouldn't that be faster?"

"Not necessarily, sir. The Romanian facility doesn't

have a jet. And the company car is in for repairs. You'll have to fly to Bucharest and drive to the lab. Do be careful. The mountains are quite snowy this time of year."

"Call the lab immediately. Tell them I'm on my way." He started to bang down the receiver, but the nurse was still talking.

"Sir, would you like an update on Yok-Seng?"

"Oh, him." Wilkerson rubbed his brow. He'd forgotten about his bodyguard. "How is he doing?"

"His appendix burst. He had a touch of peritonitis, but he should be fine. The doctors are covering him with full-spectrum antibiotics."

"How did this happen?"

"A high pain tolerance. And he's quite loyal to you, so he ignored his symptoms."

"I wasn't asking a literal question," Wilkerson said. "Don't let him die. I need a bodyguard."

He went alone to the British embassy, pushing through the jagged line of protesters. A soldier escorted him to Sir Thurston Hughes's office on the second floor. "I have an appointment," Wilkerson told the secretary, a plain, henlike woman in a brown speckled suit.

"Mr. Hughes went missing two days ago," the secretary said.

Wilkerson released an explosive sigh. Missing could mean only one thing: Hughes had been murdered. But Wilkerson didn't have any operatives in this region, except for Georgi, and he'd gone missing, too. What the bloody hell was going on?

The secretary handed him a note. Wilkerson squinted down at Sir Hughes's distinctive handwriting, which was peppered with the famed Eton *E*s.

To: Harry Wilkerson:

You misled me. There has been too much bloodshed. I know you ordered the murders of Ilya and Professor Clifford, but you will not touch me. Do not send your operatives. I know how to fight back.

Sincerely,
Sir Thurston G. Hughes

P.S. I have removed Clifford's body to a secure location. You cannot use his soul as a bargaining chip with his niece.

Wilkerson caught a taxi to the hotel and went upstairs to check on Moose. The vampire was still in the fetal position.

"I'm dying, mate." Tears streamed down Moose's broad face.

"You've had a reaction to the transfusions, but the sickness will pass. I'm fetching you a few pints of fresh blood. You mustn't leave the room. Do you understand what I'm saying?"

Moose rolled into a tighter ball and bit his own knee.

Wilkerson placed a Do Not Disturb sign on the door. Under normal conditions, he would let Moose drift into a bloodless coma. Now, of course, that couldn't happen. All of his best operatives were dead, missing, imprisoned, or incapacitated. He needed Moose.

The wheel of fortune was turning downward.

Wilkerson's phone rang, and he stepped into the hall. "Yes?" he said irritably.

It was his secretary. "Sir, I'm patching through an urgent call."

Wilkerson listened to a series of clicks, then an odd mechanical voice said, "Mr. Wilkerson?"

"Yes."

"Your trackers left a mess in Venice," the caller said. The voice sounded high-pitched and comical, rather like Donald Duck. No doubt it was distorted by a scrambling device.

"They're no longer a problem," Wilkerson replied.

"I have ten pages from *Historia Immortalis*," the caller said. "They're yours for ten million euros. One for each page."

CHAPTER 56

———

VILLA PRIMAVERINA
ISLA CARBONERA

The night wind caught the hem of Caro's dress, and the red fabric billowed around her. Arrapato ran past her, moving in a swirl of colors. But why was the wind blowing? She and Arrapato had been standing outside the powder room. Had someone opened a window?

She looked at her dress. The bottom had grass stains, and tiny leaves were stuck to her bare feet. Where were her strappy sandals? She pushed back her hair and glanced up. Stars rushed across the black sky.

A cold shudder ran through her. She wasn't in the house. Dread uncurled in the pit of her stomach as her eyes focused and Raphael's garden stretched out around her. Either she'd wandered out here in a daze or someone had brought her. Had the wine been drugged, or the grappa? Where was Jude?

Pull yourself together, Clifford, she thought, and touched the jade pendant.

Arrapato raced up the steep marble steps, toward the house. The front door stood open, and the dog paused beside it, as if waiting for Caro. Her vision blurred, but she forced herself to crawl up the steps. She followed Arrapato through the door, into the foyer. Music stained the air with black sludge, but she was lucid enough to recognize the song—Drowning Pool was singing "Bodies." She heard a screech. A moment later, Beppe strutted into the room, flailing his arms. He opened his mouth and a strange, birdlike sound came out. The noise turned colors: orange, green, red, purple.

Arrapato bumped his nose against Caro's leg, then he ran toward the arched hallway.

She braced her hand against a table. "Beppe, what's going on?"

"Caw, caw!" A thousand Beppes flapped their wings and spun around, making odd bird noises.

Caro tilted her head. Beppe had just spoken to her in raven—and she'd understood. *Caw, caw* translated into *Run, run!*

Behind him, through the arched doors, the sky flickered like a photograph negative, and she staggered toward it. The terrace elongated. The stone floor curved inward, and she felt dizzy. Jude sat in a chair, his long legs sprawled. He tilted a bruschetta, studying it.

When he saw her, he dropped the bruschetta and stood. Behind him, the water resembled glass. It rose up in a thin sheet and broke, the shards falling around him.

Father Aeneas hovered over the table, his hands tucked into his robe, blinking at the triptych. Demos leaned against the terrace rail and poured the grappa over the edge. He turned and smiled.

"Do you know what Thanatos means?" Demos laughed, a sour yellow sound that spilled above him like bile.

"Death," Caro said.

"You are a smart girl." He pulled a gun from his pocket and stepped close. "But I am smarter. Do you know why? Because I put LSD in your grappa."

He pressed the gun against her temple. "Give me the vellum pages," he said.

"They're in my bag." Her voice sounded distorted, like an old-fashioned record played on the wrong speed.

"Get them." Demos shoved her. She reeled across the terrace and fell. Her palms skidded over the rough stones.

"Don't hurt her," Jude cried. He started toward her, but his legs buckled.

"Stay where you are or I will shoot her, I swear it," Demos cried.

"Wait." Jude held up a small red key with numbers. "It opens a locker. There's a map inside that shows where the rest of *Historia Immortalis* is located. Let her go, and the key is yours."

Caro held her breath. There was no map. What was he doing? Her eyes met Jude's, and even in her drugged state, she understood. The LSD had affected his balance, and he couldn't overpower Demos, so Jude was using his brain to save her.

"Where is this map?" Demos growled.

"The Thessaloniki train station." Jude shuffled to the railing and dangled the key over the water. "The locker number is on the tag. Let her go, or I'll toss the bloody key."

Demos's eyes narrowed to slits. "I can break into every locker in that train station."

"True. But you might attract attention."

"All right." Demos lowered the gun.

"Put it on the chair," Jude said.

"As you wish." Demos set the gun on the cushion.

Jude threw the key in the opposite direction, and it clattered across the stones. Demos vaulted across the terrace, snatched the key, and tucked it into his pocket. Then he raced back to the chair and grabbed the gun. Behind him the stars melted like candle wax, leaving smoking white streaks in the dark. The triptych lay on the table, next to the amaryllis.

"Worthless!" Demos slammed the butt of the gun against the icons. Chunks of wood scattered.

"Demos, no," Father Aeneas cried.

"Shut up." Demos lifted the manuscript box from Caro's duffel bag, then he aimed the gun at the monk.

"What are you doing?" Father Aeneas yelled.

"Silence, you old fool!" With his free hand, Demos pushed the monk to the ground. Father Aeneas lifted one hand, his fingers hooked into claws. Demos hit the monk. A thin line of blood trickled down Father Aeneas's temple and curved inside his ear.

"Don't hurt him!" Caro started toward Father Aeneas. From the corner of her eye, she saw Raphael stumble onto the terrace. His ponytail had come loose, and white-blond hair streamed down his shoulders. Arrapato trailed behind, his nails ticking over the stones.

"Raphael!" she cried.

"Stay where you are," Demos yelled. An unbearable warmth invaded her shoulder. She heard a clap, and the pendant shattered. Jade pieces slashed into the air. Then she fell to the ground, red beads spilling around her.

"No," Jude cried. He staggered forward, arms stretched out.

"Idiots. I told you not to move." Demos whirled, pointing the gun at Jude, then at Raphael.

"You shot Caroline," Father Aeneas cried.

"Shut up, all of you." Demos closed his eyes and pulled the trigger. Arrapato yelped and skittered into the house.

Caro struggled to sit up, but her left arm wouldn't move. The LSD made her dress vibrate, magenta blending into crimson. She brushed her right hand over the silk and felt something damp. Then she raised her hand. Her palm was red, as if she'd touched a wet painting.

Demos pushed the box into a plastic bag. Heaving a sigh, he walked over to Father Aeneas and shoved the gun to his head. "On your feet, monk."

"No, please." Father Aeneas began to pray. Demos grabbed the monk's beard and pulled the old man to his feet. They shuffled toward the terrace steps. Demos pushed the gun against the monk's temple.

"Do not move," Demos said. "Do not call the police. Or I will kill him."

Tears ran down Father Aeneas's face. "Demos, no," he said. "Let them help Caroline. She's hemorrhaging."

"A small sacrifice. Now, move." He lowered the gun to the monk's back and forced him down the terrace steps.

Raphael rushed over to Caro. Jude tried to walk, but his legs gave way. He crawled over the stones. Their faces loomed above her, blotting out the stars. She felt firm pressure on her shoulder.

"Beppe!" Raphael called. "Help me get her into the house."

"Don't move her," Jude said. "Caro? Can you hear me?"

She tried to say *Yes*, but everything was spinning.

"She's going to bleed out," Jude said.

"I can save her," Raphael said.

No, not that. Anything but that. Her shoulder burned, and her fingers were numb.

"How?" Jude cried.

"You know how," Raphael said, holding pressure against her shoulder. Blood seeped through his fingers.

"What are you doing?" Jude cried. "Get the hell away from her."

"I am trying to stop the hemorrhage," Raphael cried.

"We need to get her to a hospital."

"There is no time. Jude, listen to me—"

"No." Jude shoved Raphael. "She won't be like *you*."

Caro felt Jude pull her into his lap. Down by the water, she heard the boat putter. A feeble light swept back and forth. The monk's voice rose up. Two quick gunshots sounded, followed by a splash.

Caro felt herself being lowered to the cool tiles. Then everything began to whirl. The pain opened like an amaryllis, each petal slick and curled.

"Mia cara?" Raphael said. His voice ricocheted inside her head. A deeper voice said, "Hold on, stay with us."

Caro felt herself rising out of Jude's arms into the melting sky. She looked down and saw the terrace. Jude and Raphael slanted over her, the red dress spilling between them.

CHAPTER 57

ROMANIA

Wilkerson's jet landed at the Bucharest airport in the middle of a snowstorm. A driver waited inside customs. He spoke little English, and he ushered Wilkerson to the car and tucked him into the backseat with a plaid blanket and a thermos filled with hot tea and brandy. Silence fell around Wilkerson like clean linen, fluttering at the edges. Perfect.

The car sped past slums, concrete buildings, and grand townhouses, and veered out of the city, into the Romanian countryside. The rounded hillocks gave way to mountains that rose up like dog teeth. Waterfalls plunged over snowy ledges into narrow gorges. Brasov was ringed by the eastern and southern Carpathian Mountains, and by the time they arrived, Wilkerson was seasick.

His mobile phone rang, but he took his time answering. It was Mr. Underwood. "Sir, they are still in Venice," he said.

"*Who?*" Wilkerson rubbed his eyes, wondering if Moose's stupefaction was contagious.

"Caroline Clifford and her companion. They're on Isla Carbonera. That's near—"

"I know where it is, you idiot."

"Shall I contact MI5?"

"Not yet. Put Caroline under surveillance. No vampires. Make sure your men stay in the background."

The car turned down an icy road and stopped in front of a gate that was laced with barbed wire. Wilkerson produced his credentials, and the guard waved them through. The driveway hadn't been snowplowed and Wilkerson saw nothing but a broad expanse of white. The car skidded up the driveway toward a modern building, gray concrete with tiny square windows. Tall, thin evergreens pressed inward on three sides, waiting and watching like starving beasts.

Wilkerson got out of the car. Snow fell sideways, and he leaned into the wind. Dr. Popovici and two men in lab coats were waiting in the lobby. As the doctor made introductions, Wilkerson waved an imperious hand. "Lovely to meet you. I'm in a bit of a rush. One of my operatives is ill. Where is the blood?"

"It is being packed in ice," Dr. Popovici said, nodding to his assistants, who scuttled into an office.

"But you knew I was coming," Wilkerson yelled. "Why didn't you have it ready?"

Dr. Popovici's cheeks blazed. "It was my understanding that you were also here to tour the facility. I have something extraordinary to show you."

Wilkerson glanced at his Rolex, trying to mask his irritation. He didn't care about his minions or their credentials; he cared about results. "All right, then, but quickly."

Popovici led him down a corridor with phones set into wall niches. The doctor pushed through a steel door into the animal studies lab. Cages were stacked to the ceiling: mice, rabbits, even a few mongrel dogs. Popovici gestured at the mice. "From the strain that were brought from the Yorkshire lab."

Wilkerson's jaw twitched. The mice represented another one of Moose's failures, and another loose end. Two years ago, a British scientist from a rival pharmaceutical company had discovered the R-99 gene. Wilkerson had hoped to recruit the man and he'd dispatched Moose and the Bulgarians to York. The research lab had burned, and the biochemist had vanished.

Popovici strode into a hall and swiped a plastic card in front of the sensor; the doors clicked open. "Stage two trials are underway," the doctor said. "We have volunteers, mostly peasants, but they are happy for the money and free blood."

"How many volunteers?" Wilkerson blinked.

"Three vampires and one hybrid—that's a half vampire. They're rare."

"The trials are going well, I hope." Wilkerson glanced at his watch.

"We've made strides with the antiaging drug. However, we accidentally stumbled onto something that might interest you."

Wilkerson smirked. Pharmaceutical "accidents" seldom interested him. Of course, penicillin was an unintended discovery, but most laboratory errors were fodder for the press, leading to ruination and bankruptcy.

"You might recall an incident several months ago, when we injected massive amounts of R-99 stem cells into humans?" Popovici smiled, showing small teeth. "The test subjects showed no antibody response to the infected blood, other than to transform into vampires. Naturally, the test subjects were euthanized, but—"

"This is old news." Wilkerson flapped his hand. "Testing humans, destroying humans, dissecting humans. You're wasting my time."

"Yes, sir, but this time we tested half vampires," Popovici said. "As you know, the hybrids aren't easily transformed. And if one is bitten, their blood causes a mild toxic reaction in the vampire. Now, we understand why. Within a few hours of exposure, the hybrid produced numerous antibodies against the vampire stem cells. We extracted the antibodies from the blood and placed them into a centrifuge. It formed a concentrate. We infused a vampire with ten cc's of the concentrate. Within minutes, the patient was dead."

"Of what?" Wilkerson frowned. He wasn't sure what Popovici was trying to prove. He didn't care about antibodies. He cared about the R-99 gene and immortality.

"Anaphylactic shock," Popovici said.

"You're saying hybrid blood is lethal to vampires?" Wilkerson asked.

"If a hybrid's antibodies are extracted and concentrated, their blood becomes a weapon against vampires. A chemical stake to the heart."

"I don't believe it," Wilkerson said.

"Let me demonstrate." Popovici stopped in front of a

window with a red 5 painted on the glass. Wilkerson leaned forward and stared into a dimly lit room. A stoop-shouldered man with long gray hair lay on a hospital bed. A unit of blood hung from an IV pole, and a red tube snaked down into the man's wrist.

"This subject is a three-hundred-year-old vampire," Popovici said. "For the last few weeks, we've kept him supplied with blood and satellite TV. He is content."

Wilkerson glanced at Popovici. "Delightful. What's the point?"

Popovici walked over to a niche and reached for the phone. "Tell Dr. Lacusta we need the drug in room five."

Wilkerson turned back to the window. The vampire's face was knitted in concentration as he watched a Romanian news show on the flat-screen television. Wilkerson ran one hand through his hair. "I desperately need to get back to Sofia. Will this take long?"

Before Popovici could reply, a door opened at the end of the hall, and a pear-shaped man in a lab coat appeared, holding a square tray with a syringe. "I am Dr. Lacusta," he said.

"What's in the needle?" Wilkerson asked.

"Concentrated antibodies from a hybrid," Lacusta said.

The portly doctor walked toward the vampire's room and swiped his card, and the door clicked open. He stepped over to the bed and chatted with the vampire while he injected the medicine into the intravenous tubing. Lacusta hurried out of the room and stepped behind Wilkerson.

Popovici looked at his watch. "The subject will be dead in three minutes. Although we can reverse it with an adrenaline injection, if you wish. You have two minutes and thirty-two seconds to make up your mind."

The vampire sat up in bed and pounded his chest. His respirations were fast and shallow, accompanied by faint wheezing. He leaped out of the bed, dragging the IV with him, and lunged forward. The IV pole tipped over and clattered to the concrete floor. He staggered around the room, blood streaming down his hand. His lips turned blue, and he clawed at his throat, gasping for air. He grabbed the IV pole and flung it into the television. The screen caved in, and fire licked out. Smoke poured out of the jagged hole.

"Notice his coloring: classic signs of hypoxia," Popovici said in a low voice. "Soon his blood pressure will bottom out. He will lose consciousness—unless you wish to reverse it with adrenaline."

"He's old." Wilkerson shrugged. "Let him die."

The vampire opened his mouth to scream, but nothing came out. He hurled himself at the window, and the glass made a zipping noise. Cracks fanned around the vampire's face in a grisly frame. He spread out his arms and slid down the glass, leaving a trail of saliva and blood. He clunked to the floor and didn't move.

"Three minutes and fifty seconds." Popovici tapped his watch. "Now, would you care to see our hybrid?"

Without waiting for an answer, Popovici led him into another corridor, with Lacusta bobbing in his wake. Popovici stopped in front of a window and opened the blinds. A woman with long red hair lay on the bed, her gown riding up on her hips.

"We had difficulty locating a hybrid," Popovici said.

"Yes, they seem to be rare." Wilkerson leaned toward the glass. "But lovely."

Lacusta stepped forward. "It is difficult for immortals to breed with humans," he said, ignoring Popovici's frown. "That's why their numbers are small. The ones we have studied exude a sexual attraction that is overwhelming."

"That is enough, Dr. Lacusta." Popovici's cheeks flushed.

"Is sleeping with a vampire the same? For humans, I mean." Wilkerson's jaw clenched as he thought of Vivienne and Grimaldi. He imagined them at the auction, exchanging flirty glances. After one taste of the filthy vampire, she'd apparently gone mad with lust.

"Yes, but it's much more intense," Lacusta said.

Two spots of color deepened on Dr. Popovici's cheeks, and he cleared his throat. "We are interested in doing further testing on the hybrid. If she were to become pregnant, by a mortal or especially a vampire, the stem cells and cord blood of the fetus could provide a breakthrough."

"What sort of breakthrough?" Wilkerson's eyebrows went up.

"Fetal stem cells are more potent," Dr. Popovici said. "They can be used to develop serums. We are also close to breaking down the genetic code, separating the genes that produce blood cravings from the ones that render immortality. We're working on the code that links sunlight, blindness, and sensitivity to ultraviolet rays."

"We are speaking of only a few amino acids," Lacusta said. "And we can create a biological product that will render immortality, albeit a temporary one. Aging will slow down, if not stop entirely, with none of the drawbacks that plague the immortals. Those who take the product will never grow old or fall prey to illness."

"How long before the drug is ready?" Wilkerson's pulse sped up.

"One to two years," Dr. Popovici said.

"Sooner if we had more hybrids," Lacusta added.

"That long?" Wilkerson pursed his lips. Maybe he should increase the lab's budget. Then he remembered Caroline Clifford. The girl had a fifty percent chance of being a hybrid. If she was, her blood was more valuable than any artifact.

Inside the room, the woman sat up, her hair spilling down. "She's pretty," he whispered.

"Indeed she is," Dr. Popovici said. "Would you like to interview her?"

Wilkerson flattened his palm against the window. A fierce desire uncurled in his belly, and his breath fogged the glass. "Yes, an interview might be helpful. Can you close the blinds?"

"Take all the time you want," Dr. Popovici said.

Wilkerson stepped into the room and shut the door.

CHAPTER 58

VILLA PRIMAVERINA
ISLA CARBONERA

Caro dreamed that she was in Oxford, watching a blue-eyed child dash across the garden. Her uncle was sitting at the kitchen table drinking Earl Grey tea and reading the *Observer*. The child's brown curls shook as he chased Dinah the cat into the cucumber patch. Caro ran after him, streaking across the sun-dappled lawn, but the child had vanished. She heard growling, then two spotted dogs crept out of the bushes.

She awakened with a start and blinked up at clouds. One cloud was shaped just like Arrapato. A moment later, a cold nose pressed against her ear and sniffed. She heard a jingling noise and felt a tongue against her cheek. Slowly the room came into focus. She wasn't in a garden. She was in a bedroom, and the ceiling was painted with clouds.

"Arrapato, I told you not to bother her," Raphael said. He lifted the black dog and set him on the floor. The dog leaped back onto the bed and stepped over to Caro.

"Welcome back," Raphael said. He smiled and touched her cheek. "Beppe, find Jude. Tell him she's awake."

"Where am I?" She rubbed her eyes.

"In my big brass bed." His smile widened. He wore a white cotton shirt that was unbuttoned, revealing an even whiter T-shirt underneath.

"I guess it's true," Caro said.

"What?"

"You really don't sleep in a coffin."

He laughed. "Were you dreaming of the dogs again?"

"How did you know about that?"

"Do you really have to ask?" He patted her leg. "The dream was prophetic. The dogs represent vampires."

She scooted her uninjured hand along the mattress and lifted the sheet. She'd halfway expected to see the red dress, but she was wearing a white cotton nightgown with thin straps. The left strap had been untied and draped across her chest like a messy ribbon, curving around a bulky gauze bandage that covered her shoulder.

"How did I get into this nightgown?" she asked.

"Maria," he said. "We helped her undress you."

She tried to sit up, but Raphael eased her down. "You've lost quite a bit of blood."

"Did you make me into a vampire?" She swallowed. "I remember you and Jude were arguing."

"No." He shook his head. "I didn't touch one drop of your lovely blood."

"What happened?" Her voice sounded scratchy. She

glanced around the room. Black walls, white bedding, clouds on the ceiling. No windows.

"The little Greek man put LSD into the grappa. He shot you."

"Beware of Greeks bearing gifts, right?" She hesitated, then bits and pieces came back to her. "I knew it was some kind of drug. I thought maybe you were responsible."

"Me?"

"After you got that phone call, everything went crazy."

"I'd been making inquiries about your problems in Bulgaria, *mia cara*. It made no sense that MI5 would be pursuing you."

"Did you learn anything?"

"Not yet."

"How long was I unconscious?"

"Almost two days."

"What's the date?"

"December ninth. You've been weaving in and out of consciousness." Raphael held up a small plastic bottle and shook it. "The bullet. Not that you want a souvenir, but here it is. Your blood type is rare, *mia cara*. AB negative. But I had it in my blood bank."

"You saved my life." She squeezed his hand. "Thanks."

"Prego." He made a little bow. "But I cannot take credit. Your necklace deflected the bullet, thankfully a small caliber; it missed the artery and nicked the great vein. Also, I suspect Demos's aim might have been off. And thank God for it—otherwise you would not have survived. The gods were smiling on you."

"The necklace was a present from Jude." Her hand rose to her chest, grazing over the empty space where the pendant had hung.

"I'm afraid the stone shattered," Raphael said quietly.

"What about Father Aeneas?" she asked. "Is he okay?"

"Demos shot him. The bastard even took a shot at Arrapato. Thank God he missed."

"Are you saying Father Aeneas is dead?"

"It appears that he is." Raphael paused. "The police have sent divers into the water. So far, they've found nothing. The current might have carried his body away. Or it may wash ashore. Time will tell."

She shivered, trying not to picture the monk floating along the bottom of the lagoon, tiny fish swimming in the folds of his robes. "Why would Demos turn on him?"

"Greed. One of the seven deadlies. He will sell those ten pages of *Historia Immortalis*."

Her vision blurred, and a tear skidded down her cheek.

"I'm so sorry, Caro. This is my home. I take full responsibility. I do not know why, but I could not read their thoughts—sometimes it is that way."

"I shouldn't have brought my bag to the terrace. But I have this ingrained paranoia."

"No need to explain. Besides, Demos wouldn't have left without his prize."

"I should have told you about my pages."

"I knew you had them the moment you showed up. I caught the edge of your thoughts—you were wondering why your Uncle Nigel had placed those ancient pages in a Venice bank. But it was brilliant. A watery city is the last place anyone would look." Raphael waved his hand. "Never mind that. I am sick that I did not protect you."

"I didn't suspect Demos. Not one bit. He has our passport numbers. Well, the fake ones."

"They are easily replaced. But you are not. You are a

rare woman. If I had not been drugged, I would have killed Demos with my bare hands. And you wouldn't have been injured. You would have your father's pages."

Another tear streamed down and she brushed it away. "Demos broke the triptych. Did he take the pieces with him?"

"No." Raphael's dark brows came together. "He thought it was useless. I suppose his rage took over. He did not understand its importance."

"Well, it's important to me; the last link to my parents. And Demos knew that. Maybe that's why he left the triptych."

Raphael shook his head. "No, *mia cara*. Men like him have no empathy. He has no idea what he has destroyed. The triptych's value is far beyond money or sentiment."

"Why didn't Father Aeneas know about the prophecy?"

"A cabal has guarded it for centuries. Only two mortals knew about the prophecy, and they're dead—your mother and your uncle."

From the hallway, Jude shouted her name. He ran into the room, squeezed past Raphael, and knelt beside the bed. "Caro." He raised her hand, as if he were lifting a baby bird. "I'm so sorry, lass. I wanted to protect you, but I couldn't. If only I hadn't drunk the grappa."

"Everyone did," she said.

"Except for Demos and Aeneas." Raphael turned to Jude. "You gave him a key. I hope it won't open Sir Nigel's bank box."

"Nothing of the sort." Jude gently released Caro's hands and turned his burning gaze on the vampire. "It was a ruse, but it worked. I didn't see you trying to help her, you bloody coward."

Raphael's lips drew back farther, showing his teeth. "You're the coward for not loving Caro."

"You don't know how I feel." Jude stood, meeting Raphael's gaze. The air around them seemed to crackle with electricity. They were like the wild dogs in her old dream. One more second and Raphael would rip out Jude's throat. Arrapato dove under the covers and nestled against Caro's leg.

"Stop it," Caro yelled. "Both of you."

Raphael stepped back, his eyes glowering. "Well, what is the real story on this key? Your thoughts have yielded nothing."

"It goes to a locker in the Thessaloniki train station," Jude said. "When Demos opens it, he'll find a bag filled with soiled clothing."

"So you tricked him." Raphael folded his arms. "I underestimated you."

"Is that an apology?" Jude asked.

"An observation." Raphael walked to the doorway and turned, his eyes sweeping longingly over Caro. "I will see you later."

He left the room so swiftly his cotton shirt billowed and sent a cold, fruity draft toward the bed. Jude sat on the edge of the mattress and pulled the blanket over Caro's chest, careful not to disturb her injured arm.

"Thanks," she whispered. She wanted to touch him but was afraid he'd rebuff her, and she couldn't have stood it. She heard a thump as Arrapato leaped to the floor. She'd forgotten he was there. A moment later she heard his nails snick over the floor, his tags clicking as he hurried after his master.

Caro stared at the M of Jude's upper lip, and she traced

an imaginary line to the cleft in his chin. He pushed his fingers through his hair. "I only took a few sips of grappa, but they were potent. My legs felt like two limp strands of linguini. Every time I tried to stand, I'd fall. But when Demos put the gun to your head. Oh, Jesus. I couldn't save you."

"In a way, you did." Her hand went to the hollow between her breasts, stroking the smooth flesh above her heart where the pendant had once rested. "Raphael said—"

"Yes, I know. The necklace. But still, we almost lost you. There was so much blood. I thought you were dying. Raphael said he could save you. All I could think about was you becoming like him—and being *with* him." His forehead tightened, and three lines appeared. "Maria heard the commotion and called Dr. Nazzareno. I was frantic that Raphael would lose control. But he didn't. He wanted to give you his blood. I wouldn't let him."

"You made the right decision." She touched his shoulder, pressing against the rough cotton fabric, feeling the taut, curved muscle that lay beneath. She waited to see if he moved away. He didn't.

"What if I'd been wrong?" He cupped his hand over hers. "I made a decision about your life—*yours*. I had no right. It was selfish. You could have died because of me."

"I almost died because Demos shot me." She pulled his hand to her breast. "Feel my heart? That's not an imaginary beat. I'm very much alive."

"The immortals have a pulse," he said. "Yours is racing. Perhaps you need another transfusion. A rapid pulse means your blood volume has been depleted and your blood pressure is low."

"Or maybe I'm excited to see you." She looked at his

throat, where the dark, springy chest hairs began, and she remembered how he and Raphael had argued.

He withdrew his hand and leaned back. His eyes were solicitous but noncommittal. She tried to hear his thoughts but couldn't grab hold of anything. Was he going to stay? She couldn't bring herself to ask. Either he was or he wasn't. He was like those ten vellum pages. She couldn't lose something if it was already gone.

CHAPTER 59

Dr. Nazzareno's wire glasses slid down his nose as he examined her shoulder. "Minimal redness. No swelling," he said. "Are you having any pain?"

"A little," she said. "Mostly it itches."

"That means it is healing. And rapidly." He smiled, and tiny wrinkles framed the edges of his dark eyes. He spread antibiotic ointment on the wound and covered it with a wide bandage, dabbing a bit on her neck, covering the scabbed bite marks.

"Keep the wound dry for another week," he said. "Don't shower, take a tub bath. As to your activities, use common sense. Don't exert yourself."

"Thank you, Dr. Nazzareno."

"You are quite welcome." He leaned closer. "We should discuss your condition."

She swallowed, and her throat clicked. "What's wrong? Did the bullet cause other damage?"

"No, not at all."

"Then what?" She blinked, searching her mind for anything resembling a medical condition. Only one came to mind. Either the doctor was psychic or Raphael had blabbed. She lifted an eyebrow. "Are you referring to my half-vampirism?"

"No, my dear." He smiled and patted her hand. "You are pregnant."

She sat there a moment, her heart punching against her ribs, and tried to absorb the news. "But how do you know?" she whispered.

"A blood test."

"Why would you check for that?"

"I've been a physician for quite a long time." He chuckled. "Not to brag, but my senses are acute. All good doctors have a second sense about their patients' health, but mine is particularly developed. The moment I saw you, I knew you were with child. I could hear two heartbeats. After you were in a stable condition, I took a small blood sample. And my hunch proved correct."

A rush of blood went to her head. "I thought it took weeks for a pregnancy test to show positive."

"The beta hCG test detects pregnancy six days after ovulation. Naturally your levels were highly elevated."

"Wouldn't that be too soon to hear the baby's heartbeat?"

He smiled. "Vampires have keen hearing. Not to boast, but my auditory skills can be trusted."

"You're sure I'm pregnant?"

"Definitely."

Streaks of joy raced through her, and she placed one hand over her stomach. A baby. Jude's baby.

"Caro, when was your last menstrual period?"

"November fourteenth."

"Let's see." He tipped back his head and mumbled to himself. "Your due date is August twenty-first."

"A summer birth," she said, imagining herself walking in clear sunlight, her hands resting on a curved belly. Then she remembered the grappa. "Demos drugged the grappa with LSD. Will it hurt the baby?"

"Raphael said that you consumed a small amount."

"Yes, just a sip, but—" She blinked. "Does he know about the baby?"

"Not from my lips." The doctor shook his head. "That would be a violation of doctor-patient confidentiality. But he is canny, as you well know. Er, he is not the father, is he?"

"No." She pressed two fingers to the bridge of her nose, trying to blot out images of Demos and the tainted grappa bottle. "But I thought LSD damaged the chromosomes."

"That was a popular theory in the sixties, but it has not been proven. However, in humans it can cause uterine contractions. When LSD was given to laboratory mice, a small percentage aborted. An even smaller percentage had stillbirths."

"Are you saying that I could have a miscarriage? Or that my baby might be born dead?"

"Did you not hear me, dear? With *humans*, there can be risks." Dr. Nazzareno patted her hand. "In hybrids, the placental blood barrier is exceptionally strong. Think of it as a super placenta."

"But I've been bitten twice by vampires."

"That shouldn't be a problem."

She would have felt better if he'd said *Absolutely not*. But at least the grappa wouldn't have a detrimental effect. A baby! She was going to be a mother.

"Can I drink coffee?" She tried to smile, but her lips wobbled.

"I don't think anyone should drink coffee." He threw his head back and laughed. "My dear, try not to worry so much. It would be different if you were completely human—the LSD would have crossed the placenta. Your baby is safe."

"You're not just trying to keep me calm, are you?"

"I do not hide the truth from my patients." He pulled a square, white pad out of his pocket. "I am prescribing prenatal vitamins. Take one daily with meals. I will send Beppe to the chemist."

"Should I do anything special? A high-protein diet? Megadoses of vitamin C?"

He flicked one finger, as if dismissing a gnat. "Eat what you like. Drink in moderation. Make all the love you wish, unless there is bleeding, of course. If this happens, call immediately. When you are back on your feet, I'd like to do a baseline ultrasound, record your weight, give you some brochures—all *normal* things for a pregnant woman."

She nodded.

He kissed her hand. "Congratulations, my dear."

CHAPTER 60

Rain slashed against the villa for two days, but Caro barely noticed. She lay curled up in the red toile bedroom while the storm raged over Venice, heaving cold surf onto Isla Carbonera.

She grimaced, fighting another wave of morning sickness, and pushed her face into the pillow. Her nausea was faintly green and spun around her like a tropical storm.

If it weren't for bad luck, she'd have no luck at all. In addition to the loss of her ten pages and a near-fatal injury, she was pregnant. By a man who couldn't wait to get away. Fine, she wouldn't feel sorry for herself, not one damn bit. Her problems were small and bearable.

She rolled over and tucked the blanket under her chin. If only her mother were here. They could discuss men, babies, and vampires. "Vivi, tell me how to be a good mother," she whispered.

And what about Jude? What would Vivi think about him? *Go on with your life*, she'd say. *Eat chocolate, paint a mural, hang wind chimes.*

Later that evening, the nausea receded, along with the rain. Caro sat next to the window and watched the lights of Venice. She craved tiramisu and risotto with leeks and carrots, which Maria sent from the kitchen on huge brass trays.

Jude and Raphael visited, bringing weather reports. More rain was predicted. Jude fed her teeny slices of Veronese Christmas cake. Arrapato jumped on her bed, showing off his red sweater.

A little after one A.M. Dr. Nazzareno stopped by to check her shoulder.

"I'm worried about her nausea," Jude said.

"Normale," Dr. Nazzareno said, winking at Caro. "It will end shortly."

Maria shooed them out of the room, leaving Caro with just Arrapato for company. She lifted his furry chin and said, "I'm going to be a mother."

Arrapato snorted and showed his teeth.

By Friday morning, Caro's nausea had passed. She craved tea and *brasadella*, a coffee cake with lemon and anise. She opened the closet and found a silk caftan that was patterned with giant poppies, then wandered barefoot through the villa. She made her way to the terrace level and paused by the arched windows. Fat raindrops slid down the glass, and beyond the stone patio, mist rose up from the water and engulfed a marble statue of Athena in the lower garden. Venice and Murano were hidden in the scrubwater clouds. Bad weather had always made Caro feel lazy and snug, as if she were hidden from the world, but today it felt menacing.

Someone is watching, she thought, and spun around, expecting to see Beppe or Maria, but the loggia was empty. She felt relieved until she turned back to the window, and a cold flutter moved through her chest. She had the distinct feeling that someone—or something—was out there.

She walked to the terrace door. This was vampire weather. They could roam on cloudy days, even though they still needed sunglasses and zinc oxide. What if those ghouls had tracked her and Jude to the island?

Behind her, music uncurled from a long, dark hallway. Nine Inch Nails was singing "Something I Can Never Have." She walked toward it. The hall twisted into a darker antechamber, where a door stood open, casting a wedge of artificial light onto the stone floor. She peeked inside. The room resembled a stylish crypt, with silver crosses hanging on the black walls. Raphael sat at a long, polished table, leaning over the shattered triptych. Beside his elbow were tweezers, a magnifying glass, and a pot of glue. Caro heard a muffled bark. It seemed to be coming from a carved bench. Arrapato's head popped up between a pile of books, and he barked again. Raphael waved one hand, and the music faded. "Come sit with me, *mia cara*. I'm trying to restore the triptych."

Arrapato leaped off the bench and followed Caro to the table. He bumped his cold nose against her leg, and she reached down to pat him. "I thought vampires slept during the day," she said, glancing at Raphael.

"We do. But Arrapato kept whining. So I came to my study. It's the darkest room in the villa."

Right, Caro thought. No windows. No chance of sunburn. She sat down and looked at the broken icons. The panels lay in five chunks; the smaller pieces had been sorted into piles. "Tell me about the prophecy," she said.

"I like a woman who gets straight to the point." Raphael smiled. "The images on the triptych are supposed to predict the future of the vampire race. According to the legend, a woman will be the link between humans and immortals—with the power to save or destroy us."

"Which images?" Her thoughts skated back to the female saint and the bleeding man.

"Let's wait until the panels are whole. It will take time because there are so many little pieces. Some images might be lost forever. If only I had thought to photograph the triptych the other night, when it was complete."

She glanced at the wooden shards; some weren't much bigger than an eyelash. "I don't see how you'll fix it."

"I've got time." He smiled. "I learned patience when I was a monk. Not that I was particularly pious. Most second and third sons of nobility joined a monastery."

Gripping the tweezers, he said a prayer, then lifted a broken fragment that showed part of the castle.

"I don't suppose you knew the Borgias?" Caro asked.

He laughed. "Yes, I knew them. The whole lot were scandal magnets."

"You aren't related to them, are you?" She felt Arrapato's paw on her leg and picked him up.

"No, my family is much older."

"How much?"

"My father was a vassal of Charlemagne. Long story short—he was one of the Lombard princes."

"You're that old?"

"Just think of me as thirty-nine." Raphael leaned back in the chair. "Are you strong enough for bad news?"

She tilted her head, trying to slip into his thoughts, but hit something solid.

"A body washed up," Raphael said.

"Poor Father Aeneas." She'd been expecting this. She briefly shut her eyes and crossed herself.

"No. Poor Demos. His body was pulled from the water."

CHAPTER 61

The room spun around, and Caro grabbed the edge of the table to steady herself. "*Demos* is dead? But he had the gun."

"Father Aeneas must have wrestled it away and shot him."

"But I thought it was the other way around."

Raphael sighed. "We'll never know the real story. Perhaps the men were in cahoots and the partnership went sour. Maybe the monk hopes to sell your ten pages and move away from the monastery. Or he could be a zealot who wishes to destroy *Historia Immortalis*."

"This is my fault. If only I hadn't gone to Meteora."

"Your uncle had no way of knowing that Aeneas would betray you."

"Why didn't Uncle Nigel send me to you?"

"Because I needed all three icons to interpret the prophecy."

"Yes, but—"

Raphael lifted his hand. "Remember, he was dying when he wrote those anagrams, Caro. He had to honor Vivi's final instructions—whatever they were—and keep you safe. Your cover had been blown, and he knew you would need to move fast. Bulgaria sits above Greece. So Nigel directed you to Meteora to collect the first icon. He thought Aeneas would protect you."

"You would have done that."

"Not in daylight." Raphael shook his head. "Even if Nigel had sent you straight to my villa, we would have needed the third icon."

"You would have brought me to Meteora."

"But I can only travel at night—I would have slowed you down. When you showed up at Varlaam, I'm guessing that Demos and Aeneas hatched a plan to steal the artifacts—or perhaps they wanted to destroy them. Either way, they needed Jude out of the way."

"Why?"

"Aeneas probably thought he could control you better if a boyfriend wasn't hanging around." Raphael's gaze sharpened. "So instead of taking you aside to explain about your parents and your hybridism, the monk blurted the news in front of Jude. And planted the seeds that you would not be sexually compatible with him."

Caro felt the color rise to her cheeks and quickly tried to clear her mind, but she was a beat too late.

Raphael opened a glue pot. "The monk used the oldest trick in the world—he wounded Jude's masculine pride."

"I'm sure Father Aeneas made that up. Because Jude and I have no problem in that department."

"The monk told the truth." Raphael lifted an eyebrow. "Humans are sexually magnetized by vampires—a bit less with hybrids. But hybrids don't have sexual chemistry with humans."

"Wrong. Jude and I have more than enough."

"Yes, after you were bitten in Momchilgrad."

She cupped her hand over her neck, grazing the scabs. Her eyes narrowed. "Did he tell you?"

"I looked into his mind. And yours." He shrugged. "Sorry, but I was curious. It's most unusual for a hybrid to lust after a human."

"So I'd feel differently about Jude if I hadn't been bitten?"

"You might have fallen for him, but the lovemaking would have been disappointing. When the Momchilgrad vampire bit you, it triggered a hormonal storm within your system. A pitch-perfect collision of estrogen and testosterone."

Indeed. "Will it lessen?"

"No." He grinned. "That's good for you. For Jude, not so much. He is riddled with doubts—your hybridism torments him. But he's a typical guy. He worries even more about his sexual prowess."

"He shouldn't." She glared at Raphael until he turned away. He lifted the tweezers, plucked a wooden shard, and moved toward the glue pot.

"I haven't seen him this morning." Caro's stomach muscles tightened. Actually, she hadn't seen him since last night. Had he left the island?

"He's here." Raphael looked up.

She felt him reach into her mind. "Stop reading my thoughts. It's rude."

"I don't want you to fret, *mia cara*. Jude is with Maria. She tried to teach him how to make panettone and focaccia, but I'm afraid he showed no aptitude for baking." Raphael slid the shard into place, then gently patted it with the tweezers. "Maria forced Jude to help her plan the *menù di Natale*. Then she insisted that he help her and Beppe put up a Christmas tree. You have never heard such complaining. But I think Jude secretly liked the festivities."

"I had no idea he was a traditionalist." She lifted the magnifying glass and examined her palm. The lines were shaped like a martini glass. "He hasn't been drinking, has he?"

"Not at all. Why?"

She didn't answer, and Raphael's gaze sharpened.

Quit snooping, she thought, but he pressed harder. Her head tipped back, and she began humming "God Save the Queen," Uncle Nigel's favorite hymn. A moment later, her chin snapped back, as if a suction had broken, and she felt Raphael's mind retreat.

The music changed, and Andrea Bocelli began singing *"O mio babbino caro."* Raphael set down the tweezers and touched her face. "Forgive me. I did not mean to intrude. I enjoyed long, telepathic conversations with your father, but he could shut me out, too."

Caro smiled. "Well, I'm glad I inherited something from him."

"You look so much like the Grimaldis—the straight nose, high cheekbones, long legs. They had blond, curly hair. Odd that yours isn't."

"Oh, I do." She lifted a dark strand. "But I needed a disguise."

"Your father had a head full of curls. My God, women loved him." Raphael pointed to an icon fragment that showed the vineyard. "The Grimaldis loved wine, too. Their vineyards were famous. In fact, they introduced the Mauzac Blanc grapes to the Languedoc region."

"If my father was a ladies' man, how did he settle for my mother?"

"Because Vivienne wasn't just any woman. She was his big love. His only true love."

"What made her different?"

"Philippe had lost the capacity to feel joy, and Vivienne found happiness in small things. Moonlight on a rug. A blooming orchid. A fresh peach."

"Why did she marry Wilkerson?" Caro scratched Arrapato's ear.

"I asked her that question. I was hoping she'd say that Wilkerson had drugged her and she woke up married. But apparently they met at a bookshop on Portobello Road. Wilkerson collected books and so did she. He romanced her. She was reeling from her parents' deaths. After he won her, he put a checkmark beside her name and moved to the next conquest. Then she met Philippe."

Caro looked up. "You knew her?"

"Quite well." He opened a drawer and pulled out a photograph that showed a laughing woman with pewter eyes and shoulder-length dark blond hair. She was sitting on a terrace with shimmering blue water rising behind the balustrades. In her arms was a black puppy with a monkey face.

"I took this photograph the last time they were here,"

Raphael said. "Vivi and Philippe had brought me an Affenpinscher puppy."

Caro looked down at Arrapato. "Him?"

"He was my consolation prize. You see, Philippe and I were both at the Sotheby's auction, bidding on those ten pages to *Historia Immortalis*. I fell hard for Vivi. But I didn't have a chance."

Raphael spread his fingers, as if to show that something precious had escaped his grasp.

"Your mother was quite upset when I named him Arrapato," he continued smoothly. "She thought he needed a more dignified name. Then she was gone, and the dog was all that remained."

Caro placed her hand under the dog's chin. "So you turned Arrapato into a vampire."

"Love will do that, *mia cara*." He pulled out another photograph that showed a bald, big-eyed baby with over-sized lips. "Vivienne sent this after you were born."

"This is me?"

"*Il bambino brutto*—the ugly baby. All the Grimaldi babies look this way. The Italians have a saying 'ugly in the cradle, beauty at the table.' You grew into a goddess."

"How did my father feel about me? Did he think I was a half-breed?"

"*Mio Dio*, no. He doted on you. The night you were born, he wrapped you in a blanket and sang you a Cole Porter song."

"Why didn't you tell me you knew my mother?"

"It is difficult for me to speak of Vivi." Raphael touched Caro's hair. "When she was here, I had a premonition of trouble. She and Philippe were hiding from Wilkerson. And the Grimaldis were furious."

"They didn't give my mother a chance, did they?"

"They couldn't." Raphael's hand fell. "It's forbidden for humans and immortals to bond."

"Says who?"

"Historia Immortalis." Raphael's voice took on a scholarly tone as he lectured her about the book's tenets and moral ambiguities—just as in today's world, the ancient vampires didn't keep their own rules.

"Exceptions were made when an immortal fell in love with a well-connected human," he said. "In other words, if you were in the peerage, if you possessed land or influence, the vamps looked the other way. Greed is a human response to an inhuman dilemma. However, when a highborn vamp romanced a lowly human, the rules were enforced, and the unfortunate lovebirds were ostracized."

Raphael couldn't cite the cases because apparently the appendix to *Historia Immortalis* was part of those ten stolen pages.

"Who took the pages?" Caro asked.

Raphael lifted his shoulders. "The pope's mercenaries, no doubt."

"Why did the Church care about that book?"

"Historia Immortalis launched the Albigensian Crusade."

"Wasn't that about the Church versus the Cathars?"

"It worked as a cover. Languedoc was a hotbed of Catharism. The Grimaldis were right in the middle of it. The crusade began centuries after your triptych was painted."

A lightness filled her chest—finally a subject that didn't involve hybrids. "I briefly studied the Albigensian Crusade. It started when Béziers was sacked."

"*Precisamente*. Pope Innocent sent Arnaud-Amay to deal with the so-called heretics."

Raphael's face darkened and he looked away from the triptych. "The knights couldn't tell the difference between Catholics, Jews, and Cathars. They asked Amay what to do. He said God would recognize His own. So they killed everyone. Thousands went to God that day. Meanwhile, Pope Innocent and his criminals cavorted at their summer residence. Not so innocent after all. One thing led to another. The Inquisition began. And more people were slaughtered."

"I still don't understand how *Historia Immortalis* was mixed up in this."

"It was at the heart of the crusade and the Inquisition." Raphael gazed down at the triptych. "The book was a threat to the Vatican."

"Why? Because the Cathars refused to tithe?" They'd been a plucky and courageous lot, from what Caro remembered of her studies.

"The pope was *always* mindful of his coffers." Raphael picked up a wooden shard and studied it. "But avarice wasn't the reason the Church stamped out Catharism."

"If it wasn't money, what was the Vatican's problem?"

"You've known about vampires for only a short while." Raphael dabbed a bit of glue on the shard and fit it onto the triptych. "You'd never believe the rest of it."

"Try me."

"Let's wait until you've had time to absorb your hybridism."

She rubbed her forehead, feeling more confused than ever. "Surely you're not insinuating that the Cathars were vampires? Or related to them in some near way?"

"No. The Grimaldis were Cathars who just happened

to be vampires. And yes, some Cathars were vampires, but most weren't." Raphael set down the tweezers. "The Grimaldis owned *Historia Immortalis*. And before you ask why anyone would care, the book is connected to one of the missing Gospels."

"A what?" she asked. But she knew. She'd studied the canonical Gospels. And no, she didn't want to believe Raphael's theory. *If* it was a theory. But it explained why people would commit murder for the book. She put her hands in her lap and twisted her fingers.

"I suppose you know the story of the lost Gospels that were found at Nag Hammadi?" he asked.

"A little." She glanced at her hands. Her knuckles were white. "Go on."

"The Bedouins found codices in jugs," he said. "The manuscripts were Coptic translations of second-century Greek originals. A Bedouin woman used the twelfth volume for kindling, but fragments were found. And they corresponded to passages from *Historia Immortalis*."

"What passages? And if fragments remained, how could they be compared to *Historia Immortalis*?"

"The twelfth volume was a Coptic translation of the original Greek text—it survived the great fire of Alexandria. There were many Coptic versions."

"Let me get this straight." Caro tucked her hair behind her ears. "You're saying *Historia Immortalis* is a Gnostic book, one that was edited out of the Bible?"

He nodded. "It's easy to see why it didn't make the canon, isn't it?"

"But the canonical Gospels are biographies of Jesus and chronicles of His teachings," Caro said. "Surely *Historia Immortalis* isn't a biography."

"No, but it's certainly a chronicle. Some scholars believe it was forged by the notorious Carpocratians—a heretical Gnostic sect. But I believe it was written by second-century monks. The language is typical of the era. It reads like a Gnostic Gospel."

"I don't understand."

"Well, the book is a treatise about the night, but the theme is resurrection. The first line says, 'This is the secret Gospel of the night.' Then it goes on to say that whoever finds the correct interpretation of the text will find eternal life." He leaned toward the carved bench and lifted out a volume. "This is the Gospel of Thomas. It opens cryptically, too, and refers to eternal life."

"Yes, after death." Shivers ran down Caro's arms.

"That's why the Church objected. *Historia Immortalis* is a chronicle of people who'd achieved eternal life on earth. Pretty radical, wouldn't you say? The Church fretted endlessly over heresy. But they also had the means to eliminate it."

Caro exhaled, and her breath made a humming sound. "So that's why it was suppressed?"

"Yes. Fortunately, many vampires were monks—and gifted translators. That's why a number of Coptic versions existed. One found its way to me at Tours. I translated a copy that went into Charlemagne's library. I also made a secret copy with pornographic illustrations. I gave it to the Grimaldis."

"Is that how the Cathars got mixed up in it?"

"In a roundabout way. Copies were made and distributed—I had a hand in that. An ambitious French monk stole a copy and delivered it to the Vatican. Claimed the Cathars were doing blood rituals and orgies. Pope

Innocent elevated the monk to a lofty position—the traitor has a statue in Saint Peter's, by the way. But I digress." Raphael reached down to pat the dog, his long fingers ruffling the black fur.

"Then the crusade began." Raphael's nostrils flared. "Pope Innocent got nearly everything he wanted. Many copies of the book were ferreted out and destroyed. Thanks to Philippe, the Grimaldis' tome was safe. As was the triptych. For a while."

Caro touched the edge of her shattered icon. "I suppose these symbols are undying, just like the immortals."

"Some of the images are mini history lessons," he said. "Pick up the magnifying glass. Study the castle walls on that large shard. Do you see the embedded symbol?"

"Barely." Caro squinted. "What is it?"

"A figure eight."

"The mathematical symbol for infinity," Caro said.

Raphael pushed up his sleeve and pointed to his tattoo. "Supposedly the symbol was invented in the 1600s by an Englishman named Wallis. But the real story is, he saw it in *Historia Immortalis*."

While he rattled on about this quirky bit of history, Caro picked at her nail polish, barely listening. Normally she loved historical gossip, but the nausea was creeping back, reminding her of her condition and her perilous relationship with the baby's father. Would Jude stick around if he knew she was pregnant? Even if he didn't reject a quarter-vampire child, she probably couldn't carry the baby to term.

"Caro?" Raphael tapped her arm.

"Yes?" She glanced up.

"Am I boring you?"

"I'm trying to work up my nerve to tell you something."

"What requires nerve?"

"I can't believe you haven't pulled it from my thoughts."

His brow wrinkled. "What's wrong?"

"Oh, God, this is too hard. I need whiskey. Only I can't drink that."

"Are you still nauseated?"

She shook her head. "Worse. I'm pregnant."

Raphael leaned back as if a bee had flown into his face. "You aren't pleased?"

"I love this baby already."

"And Jude?"

"He doesn't know."

"You must tell him immediately."

"That's why I'm worried. He won't want a child with me."

"Quiet," Raphael whispered. "He is coming."

Arrapato's ears tipped forward and he let out a muffled woof. Footsteps clattered down the tile hallway, and a moment later Jude poked his head into the room. His face brightened when he saw Caro. "There you are. I've been looking everywhere. Are you feeling better?"

"Yes." She smiled.

Raphael gestured for him to sit. "I suppose you've heard about Demos?"

"Shocking, isn't it?" Jude pulled out a chair and sat down beside Caro. "I'm thinking of hunting down that lousy monk."

"That would be a mistake," Raphael said.

"He stole Caro's property."

"But that is the nature of *Historia Immortalis*. It will

not stay put. The monk may sell those ten pages, but their new owner won't have them for long. The book possesses a type of kinetic energy."

So does the triptych, Caro thought. "But my ten pages were locked up in a bank vault for twenty years."

"Twenty years is nothing." Raphael leaned over the shattered chips, sorting them like pieces of a jigsaw puzzle.

"You're acting like the book has a will of its own," Jude said.

"A consciousness, perhaps," Raphael said without looking up. "But not a conscience."

Caro raised out of her chair to examine a large chunk from her icon. Eggshell cracks ran over the painted surface, and the corner was shattered. She examined the mitered edge. The joints had spread apart, giving a teasing glimpse into the icon's interior. It looked as if a sheet of paper were wedged inside. She picked at the gap with her fingernail. A piece of wood snapped, and the joints gaped open. She reached for the magnifying glass.

"What is it?" Raphael asked.

"Paper." She pinched the edge with tweezers and tugged until a tiny scroll appeared. It was bound with what appeared to be human hair. She handed it to Raphael. "It looks old."

"It's not." Raphael grasped an edge of the hair, and the scroll creaked open. As he unfolded it, lint wafted across the table. Spiky black handwriting was sprawled in the center of the page.

Dixit ergo Moses vadam et videbo visionem hanc magnam quare non conburatur rubus.

"This is Philippe's handwriting. Latin vulgate." Raphael's eyes softened.

"How do you know if the paper is old?" Caro asked.

"After your mother won the icon at Sotheby's, she left Harry Wilkerson. She and Philippe hid in my villa. He dismantled his icon and slipped something inside. I didn't see what, nor did he explain. I assumed it was some sort of love note." Raphael pointed to the hairs. "Those are Vivi's. Philippe was leaving a clue. In case something happened to him, he didn't want *Historia Immortalis* to be lost."

"Why didn't he just tell you or Mother?"

"Philippe trusted no one. Except for Vivi. I'm sure he confided in her."

"I don't understand my father's secrecy. If these artifacts are so important, he should have left a record."

"He'd lived two thousand years. Death wasn't part of his mind-set. Then, after he met Vivi, Harry Wilkerson had put a fatwa on them." Raphael clasped her hands. "The truth is a force of nature. Philippe knew this. He trusted this force. Now, you must trust it."

Jude edged closer. "What does the note say?"

Raphael's hands lingered on Caro's a moment, and then he moved away. "It's a verse from Exodus. 'And Moses said: I will go, and see this great sight, why the bush is not burnt.'"

"Why did Philippe put a Bible verse in his icon?" Jude said.

"It's a geographical hint." Raphael turned to the bench, slid out a thick, tattered book, and flipped to the middle. He pointed to a sketch that showed a steep mountain in the middle of a desert. The rounded hills were shaped like a woman lying on her side, her shoulders covered with a rumpled blanket. A walled fortress, the color of sand, lay nestled at the base.

"This is Saint Catherine's Monastery at Mt. Sinai," Raphael said. "The Burning Bush is inside these walls. Not to mention icons and illustrated manuscripts. Philippe was a genius. It's the perfect place to hide *Historia Immortalis.*"

He slammed the book shut and stood. "We're going to Egypt."

CHAPTER 62

VARLAAM MONASTERY
METEORA, GREECE

Aeneas walked down the aisle, gripping the box, his footsteps echoing along the church's domed ceiling. He pulled the cornerstone and the door creaked open. Cold air stirred his robe as he walked down the steps. The box felt unbearably light, but its contents would annihilate humanity. He placed the container on a broad step, then he crept up the stairs and pushed the cornerstone. The door shut with a grating noise.

God will forgive me, Aeneas thought. He shut his eyes and pictured Nigel Clifford lifting his fedora, the wiry hair sticking up like bits of wool in a flokati rug. All those years ago, the professor had arrived at Varlaam with a tiny girl. Caroline had played in the cloister while the two men had opened a bottle of ouzo. Clifford had come to discuss *Historia Immortalis* and the triptych that glorified it.

"How did you find me?" Aeneas asked Nigel, bristling with suspicion.

The professor's knapsack rustled as he pulled out the icon and photocopies of ten vellum pages. "That's what I do—uncover things. I'm an archaeologist. I made a few inquiries about icons. A vampire in Istanbul told me you'd been his physician. Apparently you saved the vampire's child? He said he gave you an icon."

"We will need more ouzo," Aeneas whispered, repressing an urge to cross himself, and left the room. The professor had brought the devil into Varlaam; but even if vampires had walked the earth during the time of Christ, it would not shake Aeneas's faith. *Historia Immortalis* wasn't the only historical record of vampirism. Other texts had vague references to immortality. The Gospel of Thomas had a startling line: *Jesus said, Whoever drinks from my mouth will become like me; I myself shall become that person, and the hidden things will be revealed to him.*

Aeneas returned with a bottle of ouzo and the icon and set both on the table. He gasped when the professor gently pressed the icons together. The images leaped out at him. A blue-black night sky, sharp mountains, a stone sarcophagus, bees and fire. The red-robed figure with an ostrich egg. The professor's voice rose and fell as he explained how the artifacts—and the child—had fallen into his life. Aeneas shifted his gaze. The little girl sat on her haunches, trying to lure a striped kitten out of the cucumber patch.

"She is a hybrid?" Aeneas said. "The offspring of a vampire and a human?"

Tears streamed down Clifford's face. Aeneas leaned back, his heart drumming. The girl was an aberration. She should have died with her parents. A half-vampire child had no place in this world. But all he said was, "You must shield her from those who will wish to harm her."

Clifford's face whitened and he reached for the ouzo. "I'll put Caro and the artifacts in a safe place."

"No," Aeneas said. "Hide the girl. Burn those ten pages. They are a sacrilege. They draw the darkness out of men. Immortality is blasphemy. Man is supposed to die a mortal death. He is not supposed to live eternally without God's judgment."

"I must honor Vivienne's wishes. She'd told me what to do if Wilkerson and his men found her. She put the icon and those pages into Caro's knapsack the night of the fire. If she'd wanted to destroy those artifacts, she would have let them burn. But she didn't."

"She was in love with a vampire. She wanted to preserve his book. You must destroy it."

Clifford rubbed his chest. "I can't."

"I will do it for you."

"No."

"Then learn to live in peril."

After Clifford and Caroline left Meteora, clouds formed a dark wall over the mountains. It rained for ten days and nights. Water surged through the valley and covered the bottom steps that led to Varlaam. God had spoken, commanding Aeneas to find and destroy the pages.

On the eleventh morning, Aeneas awoke in the half light. The rain had stopped. From the stone ledge he heard a dove cooing. He ran to the ledge, startling the bird. It rose up, white against the blue. A peregrine falcon sliced down, a dark speck moving two hundred miles per hour. Feathers boiled in the air as the hawk struck the dove and broke its back. The falcon's talons closed on the limp body and flew toward the mountains.

Another sign. Aeneas had sent the dove to its death. He should not meddle in others' lives.

That same day, a scrawny man came to Varlaam and waited for the tourists to leave. He was pale and sweaty; his shoulder blades poked through his shirt like gull wings.

"My name is Demos," the man said. "My wife and children are dead. Murdered by vampires. My house was burned." Tears gathered in Demos's eyelashes. "I stole bread in the Trikala market, and the police chased me out of town. I am seeking asylum for the night and I will leave in the morning."

Aeneas fed the man goat cheese, figs, and honeyed bread but remained skeptical. The next day, while Demos scrubbed the stone hallway outside the church, Aeneas went to Trikala and spoke with the priest. Vampires had attacked a family and burned their house. Demos had narrowly escaped. "He is a good man," the priest told Aeneas. "His loved ones perished, but Demos's life was spared for a reason. Help him find it."

Aeneas took Demos under his wing. He tutored him about the holy word and about vampirism. Together they studied Aeneas's icon, trying to decipher its symbols and secrets. Twenty years passed, eighty seasons of light and darkness. Demos spent five hours a day in prayer, begging God to forgive him for not saving his children. He fasted one day a week to atone for his theft of bread. Yet he was not without faults; he could not overcome survivor's guilt or his hatred of vampires. Each time he looked at the monk's blasphemous icon, Demos shook his fist in the air, vowing to find *Historia Immortalis* and destroy it.

Years later, when Caroline Clifford had shown up with her icon, Aeneas had thought it was God's hand. This was a chance to find the vampires' bible and destroy it. But Caroline's boyfriend had keen, suspicious eyes. The monk had offered his hospitality to the young couple, and then the police had swarmed up the mountain. The couple had followed Aeneas to the cave the way lambs scamper behind a ewe. After the police left, Aeneas shuffled to the church. Demos was waiting in the nave. He nodded as Aeneas explained about the girl and her connection to *Historia Immortalis*.

"She will lead us to the evil book." Demos made a fist. "And we will destroy it."

"I must gain her trust," Aeneas said. "But her boyfriend watches me."

"God will provide," Demos said.

And He had. After Aeneas led the couple out of the cave, he raised the subject of *Historia Immortalis*. The boyfriend's jaw tightened and fire leaped into his eyes.

He despises the immortals, Aeneas thought, and studied his body language. Defensive and angry—not on the girl's behalf, but for himself. His eyes held old wounds. Demos had acted that way when he'd first arrived at Varlaam. Father Aeneas was certain the boy had tangled with vampires. The boy would run if he knew the truth about his lady love.

Aeneas told the girl the truth, that she was half vampire. The boyfriend had fled, just as Aeneas had hoped. Later, he heard the rise and fall of voices. Aeneas crept out of bed and peered into the room. The boy had returned. He sat at the table—the fire and suspicion had left his eyes, leaving behind sorrow and confusion.

Aeneas tiptoed down to the church. Demos was kneeling in front of the altar, asking God for a sign. He glanced at the monk. "The boyfriend came back?"

Aeneas nodded.

"Then it is God's will," Demos said. "But we have another dilemma. The Bulgarian vampire is lurking. He will take what we seek."

"I will be ready."

Demos put his hand on the monk's shoulder. "Now I know why God led me to Varlaam all those years ago. You and I were meant to find *Historia Immortalis*."

It had felt like a quest, but then it changed when Demos's heart filled with greed. Aeneas should have known something was amiss when Demos had kept asking questions.

"Didn't you say that Caroline's parents stole those ten pages?" He cut his dark eyes at Aeneas.

"They belonged to Harry Wilkerson."

Demos scratched his head. "Is he a collector?"

"I do not know." Aeneas sighed. "He owns a pharmaceutical company. Perhaps he wished to exploit *Historia Immortalis*."

"I bet he'd pay anything to have those pages. In fact, I *know* he would."

"What are you saying?" Aeneas lifted his finger and drew a cross in the air. He'd told Demos too much.

"It isn't enough to burn the vampires' book. They owe me." Demos pressed his fist against his chest. "I can still hear my children's screams."

"You are God's servant," the monk said. "You cannot succumb to avarice."

Now Demos was drifting along the bottom of Laguna Veneta with a bullet hole in his chest. His death had been an accident. In the boat, he and Aeneas had argued. "You are either with me or against me," Demos said. "But you cannot stop me. I must hurry. I am meeting Wilkerson at Varlaam."

"You have betrayed me and God. And you have murdered Caroline."

"The strong do what they have to do." Demos squeezed the trigger and the bullet whizzed past Aeneas's head.

Aeneas threw himself at Demos's feet, causing him to trip. The gun clunked against the bottom of the boat. Aeneas stretched out his hand and grabbed the gun, and it detonated.

Despite his panic, he managed to retrieve the pages, the red key, and Demos's wallet. Inside was a paper with a London phone number and *Wilkerson Pharmaceuticals*. Then Aeneas caught a flight to Thessaloniki. He'd planned to burn whatever he found, but when he opened the locker, he'd pulled out a plastic bag filled with hair and bloodstained clothes. Where were the other pages to that cursed book?

Aeneas boarded the train to Kalambaka and prayed for guidance. *He who betrays shall reap betrayal.* But who, exactly, was the betrayer? If he did not set things right, the deaths would continue. He stopped in a hotel, found a pay phone, and called Wilkerson Pharmaceuticals. A woman with a nasal voice answered and identified herself as Harry Wilkerson's secretary.

"I must speak to Mr. Wilkerson." Aeneas licked his dry, cracked lips.

"He's unavailable," she said.

"This is . . . Demos." The monk paused and crossed himself. He hoped God forgave his lie. "I have an urgent message."

"I'm afraid it's impossible to leave a message. He'll return to the office next week."

"Tell him the deal is off. The pages are lost," he said and hung up.

Now, cold air stung Aeneas's cheeks as he stepped out of the church and shuffled across the cloister. No one would find those ten pages. He could almost feel the hand of God as he paused beside the windy ledge. A quarter moon hung over Meteora, a barbed tooth against the dusky sky. The winter equinox was drawing near. These dark, short days had torn his heart. A swarm of *if onlys* cut through him. If only he hadn't confided in Demos. If only he'd stopped the old man from shooting Caroline. If only Wilkerson stayed away from Varlaam.

But his unwanted guest was coming. Aeneas heard footsteps on the stone stairs. The monk decided he would greet Wilkerson cordially, then would lure him to the cave and leave him to rot in the stygian dark.

———

Harry Wilkerson's briefcase slammed into his leg as he climbed the curved steps to Varlaam, a tall, red-haired man trailing behind him. Wilkerson's eyes narrowed.

"Are you Demos?"

"He has been called away," Father Aeneas said, glancing at the redhead. His skin was white and freckled, and his teeth were too big for his mouth. He emitted the stink of ketones. *A vampire.*

"When will Demos return?" Wilkerson asked.

"He won't. He is gone from this place."

"Who the bloody hell are you?" Wilkerson asked.

"Father Aeneas." The monk swallowed and his throat clicked. "You must leave. The monastery is closed."

"Can we discuss this inside?" Wilkerson rubbed his hands together. "It's freezing."

"Your business is with Demos, not me. You must leave."

Wilkerson turned to the redhead. "Tell him how I hate the cold, Moose."

The redhead pointed a .44 Magnum at the monk. "You heard him, mate."

Aeneas led the men into the common room and poured wine, his hands shaking. The redhead wrinkled his nose and passed his glass down to Wilkerson.

"You know why we're here," Wilkerson said. "Don't bother lying."

Aeneas set the decanter on the table and tucked his hands into the sleeves of his robe. "If you have come for the pages and the icons, they are lost."

"Lost?" Wilkerson cried.

"Demos destroyed them."

"But I've already wired one million euros to his Berne account."

"I know nothing of this," Aeneas said.

"We had a deal."

"Not with me."

Wilkerson set his briefcase on the table, clicked it open,

and turned it in Aeneas's direction. The monk shook his head.

"You want *more* money?" Wilkerson asked.

"I want nothing." Aeneas waved his hand. "I do not have what you seek. Leave. Now."

"I can't do that. Not until I've seen my artifacts. Demos said they'd be here." Wilkerson pushed a stack of money across the table."

"He lied," Aeneas said.

The vampire aimed the .44 Magnum at the monk's head. "Get those blooming pages."

"Shoot me." Aeneas withdrew his hands from the sleeves and spread his arms wide. "I am ready to die."

"Don't shoot him. Bite him," Wilkerson said. "Make him like you. God frowns on the immortals."

Aeneas shrank back. He could not be bitten. God would not forgive. And he would burn. The redheaded vampire opened his dark mouth. Aeneas breathed in the sweet, calming stench.

"It's your choice," Wilkerson said. "You've got ten seconds to decide."

Aeneas led them to the church and pulled the cornerstone. The door opened, and light spilled down the first few steps.

"Where does it lead?" Wilkerson asked.

"To your precious pages."

"Don't let me stop you from getting them." Wilkerson smirked.

The monk shook his head. "I am too wobbly. Look for a box. The vellum pages are inside. With the icon." The vampire's broad shoulders filled the stairwell and he descended, counting to himself. He turned a corner and dropped out of sight. "Got it, mate," he called.

"Bring it to me." Wilkerson moved to the top of the stairs.

I'll push him, Aeneas thought, and rushed forward. Wilkerson leaped to the side. The monk tipped forward. As he fell, his robe waffled around him. He reached out blindly for the handrail and stopped his free-fall.

"Silly old tosser," said the vampire. He stepped around the monk. Then he jogged up the steps, handed the box to Wilkerson, and went back down to the monk. "Let go of the rail, ducky."

"Let me just hang here a moment," Aeneas said.

The vampire grabbed the monk's arm and tugged. The bone snapped, and the monk dropped away from the rail, into the darkness. His screams echoed up the stairwell. Moose looked up at Wilkerson. "Shall I get him, mate?"

"What's the bloody point?"

Moose ran up the steps. "He was a bit hairy at the heel, wasn't he?"

The monk's cries echoed, rising and falling. "Shut the door," Wilkerson commanded.

"But won't the other monks come sniffing around and see that he's gone missing?"

"Who cares?" Wilkerson slammed his fist against the cornerstone. The door swung shut, and Aeneas's cries snapped off.

A tinny buzz echoed in Wilkerson's pocket. He reached for his mobile phone and glanced at the display. "Yes, Mr. Underwood," he said. "This better be good news."

"I believe it is, sir. Caroline Clifford has left Villa Primaverina." Mr. Underwood paused. "Our men tracked her to an airport in Milan. I'm quite proud of our chaps, sir. They've performed admirably. Much better than your vampires. In fact—"

Wilkerson cut him off. "Where is Miss Clifford headed?"

"Sharm El Sheikh. Shall I send a crew to Egypt?"

"I'm handling this myself. Tell my pilot to register a flight plan for Egypt."

Wilkerson opened the box. He didn't see the icons, but he counted ten vellum sheets. He lifted one, and the colors leaped out. "Welcome home," he said.

CHAPTER 63

SINAI PENINSULA, EGYPT

Raphael's jet landed at Sharm El Sheikh and taxied along the runway to the old terminal.

Jude looked worried. "Isn't security rather tight in the Sinai Peninsula?"

"I've hired an excellent guide," Raphael said.

He guided Jude and Caro across the tarmac where a man in a headscarf waited. Caro saw a green armband with the insignia of the Egyptian tourist police. When he saw her, he bowed.

"Welcome to Egypt. I am Haji Muhammad Sayyid, your guide. Please call me Haji."

His lips curved, showing large, gappy teeth, but he looked intensely into her eyes. Caro looked back into his. The pupils were enormous. *Drugs?* she thought. No, he was too collected. She remembered something Uncle

Nigel had said. *The Egyptians aren't staring at you, Caro. They are studying your eyes. Tiny pupils mean boredom. Dilation means happiness or excitement.*

Haji turned to Raphael. Arabic flew into the air as the men exchanged greetings, followed by cheek kissing and handshaking. Caro saw a patch of rough skin on Haji's forehead—his *zebibah*, the praying mark, a permanent blemish caused by repeatedly pressing the forehead to the ground.

"Do not worry, beautiful lady," he said. "You will travel in safety."

He whisked them around customs into a black van. Haji drove across the tarmac and stopped next to a helicopter. Their pilot, Kareem, stowed their luggage in the back, then settled into the cockpit. His linen *galabiyyah* stretched over his wide shoulders as he surveyed the instrument panel. He bent closer, and the luminous green dials tinted his face.

The Huey's blades began to revolve. The bird veered up and over the congested streets of Sharm El Sheikh, then it passed over a road with blue barrels, indicating a security-stop point. Caro's vision seemed much sharper, and even from this distance she could pick out the soldiers that were huddled in the back of a truck, clutching AK-47s.

The helicopter dropped in altitude when it passed by Mt. Sinai. Caro leaned against the window, watching lights move up the mountain. The Huey touched down near the monastery. Sand flew past the windshield as Kareem clicked switches and the blades slowed to a rhythmic *whap*.

Haji helped Caro out of the helicopter, cautioning her to bend low. The sand rose up in thick eddies, cutting against her cheeks. She draped her pashmina over her nose and stepped over loose rocks, past Bedouin men and their sleeping camels. She caught up with the men in the court-yard. A monk stood beneath the entrance gate and lifted a kerosene lantern.

"Father Nickolas," Haji said, and gripped the monk's arm. The men turned into an arched tunnel where petrol lamps blazed down from the walls. Caro lowered her pashmina and followed the group into a large courtyard filled with narrow lanes and buildings. A monk with a shaved head joined them beside a wooden staircase.

"I am Father Konstantine." His eyes hardened into olive pits as he stared at Caro, then he turned. "Follow me to the guest quarters, please."

Raphael touched her elbow. *No woman has stayed behind these walls since the fourth century.*

How did you arrange that?

Tirari molti spagi.

Ah, he'd pulled big strings. Caro gripped the dark wooden rail and followed the monk up the stairs. They were quite steep, with twists and turns, and she was breathless when she stepped onto a veranda. At one end, Moorish arches overlooked the quad and the domed basil-ica, with Mt. Sinai rising behind the monastery's walls.

She glanced behind her. Father Nickolas was showing Jude and Raphael to their rooms. When she looked back, Father Konstantine's lips tightened. He opened her door. "Your quarters," he said, averting his eyes.

"Thank you, Father." Caro stepped into the room. It was small and tidy, with a cot at one end and a desk at the other, and it smelled of cedar incense. A carved wooden crucifix hung on the far wall with a dried palm frond tucked behind it. The walls were curry colored, brightened by moonlight that fell through an arched window. The thin muslin curtain was pulled back, and she saw lights moving up Mt. Sinai.

She dropped her bag on a chair and stretched her arms. They felt weightless. Raphael had the triptych, and Father Aeneas had taken the ten vellum pages, but in a strange way, she felt liberated. She wouldn't have to guard priceless artifacts. Her relief segued into apprehension as she pressed one hand to her stomach. The guarding had only begun.

Her door opened and Raphael walked into the room carrying along a cardboard box. "Don't get settled, *mia cara*. You and Jude are climbing Mt. Sinai."

"Tonight?" She frowned. "I've got vampires chasing me. What if they tracked me here? I'm not going on a pleasure hike."

"This is more than sightseeing, *mia cara*."

He set the box on the bed and raised the lid. Light hit the triptych and glanced off the colors. Caro remembered how he'd stayed in the back of his plush jet during the long flight to Egypt. He'd leaned over a table, trying to reassemble the triptych.

Now it was intact, more or less.

"Originally, the vampires believed that the three panels embodied the past, present, and future of the immortals. It took us centuries to understand that the images symbolized a more enigmatic prophecy."

Caro's mouth went dry. "How enigmatic?"

"Your grandfather, Etienne Grimaldi, could see the future. While the triptych was being painted, Etienne had a vision, but he couldn't interpret the symbols. Indeed, none of them made sense. The images didn't represent any past that we'd known. But Etienne was emphatic. He knew this was a prophecy, and he made sure the artist added each detail in the order he'd dreamed them. No one realized that he'd visualized the past, present, and future of a woman, and child, not yet born, who will pull the immortal race out of the dark. This duo will cause a stir, and Christianity may change—all of humankind will change, too." Raphael touched her cheek. "When you arrived at my villa and we assembled the triptych, the puzzle pieces began to merge."

He pointed to Father Aeneas's panel. "This icon represents the past. There's a castle, and it's on fire. A girl child is running away. She's holding an egg and pages from an illustrated manuscript. This child is you. The icon shows *your* past."

"But I never had an egg," she cried.

He ignored her and tapped the center icon. "See the saint with dark hair? She is you—as you are now. You are holding a complete book. Behind you is a castle in Limoux—but it could also represent Saint Catherine's Monastery. The ground has turned into a bloody battlefield."

Caro shivered. "Who's the bleeding man? And who's the monk in the background?"

"I don't know." Raphael touched the figures. "I believe they are the same person. Perhaps the monk is the soul rising."

"Could this be Demos?" She swallowed. "Or Uncle Nigel?"

"Possibly."

"What about the third panel?" Caro asked. It showed the rest of the castle, with a woman and a child. Behind them lay a graveyard of crosses. The night sky had turned to blood, with tiny glimpses of the stars.

"I believe this is you and your baby, *mia cara*."

A cold finger scraped down her spine. "I couldn't lead a bunch of tourists through Waterloo Station. I'm not at the center of this prophecy."

"You won't know until you climb to the top of Sinai. You'll find a chapel. It's surrounded by an iron fence. Your guide will take you inside. Look for a fresco on the north wall. It has these same images, but I do not know when it was painted, or by whom. Study it. Think about your triptych. Try to interpret the symbols. But I believe they concern you and the immortals.

"Have you seen them?" Caro asked.

"Yes, but they are very confusing. Perhaps they were not meant for my eyes but for yours."

"What if I can't make sense of it?"

"Then enjoy the view." Raphael smiled. "And tell Jude about *il bambino*. The longer you wait, the harder it will be."

"I'm so afraid, Raphael. What if he doesn't want this child?"

"*Mia cara*, fear waits at the edges of love. You must create a fortress inside yourself." He kissed her hand. "Let's find Jude. The mountain is waiting."

Raphael led them out of the monastery to a black Range Rover with tinted windows. Kareem drove while Haji distributed blankets and brandy. He opened a beaded purse. "*Baksheesh,*" he explained. "For tipping."

Jude leaned against the dark window. "How long does it take to climb Mt. Sinai?"

"Two to six hours," Raphael said. "Depending on camel traffic."

"I have arranged for the finest Bedouin guide," Haji told Jude. "And good-tempered camels."

They drove through the security checkpoint to the mountain and climbed out of the car. Haji called out to a young Bedouin. He jogged over, his white *keffiyeh* swirling around his feet.

"This is Abdulla, your guide," Haji said.

"I am honored." Abdulla's narrow face split into a smile.

"Take care of them," Haji said.

"Yes, yes, I shall," Abdulla said.

Caro turned to Haji. "Will you be joining us?"

"I am sorry, no. Abdulla will escort you down the mountain at dawn." Haji bowed. *"El salamo alaikom." Peace be with you.*

Abdulla helped Caro climb onto a kneeling camel. She gripped the wooden pommel as the animal lurched to its feet.

"Yella!" Abdulla cried, and the camel started up the trail, Siket El Bashait, a camel path.

Around the bend, traffic picked up. Tourists jogged up the path, Americans in checkered headcloths, and they were followed by two Bedouins who kept shouting, "You want camel?"

When they reached the summit, Abdulla pointed to a mosque and a red granite chapel. It was surrounded by a crooked iron fence. "I will take you inside, yes?"

Jude tipped back his head. "Is it open to the public?"

"It is open to us," Abdulla said.

"Raphael wants me to see something," she whispered. "It's important."

They walked by people who were kneeling in the

rocks, their heads bowed. Others stood on flat boulders and stared into the dark valley. Caro looked back and saw lights winding up the trail. All those people climbing in the dark, trusting the Fates. If God couldn't be found here, perhaps He didn't wish to be found.

Jude and Abdulla helped her over the fence, and they walked over the rocks to the chapel. "How old is this building?" she asked Abdulla.

"It was built in 1933, the year my grandfather was born. There is much graffiti inside."

She pulled Jude into the dark chamber. Abdulla pressed a halogen flashlight into her hands, then scooted back to the doorway, as if guarding it. The beam hit the wall and set the fresco to dancing. She stepped back, studying the violent images.

"What is it?" Jude asked.

"A fresco." She explained Raphael's theory about the triptych's panels signifying the past, present, and future. She hesitated, wondering if she should add that it was possibly the future of their unborn child—but she couldn't tell him about the baby in front of this disturbing artwork.

Jude whistled. "Look how the art runs together."

"Like a Salvador Dali painting," she said, fanning the light over the images. She didn't see a fair-haired child. No woman. No flames. But blood was everywhere. There were two armies—men on horseback attacked hordes of ambulating skeletons, but the men were victorious. One carried off a baby in a gilded cage—a war prize or captive?

Her pulse sped up, thrumming in her ears like bongo drums. The art seemed to pool behind her eyes, and suddenly she understood the prophecy. Raphael was right.

A woman would be the link between humans and immortals—and her baby would have the power to save or destroy them all.

She studied the figures on the battlefield. *A puzzle piece is missing.*

Jude walked up behind her. "What sort of battle is this?"

"This isn't a battle," she said. "It's an apocalypse."

She could almost hear thundering hoofbeats, the cries of wounded men, and a baby's plaintive wail. In the future, humans would be pitted against the immortals. And somehow her baby was involved. She placed her hand on her stomach and took a deep breath.

From the doorway, Abdulla stirred. "Come, it's time to find a place in the rocks or they will all be taken."

Jude rented blankets at the refreshment hut, and when he gave one to Abdulla, tears welled up in the man's eyes.

"Sleep," Abdulla told them. "I will wake you at dawn."

Jude found a flat rock and helped Caro get settled. He pulled the blankets around them. She pushed the fresco out of her thoughts. For all she knew, teenagers could have painted it—wild, drug-induced graffiti.

"The stars look so close," she whispered. The air was thinner, and she struggled to catch her breath. A Babel of voices floated around them, hushed and reverent. Even the wind sounded like a chant. Caro felt something powerful swelling up from the mountain, and from the people. If Uncle Nigel was up there, she hoped he would help her find the right words.

"Jude?" she said. "Do you notice anything different about me?"

"Your eyes." He smoothed her hair. "They don't look

silver tonight. Your irises are shot through with turquoise. When I was young, I made a blue fire with copper chloride. It was a clear hue. The color of your eyes."

"Mmm-hmm. Anything else?"

"Your cheeks are pink. But it's a cold night." He glanced at Abdulla. The little guide was curled up on a rock, the blanket tucked around his shoulders. His eyelashes lay on his cheek like sable paintbrushes.

"Caro." Jude cupped her cheek. "We need to talk."

Do we ever, she thought, but she just nodded.

"Can you ever forgive me?"

"For what?"

"I acted like a bloody bastard that night at Varlaam. And in Venice."

"You don't have to explain."

"I know it's happened so fast. But I can't hold back another second." He inched closer. "I'm in love with you, Caro."

She traced his upper lip. "I fell a while ago. That first night in Momchilgrad. But you already knew that, didn't you?"

"I need to hear it," he said.

She took a breath and released it. "You're the one I'll always love."

He kissed her face, wet with tears, then drew back. "What's all this?" he asked, running his finger through a damp streak.

"I need to tell you something. But I don't know how."

"Just say it, darling."

"Okay." She took a breath. "We're going to have a baby."

He stared so long that she began to panic. "Baby?" he asked.

"I wanted to tell you sooner, but I was frightened. I thought—"

He pressed his fingers to her lips. "Don't say what you feared. I couldn't bear it. I gave you reasons to doubt me. But if I could go back to the day we met and do it over, I wouldn't change a thing. I want our baby. Because I love his mother. And I will never stop. Not in a thousand years."

His hand pressed against her belly. She was afraid to be this happy. Too much happiness was a jinx. She remembered her dream of the blue-eyed child, his laughter in the garden. She fell asleep to the singing voices. A long while later, she felt a presence standing behind her.

The vampires have found us, she thought. A hand grasped her shoulder. She sat up and pulled away, but it was only Abdulla. His face split into a grin.

"The sun, she is coming," he said.

Jude helped Caro to her feet. A gold slash broke over the mountains. People chanted and prayed; others sang. As the different languages passed through the light, a kind of metallurgy occurred, each voice hammered and shaped, rising into one sound.

CHAPTER 64

ST. CATHERINE'S MONASTERY
SINAI PENINSULA, EGYPT

Pink clouds cast a reddish stain over the mountain as Abdulla led the couple down the path to St. Catherine's. The sudden drop-offs made Caro dizzy. One wrong step and she would plunge over the edge.

"How much longer?" she asked.

"We've gone one hundred steps. Only two thousand nine hundred to go."

"How did we make it up here without falling?"

"You trusted that you would not stumble," Abdulla said.

By the time they reached the outer walls of St. Catherine's, the sky had turned muddy blue. They walked past Bedouins selling trinkets and herbal cures. Tourists sat on the low walls by the center tower, waiting for the monastery to open.

"What time is it?" she asked Abdulla.

"Eight A.M."

The camels blended into the sand, their legs tucked beneath their massive girth. One beast lunged forward, showing crooked yellow teeth, and bit another camel. It hissed, flinging out a rope of saliva. The Bedouin man said something to the animals and they settled down.

Abdulla pointed to mountains behind the monastery. "Tomorrow, I take you to the caves to see the wall paintings. It is very dangerous terrain. Bandits and weapon trafficking. But worth it."

"How far are the caves?" Caro asked.

"A thirty-minute camel ride. Just beyond the palm trees." Abdulla steered them past a guard in a black beret and led them across the quad. They moved through a dark corridor that smelled of freshly baked bread.

"Are all of Saint Catherine's monks vampires?" Caro asked.

Abdulla laughed. "No, no. Most of the fathers are human. The blood drinkers shave their heads and have tattoos. They are devout, but in an extreme way. They call themselves *the brethren* and belong to a cult. Very elite and high-born."

Jude pressed his lips against her ear. "The Princes of Darkness," he said.

She pinched his cheek and grinned.

Abdulla's *keffiyeh* billowed as he led them to another courtyard. He pointed to a ragged bush that jutted up from a bowed rock wall.

"I present you the Burning Bush," he said. He plucked a leaf and held his lighter beneath it. A broad grin spread across his face when the leaf did not ignite. He escorted them to the guest quarters. Jude handed him the beaded bag, and the guide reached into his pocket and pulled out the leaf.

"For luck," he said, then hurried across the veranda and disappeared around the corner.

A note was taped to Caro's doorknob. She reached for it.

Caro and Jude—

Welcome back from the mountain. After you have rested, please join us in the library at midnight.

—Raphael

"Why so late?" She yawned and rubbed her eyes.

"Vampires don't keep banker's hours," Jude said.

"I suppose not." She laughed, then tucked the note in her pocket and opened her door. "I'd invite you in, but the monks haven't allowed a woman inside these walls in centuries. We should probably sleep in separate rooms, right?"

"Yes, absolutely." He nodded. "I'll fetch you a little before midnight." She hadn't realized how tired she was until she flopped onto the bed and tumbled into a place that smelled of blood and dirt. The dogs were closing in, their red incisors clicking. She clawed her way out of the dream and sat up. Perspiration slid down her backbone. Moonlight cut through the thin curtain and fell into her eyes. The basilica was outlined against a dark lapis sky. Was it dawn or dusk? How long had she slept? She was forgetting something. But what?

From the courtyard, she heard a gagging sound. She strained to listen, but she heard nothing else but faint chanting from the basilica. The four A.M. mass. Damn. She'd slept through the midnight meeting with Raphael. She pulled on a dress, grabbed the pashmina, ran onto the veranda, and opened Jude's door.

"We overslept," she said.

"Bloody hell," Jude sat up in bed and pushed back his hair.

"Maybe I can still catch Raphael."

He rubbed his eyes. "I'll catch up with you in the library."

"I'll be waiting." She draped the pashmina over her head and shut his door. The sky had darkened and the narrow moon was starting to set. She walked down a corridor, stirring the petrol lights as she hurried toward the library.

"Caro?" a voice called.

She tilted her head and listened, as if straining to hear music. Was Raphael sending her a message? No, this wasn't his voice. It was feminine and eerily familiar.

"Come to the Burning Bush, Caro." The words held in the air like a clap. "Hurry, my darling girl."

Vivienne had called her *my darling girl*. Caro's heart thrummed like a cello string. No, it wasn't possible. Her mother hadn't survived the fire. Caro felt dizzy and placed one hand against the rough wall. But what if her mother had escaped? What if she was *here*? That wasn't crazy, was it? Everything that she had believed about herself had been a lie. In this new, fantastical world, anything was possible.

Caro followed the voice into a courtyard. The Burning Bush fanned out against the stones, the leaves trembling as the monks' voices rose and fell on the other side of the wall. A man squatted beside the bush, his face hidden beneath a brown hood.

"Are you all right?" she asked and stepped closer. The man raised his head, and the hood fell. Curly red hair tumbled out. A broad, masculine face looked up and grinned, his canines pressing into his bottom lip.

She ran toward the corridor, but icy hands pulled her back. A rough palm clapped over her nose and mouth. His sweaty flesh reeked of ketones. Vampire. She stamped at his feet, but he shifted out of the way.

"Be still." He wrenched her elbow, and pain throbbed into her injured shoulder.

"You're hurting me," she said into his palm. How had he known what her mother had called her?

He mewed. "I sound like Tom Kitten himself, don't I? Your flatmate thought so."

Caro breathed in his sour-sweet smell. He'd murdered Phoebe? Her lungs contracted as she struggled to draw in a breath. If he didn't loosen his grip, she'd suffocate.

"I've got you now, ducky," the vampire said.

"Don't hurt her, Moose," a man said, his cut-glass English accent echoing. He stepped out of the shadows and smoothed his cropped gray hair. "Lovely to finally meet you, Caro. I'm Harry Wilkerson. Your father."

Father? He'd been Vivi's husband? Caro whipped her head from side to side.

"Yes, I was rather shocked to find out about you, too." Wilkerson pulled duct tape from his pocket. He picked at the roll with his fingernail, then tore off a strip and stepped toward her. She barely had time to draw in a breath when he pressed the tape over her lips.

"Scream, if you like." He smiled. "But not too loud.

Moose hates screamers. He's already killed one loud-mouth tonight."

A tear slid down Caro's cheek. She wasn't listening. Had Raphael or one of the monks come this way? What was that shadow by the far wall? A body? She twisted her head, trying to see. She tried to pull away from Moose, but his grip tightened.

"I never wanted a child. Yet here you are." Wilkerson's smile widened, but it didn't touch his eyes. "Vivienne broke my heart. I gave her everything she wanted, and she left me for a dead man. She took a few things that belonged to me. She took my artifacts. And she took you."

Caro shook her head. No, Philippe was her father.

"I would have found you sooner if I'd known that Vivienne had relatives. How clever of her to stash you with Sir Nigel. But not that clever." His eyebrows went up. "Do you have any idea how much I paid for those bloody pages? One point two million pounds. Think what they're worth now. At least ten times that amount. And I don't even need them anymore. My scientists are worth twenty books. But it's the principle of the thing. I paid for the book, I might as well keep it." His eyes shimmered. "You don't know what I'm talking about, do you? Your Greek monk stole your ten pages. Then he tried to keep me from them. A big mistake. He won't be bothering me again, will he, Moose?"

"Not bloody likely, mate."

"Those pages were rightfully mine—and so was the icon." Wilkerson leaned closer. "Do you have it?"

Caro flinched as the smell of whiskey hit her face. She shook her head.

"A pity. But I'm sure you won't mind if I take a little of your blood." His eyes held a glint of wildness.

Oh my God. He's going to bite me. Caro focused her thoughts to a pinpoint. *Raphael, help me.*

"Don't pull a face." Wilkerson laughed. "Moose is the vampire, not me. I want your blood for the DNA—to see if you are Grimaldi's bastard. You *do* know that your mum was a world-class slut? She had a weakness for vampires. Your father could be anyone, alive or dead."

Wilkerson snapped his fingers. "Moose, hold her down."

The vampire pushed her against the wall and flattened her right arm against the stones. She screamed and screamed, but the tape across her mouth muffled the sound.

"Hold her steady, Moose." Wilkerson tied a tourniquet around her arm, then slapped the inner curve of her elbow until a blue vein popped up. She barely felt the prick when he jabbed a needle into her flesh. Blood swirled into the Vacutainer, a flash of red. Wilkerson was a madman. Off the rails.

"There we go." He withdrew the needle and released the tourniquet without bothering to bandage the nick. Blood streamed down her arm, curved to her wrist, and splattered against the stones.

"Don't look, Moose." Wilkerson chuckled.

The vampire cursed. Caro released a lungful of air, and the harsh breath loosened a corner of the duct tape. She ran her tongue on the inside of the tape, trying to undo the adhesive.

Wilkerson's eyes glittered. "Do you remember the night your mother died? My Bulgarians let Vivienne watch as her immortal beloved was decapitated. Not so immortal, after all."

Raphael, hurry.

"They told me how Vivienne begged for his life," Wilkerson continued. "Funny, but she didn't mention *you*. Not a single time did she ask for your life to be spared. So much for maternal love. But she burned. She burned with her fanged lover."

Two veins appeared on Wilkerson's forehead. "Come now, my darling daughter. We can make this easy or hard. Where is the icon? Don't be bashful, or I'll start taking lives."

"It's gone," she yelled into the tape.

"Didn't quite catch that." Wilkerson tilted his head.

"Want me to rip off her gag, mate?" Moose glanced up. The sky had lightened to that colorless time between night and dawn, the clouds gray and rippled like an oyster shell.

Wilkerson knelt beside her. "If I remove the tape, you promise not to scream?"

She nodded.

"Good. Because I'd hate for Moose to break your arms. That would really make you yell." Wilkerson ripped off the tape and rubbed his thumb across her mouth. "You have Vivienne's lips. She left without telling me she was pregnant. The bloody bitch. She took everything."

"I'm not your daughter," Caro said. "Run your tests. You'll see."

"Vivienne and I were never divorced, so legally, you *are* my daughter. I don't want your DNA to prove paternity."

Hurry, Raphael. Please hurry.

"If you *are* Philippe's spawn, you've got the R-99

gene," Wilkerson said. "I'll lose a daughter—well, of a sort—but I'll gain a guinea pig."

Moose stepped forward, dragging Caro along. "What's this about genes, mate?"

"You'd be bored with the science." Wilkerson flipped his hand. "In a nutshell, I suspect Caro might be half vampire. My researchers are testing the blood of hybrids. They're working on a biological agent."

"For what?" Moose's forehead wrinkled.

"To stop aging. Imagine living forever without having to ingest blood. No light blindness. Walking freely in daylight." Wilkerson turned to Caro. "And your genes may be at the heart of it."

"I'll have a go at it," Moose said.

Wilkerson shook his head. "Sorry, that drug will be contraindicated for vampires."

"You're lying," Moose said. "You just want to keep it for yourself."

"Don't be wet. If you concentrate the blood of a half vampire and inject it into someone like yourself, it's fatal. Of course, concentrating hybrid blood requires a state-of-the-art lab. Which I have, of course. Sorry, old chap. I guess you shouldn't book a trip to Bali just yet."

Wilkerson stroked Caro's cheek. "You are lovely, but it's hard to look at you. Because you resemble *her*. Maybe you are Philippe's child. Just think, he gave you life, and I shall take that life and destroy all of his kind."

"You're mad," she said.

"And a wanking liar." Moose released her arm. "What a load of cack."

"I wasn't speaking to you," Wilkerson told the vampire. "I wouldn't be in this godforsaken desert if you hadn't botched your assignment. All I wanted was a blood sample, not a bloodbath. Besides, you aren't my confidant. You're a plonker from the East End."

"Shut it, you toffee nose." Moose sprang onto Wilkerson and bit a plug out of his neck. They fell to the ground and rolled. Wilkerson fumbled in his pocket, blood streaming down the front of his shirt, then dragged out a small pistol. He pulled the trigger. Moose jerked back. A spot of red bloomed on his shirt. The vampire watched it a moment, then laughed.

"It'll take more than a fucking .38-caliber to bring me down."

"Not if it hits your brain." Wilkerson raised the pistol. Before he could pull the trigger, Moose bent his legs at the knees and vaulted over the wall. There was a thump on the other side, then a scrabbling over the rocks.

Caro bolted toward the corridor, but Wilkerson snagged her wrist. His hand was slick with blood. It cascaded down his neck, dark as treacle. "You're going with me," he said, and pulled her in the opposite direction, toward the narrow alley that led to the church.

"No." She screamed for Raphael and the monks. Wilkerson shoved his hand over her mouth, and she bit his palm. His blood tasted bitter, but she bit deeper. Then she felt the pistol crash against her head. Her ear rang. A warm trickle ran down her neck. He hit her again, and the courtyard spiraled. As she fell, she saw rocks, bush, sky, walls. Pain sliced through her stomach as if she'd swallowed pebbles.

You will not faint. Her pulse slowed and she sat up. The desert wind whipped her hair, and she heard the distant wail of dogs.

"Caro?" Jude's voice rang out from the corridor.

"No!" The pebbles in her stomach grew into razor-edged rocks. He didn't have a weapon. "Stay back. Wilkerson's got a gun."

Footsteps echoed over the stones, and then Jude rushed into the courtyard. As she scrambled to her feet, something hard and cold dug into her scalp. The rocks in her belly had coalesced into a boulder that pressed hard against her lungs.

"Nice of you to show up." A tight smile creased Wilkerson's lips. "But we were just leaving."

"The hell you are." Jude leaped in front of Caro.

Wilkerson squeezed the trigger. The bullet ricocheted against the wall. Jude pushed her from behind, guiding her to the corridor. The gun went off again and again. Jude's hand fell away from her shoulder. She whirled. His eyes widened as he lurched toward the wall.

She swallowed. Dear God. Had he been hit? A bullet whizzed past her ear. She grabbed Jude's arm, trying to hold him up. Red commas spurted out of Jude's sweater and pattered to the floor. She swallowed hard, pushing down those rocks, and pulled open the edges of his jacket. Blood pulsed through a hole in his shoulder. She mashed her hand against it.

"Are you all right, lass?" he asked. He didn't seem to know he'd been hit.

"She's fine," Wilkerson called, aiming the gun. "But you're toast."

Tears burned the backs of her eyes. A surge of adrenaline rippled through her, and she pushed Jude toward the tunnel. She couldn't think beyond the immediate danger. Jude was bleeding. He needed a doctor.

Wilkerson fired again. A hole cut through Jude's leather jacket, and he bent over. Caro cut in front of him and grabbed his elbows. A fist-sized chunk of the sweater had been blown away, and the rest of it was damp and glossy. A high-pitched whistling noise came out of the wound. A needle prick of dread stabbed through her. Oh, God. Had the bullet hit a lung? She pressed her hands over the jetting blood. *No, please.*

"It doesn't hurt," he said. He coughed, and frothy pink bubbles spilled over his lips. No, he couldn't die. She'd get him to a hospital. She flattened her hand over the wound.

Wilkerson kept fiddling with the pistol. The bastard was trying to reload. She couldn't let that happen. He'd have to kill her, too. Gritting her teeth, she strained to hold Jude upright, but he was too heavy. She felt as if they were straddling an abyss, and she was wrenching him away from the dark pit while gravity tugged him over the edge.

A clatter echoed in the passage, and Haji sprinted into the courtyard. He aimed his gun at Wilkerson. "Drop your weapon," he shouted.

"I don't take orders from the likes of you." Wilkerson fired twice. Each bullet seemed to move in slow motion, floating through the grainy light, and then Haji fell to one knee. Dark, damp circles widened on his *galabiyyah*. He fell sideways. Caro looked down at Jude. Those eyebrows she loved so much were knitted together. His face was pale, beaded with perspiration.

"We've got to get help," she whispered. "Can you stand?"

"Don't worry about me. Run!" Jude nudged her toward the corridor. "Go."

"Your gallantry is admirable but ill-timed." Wilkerson turned the gun on Caro.

"No." Jude struggled to sit up and spread his arms in front of her.

Wilkerson fired into Jude's knee. There was a crunch of bone and Jude went rigid, every muscle tensed with obvious pain.

"Get away from him," Wilkerson said.

"Never."

"Don't make me shoot you, Caroline."

Raphael ran out of the corridor and tackled Wilkerson. The pistol clattered across the courtyard as the men fell over backward and rolled over the stones.

Jude gasped, his nostrils flaring. Caro pressed both hands against his chest. With each heartbeat, blood shot through her fingers. Dark red, not arterial. His face was alabaster, with a faint blue tinge around his mouth.

"I'm cold." He shivered. "So cold."

She lifted one hand from his chest, yanked off her pashmina, and draped it around him. The tang of blood and gunpowder hung in the air, making her stomach fold back on those sharp rocks. Jude cut his eyes toward Raphael and Wilkerson as they thrashed on the ground. Wilkerson's hand strained for Haji's gun.

"Haji, look out," Jude yelled, then coughed up another mouthful of pink froth.

The Egyptian stirred. He rose and shook his head. He scrambled to his gun, then grabbed Wilkerson's hair and pulled hard, bowing the man's neck.

"What did you do with Caro's pages to *Historia Immortalis*?" Raphael asked.

Wilkerson laughed. "She doesn't own any bloody pages."

Raphael pressed his hands against Wilkerson's skull.

The wind scraped through the courtyard, and then everything went still. Raphael's brow knitted in concentration, and Wilkerson began to scream.

"Get out of my mind, you fucking vampire," he yelled.

Raphael's hands sprang away from Wilkerson as if he'd touched burning chemicals and he turned to Haji. "The pages are hidden in a hotel room. Saint Catherine's Plaza."

Caro's hands were slick and red. She could feel Jude's blood pumping. She lowered him to the ground and put his head in her lap. She barely noticed when Father Nickolas hunkered beside her.

"He has a sucking chest wound," the monk called to Haji. "Where is Kareem? We need the helicopter."

"Don't bother. He's finished." Wilkerson laughed. "Unless you plan to bite him."

"Do not speak or I shall cut out your tongue." Raphael kicked Wilkerson's jaw. The bone cracked, and a tooth skittered across the courtyard. A crimson jet sprayed down Wilkerson's chin.

Raphael pulled off a long strip of duct tape and plastered it over Wilkerson's mouth.

"Drown in your own blood," Raphael said.

CHAPTER 65

Jude's blood pattered to the stones as the monks carried him into the corridor. First light was breaking over the mountains, and the monks' hands instantly reddened, the flesh covered through with blisters.

"Where is Kareem?" Raphael yelled.

"He's flying from Cairo." Haji gave his gun to a tall monk and pointed to Wilkerson. "If he tries to run, shoot him in the balls."

Caro followed the monks. Their sandals chafed over the ground as they turned down a narrow vestibule that twisted and turned, then stopped in a T-shaped passage. Torches blazed from the stone wall, casting shadows on a row of doors, all wooden and heavily carved, except for one—it had been painted blue.

A monk rushed ahead and flung open the door, and the others ran into the room and set Jude on an iron bed. Candles were set into the wall, blazing from shallow niches. She squeezed past the robed men and sank down beside Jude. He lifted one finger and grazed her cheek. "Tell me something, lass."

She couldn't speak. Her hand slid under his arm. Cold. A thready pulse jumped in his wrist.

Raphael stood on the opposite side of the bed, his pale hair loose, streaming over his *galabiyyah*. He started to lift Jude.

Father Nickolas pushed in beside her, gripping scissors. He cut open Jude's sweater and pulled back the wool. Caro stifled a gasp. Jude's chest was red and slick. Blood streamed through multiple holes, ran off the side of the cot, and tapped against the floor.

Jude grabbed Raphael's hand. "Take care of her. And my child."

"Nothing's going to happen," Raphael said.

Yes, it will. Caro's neck prickled.

Jude's fingertips grazed her chin. "Just let me look at you. I didn't get to say all that I meant to. But . . . I loved you the moment I saw you."

His chest sawed, as if he couldn't get air. The linen beneath him was crimson. No one could lose this much blood and survive. She opened her eyes wide, trying to keep the tears from spilling down, then reached for his hand. This was her fault, all of it. The moment their lives had intersected, he'd been doomed, like everyone else. Her parents, Uncle Nigel, Phoebe.

"He needs to be in a hospital," she whispered to Father Nickolas.

"There's a clinic in Saint Catherine's City," he whispered back.

"What about Dahab?" Raphael said.

Father Nickolas leaned over the bed. "We need to fly him to Sharm El Sheikh."

Caro made a fist. They were talking as if Jude couldn't hear. She took slow breaths, trying to calm herself. If he sensed her terror, his heart would beat faster, spilling more blood.

His hand grazed her cheek. *"Vous êtes mon air,"* he said under his breath. *You are my air.*

"Don't you dare leave me," she said. "I won't let you."

"Lass?" Jude's hand fell to her sleeve.

"I'm here."

He was quiet for a long moment. Then his brow furrowed. "Don't go outside."

"I won't." She looked up at Raphael.

Delirious, mia cara. Raphael shook his head.

"Momchilgrad isn't . . . safe." Jude's hand dropped to the bed.

"No!" Caro's stomach heaved, the rocks churning. She folded her shaking hands around Jude's. This wasn't happening. If only they'd stayed in Momchilgrad—anywhere but this room with the blue door. He was cold. So cold. If only Wilkerson had shot her. Jude had protected her and now he was dying. Every second of every day she would ache for him.

Jude plucked the sheets. Raphael reached across the bed and grabbed Caro's hands. "We can save him, *mia cara.* But I cannot do it without your consent."

"Make him into a vampire?" She shook her head. "You know how he feels."

"No time to debate. Decide."

"I can't allow it." She pressed her face against Jude's cheek. A tear ran sideways into her mouth. *My love. My only love. I can't let you go.*

"No time to think!" Raphael shook her arm. "We will lose him."

She lifted her face. "Do it," she whispered. Fear had made her voice weak and raspy.

Raphael picked up the scissors and drew the pointed tip along his wrist. He held his hand above Jude's mouth. The blood made faint tapping sounds as it hit Jude's teeth. "Hold his lips, *mia cara*."

She slipped her hand under Jude's chin, feeling the stubble graze her palm. His eyelids fluttered.

"Oh, thank God. He's coming around." She glanced up at the monks. "Isn't he?"

Raphael wrapped gauze around his wrist and didn't answer. The monks found an intravenous kit in the first-aid drawer and set up a makeshift transfusion. Father Nickolas inserted a needle into Father Konstantine's arm and attached plastic tubing to the catheter. A monk with a shaved head started an IV in Jude's arm, and the two lines were joined. A thin line of vampire blood raced down the tube into Jude's veins. His eyes opened. The pupils were large, as if dark water were slowly filling them.

"He is not responding," Father Nickolas whispered to Raphael.

"What do you mean?" Caro said, her voice rising.

"She shouldn't see," Father Nickolas said.

"Why not?" she cried.

Because the monks will do more than infuse blood into

Jude's veins. They must bite him. Please don't cry, mia cara. *A vampire's saliva is filled with a substance that facilitates the change.*

Stem cells. She pressed her face into the blood-soaked linen. She kept seeing Jude charge fearlessly into that courtyard without a weapon. An icy hand touched her arm, and she looked up.

"Come, *mia cara.*"

"No." She wrenched free and grabbed Jude's hand.

Above her, the monks' voices sparked like cinders caught in an updraft.

"When will Kareem be here?" one asked.

"It's too late for the helicopter," another said.

"No, it isn't," she cried. "You can't give up, not yet."

"*Mia cara*, they are doing everything they can," Raphael said in her ear. "He's hemorrhaging."

"Give him another transfusion."

Raphael cast an edgy glance at the narrow window, where a monk struggled to close the wooden shutters. "We should go, *mia cara*. The sun has risen."

"Then leave." Caro wiped her face. Even she could see that it was too late. A red stream spilled over the edge of the mattress to the floor, a dark torrent carrying him away.

"I will not leave without you," Raphael said. Before she could protest, he lifted her into his arms.

"Set me down." She slammed her fist against the vampire's chest. Her knuckles stung, as if she'd hit limestone.

"You cannot see this." His grip tightened.

"You're hurting me, dammit. Let go. Jude's by himself. He needs me."

"He isn't alone. The monks will anoint him and pray."

A bald monk leaned over the desk, burning something that looked like wheat. Another monk smeared oil on Jude's forehead. Others knelt in blood and traced crosses in the air, speaking in a dead language. Each man bore an infinity tattoo, identical to the one she'd seen on Raphael's arm.

He turned to her. "He would not want you to stay, *mia cara*."

Father Konstantine opened the blue door and beckoned Raphael to follow him into the wide, torch-lit hall. Raphael stepped over the blood spatters and carried her away from Jude, into the winding maze. As she pushed against his chest, a fury burned in her throat, a pyroclastic flow that threatened to dissolve everything in its path. Her head jolted painfully against Raphael's chest when he followed Father Konstantine into a brightly lit, square room.

Raphael set her down but held on to her shoulder. As her eyes adjusted to the light, she saw red altar candles burning on a table. Beyond the candles, monks were seated around a long pine table. At the far end, Haji bent over a cup of blood. A bulky bandage covered his shoulder.

"The tourist police arrested Wilkerson," Haji said.

"Arrested him?" Caro cried. "Why didn't you shoot him?"

Haji's eyes widened as he caught the edge in her voice, then looked away. "The police are tracking his vampire—he will be in custody before dawn."

"No one will chase you now." Raphael led her to a chair and draped a blanket around her shoulders. "And your father's artifacts will be returned."

The monks began whispering. Father Konstantine flashed

a basilisk stare. "That might be difficult," he told Raphael. "The antiquities police will need to establish provenance."

"There is no way to show provenance." Raphael sat next to Caro. "Sotheby's had a damned hard time proving it."

"What is the history of these pages?" Haji asked. "Who owned them before the auction?"

Father Konstantine rose from his chair. Before he tucked his hands into his sleeves, Caro saw an infinity tattoo on his wrist. "During World War II, ten vellum leaves were found in the basement of the Louvre and were taken back to Berlin. A Munich collector bought them. Not long afterward, his only son hanged himself. The pages were sold to an Austrian violinist. Days before her murder, she sold the pages to a South American dictator who couldn't get rid of them quickly enough. Before he could find a buyer, the pages were stolen. Decades later, they ended up at Sotheby's."

"How many people have died because of your damned book?" Caro flung off the blanket.

Father Konstantine glared, but the others began whispering. The murmurs changed into a strident hum, like bees getting ready to swarm. She thought they might attack and sprang from the chair.

"Where are you going, *mia cara*?"

"You know where. He's all I have. I'm going. Don't try to stop me."

"The brethren are with him." Father Konstantine looked alarmed.

Raphael steered her back to the chair. She gaped up at him. "We shouldn't have come to Egypt. I shouldn't have been born. Then my uncle and Jude would be alive."

"You don't know what you're saying," Raphael whispered. "You're in shock."

"I'm in pain. I want the pain to end."

"Sometimes there *is* no end."

"When Wilkerson and the vampire snatched me, I screamed for you in my mind. But you took so long to come."

"I didn't hear." He shook his head. "I am sorry."

"I'll never forgive you."

Father Konstantine's eyes narrowed. "Signore Raphael was too worried to hear your thoughts. He was waiting for you in the library. All of us were waiting. Blame yourself for the young man's death."

"Death?" Caro released a shuddering sob. Jude had died? How did the monks know? Maybe they were in telepathic contact.

She clasped her hands. "Jude was still alive when we left him."

Father Konstantine crossed himself, then turned to Raphael. "She is agitated, Signore. This could have dire consequences."

"For whom?" Caro frowned. She hated the way he was glaring, as if her skin were covered with oozing sores.

The monk ignored her. "We heard what the criminal Wilkerson said about her blood. She is tainted, Signore. Please, remove her from our presence or we cannot be responsible for our actions."

Dizziness spiraled through Caro, and she shut her eyes. Now she'd be hunted by Wilkerson and vampires. She was the genetic bridge to the immortals' extinction.

"Signore, take the whore to her room or I shall be forced to sedate her."

Father Nickolas stepped into the room, clutching Jude's

leather coat. "What shall I do with Mr. Barrett's belongings?" he asked.

"Save them, Father," Raphael said. He led Caro into the corridor, and the torches along the wall flickered, casting shadows over the stone floor.

"Where are you taking me now?" she asked.

"To a safe place." He squeezed her hand and pulled her toward a bright circle at the end of the tunnel. Beyond the tunnel lay a small courtyard and a staircase that led to the guest quarters.

"Stay here," she said. "I know the way to my room."

"I'm going with you."

"But the sun—you'll burn."

"Fuck the daylight. I will not leave you alone."

"Why not just—" She felt the pull of gravity, the whoosh of cold air as he picked her up and sped toward the courtyard. Why in bloody hell was he always carrying her—a remnant of loyalty he still felt for her family? The courtyard and stairs blurred together, and then a door flew open and everything went still.

They stood in the center of her room. Sunlight blasted through the arched window and hit the crucifix on the far wall. As he set her on the bed, she smelled incense, heard the creak of a mattress, and her shoulders sank into a scratchy woolen blanket. Through the thin muslin curtain she saw the basilica and mountains beneath a cloudless, whitewashed sky.

Tears gathered in her lashes, and the room blurred. *Oh, Jude. Please don't be dead.*

Raphael shut the curtain and the room darkened. He walked to her bed and sat down. His hands and cheeks were covered with blisters.

"You should put salve on those burns," she said.

"I'll be fine. I'm more worried about you, *mia cara.*"

She dug her fingers into the blanket and scraped her nails over the wool. "Did Father Konstantine tell the truth? Is Jude dead?"

Raphael's brows drew together. "I do not know. He was shielding his thoughts. But I will find out. I will also talk to the antiquities police. Perhaps they have recovered your vellum pages."

"I don't want them." Her gaze held his. She hoped he read her mind. She could summarize the book in three parts: death in the beginning, death in the middle, death at the end. Especially at the end.

"Those pages were your father's," Raphael said. "Now they are yours. The rest is here at Saint Catherine's. Your father brought *Historia Immortalis* here for safekeeping, just as he indicated on the scroll. I have listened to the monk's thoughts. I know where they hide the manuscript. It's in a room behind the altar."

"Keep it. And while you're at it, hang the triptych on your wall. Use it for kindling."

"But these artifacts are your legacy. Your father—"

"Do you think he'd still want me to protect objects that killed him and Mother?"

"Yes."

"I don't want a reminder of that bloody book. It has cost me everyone I've ever loved."

"You are overwrought," Raphael stood. "And *il bambino* needs his rest. You, too. Sleep, *mia cara.*"

Caro dreamed in fragments—pottery shards, torn gilt pages, scattered bones. The images coalesced into dogs with monks' heads. She awoke with a gasp. For a panicky moment, her lungs contracted and she couldn't get a satisfying breath.

Jude. Oh, no. She hadn't dreamed it.

She sat up and pushed her hair out of her face. Through the window, lights wound up the hulking black mountain. It was night again. And she was alone. Raphael had not returned. She yanked off her bloodstained clothes, then slid off the bed and unzipped her bag. She had to find Jude's body before the monks took him away. Before Raphael returned. She pulled out a chalk-colored *galabiyyah* and an ivory pashmina, heavily fringed. White, the absence of all colors, the symbol of purity, traditional desert garb to reflect the sun, but her grief was hard-edged and black.

Tears hit her arm and slid to her wrist. Jude had saved her in downtown Kardzhali. Then he'd attacked the vampires in Momchilgrad and Varlaam. Here at St. Catherine's, he'd sacrificed himself to protect her and their unborn baby from Wilkerson's bullets.

She dressed slowly, as if a cup were trapped inside her chest, its contents sloshing over the edge. If she rushed, the cup would overturn and unbearable sadness would spill through her. On her way out of the room, she lifted a red robe from the hook on the wall and pulled it around her. The cold stones shocked her bare feet as she stepped onto the veranda. The night wind smelled of baking bread with faint undertones of curry. The aromas made her queasy, and she held her breath as she rushed down the stairs.

When she reached the main courtyard, she moved into the shadows. The monastery looked deserted, but she heard clanging from the south corridor. She turned toward the sound, into a tunnel with a low ceiling. The dark, cool air hit her face as she groped her way along the rough walls toward a circle of light. She passed into a moonlit courtyard where a silver-haired monk squatted beside a rectangular pine box. His robe puddled around his feet as he hammered nails into wood.

"Father, what are you building?" she asked. But she knew. She clasped her hands, trying to stop them from shaking.

The monk looked up, his eyes red-rimmed. "A coffin."

At the far end of the courtyard, she saw the Burning Bush. A Bedouin man pushed a mop over the stones, leaving a film of suds and blood-tinged water. She followed a trail of dried blood into an arched tunnel that reeked of copper and petrol. The spatters led her down a maze of narrow halls, around corners, and ended in a familiar T-shaped passageway with the blue door. It was heavily carved, with an egg-shaped knob.

She grasped it, then let go as a shivery panic seized her. She hugged herself, cupping her palms under her elbows. She didn't want to know what was in that room. Why in God's name had she come?

Yet the door seemed to hypnotize her, pulling her closer, as if whispering secrets. An image rose up, and she saw herself sitting in the library, surrounded by illustrated manuscripts, studying the images and colors. This door held meaning to the monks at St. Catherine's. It was lighter than the blue in a Greek talisman, the one that repelled the evil eye. Blue represented the throat chakra. Blue was sad, serene, cold, and sheltering. Blue had been made in the antiquities by fusing copper, iron, and calcium—components of blood.

On the other side of the door, she heard a bang. She pressed her ear against the smooth wood. The noise was erratic, as if someone were slamming dresser drawers. Her hand molded around the cold knob, and the metal instantly chilled her skin. She opened the door and her pupils constricted painfully in the candlelight. Shadows undulated over a freshly scrubbed stone floor, rippling over an iron bed and pristine white linen. A small table held a candle, and the flame bent sideways as a breeze rushed through the open window and banged the wooden shutter against the wall.

She swallowed. She was too late. The room had been cleaned and emptied. She started to leave when she saw movement at the other end of the room. A crop-haired monk rose from a pine desk, his white *galabiyyah* stirring around his bare feet.

"I'm sorry to bother you," Caro said. "I was looking for—"

Her throat clenched as she stared into the man's blue eyes. She studied them the way the Egyptians did. The eyes told the truth. But the shorn hair told another story.

"I've been waiting for you, lass," the man said.

Her hand flew to her lips. The hair might be gone, but Jude's soft Yorkshire accent was intact. Oh, thank God. Thank God. "You're alive," she whispered.

"In a fashion." He grinned.

"But they said—" Her vision blurred. Tears gathered on her knuckles. She extended her other hand, fingers shaking, and then her knees buckled. Jude vaulted from the chair and grabbed her. She fell against him and pressed her damp cheek against his neck. Cold, so cold.

His neck smelled spicy, but there was a muskiness surrounding his body.

He pulled back, eyebrows slanting over the pale skin. "I kept asking for you," he said. "Didn't the monks tell you?"

She shook her head. Why had Father Konstantine lied? Or had she dreamed it? Questions darted around her, each one a silvery minnow that flitted through black water, just out of reach, but they could wait. A deeper want rippled through her, the need to merge with him physically, and then she would be ready to hear those elusive answers.

Jude's fingers tangled in her hair. "Caro, you were the thread in the maze. I lost my way for a bit. But I followed the thread and made my way back."

"It's a miracle. I'm over the moon." She flung her arms around his neck, flattening her breasts against him. He leaned in to kiss her. Their lips fused, the way a finger will adhere to dry ice, and a current moved between them. His mouth tasted sweet, as if he'd been eating ripe, red fruit. Then the kiss changed into a crackling vortex. Oh, such pleasure.

Jude led Caro to the bed. The mattress creaked as he slipped in beside her. She helped him pull off his *galabiyyah*. There were no wounds or gauze dressings on his chest. Only two square Band-Aids. Her hand slid over the smooth flesh, past the springy hairs.

He kissed her, and the icy sweetness melted on her tongue. He was one of *them* now. Could he hear her thoughts? She pushed words in his direction: *Please don't be angry with me.* But he didn't respond; he hadn't heard.

A ticklish sensation leaped under her flesh as he swept back her robe. He slipped her bra strap down over her shoulder, then drew his fingers back and forth over her collarbone, barely touching her. Her body tensed with anticipation. She closed her eyes, feeling his desire for her blood, but something strong and protective moved beneath it. If he asked, she could grow acquainted with the night. She could give up the sun without regret. The night would be her new world, and as long as he was with her, she wasn't afraid. If he asked, she would leave her life and go with him.

He pulled off her *galabiyyah*. Cool air blew around her as he moved her hand to the pulsing between his legs. The shaft widened and curved. She wanted to feel it, taste it, rub down his length. Tingling started in her throat and shimmied into her chest. Tremors moved through her belly, then deeper into the very core of her being. As vibrations pulsed into her legs, she pointed her toes, and her calves trembled.

"Stop." He tipped back his head, and his incisors lengthened. "You're pushing me to the edge."

But she couldn't stop. She wanted to taste him again and again. All around her, the room glimmered, all hazy at the edges. Her hair drifted against him, each strand taut as thread, moving across his skin like a binding spell.

"Caro, no—" His face contorted. The muscles in his thighs and abdomen tensed. Cool, milky fluid jetted against the back of her hand and curved around her wrist. A thrill shot through her, and the thread tightened. Every square inch of her body thrummed, but she held still, afraid that if she moved, the fine cord would break.

Jude's breathing slowed, and he smiled a crooked smile, as if to say, *Let's have another go, shall we?*

She smiled back. *Quite the randy fellow.* She'd just had the most intense sexual reaction in her life, and they hadn't been physically joined. Now she knew why vampires had groupies. The sex was transcendental.

He blinked as his length rose from the tight curls between his legs. She drew in a sharp breath.

Yes, oh, yes. She reached for him, and he caught her hand. The M of his upper lip sharpened as he stared at her throat. "What if I lose control?"

"So could I."

"But I want you more than I want air." Candlelight flickered over his teeth. He kissed her neck, and his lips lingered on her pulse beat. She wanted him to press those fangs into her flesh. No, he mustn't. Wilkerson had said her blood was lethal to vampires. After the Turkish man and Georgi had bitten her, they'd suffered brief, but extreme, reactions. Coincidence? Or maybe Wilkerson had lied. So many untruths swirled around her; she didn't know what to believe. But she could not put Jude in danger.

"I'm not scared for myself, just for our baby," she whispered. "But I don't think I can stay away from you."

"There's got to be a way," he said.

"Too bad we aren't in a city. I'd buy a dental device." She smiled and touched his front teeth. "Like the wax that teenagers use for their braces. Or a mouth guard, like for sports."

"You've given me an idea. Hold on." Jude turned to the nightstand, lifted a burning candle from the holder, and rolled back to her. He drew in a breath and exhaled. The flame spit out and a dark ribbon curled up. Wax trickled onto Jude's wrist and instantly hardened.

"I won't be able to last. So no foreplay this time," he said, shaping the warm candlestick into a U. His teeth sank into the soft candle, to keep him from biting her in his ecstasy.

He moved closer and drew his finger over her nipples, down to her navel, then inched lower and lower until he reached her cleft. She gasped and arched her back.

He moved into the space between her legs, smelling of cedar and incense, and then his face was directly above hers. He took a breath and sheathed himself inside her. She cried out, clutching his back. He withdrew and she lifted her hips to keep him inside her. With each thrust, his shoulders grew warmer, as if sucking heat from her flesh.

He pulled back again, teasing her, and she pressed her fists into his hips. A luminous rush of ice and fire surged just beneath her skin, stoking flames in her belly.

She wanted to kiss him, but she didn't dare dislodge the candle. She pressed her face into his chest. He lunged inside her, their bodies slick with perspiration. Her thoughts rose straight up and began to spin. Then she was spinning with them, weightless and twirling, sparking into a vast, black chasm.

He shuddered and a cool rush filled her. He groaned and bit the candle in half. Shards pattered in her hair and skittered to the sheet. The spinning slowed into lazy spirals, and the air went still.

A thundering noise sounded in the corridor. The door banged against the wall and Father Konstantine charged into the room.

"What the bloody hell?" Jude cried.

"This is not a sacrament." Father Konstantine's cheeks pinkened as his gaze swept over the wax-strewn linen. "You are not man and wife."

"Why are you here?" Jude blinked. "What in God's name is going on?"

"Yes, I want to know, too," Caro said. "You told me Jude was dead."

"Silence!" Father Konstantine reached for Caro's *galabiyyah* and red robe. He threw the clothing at her.

"Whore, cover your nakedness," he said.

Jude's eyes blazed. "How dare you call her that? And why did you lie to her? What purpose would that serve to you, a man of God?"

Father Konstantine looked away. Caro's hands shook as she pulled on the clothing. Did the monk think Jude's condition was too precarious for lovemaking? More likely, he was morally outraged.

"Your whore does not understand." Father Konstantine tucked his hands into his sleeves. "Your wounds have healed, but internally, you are still transforming. The urge to feed is all-powerful."

"I've been bitten before," Caro said. "And I'm not a whore."

The monk gave her a freezing stare, then faced Jude. "Your unborn baby is a miracle. He is the last bit of you that is human. You can have more children, of course, but they will carry your immortal genes. The child must be protected. Therefore, the whore must be protected from your carnal desires."

"I'd rip out my heart before I hurt her or the baby," Jude said.

Father Konstantine shook his head. "You cannot be with her. You must fulfill the blood oath."

"What ruddy oath?" Jude cried.

Two portly monks entered the room and seized Jude, pinning his arms behind his back.

Father Konstantine's hand clamped on Caro's elbow, and he steered her through the blue door, into the corridor. "Let me go, you stupid monk! My place is with Jude."

"You have no place in this world." Father Konstantine's voice pierced the empty hallway. "Jude is ours. And you are little more than seven pints of blood."

"And you're a bloody cue ball!" She squirmed away, clawing his wrist. He grasped her shoulders, and shook hard. Her teeth clattered, and she bit her tongue.

"You set this in motion, woman. You gave permission for the cabal to turn him."

"Cabal? What are you talking about?" *Raphael, where are you? Damn you.*

"You need to know only one fact." Father Konstantine's lips curled over his teeth.

Like the wild dogs in my dream. Blood pooled in Caro's mouth, and she swallowed.

The monk's eyes narrowed. "Jude resisted the change because he did not want to be immortal. Now, he's become the one thing he despises. And you gave the order."

"To save him." She struggled to control her voice, but little streaks of terror broke loose.

"Yes, you saved his life, but the cost was his soul." The monk's bitter laugh held in the air. "Now he will live a thousand years. And a thousand more. In the dark."

She kicked him in the groin. An explosive gasp hissed through his teeth, but he didn't loosen his grip.

Raphael, please hurry.

Konstantine slapped her, hard. She fell against the wall,

stunned, as if a pot of cold, black coffee had spilled behind her eyes. He pulled her out of the corridor, across the courtyard, toward the main entrance of the basilica.

"Where the hell are you taking me?" Her words struck the cold night air like a series of claps.

As he still gripped her, his free hand flung open the church's carved wooden doors. He pushed her inside, and she sprawled in the aisle. His robe waffled as he scurried back into the hall. He slammed the doors and a scraping noise reverberated, as if a bolt were dropping down. Oh, God. No. He was locking her inside the church.

She scrambled to her feet and slapped her hands against the doors. Damn him. "You can't hold me captive!"

"You will be released when Brother Jude has left Egypt," the monk called from his side of the door. "Until then, I will pray for the soul of your bastard child."

CHAPTER 66

CHURCH OF THE TRANSFIGURATION
ST. CATHERINE'S MONASTERY

White altar candles fluttered as Caro ran through the basilica, searching for an exit. All doors were fastened, and the windows were ten feet above her head. She shivered, and her breath rose in an ivory thread. She pulled the red robe around her and started down the center aisle, past flaming candelabras in tiered brass holders.

Shadows flitted over the gilded iconostasis as she slipped into a pew and put her face into her hands. Great, gulping sobs escaped her throat. She cried so hard it hurt to breathe. Each intake of air sent a sharp crackle through her ribs as if the bones were made of glass. How long did Father Konstantine plan to keep her locked up? Until the baby was born? How many other monks were on his side?

She wiped her face on her robe and tilted her head. Above her, ostrich eggs hung from the ceiling by slender chains. The egg, an ancient symbol of rebirth. Her chest tightened, stirring sharp, insatiable pangs. Jude's whole biology had been altered, along with his concept of time, and it was her fault. Now, he was on intimate terms with darkness. As long as human blood flowed through her heart, their time together was finite. Years after she and their child had turned to dust, Jude would be here. Time would flow around him like the fine bits of sand that passed through the monastery's outer walls.

Raphael's voice floated into her mind just as clearly as if he'd been sitting beside her. *Hold tight,* mia cara, *I am coming.*

A shuddering noise echoed outside the church. The doors creaked open, and a draft stirred the candles. Raphael shut the doors, then walked down the aisle gripping a metal briefcase and a burlap sack.

He genuflected in the center aisle, then squeezed into her pew next to her and set the briefcase and sack on the floor.

"It's about time you showed up," she said. "What's in the sack? It better not be ticking."

"No bomb, *mia cara.*" Raphael's jaw tightened, and tears beaded in his lashes. "This is all my fault. I shouldn't have brought you and Jude to Egypt."

She grabbed his sleeve. "I want answers."

"Jude's being moved to a treatment facility near Istanbul."

She sprang to her feet "Is he still injured?"

"Sit, *mia cara.* His wounds have healed, but his body chemistry is still evolving. He'll need transfusions and a complete orientation to vampirism."

She eased back into the pew and cast a sidelong glance at Raphael. "How long will it take?"

"Six months. Maybe less."

"Then I can be with Jude?"

Raphael shook his head.

She narrowed her eyes. "When?"

"Never."

"What?" A sick feeling uncurled in her belly, and she grasped the pew in front of her.

"Jude will eventually be put to work in a laboratory," Raphael said.

"A lab?" She let go of the pew and crossed her arms. "He won't go."

"It's mandatory."

"Says who? You and Konstantine?"

"I have no part of this."

"Who does?" Her breath came in short gasps.

"The monks who resurrected Jude are members of the Salucard Foundation."

"The what?" she asked.

"It's a nonprofit organization. Trustees and directors are composed of influential vampires from around the globe."

"And that includes bald monks with reptilian eyes?"

"They're dedicated to the protection and preservation of immortals. The cabal at Saint Catherine's safeguards our history, culture, and artifacts. They are maniacal about the prophecy. They believe the child you carry is the baby in the fresco on Mount Sinai."

"How would they know I'm pregnant? I'll tell you how. You told them!"

"No, I swear it. One of them must have read our

thoughts. I learned their intentions only fifteen minutes ago. Father Nickolas told me. He is on your side, *mia cara*."

"Why should I trust him?" *Or you.*

"He knew Philippe." Raphael inched closer. "Let me explain what's going on. Jude is now a member of the cabal. These brethren saved him. He is in their debt. That's why his head was shaved. It's the first step of initiation. The cabal will take Jude away, but they plan to detain you at Saint Catherine's."

"Why?"

"Haven't you figured it out? You will be used as an incubator for the child. After he—or she—is born, the brethren will raise the baby."

"Incubator? No one is taking my child. And they can't separate me and Jude." She started to rise, and he caught her arm.

"You don't understand what is at stake. After the baby is born, you will be eliminated. Jude's life will be spared because he will be useful to the foundation as a biochemist. But he will be held captive as long as you breathe. Then he will be free."

She shook violently. Her palms skidded down the front of her robe, leaving a damp smear on the red wool. She had to escape, had to warn Jude. If she had to rip down these walls, she'd find him.

"But you have an infinity tattoo." Her voice was low, but a scream perched in the back of her throat. "I've seen it."

"I'm a member of the foundation. As was your father. But I am not in the hierarchy." Raphael pushed back his sleeve, and his tattoo gleamed in the candlelight. "I am too radical for their tastes, *mia cara*. I am not privy to their secrets. If I had been, I would never have brought you and Jude here. I would have hidden both of you from the world."

"Why should I believe you? Why are you telling me these things?"

"Because I want to help you and Jude escape. Haji and Father Nickolas are making arrangements as we speak." Raphael swallowed, and his throat clicked. "It's only a small chance, and you'll have to leave now. Members of the cabal are being transfused. They should be finished in thirty minutes. Then the brethren plans to sedate Jude—if they haven't already. A helicopter will arrive and take him away. If you don't find him, you must leave. A Bedouin man is waiting with camels just beyond the south wall. He is trustworthy and will lead you to the caves in the desert, near Libya."

"What if the monks are listening to our thoughts?"

"It's a risk. But they are less telepathic while they are feeding."

"But even if I find Jude, he'll need blood."

"The Bedouin will provide what Jude needs. Do everything the man says, *mia cara*. Sleep by day and travel at night. I will catch up with you in the Gilf Kebir. And I swear on my father's grave, I will take you and Jude to safety."

"Why would you and Father Nickolas betray your own cabal?"

"I cannot speak for Nickolas. As for me, I am an outsider. And I loved your mother. She was my heart. I still love her. Above all else, she would want you to be with Jude."

He opened the burlap bag and pulled out beaded slippers and two black hooded capes.

"Your birthday is tomorrow, so here is an early present."

"I'd forgotten about that."

He smiled. "There's a full moon tonight. You'll need camouflage."

She tossed aside her red robe, making the candlelight wobble, then put on the slippers and cape. "As much as I want to leave, I'm worried about you and the others. What will the cabal do when they find out what you've done?"

"Do not worry about us."

She wiped her eyes, then leaned closer to kiss his cheek. "Good-bye, Raphael. And thank you."

As she gathered Jude's cape, she felt pressure on her arm and glanced up. Raphael squeezed her. "Two things, *mia cara*. First, do not make the mistake of thinking you can trust Jude during the act of love. He's physically weak, which is to your advantage. But when he is stronger, sex will alter his consciousness, and his drive will be an unstoppable force."

"We'll be careful." She could feel him reach into her mind, prodding and searching, and she willed her thoughts to go blank.

"What's in the briefcase?" she asked.

"That is number two." He flashed a quick smile. "The antiquities police brought Wilkerson's ten million euros and your vellum pages. I stole them. I also added the triptych and the rest of the book—more birthday presents for you. So you now have the only complete copy of *Historia Immortalis*."

She recoiled. "It's not a present. It's a curse. I don't want it."

"I raided the monks' library and can't very well return the stolen property, can I? Besides, these pages are your legacy, *mia cara*. Guard them well. They are not ill-omened. We make our own destiny. But this is no time to hypothesize.

"Is there anything else?" she asked.

"Number three." He gripped her arm. "Haji has connections through the embassy. He learned that your uncle is in Prague. Nigel is adjusting to the night. And he will find you, *mia cara*."

The candlelight swirled. Her breath rose above her head and soared. Oh, thank God. She'd see Uncle Nigel again. He could fill in the missing pieces. "But how did he get to Prague?"

"A fellow named Hughes brought him. But we will talk later," Raphael said. "When I meet you in the Gilf Kebir."

As she ran out of the basilica, his thoughts chased after her: *Mia cara, do not be afraid.*

Caro raced breathlessly through the empty corridor, her slippers rasping over the dry stones, and then she stopped in the T-shaped hall. The blue door was closed, as were the other doors. No monks stood guard, thank goodness, but when she turned the knob, it wouldn't budge. The bastards had locked Jude inside. Were they with him?

It didn't matter. Despite all risks, no man—or vampire—could keep her away. Her cape billowed as she ran into the next room, pushed open the window, and climbed onto the tiled roof. Tattered clouds glided over a December moon. In the distance, lights moved up Mt. Sinai. As she inched along the ledge, the wind blew her cape, showing a flash of her white *galabiyyah*. If she was caught, she and Jude would be separated and escape would be impossible.

She paused outside Jude's window. He sat on the bed, his back to the window. Pains shot through her chest. Never again would he feel sunlight on his face. Oh, how he'd loved it. He'd miss the pink sky at dawn. Nor would he see himself age. He would never have gray hair or laugh lines. He was a perfect male specimen, caught in his prime.

And she was drawn to him. Without even meaning to, she'd started to crawl through the open window. At the last moment, she craned her neck, glancing around the room, making sure he was alone.

"Jude?" she whispered.

He vaulted from the bed and whirled. "Jesus, Caro. They'll be back any second."

She pushed the briefcase into the room, then climbed in after it and tossed him the black cape. "Put it on, and hurry. We're breaking out of this bloody jail."

He gave her a long, level gaze, then pulled on the garment.

"I don't have time to explain," she said. "Raphael has put his life in danger to help us. He's arranged for us to escape. If we don't, the monks will separate us permanently—very permanently. They'll murder me, turn you into a lab rat, and take our baby."

"Bloody bastards. Let's go, lass."

He held the briefcase while Caro climbed out the window, and then they picked their way over the red tiles, to the edge of the roof. It was just a low drop to the staircase, but when Caro started to climb down, she heard voices. Had the monks already transfused themselves? If so, she and Jude wouldn't make it out of the monastery.

"They're on the far side of the courtyard," Jude said,

then sniffed the air. "They're mortals. And they're arguing about a fine point in Exodus."

They jumped to the landing, then hurried down the steps. They started to bolt into the orchard when the voices got closer.

"Down," Jude said, pulling her against a wall, his cloak waffling.

Caro reached out to grab it. Nausea and terror rose to a peak and hovered in the back of her throat as two monks passed by, their voices low and tangled. Then they turned the corner and their sounds faded.

"Now," Jude said. They ran through the straight rows of the orchard and cut toward the wooden door in the south wall. It stood ajar, and the lock looked as if it had been recently smashed—bits of metal glinted on the sand.

Caro's terror lessened when she grasped Jude's arm, and they dashed into the shadows, tripping over loose stones. Each time she stumbled, he held her aloft. She wouldn't allow herself to think what might—or might not—be lurking ahead. All around them the terrain dropped off into a murky haze, with faint halos rising from the monastery.

The Bedouin guide waited in a clutch of palm trees, just as Raphael had said. The man helped Jude and Caro onto the camels and handed them heavy woolen shawls.

"Wrap yourselves," he said. "It hides. And the night air is cold. The blowing sand cuts like shattered goblets."

He secured the briefcase in a canvas satchel and strapped it to Caro's saddle. She settled onto the tasseled blanket, arranging her cape beneath the shawl. Her camel lurched upward, and she gripped the wooden pommel. For one moment she felt weightless. She looked around for Jude. He huddled beneath the shawl, blending into the gloom. A shadow within a shadow.

"Yella!" the guide called, and the camels trotted out of the palms. Caro looked over her shoulder and saw the blurry lights of the monastery; farther away, a curved glow hung above St. Catherine's City. She abruptly turned. As her eyes adjusted to the dark, the plains spread out beneath the moon, ringed with mountains. Here, in this deeply symbolic land, the Israelites had waited for Moses to climb down Sinai.

She crossed herself and said a prayer. The dark world around them had boundaries, but it was filled with hope. She and Jude had been touched with Raphael's grace. He'd promised to lead them out of Egypt, but at what cost to himself?

"Wadi ed-Dier," the Bedouin said, waving his arm. "The Valley of the Monastery."

They hadn't gone five hundred yards when Caro saw a flash of light. She turned in her saddle, gripping the pommel. The beam from a helicopter spangled through the night sky over St. Catherine's City and veered toward the monastery.

"Can't we ride faster?" she asked the Bedouin. "The monks are bound to know we've escaped. They'll come after us."

"No, madam," he said. "They will not."

His camel spat, and a moment later, a boom shook the ground. Caro muffled a scream and whirled. Below the mountain, just outside the monastery, an orange fireball exploded.

"Ruddy hell, what was that?" Jude cried. "Did the helicopter crash?"

The Bedouin man's mustache twitched as he watched smoke blot out the moon. "Signore Raphael planned a small diversion. But do not fear. He is safe."

The Bedouin moved ahead before she could ask more questions. The wind snapped Jude's cape as he steered his camel next to Caro's. She leaned against him the way night touches day, and daylight slants into dusk, their boundaries inseparable. The wind stirred her blanket, and her cloak escaped and fluttered out, melting into Jude's. Both garments hovered above them, beating like hundreds of wings.

"We will reach the caves before dawn," the Bedouin called over his shoulder.

The stars curved above Caro and Jude as they followed the Bedouin into the valley. Their camels slogged toward the jagged mountain peaks, their breath stamping the cold air, hooves clicking over the rocks. Straight ahead, the night spilled down like a bowl of black water. As Caro listened to the singing wind, Jude reached for her hand and laced his fingers through hers, and they rode toward the sheltering dark.